AF253365

A BRIDE FOR MARCUS

ANNE GRACIE

DEDICATION

To all the wonderful readers who waited so patiently for Marcus's story and who sent me hundreds of emails and messages of encouragement — this book is for you! With my heartfelt thanks.

DEAR READER,

Back in 2012 the fifth book in the Devil Riders series was published by Berkley. I wanted to write a sixth book, about Marcus, the Earl of Alverleigh, the oldest of the Renfrew brothers, and although my editor initially gave me the okay for it (in person) she later withdrew her permission, and asked me to begin a new series instead. So I started work on The Autumn Bride.

But emails and messages kept coming in from readers asking for Marcus's story, more and more emails all the time. Years later I was still getting two or three "Marcus" emails a week. I wanted to write his story, but my contracts forbade me to self-publish anything longer than a novella, and I knew Marcus would need a full novel.

Fast forward to 2025, when I was finally out of contract with Berkley, and could start on Marcus's story, with the aim of self-publishing it.

So now, here it is. I hope you enjoy it.

PROLOGUE

THEY WERE AT it again, yelling, screaming, tearing each other to shreds.

Marcus couldn't stand it. He wrenched open the door and raced across the lawn, heading for somewhere, anywhere. He didn't care, as long as he was far enough away not to hear his parents arguing—yet again.

They were unbearable—one minute slinging the most vicious insults at each other, the next falling into each others' arms, cooing soft endearments and making passionate love.

Until the next time.

If only he'd been allowed to go and stay with a friend for the school holidays, like his brother Nash. But Marcus was the heir, and his father wanted him here to learn how to be a proper earl and to oversee the management of the various estates— not to manage them himself, of course, but learning how to keep a stern, supervisory eye on those they employed to do the work.

He wouldn't have minded so much if that had happened, but he'd come home to find his parents in one of their periodical reconciliations, if you could call it that. It was feast or famine with his parents—screaming jealous arguments or passionate love-making—there seemed to be no middle ground.

It didn't matter which to him—both made him sick to his stomach. If that's what love was, you could keep it.

Normally Marcus would have headed for the stables and taken his horse, Jetta, out for a long, cleansing gallop, but Jetta had thrown a shoe the day before, and was being taken to the blacksmith. There were other horses in the stables, but even though he was fourteen, the grooms wouldn't let him ride one of his father's precious hunters, not without his father's permission, and Marcus didn't want to ask. He didn't want to talk to his father at all.

His second favorite place to retreat was the maze in the garden with hedges high enough to conceal him. Taking himself to the center and sitting down on the bench in the middle with a book, and breathing in the sharp, clean fragrance of the yew hedges that enclosed him always made him feel calmer. Somehow cleaner inside. But the hedging had to be trimmed regularly and today the maze was filled with gardeners busily clipping away. No peace to be found there.

So he made for the forest that bordered the estate. The neighboring estate was called Ferndale, and it—and the forest—belonged to their neighbor, Lord Blaxland, who neglected his land shamefully. He was what they called an absentee landlord, a gambler, Marcus had heard, who lived in London and was almost never home. Marcus hardly ever went there but he wanted—needed—to be alone, and wherever he went on his father's estate, there would be people wanting to talk to him, asking questions, happily chatting.

He couldn't chat happily at the best of times, and at times like these, when he was full of anger and frustration, he could barely even talk.

The forest was a tangled, wild place, but it was cool, shady, and peaceful. The only sound was the twittering of birds and the soughing of the breeze sifting through the leaves. The air was fragrant with the scent of fresh greenery and the moist, rich earth beneath the soft carpet of leaves. He breathed it in deeply and felt his heartbeat and his breathing slowing, settling, calming.

Even though his newly trained landowner's eye could see the neglect, the tangle of blackberries and vines, the weeds choking off new growth, the need for pruning and thinning, he had to admit the forest was beautiful in its wildness.

Thoughts of his parents intruded: he thrust them aside. He wasn't going to think about them, not here. This would be his own special place to escape to. None of his father's employees would venture onto Blaxland land, and nobody would think to look for him here.

Several faint pathways meandered through the undergrowth, made by animals, he presumed. He followed one, pushing aside fronds of bracken and other weeds. Thorns caught on his clothing. His father's valet would scold him, but Marcus didn't care.

A crashing sound ahead made him look up from his contemplation of the path. Something, some creature was coming toward him, pushing through the undergrowth in a rush. He tensed.

A little girl burst out of a clump of greenery, then stumbled to a halt, panting as she stared at him out of wide blue eyes. She was small, maybe eight or nine, and dressed in a shabby, ill-fitting dress. Her hair was a tangle of silvery blond elf-locks surrounding a face that was dirty and tear-streaked. A gypsy child perhaps? Though that coloring was unusual in gypsies. For a moment they simply stared at each other.

"You have to help me." She was distraught, still gasping for breath. The words burst forth in a pelter. "She's going to die and then her babies will too and I can't bear it. Will you come? You have to come! Please?" She swiped at her tears with a grubby paw, leaving her face even dirtier.

Marcus nodded. "Of course. Who is going to die?"

She gave him a wary look. "My friend." She grabbed his arm and pulled him back the way she'd come.

Bemused, Marcus let himself be towed through the forest. If her friend was badly hurt, it might be better to go back home and get help—adult help. But until he knew the situation, he couldn't know what was needed. And Father would be furious if Marcus pulled workers away from their duties for the sake of a gypsy child.

"She's there." The child pointed. "I tried to get her out but I couldn't open it. She's trying to chew her leg off—see? It must hurt terribly but she's desperate. She's got babies to feed."

Marcus stared, shocked. The little girl's 'friend' was a vixen caught in a trap. She was snarling and growling and was indeed, he saw, disturbed, trying to gnaw off her own leg in order to escape. The leg was bloody and raw.

He looked around and selected a sturdy piece of fallen branch.

The little girl grabbed his arm. "What are you going to do with that? You're not going to kill her, are you? I won't let you!"

"No, I'm going to try to pry open the trap with it." He moved cautiously forward.

The vixen turned to face him, snarling. Murmuring what he hoped were soothing sounds he approached. Her savagery worsened.

"It's all right, Russet, he's going to help you," the little girl crooned.

The vixen bared her teeth at Marcus. They looked very sharp. He pulled off his jacket and wound it around his hand and arm, then eased closer.

He carefully slipped one end of the branch in between the teeth of the trap—it wasn't easy—and then pushed it hard to lever the metal jaws open. The trap was strong and stiff, but "It's moving," the little girl crowed. He put all his weight into it and the trap opened, just enough for the vixen to escape. She was gone in a flash, fleeing unevenly through the brush on three legs.

Marcus pulled the branch out, the trap snapped shut with a loud crack! and the little girl clapped her hands, "Oh, thank you, thank you. I tried to open that horrid thing myself but I couldn't budge it."

His eyes widened. "You tried to open it yourself?"

"Yes of course."

"But that's dangerous. You could break your arm on that wretched contraption, and in any case, that vixen could have bitten you."

She snorted. "Of course she wouldn't. I told you, she's my friend."

People *hunted* foxes. He'd never heard of anyone being friends with one. "Maybe, when she wasn't mad with pain, but trapped like that and with her leg half chewed off, she would bite anyone. It's instinct."

He tossed the branch into the undergrowth.

"Don't," the little girl said, but it was too late. "I could have used that."

"Used it for what?"

"Tripping the other traps. I do it every day."

Marcus stared at her in shock. "You trip animal traps?"

She nodded. "I hate them. They're horrid and cruel."

"Yes, I know but . . ." He didn't know what to say. His father didn't use traps on their land, but only because he preferred to hunt foxes, instead of trapping them. "It's dangerous."

She shrugged. "I know what I'm doing."

"Who are you, anyway?" he asked. "Where do you live?"

"I'm Tessa. I live over there." She gestured, but all he could see were trees.

"In the village?"

She laughed. "No, silly. At Ferndale." When he still stared at her blankly, she added, "I'm Tessa Blaxland."

Blaxland? Marcus blinked. "You're Lord Blaxland's . . .?" He trailed off. Dressed as shabbily as she was and clearly allowed to run wild, she must be one of Lord Blaxland's bastards.

She nodded. "His daughter, yes."

He said awkwardly, "Shouldn't you be in school or something?"

She laughed. "I escaped from NannyJune, who was my nanny and is now my governess. She was my mama's nanny too, when Mama was small, but she's ancient now and is always falling asleep."

"Governess?" If she had a governess, she must be Lord Blaxland's legitimate daughter. But if so, why was she dressed in shabby, faded, ill-fitting clothes? And left to run wild and unsupervised.

"Can I trust you?" she asked abruptly.

"Yes." He hoped so, anyway. It was foolish to make a promise when you didn't know what you were promising. And as a gentleman, his word was his bond, and therefore unbreakable.

"Would you like to see her kits?"

"The vixen's, you mean?"

She nodded, and without waiting, she grabbed his hand and pulled him down another barely perceptible pathway. Ten minutes later she stopped.

"Shhh." She put a finger to her lips, then crept toward an opening in the underbrush. Marcus followed suit.

There in a grassy clearing, the vixen lay, panting, licking her injured leg while three small, fluffy fox kits fed from her. He watched, fascinated, as one by one they finished feeding and started frolicking around her, wrestling and mock-growling, playing just like puppies.

He must have moved or made some kind of sound, because the vixen scrambled to her feet, made a yipping sound and in an instant she and her babies had vanished under a thicket of brambles.

"That's their den," Tessa told him. "I've been watching them ever since the kits were born. Aren't they sweet?"

"Mmm," Marcus made a noncommittal sound. The kits were charming, but foxes were vermin, weren't they? Everyone said so.

"Their mother takes good care of them, doesn't she? Even though she hurt her leg in that horrid trap, the first thing she did was feed her kits. Have you got a mama?"

He blinked at the abrupt question. "Yes."

"And you live with your mama and papa?"

"Yes. And my younger brother." What was she getting at?

"I don't have a mama. I killed her."

"You *what*? Who told you that?"

"My brother Edgar. He said I killed Mama when I was born. He says it's why Papa doesn't like me."

"That's nonsense, and it was wicked of your brother to say so," Marcus said forcefully. "Women sometimes die giving birth to babies, but it's not the baby's fault, never the baby's fault. How could it be?"

The little girl gave him a long thoughtful look. Her eyes were almost violet, not simply blue, as he'd first thought, but a deep violet-blue. "I haven't seen you here before. Why not? What's your name."

"Marcus. Marcus Renfrew. I live over at Alverleigh,"—he gestured—"but most of the time I'm away at school."

"My brothers went away to school, too, but they hardly ever came home. Louis did sometimes, when he could, but not Edgar. He's like Papa and prefers London."

Marcus knew both Blaxland boys slightly. He'd only known Edgar— known at school as Blaxland Major—the oldest brother, for a month or two before he left school. He had a reputation as a bully and a gambler who wasn't above fudging the cards, though nothing had ever been proven. Louis, — Blaxland Minor—was the younger of the two and a year above Marcus. He was quiet and seemed harmless enough. He'd left school at sixteen to go into the army.

Tessa glanced in the direction he'd pointed. "I don't go over there. I did once and a man yelled at me. Besides, it's all so . . ." She wrinkled her nose. "Neat."

He hid a smile. Yes, the grounds of Alverleigh were very neat, constantly maintained by an efficient team of gardeners. "There's a very good maze, though. Have you tried it?"

She tilted her head like a little bird. "Maze?"

"It's a puzzle on the ground, with lots of paths bordered by hedges. You have to try to find your way into the center—and then out again—but lots of the paths are dead-ends, which makes it difficult. It's fun."

She considered that, then shook her head. "I've got plenty of paths here. The animals make them." She gave him a mischievous look. "I come out at night sometimes and watch the badgers."

"You come out at night? By yourself?" Marcus was shocked. She was too young, surely, to be out at night on her own.

"Of course by myself. Most people make too much noise and frighten the animals away." She gave him a speculative look. "If you like, I could show you the badgers. But you'd have to be quiet."

"Now?"

"No, not now, tonight when the moon is up. That's when they come out."

"All right," he said cautiously. She probably wouldn't show, was no doubt boasting about coming out at night. But he was curious. He didn't know much about little girls; he only had brothers—no, just one brother, Nash.

Papa insisted that those other two boys were not his sons.

Marcus wasn't so sure.

"Well?" the little girl said. "Will you come or not?"

He ought not, he knew. She was a young child, with nobody looking after her. He ought to report the situation, have something done about it, but he was somehow reluctant to do so. She seemed to relish her wild and unsupervised life. Marcus had no idea how that might feel.

Well, why not? He had nothing better to do, and anyway, he was curious. Besides, he'd given her his word. "I'll come. Moonrise, you said?"

She nodded. "Thank you for saving Russet." She skipped off down an almost invisible pathway and disappeared from view.

Marcus slowly made his way back through the tangled forest. What an odd, interesting little girl. Normally he wouldn't associate with children of that age, but there was no-one else here for him to talk to, only adults, and they usually did all the talking. He was supposed to just listen and learn and be trained in the correct behavior of the heir to Alverleigh.

But while Papa's attention was wholly on his latest explosive reunion with Mama—which everyone except Papa knew wouldn't last—Marcus was left to his own devices.

Could this grubby little girl truly be Lord Blaxland's legitimate daughter? Running wild in the forest, day and night, with a dirty face, and dressed in rags? If he'd been the credulous type, he might even have thought her a fairy. But he wasn't. He'd ask one of the servants about her, Cook, probably. Cook and her family had lived here forever, and she knew everything about everyone.

"Oh yes, Master Marcus, there is a little girl." Cook's floury hands kneaded the dough briskly as she worked. The kitchen was his favorite place in the house, and though he wasn't supposed to go there, Cook always welcomed him, and always gave him something tasty to eat, often jam tarts, which she knew were his favorite.

She continued, "But that Lord Blaxland, he takes no interest in the poor little mite. Left alone in that big old house year after year, she is, with naught but an old woman to tend to her—her ma's old nanny, I believe, and her with nowhere else to go, poor old soul. And a bare skeleton staff to keep that big house running—though most of the rooms are closed off, I hear. A disgrace it is."

She rolled the dough out and started cutting out shapes with a metal cutter. "Mind you, the whole estate is going to rack and ruin—everybody knows it. Every penny it earns goes straight to some London gambling hell. The master doesn't care. And I'm told his heir is a chip off the old block, which doesn't bode well for the people dependent on the estate. Now, if you come back in half an hour, Master Marcus, these jam tarts will be ready."

That evening, at moonrise, Marcus slipped out of the house, several jam tarts in his pocket, and headed for the forest. He found her waiting. "Would you like a jam tart?" he offered. She didn't hesitate.

"I didn't think you'd come," she said, munching on a tart. It was chilly out and Marcus had put on a coat, but Tessa was in the same ill-fitting cotton dress. There were goosebumps on her skinny little arms.

"Here, you must be cold, take my coat," he said, but she laughed him off.

"I'm not a bit cold. Anyway, moving keeps me warm. Now come on, the badgers will be coming out soon. Walk quietly."

She took his hand in her grubby little paw and led him through a wild maze of pathways, barely lit by the moonlight. She practically skipped along; he found himself stumbling in the dim light and almost tripping on the undergrowth. He was stunned. She must know this forest like the back of her hand.

Eventually she slowed, signaling to him to stay quiet. She lay down and wriggled forward on the ground and patted the earth beside her. Marcus joined her.

Through a gap in the undergrowth he could see a grassy mound with a hole dug into it. They watched for a time, but nothing happened. Marcus started feeling restless, but the patient watchfulness of the little girl beside him shamed him into staying still and silent.

Then she nudged him, and he saw a black and white striped muzzle poking out of the hole, sniffing cautiously around. A badger emerged and was followed a few moments later by three small cubs. They foraged around, snuffling in piles of leaves and digging in the earth, and occasionally wrestling and tumbling around—and again, they were just like puppies.

Eventually they wandered off and disappeared from sight.

Tessa turned to him, her grubby little face alight with pleasure. "Aren't they wonderful? Aren't you glad you came?" She scrambled to her feet, beaming.

Marcus had quite enjoyed it. He wasn't sure

badgers were wonderful at all but he did, however, like her enthusiasm. "How do you know about all this?" He gestured around him.

"Oh, I just watch, and when I want to know more I find a book. We have a very large library, though Papa has sold off the more valuable ones. I hid my favorite ones though, so he couldn't sell them."

"Do you come out here every night?"

She shook her head, setting her elf-locks dancing. "No. Sometimes I stay home and read—NannyJune taught me to read and write. And I try to draw the animals"—she laughed—"but I'm not very good at that. But there's always plenty to do so I'm never bored."

Marcus was frequently bored.

Then in the abrupt change of subject he was getting used to she went on, "I'm going to learn to ride soon. Phillips—he's our groom—told me he's going to borrow a horse for me. He's going to teach me. He taught my mama to ride when she was my age. Well, I'm off now. G'night."

She skipped away and vanished into the darkness, leaving Marcus to make his way home, stumbling in the faint, filtered moonlight, and feeling large and clumsy compared with the small, quicksilver fairy-child.

From time to time over the next few years Tessa met up with the boy from Alverleigh. He was nice, for a boy. He didn't say much, but he listened to what she had to say. He also brought her little treats—jam tarts and meat pies, sandwiches and biscuits that they shared, like a picnic.

In return, she shared with him some of the treasures of the forest: a perfect fairy-ring of fragile, frilly, parasol-shaped toadstools; a squirrel gathering nuts for the winter, a gossamer spider's web strung with glittering crystals in the morning sunshine; the wonder of a delicate fern frond slowly unfurling, the otters that frolicked in the stream.

She liked that he didn't mock her for loving the forest and the wild animals that lived there. And most importantly, he never broke her trust in him.

Each year she took him to visit their vixen, still alive and running on three legs, the fourth one dangling, too damaged to heal. And each year there was a new litter of kits. She knew now that Marcus wouldn't tell on her, or on the animals, even though some of them were regarded by the famers around as pests to be eradicated. As far as she was concerned, they were all God's creatures and had the right to live there.

And one day Ferndale would be hers and she would be better able to protect the forest and all the creatures that lived there.

When Phillips acquired a horse for her it changed Tessa's life. She took to riding like a duck to water—just like her mama, Phillips said. He was a strict taskmaster, making her learn to ride sidesaddle and frowning when she sneaked out and rode astride. But he wasn't really cross, she could tell.

She wore her mother's old riding habits, which were, of course, much too big, but she and NannyJune altered them, not very elegantly. But nobody ever saw her so what did it matter? She always stayed within the Ferndale grounds—she'd promised Phillips she would, and she would never break a promise. Phillips would get into trouble if she ventured outside the grounds, she knew. She loved Phillips. He was more like a father to her than her real father. And NannyJune, old as she was, had been her only mother.

And if her life was sometimes a little bit lonely, she gloried in the freedom of it. Ferndale was her own little kingdom and she was its caretaker and its queen.

Then one day, just after her fifteenth birthday she was out riding, and saw a traveling carriage turning into the Ferndale driveway. They never had visitors so, curious, she cantered down to meet it. It was probably someone who'd taken a wrong turn or were lost.

The coach had pulled up, and a groom jumped down to let down the steps. To her amazement, her father and Edgar stepped down, just as she rode up to them. It had been at least two years since their last visit.

"Papa, Edgar, what a surprise!" She tried to think what might have brought them here. Could it be to celebrate her birthday?

Her father and Edgar stared up at her, their expressions blank, as if they didn't know who she was. "It's Tessa, Papa." She lifted her leg over the pommel and slipped to the ground.

Papa and Edgar looked her up and down, as if they could hardly believe their eyes. Then they turned to each other. "Looks like we have another asset," Papa said.

Edgar nodded. "Will need a bit of cleaning up, but yes. Definitely."

Tessa stared, puzzled, but they didn't explain, just went inside.

Asset? What did they mean? Were they talking about the house? People called houses and land assets, but they couldn't sell Ferndale, she knew. The estate had been Mama's home before she was married and it had been part of the marriage settlements that when she died it would go to her first-born daughter. Which was Tessa. NannyJune had explained it all to her years ago.

She took her horse to the stables, leaving it to Phillips's care instead of doing it herself, as she usually did, then hurried inside, hoping for an explanation.

She never got one.

Three days later, the traveling carriage, containing Tessa, her father and Edgar, left Ferndale. Tessa was distraught. Her father had closed the house and dismissed Phillips, NannyJune and the remaining few servants, turned them off without even a pension, even though they'd worked for the family their whole life.

She'd argued and argued, but Papa ignored her, until he got fed up and slapped her—hard, twice— and told her if she opened her mouth again, she would suffer the consequences. She did, of course— insisting that NannyJune and Phillips should have a pension, at least—and he beat her severely, in places where the bruises wouldn't show.

And now he was taking her away from her beloved Ferndale, and the few people in the world who cared for her, going to who-knew-where for who-knew-what-reason. Papa hadn't said a word to her since the beating and Edgar ignored her. He'd ordered poor NannyJune to pack a bag for Tessa, and then told her to pack one for herself and be gone by the end of the week.

Tessa stared out of the carriage window, dry-eyed but heartbroken, watching her beloved home fade into the distance. The moment she turned twenty-five, she vowed silently, she'd be back.

CHAPTER ONE

*Alverleigh, hereditary seat of the Earls of Alverleigh.
England*

"YOU'RE LEAVING? NOW?" Maude, Lady Gosforth trained her lorgnette on her eldest nephew with exasperated indignation.

"I am." Marcus Renfrew, the seventh Earl of Alverleigh, was in his library, sorting through a small stack of documents on the desk in front of him. Outside a footman and valet were loading baggage into his traveling coach.

"But I only just arrived from Bath."

"I'm sorry Aunt Maude. Had you notified me you were coming, I might have been able to delay my departure. But I have appointments in the city I cannot put off. Peverill and Cook and several other servants have gone ahead to ready Alverleigh House, but the under-butler and Mrs. Allen and the remaining staff will take good care of you, I'm sure." His aunt periodically descended on him—invariably without warning and with a purpose of which he was well aware. And so, since he really did have appointments to keep, he saw no reason to delay his departure.

"If you had a wife, *she* could take good care of me," she said pointedly.

Marcus didn't respond. His aunt managed to introduce the subject of his wifelessness into almost every conversation she had with him. She watched him now, shuffling through papers.

"You're going to London, I assume."

"I am."

"At *this* time of year?" she said with faint emphasis.

"Yes. Why not?" he said indifferently. "The worst of the winter weather has passed, and since there has been little rain in recent days, the roads will be in good condition."

"Pshaw! I'm not talking about the roads."

Marcus knew very well she wasn't. But though he was fond of his aunt, he had no intention of dancing to her tune. No doubt if he stayed at home, within a few days, she would invite 'friends' to stay, the kind of friends who brought marriageable daughters, nieces or granddaughters with them. It had happened before.

"It is May, Marcus, and the season is well begun. So, are you going to London to seek a wife? At last?"

"No, I am going to London on business. And as you very well know, the season coincides with the sitting of Parliament, and my presence is required in the Lords, as is my duty." Marcus selected a document and set it to one side.

"Duty!" She made an impatient noise. "Then while you are there you can begin the search for a wife—which is another of your duties."

Ignoring her—it was an old song she sang—he concentrated on the documents.

She stamped her foot. "You are one-and-thirty years old, Marcus. It's high time you married and got yourself an heir."

"I have several heirs already."

"Pah! Your brother Nash is in Saint Petersburg, and has no intention of returning to England to live. And don't tell me Gabriel is next in line because as the Regent of Zindaria, he has his hands full, and will until little Prince Nicky comes of age, which is at least a decade away. So with both heirs out of the country indefinitely, what would happen to the estate if something happened to you?"

Marcus slipped the documents into a slim leather folder. "I understand that Nash's wife is in an interesting condition and Gabriel's wife has already given birth to a girl, and may well be breeding again, so the next generation is well on its way, and thus the succession will be secured. Now, while I am gratified by your concern for my continuing health, Aunt Maude, it is time I left."

"I am not talking about your dratted health," she said acidly. "You are as healthy as a horse—and just as stubborn—and yes I know it's mules that are the stubborn ones, but you know what I mean. There are such things as accidents, Marcus, as you very well know. How would the estate fare if you had one?"

"Leaving my brothers aside, I have a number of excellent employees maintaining all aspects of the estate, so if I did happen to slip from this mortal coil, I'm sure everything would continue as usual. I hope that reassures you."

She narrowed her eyes thoughtfully. "It's your parents, isn't it?"

He raised an eyebrow. "I understood they were dead."

She made an impatient gesture. "You know perfectly well what I mean. Their marriage was a disaster and it has put you off the very idea of marriage."

"You are mistaken, surely," he said dryly. "I was under the impression they were passionately in love."

She snorted. "I wouldn't call that love. Obsession maybe, and utterly destructive. Their frequent tempestuous quarrels and dramatic reconciliations tore this family apart—literally!—and I know how damaging that was to *all* you boys." Her voice softened. "I know you've done your best to repair the damage, bringing your brothers—even Harry—back into the fold and reuniting the family again, and for that I praise you. But Marcus, dear boy, I fear the worst of the damage was to your heart."

"Nonsense," he said crisply.

"It's not nonsense. Now, listen to me. Nash and Harry were chary of the whole idea of marriage and courtship, and each of them turned to me for assistance in finding them a suitable bride. And look at them now—both of them married and blissfully happy. You could be the same. Let me help you as I helped them."

Marcus turned away, hiding a smile as he perused some books on a shelf. While it was perfectly true that both Harry and Nash had initially sought Aunt Maude's assistance in finding a suitable bride, the brides they'd ended up choosing had never been anywhere near Aunt Maude's list of ideal candidates.

His half-brother, Harry, had found Nell sitting on the back of a dray, muddy, drenched, exhausted and in utter despair. And Nash had found Maddy living in poverty in a small rural cottage trying desperately to keep herself and a gaggle of children alive. Actually, you might say that it was Maddy who found Nash when he came off his horse and crashed into a stone wall, unconscious.

For all that Aunt Maude claimed the credit for

their happy marriages, she'd had nothing to do with arranging them.

"Marcus, dear boy, let me help you find the perfect bride. I know the sort of gel you need, and most of the gels coming out this season—"

"Aunt Maude," he said firmly. "I thank you for your concern but I am not going to London in search of a bride and I don't need your help." He picked up his document folder, selected a book and turned to leave. "In the meantime, stay as long as you want. Make yourself at home. Anything you need, ask the under-butler or Mrs Allen."

She followed him out of the room. "One-and-thirty, Marcus—one-and-thirty! If you wait much longer, the new crop of gels will be young enough to be your daughters."

He turned and said dryly, "You flatter me, aunt, but I was not quite as enterprising at thirteen as you obviously imagine."

She made a frustrated noise. "Mark my words, Marcus Renfrew: you will rue the day you refused my assistance."

"Undoubtedly." He walked toward the door.

She snorted. "You're just like my stupid, stubborn, rigid, impossible brother."

Marcus didn't wait to hear her response. "Who else should I be like but my father?" he tossed over his shoulder.

"Yourself, whoever that might be — but you won't, unless you get that stick out of your arse."

Marcus whirled, shocked. "*What* did you say?"

Aunt Maude gave him a gimlet look. "You heard."

Marcus shook his head. "Goodbye, Aunt Maude." He kissed her cheek, climbed into the carriage, and tapped on the roof to signal the driver to move off.

His aunt watched, and as the carriage rolled away, muttered, "You stupid boy, don't you realize how lonely you are?"

As the carriage passed through the front gates and turned onto the main road, Marcus settled back in his seat. His aunt's never-ending and unsubtle efforts to get him leg-shackled might amuse him if they weren't so irritating.

Stick out of his arse? What nonsense. He was rational, that's all. Level-headed. Responsible.

His aunt was getting more outrageous the older she grew.

As for the way she prated to him of his duty, he didn't need her to remind him. His estate—and those under his supervisions that would eventually pass to his brothers—were in excellent order. He did his duty by his family, his tenants, his dependents and his country, just as his father had raised him to. He was a damned dull dog, in fact.

But he would *not* marry to order. When the time came for him to choose a bride—which would be if and when *he* decided—he would choose one soberly, dispassionately and prudently. And if that was cold-blooded, all the better.

He wasn't opposed to the idea of marriage, but he was wary of the idea of choosing a bride from the *ton*. The young ladies one met in society showed the world one face, one wholly agreeable face, intended to lure a man into proposing. But after marriage . . .

The beautiful Lady Anthea Quenborough came to mind.

Better to remain single the rest of his life than leg-shackle himself to one like that.

If he ever did decide to seek a bride, he would make a practical, unemotional marriage, entirely without his aunt's so-called assistance. And ensure that his bride understood that.

Even so, he shuddered at the thought, imagining the kind of fuss and botheration his wedding would entail. His aunt often complained that his brothers had done her out of a grand society wedding, but that his own would be done properly, as befitted an earl. Aunt Maude adored a fuss, the bigger the better.

All the more reason, should he ever consider marriage, to go about the business quietly and discreetly. Or not at all.

On arrival at Alverleigh House in Mayfair, Marcus dropped his luggage and valet off, and checked that everything was all right there. He kept the town house perpetually open, running with a skeleton staff, in case any of his brothers or Aunt Maude wished to stay there.

His cook had already taken charge of the kitchen, but for his first evening in town he decided to eat at his club. He was bound to find one or two acquaintances and possibly even a friend there, though he didn't have many close friends.

The trouble was, by eating at his club, the word would go out that he was in town, and that would, he knew, result in invitations.

He was, after all, a single earl in possession of a large fortune, as it said in that wretched novel from which his aunt incessantly quoted.

But he wasn't in want of a wife, and invitations could be refused.

As expected, before he even got to the pudding course—plum duff with custard—he'd been invited to a party that very night, and two more acquaintances had promised him invitations to upcoming events.

By the end of the first week, despite his intention of avoiding the marriage mart, he'd attended several social events. He'd met many perfectly pleasant eligible young ladies, and their mothers had delicately hinted—and others much less delicately—that his attentions would be most welcome.

He deflected the hints as gracefully as he could. Though he wasn't the kind of man that grace came naturally to. Blunt was more his style.

Almost any one of them would make him a suitable wife—on the surface, at least. But they were all so very young. His aunt's words came back to him. *If you wait much longer the new crop of gels will be young enough to be your daughters.*

They already felt like it.

They all showed him the pretty society manners he had learned to distrust, fluttering fans and eyelashes at him, and trying to entice him with sweet smiles. Hanging on his every word and laughing at the mildest pleasantry, treating him as if he were the wittiest man in London. Which was ridiculous. And irritating.

Choosing a wife that way was like entering a lottery. Courtship was all for show. You never knew who you might end up with.

He'd met a number of widows, too, who'd also subtly indicated they were open to an offer of marriage—and several who, much less subtly, indicated they were open to less respectable offers. He had nothing against widows, and most of them seemed quite pleasant, but he had no plans to take a mistress, not from members of the *ton*, anyway.

He wasn't a talkative man, and he didn't find it easy to make light conversation. The young ingenues were either dreadfully shy and it was hard to pry a word out of them, or they prattled happily of people and events he knew nothing about and cared even less.

And the widows tried to flirt with him. Marcus was hopeless at flirting. He was a dull dog, and he knew it.

He stood sipping wine, his bored gaze running over the crowd crammed into somebody's ballroom and listening with half an ear to Barney Wimple, a friend from his schooldays, relating some tale about the triumphs of the recent hunting season.

Marcus had no interest in hunting. It was the one thing he and his father had disagreed on. That and marriage.

The amount of attention Marcus had been getting since he arrived in London was already verging on the unbearable. And Aunt Maude had written to say she had recovered from the journey from Bath to Alverleigh and was now following him to London. Her presence would only make it worse. He didn't want a wife, and he wasn't looking for love—most emphatically not.

His aunt was correct in her assumption that his

parents' tempestuous marriage had given him a distaste for a love match. Not to mention the disastrous experience of Lady Anthea, which thankfully—and miraculously—his aunt knew nothing about.

His brothers might have managed happy marriages, but Gabe and Harry had been raised initially by Great-aunt Gert and later Aunt Maude. They'd never had to live with his parents' constant drama, and Nash, who had, was blessed with the kind of personality that enabled him to vanish whenever things got ugly.

Marcus, being the heir, had had to stand there and endure it.

And if those memories weren't enough, there was the lesson he had learned from Lady Anthea Quenborough.

Both Marcus and his estranged half-brother Harry had—unbeknownst to either of them—fallen madly in love with the beautiful Lady Anthea, the dazzling toast of that year's season. Charming, modest, sweet-natured, she'd been courted by dozens of high-born young gentlemen.

Harry, young and impulsive and seemingly her favorite, had asked her father for permission to court her.

And had received a thorough, vicious horse-whipping in answer.

Her father and brother had dumped the bleeding, barely conscious Harry on Lord Alverleigh's London doorstep, proving they knew Harry's true parentage.

It seemed that Lord Quenborough had no interest in acquiring a relatively penniless Earl's by-blow for a son-in-law.

He made it clear, however, that he would smile on the legitimate son and heir of an Earl—Marcus.

Later Marcus later learned that not only had Lady Anthea repeatedly seduced Harry—which had prompted that honorable young fool to seek permission to marry her—but that she'd actually watched her father horse-whipping him with every sign of enjoyment.

That had shocked Marcus deeply. Any faint remaining shreds of tenderness he'd felt for the girl turned to disgust and revulsion.

Harry's beating had resulted in a lucky escape for Marcus. And marked a change in his attitude towards his formerly despised half-brother.

Lady Anthea had married some other rich, titled unfortunate, but rumor had it that she slept with everyone, from her husband's friends to his servants and even the stable-lads.

The whole distasteful affair had been an object lesson for Marcus. Before his eyes had been so shockingly opened, he'd thought Lady Anthea a sweet, charming, innocent girl.

And ever since, he'd observed dozens of sweet, charming, innocent-seeming girls, and wondered what they were really like behind their delightful, deceptive facades.

No, if Marcus ever took a wife it would be someone who stirred his senses not at all—that way madness lay. If he did choose a woman to wed, it would be as a pleasant companion, someone well-born, of course, who wouldn't lead him a merry dance, and who would be happy to spend most of the year at Alverleigh.

And—he thought of his mother—someone who wouldn't be constantly demanding his attention and requiring him to prove his love for her over and over. He shuddered.

In recent years, seeing his brothers so content in their marriages, he'd occasionally wondered if perhaps he might risk it. Find some young woman who would be a companion, and who wouldn't stir his senses. But how could he be sure that any woman he considered would be suitable? Society courtships worked to ensure there was no way to really get to know a young woman, not until after the wedding. And by then it was too late.

His friend, Barney, droned on, something about an exceptionally cunning fox. There was a slight stir at the entrance, and the crowd's attention shifted toward it. There was a perceptible hush and then a buzz of conversation rose. Marcus glanced across the room, faintly intrigued.

Three people had entered the ballroom, a man and two women. The man was Marcus's own age or a little older, thin, elegantly dressed and with an air of sophisticated dissipation. The older of the women trailed behind, bearing all the hallmarks of a duenna or companion, rather than a wife. But it was the young woman on the man's arm who caught his eye.

She was perhaps twenty-three or four. Of medium height and very slender—perhaps too slender—she was exquisite looking, with pale, almost luminous skin, and silver-gilt hair pulled back in a smooth, sleek chignon, not a hair out of place. Her face was a perfect oval, a little on the thin side, or was that the effect of her high cheekbones? Her nose was small and straight, her eyebrows delicate arches. He couldn't see the color of her eyes from where he stood, but they were large and striking. Her mouth, full-lipped and deep rose red, was the only color about her.

The very sight of her stole his breath. He'd never seen such a beautiful woman, her expression serene, almost blank, looking as remote as the moon.

Her dress showed just the palest hint of lilac, silk from the sheen of it, and cut low across her small breasts. It was very plain, without a frill or flounce or contrasting trim. But even a man such as he, unversed in female fashions, could tell it was superbly cut, for as she moved it floated with her, emphasizing her slender curves.

She wore no jewelry at all, which again was most unusual. She should have looked plain, but instead she made all the other ladies present look overdressed and fussy. He knew he'd never seen her before—he would never forget a woman like her—and yet something about her tugged at his memory.

He turned to Barney, who was the sort of fellow who knew everyone.

"And then the blasted fox dived right into a bramble thicket, and m'horse—"

Marcus cut off his friend in mid-chase. "Barney, who is that?"

"Eh? What? Who d'you mean?" Barney blinked and looked around.

"Over there, just come in. The blonde in the lilac dress."

Barney looked. "Hah. Out of her weeds again, I see. She's oddly punctilious in observing her mourning. Her year must be up."

All Marcus understood from that was that the woman was a widow — the rest made little sense to him. "But who *is* she?" She seemed somehow familiar, and yet he was certain he'd never seen her before.

Barney shook his head. "Don't even think of it, my friend. That's Lady Hewitt, the Ice Widow. She's beautiful, I grant you, but"—he shuddered—"cold as ice, and venal as all get."

The Ice Widow? Marcus watched as she glided through the crowd, serene—indifferent?—her hand resting lightly on her escort's arm. She made no attempt to engage anyone in conversation. The man she was with did all the talking, all the greeting— and he spoke only to other men. No women spoke to her, none greeted her, and the few who looked at her did so with sour expressions, murmuring something to their companions—something even from this distance Marcus could tell was disparaging.

She just stood there looking beautiful. Seemingly indifferent. And, admittedly, cold.

"Who's her escort?"

"Her brother." Barney gave him a curious look. "Don't you recognize him? It's Blaxland Major, from school."

"Blaxland Major? You mean Edgar Blaxland?"

"That's the one. Not the younger brother of course. Died at Waterloo, I heard. Pity. He was the best of that family. And Blaxland Major is Lord Blaxland now: the father died a few years ago."

Marcus stared at the woman and her escort. His head was reeling. It couldn't possibly be . . .

But if she was with her brother, Edgar Blaxland, it *had* to be.

The beautiful, serene and apparently cold-as-ice widow was also Tessa, his wild and grubby little sprite from the forest.

It made no sense.

As he watched, Edgar Blaxland seated his sister and said something that made her stiffen. She shook her head and rose. It looked as if she was ready to leave. But Edgar simply shoved her back into her seat. He turned to the companion, said something that made the woman nod, sit down beside Tessa and take her arm in what looked like a firm grip.

Marcus frowned.

Then Edgar made a 'stay there' sort of gesture to his sister and headed for the card room.

Tessa watched him go, her expression, what? Mulish? Angry?

What on earth was going on? Marcus could only surmise, but whatever it was, he didn't like it. But not a soul in the ballroom had seemed to notice, or if they did, it hadn't seemed to bother them, not even when Edgar pushed his sister into her chair, and not gently.

The moment Edgar disappeared, the companion or chaperone or whatever she was, started looking around and gesturing with her free hand, trying to catch the eye of a waiter. After a few unsuccessful minutes, she stood, made a 'stay there' gesture to Tessa, and hurried away.

Abandoning his friend in mid-sentence, Marcus strode across the room. He had to talk to Tessa. As he approached, weaving through the crowd toward her, their eyes met. For a moment he thought hers lit up with a welcoming expression, but then she looked away, biting her lip and looking first one way, then another, as if looking for someone. The chaperone? Her brother?

Had she not recognized him? Her eyes were still that deep violet-blue he remembered, but now he couldn't read them.

But as he reached her the cool, frustrated, faintly worried expression vanished and she smiled up at him. "Marcus."

"Tessa, what a wonderful surprise. I had no idea you were in London, let alone that you would be attending this party."

"It was a last-minute decision. We've only just returned to London—or at least I've only just returned." Again she glanced quickly in the direction her brother had gone, and the furrow between her brows deepened. If he hadn't been watching her so closely he might have missed it.

"How long has it been? Remember how we freed the vixen from the trap that day?" Lord, but he was hopeless at making polite conversation with women.

Her smile was half-hearted, a little distracted. "Of course I do. And have often wondered whether she has survived in the years since."

She kept darting sideways glances in the direction her brother had gone. Why? Was she nervous in company? The child he remembered hadn't been nervous or the slightest bit shy.

"I don't often come to London," he told her, "But I'm delighted to see you here." Lord, where was witty banter when he needed it?

She glanced around. "I rarely move in *ton* circles."

"I gather you are widowed. My condolences on your loss."

She didn't reply, just glanced again in the direction her brother had gone, absently pulling off her gloves and smoothing them on her lap with restless fingers.

"Are you looking for someone?" he asked.

She started and gave him a swift smile. Again it felt forced. "No, I don't know anyone here. Just my brother. And you." She looked up at him with a serene expression, but he noticed she was picking at her nails with nervous fingers.

Marcus frowned. Was his presence unsettling her? He wasn't much of a conversationalist it was true, but surely . . . Was he looming? He edged back—but no, she leaned slightly toward him, so it wasn't that.

"What have you been doing in the years since we last met?" she asked him. "I suppose you're married."

"No," he said bluntly.

She was about to say something in response when the chaperone returned with two brimming glasses of wine.

The woman pushed her way in between them, saying, "I mush ask you to leave, sir." She plopped unsteadily down in the seat next to Tessa, drained one of the glasses and tucked it out of sight under her chair. "S'most improper, you haven't been introdushed." She sipped daintily from the second glass. It was clearly not her first glass of the evening.

"Nonsense," Marcus said crisply. "Lady—" he broke off, unable to recall Tessa's married name. "The lady and I have known each other since childhood."

"Nev'r'thless, I have my instrusch'ns," the woman said.

"Oh no," Tessa muttered, looking past Marcus. "I *told* him!" Her eyes flashed and she made a low, angry sound.

Marcus followed her gaze, to where Edgar Blaxland was making his way toward them, accompanied by a nattily dressed elderly man.

"You'd better go, Marcus," Tessa said. "This is going to get ugly."

"Yesh, go 'way," the chaperone said, flapping a hand at him.

Marcus had no intention of leaving, especially if things were going to get ugly. He hadn't liked what he'd observed earlier, before he'd even spoken to Tessa, and from her expression now, it was going to be more of the same.

Her brother seated the old man on a settee outside a small, curtained anteroom and glided up to meet them. He lifted a quizzing glass and regarded Marcus through it. "Good lord," he drawled, "Renfrew, is it?"

Marcus inclined his head. "Though now I'm Alverleigh."

"And I am now Lord Blaxland. So melancholy, is it not, that our esteemed papas have both passed away? Still, life goes on. You wish to be introduced to my sister, I gather. Theodosia, Lady Hewitt, Lord Alverleigh."

Marcus was about to point out that he and Tessa had known each other as children, but the expression on her face froze the words in his mouth. "Delighted," he murmured, as if they were strangers, and bowed over her hand.

She murmured some polite phrase in response but before she'd even finished, her brother had taken her elbow, saying, "And now that dreary convention has been observed, I must tear you apart. Come, Theodosia, there is a gentleman who is anxious to meet you." He gestured to where the elegant, white-haired old gentleman waited, watching them with a look of eager expectation.

Tessa's mulish expression hardened. "No, Edgar, I'm *not* meeting him. We discussed this."

"Now, now, don't be shy, dear sister, come along." Edgar gripped her arm and nodded to the chaperone, who drained her glass and grabbed another one from a passing waiter.

For a moment Tessa sat there, stiff as if refusing to move, but just as Marcus was about to intervene, she glanced at him and shook her head. He stepped back. He didn't like what was happening, but he didn't know what it was all about, but she'd signaled clearly—twice—that she didn't want him to get involved.

And it was clear that if he did intervene, there would be a scene.

"Very well," she told her brother, "I'll meet him, but there's no point. I told you, I'm not doing it again."

Edgar laughed as if she'd said something silly. "Come along." His voice was implacable.

Marcus watched as her brother introduced her to the old gentleman, with what looked like a lot more charm than the perfunctory introduction he'd given Marcus. He couldn't see how Tessa was responding to the old man's remarks—her back was to him. But the old man, whoever he was seemed delighted with her.

"Told you," Barney said at his elbow.

Marcus turned. "Told me what?"

"Not to bother with her. She's not for the likes of you—or me, for that matter, not that I'm looking for a leg-shackle just yet. Didn't think you were either."

"What do you mean, not for the likes me?" He wasn't looking for a wife; he was just reconnecting with a childhood friend.

Barney nodded to where the dandified old man was beaming down at Tessa. She'd turned a little and he could see her better now. Her expression was remote as the moon again and she seemed to be saying little, but her brother looked on complacently, clearly pleased with whatever was going on. "Lay you a pony he'll be her next victim."

Marcus frowned. "Victim? What are you talking about?"

Barney shrugged. "Victim, husband—not much difference when you boil it down."

Marcus stared. "Do you mean to say she's planning to marry that old man?"

"Not sure what she's planning but unless I'm mistaken—and I rarely am—her brother is certainly brokering the deal this very minute."

Brokering the deal? Marcus was revolted at the suggestion. "But she's only twenty-four or five. That old goat's old enough to be her grandfather."

Barney glanced at the little scene again and said,

his voice full of disgust, "That's how they like them, those Blaxlands—old and rich."

"I don't believe it." He couldn't imagine the passionate, animal-loving little scrap he'd known all those years ago becoming in the least bit venal. And on Tessa's behalf he resented her inclusion in '*those* Blaxlands.'

Barney shrugged. "Believe what you like, but you'll see I'm right. Oh, look, there's Monty. I haven't seen him for ages. Hey, Monty!" He hurried off to greet his friend, leaving Marcus thoughtful and disturbed.

He could believe anything of Edgar Blaxland, but Tessa? No.

And yet, Barney had always been up-to-the-minute with the doings of London society. And Tessa had been behaving oddly, far from the open-hearted little girl he remembered. What was going on?

He looked again to where the old gentleman was seating Tessa beside him on the settee, patting her hand, with her brother smiling benevolently on. Her expression was blank, cold and distant as the moon.

He hadn't seen her for years, but it was only natural that she'd changed.

Was she being forced into some hideous mismatch? Was her brother exploiting her? Was she frightened of him? Did he mistreat her, was that it? There had been definite undercurrents in their brief exchange, undercurrents he didn't understand, and didn't like.

The questions hammered at him. The contrast between this reserved young woman and the warm and passionate little scrap was . . . unsettling. He had to speak to her, in private.

After a while the old man rose and after a brief exchange with Blaxland, he kissed her hand, shook the hand of her brother and tottered off.

Immediately Tessa turned to her brother and said something that made him throw up his hands in apparent exasperation. Then he jerked his head and the small party rose and turned toward the exit.

Marcus hurried to catch them. "May I have the next dance, Lady Hewitt?" he said.

She opened her mouth, but her brother answered for her. "My sister is still in mourning and doesn't dance."

And yet he'd brought her to a *ton* party and though she hadn't danced, she was not wearing black as she would be if still in full mourning.

"In any case she's tired and we're leaving," her brother added. She didn't look the slightest bit tired, but she didn't try to contradict her brother. And when Marcus caught her eye, she gave a barely perceptible shake of her head. It was very odd.

"Then may I call on you, Lady Hewitt?" Marcus persisted.

"She doesn't wish for callers either," her brother snapped. "Goodbye."

Marcus looked at Tessa, willing her to indicate something—anything—that would help him to understand her situation. But as her brother urged her out the door toward the waiting carriage, she looked back at Marcus and though he searched her face for signs of regret—or any other emotion—she simply said, "I'm sorry, Lord Alverleigh. Goodbye." She looked pale and . . . brittle.

He watched her leave, puzzled and more than a little disturbed.

CHAPTER TWO

TESSA WAITED UNTIL the carriage moved off, then she turned to her brother. "How dare you introduce that man to me! And indicate I was willing to accept his attentions with a view to marriage! I've told you and told you, Edgar, I won't marry again—not to another old man, not to anyone! And I really, really mean it!"

It was gloomy inside the carriage, but she could see her brother give an indifferent shrug. "It was just an introduction."

Tessa thumped her fist on the worn leather upholstery of the rented carriage. "It was nothing of the sort! It was clear to me Sir Henry thought it was all agreed, and that any "courtship" would be for the sake of appearances. But I won't marry him—or any other man!"

There was a short silence, broken only by the sound of the horses' hooves clattering over the cobblestones.

"Speaking of other men, you behaved like a whore tonight."

She stiffened in indignation. "A whore? I did not!"

His voice hardened. "I told you to wait where I put you and not to talk to anyone, and when I got back, there you were, flirting with Renfrew."

"I was *not* flirting. I barely spoke to him. And he came up to me. I didn't move."

"Well, don't do it again. He's no use to us, so don't even think about it."

No use to us. That was true enough. Not to any scheme Edgar had hatched. But she was having no more of Edgar's schemes. Never again. She made a frustrated noise. "Oh, why won't you listen? How many times must I tell you, Edgar, I won't marry Sir Henry. Or any other man. And I'm of age now, so you can't force me."

He gave her a bored, basilisk glance, but didn't otherwise respond. He glanced at the chaperone, lying slumped in the corner of the coach, snoring gently. "That Thracknell woman is useless. Look at her—drunk again, damn her eyes!" He pulled a flask from his coat pocket and took a long pull. "I ought to sack her."

Tessa said nothing. There was no point. She knew he would keep Mrs. Thracknell on. Edgar owed her several months' wages, but the woman had nowhere else to go and was too intimidated by Edgar to demand her wages. Tessa might have sympathized with her, but Mrs Thracknell was also a bully, and treated Tessa like a prisoner.

But that was going to change: she had a plan.

The carriage continued to rattle along. The house they were currently renting was on the very edge of fashionable London—funds were scarce, again, which presumably was why Edgar was courting Sir Henry Lester. He was in debt again. But Edgar's debts were his problem, not hers.

He'd had told her that bad men were after him and that only her marriage to a rich old man would save his life. It was the same old story. Twice now she had married a rich old man—the first time when she was still a naive child, because she believed her father's life was in danger because he couldn't repay his debts. And because she thought he loved her.

The second time was because... She wasn't quite sure how that had happened.

Tessa tried to put it all out of her mind. She just had to stand firm. Edgar couldn't *make* her marry anyone.

Her thoughts returned to the real surprise of the evening. Of all the people she'd expected to see in London, the very last was Marcus, her friend from the forest. She hadn't recognized him at first, but despite the crowd at the party, her gaze had been drawn to him, tall and grave and somehow separate from the crowd. And compelling. To her, at least.

"Wait here," Edgar had told her. "I'll be back in a few minutes. And don't speak to anyone."

There was little chance of that, she knew. The men might ogle, but they knew better than to approach her while Edgar was in the vicinity—as he invariably was. As for the ladies, the few times she'd mixed in society, they'd made it all too clear that they despised her.

She hadn't wanted to attend this party—there was no point, after all: she'd made that clear to Edgar. But he'd been very insistent, and despite her wariness about his motives, she was fed up with staying inside day after day, going nowhere and seeing no-one. Edgar occasionally took her to the park in a hired carriage, but though it felt good to be out in the fresh air—not that London air was particularly fresh—they never stopped to talk to anyone. He was only showing her off, like putting a prize mare through her paces.

So she'd gone to the party in the hope—she knew even then it was unlikely—that she might find someone to talk to. Make a friend, even. But as always, the gentlemen eyed her from a distance and the ladies snubbed her.

London society had taught her that even surrounded by people, you could still feel achingly alone. And yet as a child, she'd spent most of her days alone and had never felt lonely. She couldn't wait to leave London, to go home to Ferndale. Just another few months and Ferndale would be hers again.

She'd sat quietly, listening to the talk swirling around her, doing her best to ignore the slighting glances she received, and the waspish shreds of conversation she was meant to overhear.

She sat quietly and watched Marcus—though she hadn't realized who he was at that point. His friend had been doing all the talking while Marcus stood still and silent. He seemed to be all hard edges. Tall and lean, with long legs and broad shoulders, he was dressed conventionally in black, his waistcoat a kind of dull silvery gray, but something about his stance set him apart from the other men at the party. Like a rock. An island in the swirling throng of society.

The women flocked around him, but he gave them scant encouragement and they soon drifted away. Who was this man, actively courted by so many women, yet so apparently indifferent? And why so grave-looking?

His white shirt emphasized his unfashionable tan. A man who spent a lot of time out of doors, then. Not a Londoner. And not somebody she would ever be allowed to know.

Her gaze kept getting drawn back to the tall,

grim-looking stranger. She hadn't been able to help herself. And then he saw her. It felt almost physical when his cold gaze clashed with hers. He stared for a long time, then said something to his friend, who turned to look at her.

She didn't need to hear it to know exactly what the friend would be saying. It was the same everywhere. Her reputation was set in stone.

But then he'd left his friend and made his way purposefully across the dance floor toward her. Hardly able to breathe, she watched him approach.

And when he was close enough for her to see his eyes, those unusual piercing light gray eyes in that grim face, she knew at once who he was.

The boy from the forest. Marcus. All grown up. Taller, bigger, stronger.

Harder.

For a moment she'd panicked. Years of training enabled her to keep her expression serene, but inside her heart was pounding.

Too late, too late, too late.

There was no boyishness about him now. He was all man, and somehow. . . beautiful, in a hard-edged, masculine way. Dark lashes fanned over the lightly tanned skin. His eyes were the same light gray. But tonight they seemed cold as well as gray. Icy.

On the boy those eyes had lit with laughter, danced with amusement and sometimes widened in wonder. Now, on the man, they seemed to slice through her.

She ought to have appeared indifferent, uninterested, but she couldn't prevent the leap of her heart when she realized who he was. And it was only when his gaze softened and he smiled at her that she realized she was smiling at him.

And oh, that mouth. It drew her, like a moth to a flame. Chiseled by a master sculptor, it fascinated her. It was, quite simply, beautiful. She'd never thought of a man's mouth being beautiful, but his was. Yet there was nothing feminine about it.

But he was not for her. No matter what Edgar said—what anyone said— she would never marry again. She'd had enough of men and marriage.

She grimaced ruefully at her ridiculous presumption, thinking, even for a moment, that this tall, beautiful man, courted by the highest-born, most beautiful, most respectable ladies in the land, might want to marry her. *The Ice Widow*. Oh yes, she'd heard the name she'd been given. And worse.

She'd tried not to let it upset her.

The carriage rattled on. She gazed out of the window, watching the gaslights in the street glow and fade as they passed. So, Marcus Renfrew was now Lord Alverleigh. She'd wondered about him from time to time, what he was doing, how he'd turned out.

As a naive young girl she'd dreamed of a future with the boy. After school he'd go away to university—Cambridge or Oxford—and four or five years later he would graduate and come back to Alverleigh.

He would be twenty-four and she'd be eighteen. She'd fantasized about how they would meet again as adults. Perhaps he'd come and find her in the forest. Or at their secret pool, where the otters played. Or maybe she'd be out riding and he'd appear silhouetted on the ridge, mounted on his magnificent black stallion, and he'd see her and canter down to meet her.

The very last place she'd expected to see him was at a London party, striding toward her, cleaving through the crowd, his eyes burning. Or staring after her as she left, with unreadable, ice-gray eyes, as hard and cold as if they were carved from marble.

She hugged her shawl around her. She'd put her childish dreams away when she turned sixteen and learned what life was really about. Besides, dreams were too painful.

Too late, too late, too late.

Edgar glanced at her. "Very quiet you are tonight, little sister."

"I'm tired," she murmured. It was dark in the carriage, but she could feel his eyes boring into her. And she was weary of arguing with him, going round and around in circles.

"You might not care about what happens to me, but I didn't think you'd be so indifferent to the fate of Ferndale."

She turned her head sharply. "Ferndale? What do you mean?"

He shrugged again. "Just that Ferndale is mortgaged to the hilt, and if we don't pay up, the mortgage holder is threatening to sell it."

"Sell it? He can't! Nobody can. Ferndale belongs to me."

He made an indifferent gesture. "At the moment it does, but if we don't pay up soon, the mortgage holder has every right to sell it. Effectively the entire estate belongs to him."

"But it *can't* belong to him. Ferndale was willed to me by my mother, and by the trust my grandfather set up. Only I can sell it, and I'd never do that—never!"

He shrugged again. "The law is the law."

Tessa stared at him in frustration, her pulse pounding. "How could such a thing happen. It must be a mistake."

Edgar simply shook his head and turned away, a signal that as far as he was concerned the conversation was over.

Tessa sat in silence, her thoughts in turmoil. How could Ferndale be sold? It was hers! Who was this man who held a mortgage and was demanding payment? And how did mortgages work? She had no idea. Her father, Edgar and both her husbands would never discuss finance—or anything important—with her. Even though she was the one who saved Papa and Edgar from the violence of debt collectors.

Ferndale. . . Her beloved home. It was the key to her plan. As soon as she amassed enough money—and she had almost enough to hire a carriage to travel there—she planned to leave London and go to Ferndale and live there in peace for the rest of her life.

But without Ferndale, she would be homeless. And dependent on Edgar for the rest of her life.

"There must be another way," she told her brother. "You're always getting loans—why can't you get a loan to pay off this mortgage?"

"Loans are not so easy to come by," he said. "Besides, it's only the interest the mortgage holder requires: he will still be holding the mortgage over our heads."

Tessa felt a surge of hope. "The interest—it's less? How much do we need?"

He told her the sum and her heart sank. That was just the interest? It seemed impossible.

"Nevertheless, we must try. Tomorrow you must go out and try to raise the money. I won't have my home sold out from under me, Edgar, I won't allow it."

"If you married Sir Henry—"

"No! I won't marry again, not even to save Ferndale."That might be a lie, she thought. She'd do anything to save Ferndale, but before she reached that stage of desperation, she would try every other possible way.

A loan, that was the solution. *If* Edgar could manage it. He had to. Her nails bit into her palms. It was infuriating that females weren't allowed to do any business. She'd tried several times in the past but had been politely but firmly rebuffed. "Anything you own, madam, belongs to your husband.There is no need for a lady to have a bank account."

But thanks to Grandpapa's trust and Mama's will, she did own Ferndale.

"So, Edward, tomorrow morning you will go out and seek a loan—yes?"

Edgar sighed theatrically."It won't do much good, but very well, if you insist, I'll try. But marrying Sir Henry would be easier."

She shuddered."Not for me."

Sleep came hard for Marcus that night: he found himself mulling over his brief interaction with Tessa. Something wasn't right.

At first she'd seemed pleased to see him, but then . .. those frequent glances off to the right, as if looking for something. For what? Or whom? And the image given by her demure, ladylike posture and pleasant conversation was contradicted by the way she had removed her gloves and was picking at her nails.

He'd itched to reach down and stop her, place his hand gently over hers and see her anxiety fade.

And when her brother had arrived with that elderly gentleman in tow, she'd stiffened. He was sure he saw her eyes flash with anger but an instant later it was as though a mask had dropped over her face, and she looked cool, serene, even bored.

But her fingers kept picking at her nails. Worse than ever.

Marcus had left them—Edgar had made it clear he wasn't wanted, which normally would have made no difference to him, except that Tessa had sent a subtle silent signal that he should leave too.

The tense undercurrents were almost tangible.

Something was very wrong. Something or someone had turned the carefree, exuberant, open child he remembered into this cautious, restrained, tense young woman. Her brother? Her marriage? His every instinct told him she was far from happy.

But was he simply reacting to her cool reception? And her parting words that had seemed a clear message: stay away.

He'd never been rejected by a young, eligible lady or widow. Quite the contrary.

Was he the sort of coxcomb who was only interested in the hard-to-get? Who forced his company—unwanted—on women? He didn't think so. Having experienced unwanted attentions himself, the very idea revolted him.

But he wasn't generally given to much self-examination.

In any case, he wasn't thinking of her as potential partner. She was simply an old friend who seemed . . . unhappy? Lonely?

In the time he'd been observing her, not one person had greeted her, not a soul had talked to her. Not even that chaperone woman. Only her brother and the old man.

Not for the first time he wished he'd overheard the conversation she'd had with her brother when they first arrived. From the distance it had looked like a dispute. And Edgar had certainly taken charge when he returned, making it clear to Marcus that his sister was off limits.

But why?

The questions nagged at him, and one thing became clear: he needed to find out more about her and her recent history, and for that he would seek out his friend Barney. The idea of discussing her behind her back was distasteful, but he needed to understand.

First thing in the morning he headed for Barney's

lodgings. He found his friend dressed in a violently patterned Oriental silk dressing gown and addressing a large breakfast. He invited Marcus to join him, but he only accepted coffee.

When Barney had dealt with most of his breakfast, and was onto his third coffee, Marcus broached the question. "Tell me about Lady Hewitt. Everything you know about her."

Barney buttered a piece of toast and spread it with marmalade, shaking his head sorrowfully all the time. "Marcus, you madman. Did I or did I not warn you against that woman? She'll eat you alive, man—or her brother will, which is just as bad."

Marcs snorted. "Eat me alive?"

Barney crunched down his toast, drank some coffee, swallowed and said, "Hard to believe, isn't it, but trust me, she's as cold as ice and worse—she's heartlessly, ruthlessly avaricious. She's already bled two husbands dry and if she was at the party the other night, it means she's on the hunt for a third. It's the only time she ever appears in society, so be warned."

Marcus was stunned. *Two husbands? At her age?* "You mean she'd been married before Hewitt?"

Barney, his mouth full of toast, nodded. He swallowed. "The first one was old Lord Holgrave."

Marcus had never heard of Lord Holgrave. Nor Lord Hewitt for that matter. His brain was still reeling at the thought that Tessa had been married twice before. "What do you mean 'old' Lord Holgrave?"

"He was past eighty when he married her."

Marcus's jaw dropped in shock. "Past eighty? And she must have been—?"

"Very young." Barney grimaced distastefully. "Holgrave liked them young."

"Good God! She can't have wanted him."

Barney shrugged. "Word is, her father brokered the match. Was in debt to the eyeballs. Worked too. As I said, she—or rather her dear papa—bled the old man dry. By the time old Holgrave died, he was a pauper. But a happy one, I gather, with a beautiful young girl in his bed."

Marcus felt ill. It was a most unsavory tale. "You say she lost her second husband, too? What did he die of?"

"Old age." Barney buttered another piece of toast and spread it lavishly with marmalade. "Are you sure you don't want some toast? This marmalade is dashed good."

Marcus ignored him. "*Old age?*" he repeated, stunned. "You mean she married *another* old man?"

Barney nodded. "Bled him dry too. I expect they're looking for a third rich old octogenarian for her to wed. She's obviously making a career out of it."

Marcus swore silently. The story appalled him,

disgusted him. Tessa couldn't be more than twenty-four or five. Two elderly husbands and both dead and stripped of their wealth? And now there appeared to be a third octogenarian courting her. If that was true, she must have a heart of ice, as Barney had suggested—or no heart at all.

But was it true? She hadn't appeared to encourage her elderly swain at all—far from it. Though some women did play hard-to-get. And some men loved it.

Barney was up to date with every bit of *ton* gossip, but Marcus was sure there was more to the story. There had to be.

He simply couldn't believe that the wild little scrap who loved the forest, who called foxes her friend and slipped out at night to watch badgers and otters and their cubs, could turn into a coldly mercenary young woman who would barter her body to old men and strip them of their fortunes.

He needed to speak to her in person. "Do you know where she and her brother are staying in London?" he asked Barney.

"Brother keeps their address pretty close," Barney explained, waving a triangle of toast vaguely. "Always a rented house that changes every few months. Don't want callers." He snorted. "If you ask me it's debt collectors—or worse—he don't want calling."

Marcus swore under his breath.

Barney eyed him, then shrugged. "I did hear a whisper that his current abode is in Cressy Lane. Not exactly a salubrious address, but neither is it quite in the slums."

"Excellent, thank you. I'll track him down."

It took him a day or two, but by sending a footman to Cressy Lane with a letter addressed to Lord Blaxland, the man, by dint of trial and error, eventually found which house it was. The letter, of course, was blank inside. Marcus had no intention of warning Edgar Blaxland of his interest.

He was shocked by what Barney had told him. Two marriages already, and both to wealthy old men. He could scarce believe it.

It was almost eleven in the morning when he turned the corner to approach her house. As he did, the front door opened and Edgar ran down the steps, climbed into a hackney cab and drove off.

Perfect. He could speak to her without Edgar's interference.

He rang the doorbell. A man—a shabby sort of butler—opened the door, but when Marcus asked for Lady Hewitt, he said indifferently, "Milady is not at home."

But Marcus could see Tessa standing on the landing of the stairs behind the butler, looking cool and serene in a pale green dress. She said nothing, just stared down at him, a troubled line between her brows.

The chaperone from the other night seized her by the arm and pulled her back. "She is not at home," the woman called down.

Marcus pushed past the butler and stepped inside.

"I told you, Milady does not accept callers," the butler said crossly and, grabbing Marcus by the sleeve, tried to pull him away.

Marcus didn't move. The man's ineffectual attempts to oust him had no effect whatsoever. He just looked up at Tessa and waited. If she wanted him gone, he would go, but until then . . .

She had a low inaudible conversation with the chaperone, then shook off the woman's grip, saying, "It's all right Hodges, Lord Alverleigh can enter. Show him into the drawing room and bring us a pot of tea, if you please."

The woman shrugged and went back up the stairs, leaving Tessa alone with Marcus. Strange behavior for a chaperone, he thought, though he welcomed the privacy.

"Why did you come?" Tessa said once they were settled and the butler had departed.

"I had to see you, speak to you."

"It's very kind of you, but really"—she hesitated—"I don't see the point."

"Why? We were friends as children, and now

we are adults, why should we not continue that friendship?"

She glanced away. "It's all different now."

"In what way?"

The butler returned with a tray bearing a pot of tea, cups and saucers, sugar and a plate of biscuits. Tessa busied herself pouring the tea and passed Marcus his cup.

She sat back. There was a short silence. Marcus sipped his tea—he didn't want it: he was just being polite. But the ritual of serving tea was a soothing one.

After a few minutes' silence, he set his cup down and repeated the question. "Why is it all different now?"

"Because we are different people now, of course."

"We're both older, that's true. But I don't see that as a problem."

She sipped her tea, avoiding his eyes. He waited, then added, "I'm worried about you."

"Worried?" she said with a brightness that didn't ring true. "Whatever for?"

He wasn't sure what to say. He didn't want to reveal what Barney had said about her and her brother. "I didn't like the way your brother treated you at the ball the other night."

She made a dismissive gesture. "That was nothing. He was a little bit drunk."

"Nevertheless—"

"I can handle Edgar."

He set down his cup. "To be frank, I heard a rumor that your brother was arranging a marriage for you—"

"No."

"—to the gentleman your brother introduced you to the other night at the ball." He waited, holding his breath.

There was a short silence. Outside a carriage rolled past. A dog barked.

She stirred her tea slowly, then lifted her chin. "It's true that Edgar wishes me to marry again but I'm not doing it. Sir Henry Lester has asked for my hand, but I have refused him."

Marcus swallowed. The relief he felt at her cool, firm words surprised him.

"I married twice for the sake of my family, and that was enough. I will never marry again."

Never? He frowned at the coldness in her voice, then asked her the question that had been eating at him since Barney first told him about her. "How old were you when you married your first husband?"

She looked away, pressing her lips together, and for a long time he thought she wasn't going to answer him. He waited. Eventually she met his gaze and said in a level voice, "Almost sixteen."

Almost sixteen? So, she'd been fifteen—still a child.

"Good God, why?" The question was out before he could stop himself.

There was a short silence, as if she was debating with herself whether to speak or not. He ate a biscuit and waited. Finally she said, "Papa was heavily in debt to some bad men. They were threatening to hurt him, maybe even kill him. Lord Holgrave was a friend of his, and he offered to pay all Papa's debts if I married him." She spread her hands in a gesture of helplessness. "I didn't want to marry him, of course, but with my father's life at stake, what could I do except agree?"

Refuse, Marcus thought, but he could see that at such a young age it would be hard to go against her father. But what sort of a father would do such a thing, sell his innocent young daughter, not yet sixteen, to a man old enough to be her grandfather? A perverted old man at that, who would take a child-bride to wife.

"And Lord Hewitt?" he asked when he had mastered his anger.

Her eyes dropped again. There was a short silence, then she said quietly. "Papa was dead by the time I was widowed, but gambling is in the Blaxland blood: they can't help it. This time it was Edgar who was in trouble with bad men. I didn't want to do it then, either, but"— she shrugged—"it happened anyway." Marcus pursed his lips. There was something in her expression that made him think there was more to that than she was saying.

He had his doubts about the 'bad men'. Oh, he could well believe that there were debts—the Blaxlands were notorious gamblers—but he couldn't believe that first her father and then her brother had been in such dire straits as to have to sell a child in marriage. They'd counted on her youth and innocence—and loyalty.

Her father and brother had rarely visited Ferndale when Tessa was growing up wild and neglected and unloved, except by servants. The lonely little girl would have been eager for their approval, desperate for their love.

Putty in their hands.

Marcus frowned. "You're a beautiful woman. Why not marry a young man and settle down to raise a family—you don't yet have children, do you?"

She flushed and looked down. "No," she said in a low voice. "No children."

"Do you gamble?"

She gave a huff of humorless laughter. "Never. It doesn't appeal to me at all. I don't even like playing cards, though of course I do to be polite. Though not for money—chicken stakes if I must. But I avoid it when I can."

"And Edgar is planning a third marriage for you. What is his reason this time? Is he in debt again?"

She was silent a long time. She picked up her cup, hesitated, put it down, then sighed. "It's much worse than that. He says I must marry again to save Ferndale."

"Ferndale?" he repeated, surprised.

She nodded. "It's my home, you see, and belongs to me."

"I know that, but—"

"It belonged to Mama, not Papa. It was in her marriage settlements that it would come to her first-born daughter—which is me—on my twenty-fifth birthday. That's later this year. I would have gone to Ferndale immediately after Lord Hewitt died, but there was his estate to be disposed of which was a lot of work. And since he'd willed everything to me, I had to remain to sign the various documents. Edgar handled it of course, as he'd overseen the disposal of my first husband's estate and knew what had to be done."

In other words, Edgar had been stripping every last penny from their estates.

"I also needed to arrange pensions for his servants. Some of them had been with him for decades."

"Then after that was done, why did you not leave?" Marcus had a creeping suspicion of what was to come, but he wanted to hear it from her.

"Because as it turned out there was not a penny left. And then there were the mortgages to be sorted, of course. I didn't realize—Edgar manages all that side of things for me, as Papa did before him. And, of course, banks and lawyers and people who arrange mortgages won't do business with females anyway. Which is very frustrating, but what can you do?"

"Which mortgages are these?"

"The Ferndale mortgages. Apparently the estate is deep in debt and has been for years—mortgaged to the hilt, Edgar said. I had no idea. And the man who holds the mortgages is threatening to foreclose. I couldn't have that, I just couldn't. Lose my home?" She shook her head vehemently. "Never! And since we have no money to pay the mortgages, Edgar insists that the only solution is to arrange another marriage for me—which would be my third and my last. If I married Sir Henry Lester, he would pay off the mortgage." She shuddered. "But I won't do it—I couldn't bear it. There *must* be another way."

There was a short silence. Marcus couldn't speak for the anger that was choking him.

"Edgar has apologized about the mortgages. He says he forgot the last few payments, but I'm sure it was a lie. My brother, like our father before him, is a hopeless gambler—it's in his blood—and neither of them have been particularly lucky. I'm sure he had the money ready to pay the mortgage but then, no doubt . . . *'There was this horse. And it was a dead cert to win.*'" She shook her head sadly. "Of course, it didn't. None of his 'dead certs' ever do."

She stared into her tea for a moment. "But I've made it clear to Edgar that I will never marry again, not to Sir Henry, not to any man. And so he has gone out this morning to try again to get a loan to cover the mortgage interest payments. He's trying very hard, but it won't be easy."

Marcus gritted his teeth, holding the words back. He rose and strolled toward the mantlepiece, his back to her, as if warming himself—though the grate was empty—while he tried to master his rage and work out how to tell her. And how much to tell her. Would she even believe him if he told her the unvarnished truth?

Probably not. Nevertheless, she had to be told. He couldn't let her be persuaded to sacrifice herself a third time because of the lies her swine of a brother had told her—and this time Marcus knew for certain it was a lie—a big one, possibly the worst of all.

She wasn't the mercenary ice-maiden Barney had warned him about.

He understood more now, and when she'd talked about her beloved Ferndale, her voice had warmed and he'd caught a glimpse, beneath the cool, polished facade, of the scruffy little girl who'd been passionate about her forest and the wildlife in it, and who cared nothing for riches or position. She wanted her home back.

But it was the one thing she couldn't have.

It was none of his business—*she* was none of his business—but he couldn't help himself. She was his little friend of the forest, and her company had made his adolescent years at Alverleigh almost bearable. He was damned if he let her go on thinking her sacrifice would save her home, but how to explain it without telling her the whole story? It was the devil of a coil.

He resumed his seat. "You say Ferndale is mortgaged to the hilt?"

She nodded. "Yes, and the mortgage holder is threatening imminent foreclosure unless we pay him immediately. That's why Edgar was in a hurry to get me married. But I've convinced him to look for a different solution."

Marcus took a deep breath. "I don't quite know how to tell you this, Tessa, but the Ferndale estate was sold two years ago."

She stared at him, then shook her head. "No, you're mistaken. It can't have been sold. The Ferndale estate belongs to me and came to me from my mother. She—or more likely my grandfather—must have known of the Blaxland tendency to gamble, and so it was written into her marriage settlements. So you see it can't possibly be sold without my permission—and I would never sell Ferndale. Never."

"Nevertheless, it was sold two years ago."

Two spots of color rose in her cheeks. "You're wrong, I tell you. It's not possible." Her knuckles were white around her tea cup.

"Do you think I'd make such a mistake about an estate that borders my own? Ferndale has changed hands. Another family is living there now."

"No." Her complexion turned chalky. "It can't have been sold. It can't." She was almost whispering, as if trying to convince herself. But he could tell she more than half believed him.

She rallied. "Edgar can't have sold it, not without my permission. And I would never give it, never."

"You mentioned he used to get you to sign documents."

She stiffened. "Sometimes."

"And do you read them—every detail?"

She looked at him, stricken. Her expression said it all.

There was a long silence. She put down her barely touched tea cup and pushed it away. The clock in the hallway chimed the hour and she jumped and rose to her feet. "My brother will be back soon, and he won't be happy to see you here. He dislikes callers and can get quite unpleasant about it, so I will bid you good day, Lord Alverleigh. It was kind of you to call." He could tell her mind was still elsewhere, no doubt reeling from the news he'd given her.

Marcus rose. "We used to be Marcus and Tessa."

She shook her head sadly. "Goodbye, Lord Alverleigh."

He moved toward the door, then turned back. Producing his silver card case, he took out a card and handed it to her, saying, "If there's ever anything I can do for you, let me know."

She glanced at it, but made no move to take it, so he placed it on a small side-table and left.

The butler slammed the door behind him.

CHAPTER THREE

THE MINUTE TESSA heard the front door close, she sank back on her seat. She was shaking. Ferndale sold? Two years ago? She couldn't believe it.

But Lord Alverleigh had sounded so certain. And since the Alverleigh estate shared a border with Ferndale, he would surely know. Why would he lie to her about it? He had nothing to lose, while her brother. . .

Oh, Edgar. Had he really tricked her, sold her home and lied about it? And was even now pretending to raise a loan to pay for non-existent mortgages? Which of course he wouldn't be able to get, and so the only choice left for her would be to marry Sir Henry Lester.

She could challenge him on it, of course, but if Lord Alverleigh was right—and she had a sickening feeling he was—Edgar had been lying about the mortgages all along.

He *knew* she hadn't intended marrying ever again. She hadn't wanted to marry the first time—or the second—but had endured both marriages in the sure and certain knowledge that it was her duty to her family, to save Papa's life, and later Edgar's.

Had those been lies too? She picked up her tea cup and tried to swallow some of the cold tea but a lump in her throat made it impossible.

She took a deep breath. She wouldn't ask Edgar about Ferndale; she couldn't trust him to tell her the truth. She would have to find out for herself. But how?

She glanced at Lord Alverleigh's card sitting on the side table. If Edgar saw it, there would be questions. And nasty repercussions. She picked it up and tucked it into her reticule, out of sight.

She rang for another cup of tea and, over a gently steaming cup, pondered her choices. There was really only one thing to do—to go to Ferndale and see for herself.

The yellow bounder raced along. Inside, Tessa clung to a leather strap, bouncing and swaying. The little yellow carriages certainly lived up to their nickname, she thought. Not that she minded. She watched the countryside flash by, half excited by the prospect of going home at last, half dreading what she would find.

She'd given Edgar the slip, and hired the carriage herself, using the money she'd secretly squirreled away over the last year. It was her first real act of independence and she felt quite proud of herself. Hiring a carriage had been fearfully expensive, but time was of the essence.

Edgar had gone to a country house party and would be gone for a week. "There's a good chance I'll be able to raise the money for a mortgage," he'd told her. It was just an excuse. It would be a bachelor affair, all gambling and shooting and loose women, she knew. Tessa would never be invited to such a gathering. Edgar was very strict about her reputation.

So he'd left her at home with Mrs Thracknell, the grim woman he'd hired as her chaperone. Tessa had given her the slip too, leaving a bottle of brandy out the night before—Mrs Thracknell could never resist alcohol—and slipping out at dawn. She knew the woman would report her to Edgar eventually, but she'd deal with that when it happened. She'd left a note to say she'd gone to stay with a female friend—unspecified.

She had no female friends. Ever since Edgar and Papa had brought her to London, she'd always been with a husband, or with Edgar or with Mrs Thracknell. Personal friends were not encouraged— were actively discouraged, in fact. Not that any had tried.

Through the big glass front window of the carriage, Tessa watched the countryside slide by. Ferndale, how she'd missed it. She'd never been lonely there, even though she hardly saw anyone, only NannyJune and Phillips. While for the last ten years she'd almost never been alone but was constantly lonely.

She dozed a while, only waking when they stopped at a posting inn to change the horses. Sometimes she stepped down to stretch her legs, or to visit the facilities or have a hot drink. No food, despite the fact that she hadn't eaten all day. She was too nervous to eat. They were moving ever closer to Ferndale.

She loved it so much, had thought of it so often over the years, planning what she would do to it, once she was free to go home. The house had been terribly shabby. She'd realized that in retrospect— not that she'd cared at the time—and would be even more so now. And the estate would need a lot of work to bring it back to profitability.

Neither Papa nor Edgar had ever shown an interest in it, even though they spent any income the estate earned. But she'd learned a bit about land management during her marriages, and she knew exactly what she would do once she was home again at Ferndale.

Her stomach cramped. It couldn't have been sold, it just couldn't.

Not long now. The countryside was becoming more and more familiar as they passed. The shape of those hills, that old stone bridge, the tumbledown cottage with the crooked roof: small landmarks that she didn't even know she'd memorized, but they brought a lump to her throat.

Home.

The carriage slowed and turned in between two tall wrought iron gates. Dread swamped her. Lord Alverleigh had told her the truth. In her memory those gates had been old and rusting: now they gleamed with black paint.

Her heart was pounding. She could barely breathe as they drove down the curving driveway toward the house and she took it all in, all the changes. Everything was as neat as a pin. The lawn, which she'd only ever known as shaggy grass filled with weeds and wildflowers, was now green and smooth as velvet. Here and there were well-tended flowerbeds, bursting with spring flowers. In the distance she could see the old orchard and even from here she could see the trees had been neatly pruned. Some were in blossom.

She glanced toward the forest, her heart heavy

with the burgeoning realization that this would be the worst of all. She couldn't tell from this distance, but she already knew it would have been cut back, dozens of trees cut down and harvested, the beautiful tangle of undergrowth cleared away, not a fern or a bramble in sight. No place for foxes or badgers to hide and bring up their young.

Her stomach clenched and she felt as though she might throw up. Despite having eaten nothing all day.

Her brother had sold her home. Sold Ferndale. And lied to her about it. In the worst way, and for reasons that made her want to scream. Or curl up and whimper.

How could he?

The carriage pulled up in front of the house. Tessa didn't want to get out, didn't want to have her worst fears confirmed—she'd seen enough—but the front door had opened and a butler stepped forward, a man she'd never seen before. The postilion let down the steps and gathering what remained of her poise she alighted.

Acid rose in her throat, but she managed to say, "I'm terribly sorry, but I think I've come to the wrong house. I was looking for the . . ."—she pulled a name out of thin air—"the Taylor family."

The butler's brow wrinkled. "I don't know any

Taylors hereabouts, madam. This is the home of Mr and Mrs Sanderson and their family."

Tessa nodded. She could hear childish shouts and laughter coming from behind the house. It felt like her insides had been gutted. She managed to say, "Perhaps the Taylors were before your time. Have the Sandersons lived here long?"

"Coming up to two years, madam. I came with them from their previous abode outside of Bath. Would you care to come in? I'm sure Mrs Sanderson would like to meet you. And she might know more about the previous residents." He hesitated. "Though I think the name was Blackstone, or Blaxland—something like that."

"No, no thank you. It's getting late and I must get on and find my friends," Tessa said hurriedly and turned away, fearing she might throw up.

He inclined his head. "Good luck finding them, madam."

She climbed back into the carriage, and it drove back down the driveway. Tessa didn't see much. Her eyes were blinded by tears.

Two years! The Sandersons had moved two years ago. It was just as Lord Alverleigh had said.

So much for Edgar's claim of mortgage arrears. Her beloved home had been sold and was lost to her forever. Strangers lived there now. It was lost to her. Forever.

By the time she reached London again, Tessa had cried herself out, slept a little and commenced some serious thinking. She'd been a fool, a stupid, trusting fool to think that her brother—and no doubt her father too—had been looking after her interests, as they'd claimed.

She thought back to the day they'd arrived at Ferndale, when she was fifteen, and Papa had looked her up and down and then said to Edgar, *'Looks like we have another asset.'*

She'd asked them about it later, but they just shook their heads and told her it was business—men's talk. And naive little idiot that she'd been, she'd accepted that.

Stupid, needy, *ignorant* little girl, imagining that Papa and Edgar had come for her because they cared about her. That feeling had lasted all through her first weeks in London, when Papa, with the advice of a lady friend, had purchased all new fancy grown-up clothes for her, and put her on a strict beauty regime, attempting to tame her wild hair, and using endless lotions on her skin, which they said was dreadfully tanned from all the time she spent outdoors.

She learned to keep her hands clean and to grow and polish her nails, to keep herself and her clothes tidy, to get used to a maid dressing and undressing her.

She was never alone, which had been very hard for a girl used to solitude and freedom.

They trained her relentlessly, in etiquette, and how to dance, and to serve tea elegantly. And to talk to men. She'd been horribly shy at first, but when they'd introduced her to the man who became her first husband, he'd claimed he found her shyness delightful.

Not that she knew he was to become her husband then—he was just an old man who was a friend of Papa's. She didn't much like the way he stroked her hand and sat rather too close. And his breath stank. But she'd learned to be polite and to hide her discomfort.

The day Papa informed her, with tears in his eyes, that bad men were after him, threatening to kill him—slowly and painfully—unless he could pay them the money he owed, she'd been so distressed and frightened on his behalf.

Foolish, gullible child.

And then a few days later, after she'd lain awake through several nights, tossing and turning, conjuring up schemes to save him—wild, impossible schemes—he'd come to her and told her that old Lord Holgrave was willing to give him the money that would save his life. She'd been so relieved. Even grateful.

Until she heard Lord Holgrave's condition for the gift.

Marriage.

The thought had horrified her, and she'd refused and refused. But Papa and Edgar were adamant: if she didn't marry Lord Holgrave, her father would be murdered. Violently and painfully. What sort of daughter would put her own silly, childish female preferences before her father's life?

And so she'd gritted her teeth and done it. And it had not been so very dreadful. He hadn't beaten her, at least. She'd learned to endure the marriage bed, and apart from that, Lord Holgrave had been an indulgent husband, buying her jewels and other pretty baubles, treating her like a little doll. Not that she cared for such things. Papa usually took the jewels for safekeeping, saying she was a careless chit—which she had to admit she was. She had no interest in jewels.

Then Papa had collapsed and died in bed—no bad men involved—and from then on, Edgar had looked after her jewels for her. And not long after Papa's death, Lord Holgrave had died, and she'd thought she was free, at last.

But then the bad men came after Edgar, and marriage to another wealthy old man was his solution. She'd refused, of course—once was enough—and she'd felt so guilty, because she didn't love Edgar the way she'd loved Papa.

But somehow—she still wasn't clear quite how it had happened—she'd found herself married to Lord Hewitt.

What was that expression? *Fool me once, shame on you. Fool me twice, shame on me.*

She'd even been about to fall for the lies a third time. So what did that make her? A stupid, naive, trusting fool. Worse.

Well, no longer. The scales had well and truly fallen from her eyes now, and she wasn't shamed— she was furious. And the moment Edgar returned, she was going to confront him.

"Did you enjoy your house party?" Tessa asked her brother shortly after he'd arrived home. They were seated in the drawing room. She was sipping tea, he, brandy.

"Yes, it was very pleasant. Now, I was speaking to Sir Henry Lester and—"

She cut him off. "Lose much money?"

He shrugged indifferently. "Won some, lost some. Now about Sir Henry—"

She could tell from his expression that the losses

greatly outweighed the wins. Had he come away flush with his winnings, he'd be crowing about it.

"No bad men confronting you about your debts?"

"No, what bad—Oh, them. No, thankfully they've agreed to wait until after your wedding."

"In that case, they'll be waiting forever," she said calmly. Inside she was fuming. He hadn't even bothered to get his story straight—that it was the mortgages needing to be paid, not bad men after his gambling debts.

He caught himself up. "Besides, it's not my debts that are the problem, remember? It's the mortgage arrears. And the mortgage holder is pushing very hard for payment."

"No he's not."

His brows snapped together. "What the devil do you mean by that?"

"There is no mortgage on Ferndale."

"There damned well is. I should know. What does a chit like you know about mortgages anyway?" His tone was an uneasy mix of cajolery and contempt.

"Not a lot," she said. Though that would change. Never again would she trust her security to her brother—or to any man.

"Exactly. You have no idea—"

She continued, "But I do know that when you've sold a property you no longer have a mortgage to pay."

His eyes narrowed. "What do you mean, 'sold a property'?"

"Don't bother denying it, Edgar. Ferndale was sold two years ago."

"Who told you that piece of nonsense?" he blustered. "I tell you—"

"I've been there."

His jaw dropped. "You've—"

"Been there, yes, to Ferndale. While you were away. Seen it with my very own eyes, seen how money has been poured into it to bring it back to—"

"Well of course, I authorized repairs."

She snorted. "You've never spent a penny on Ferndale, so don't lie to me. Neither you, nor Papa, for as long as I've been alive."

He opened his mouth to argue, and she added, "Besides I've met the people living there now— which they have for the last two years."

He stared at her. She could see he was trying to come up with a story to placate her. Another set of lies he would expect her to tamely swallow.

But she wasn't the naive fool she had been.

She made a dismissive gesture. "Don't bother, Edgar. You've been lying to me all along, I know that now. Papa too, I have no doubt," she added bitterly. "So there will be no more marriages to wealthy old men for me, no more marriages at all, in fact. From now on, brother dear, you and your debts are on your own."

He drained his glass of brandy, poured himself another one, drank it down in one go and leaned back in his chair, eyeing her with a brooding expression.

"There's no need to look so smug, sister dear. My problems are your problems."

"Not any more."

He gave a humorless laugh. "Believe that if you like. But I ask you— what do you intend to do? Because unless you marry Sir Henry Lester, you'll be destitute."

She frowned.

Edgar continued. "We are behind in the rent on this house—if we don't pay up by the end of the month, we'll be out in the street. And you needn't look at me like that—I don't have any money—not a bean. As you so rightly pointed out, all I have are debts."

"What about my jewels?" she asked hopelessly, knowing better.

He huffed a laugh. "Sold ten minutes after you handed them over."

She'd guessed as much. "Lord Hewitt left me a substantial sum—I know it is true because he told me." It was her last hope.

Edgar shook his head. "By the time Hewitt

breathed his last he had barely a penny to leave. And we—all right, *I* then—sold everything after his death, and if you're thinking there's money left over, I can assure you there isn't, not so much as a groat."

Her stomach sank. "You stripped him of everything?"

"Indeed." Edgar inclined his head in ironic assent. "So you see, you haven't a choice. It's Sir Henry Lester or debtors' prison. Think about it, my pretty sister—do you really want your next address to be 'care of The Marshalsea'?"

She shuddered. She didn't know much about The Marshalsea except that it was a notorious prison for debtors. "I won't marry Sir Henry, and I won't be going to The Marshalsea," she told her brother.

He gave a cynical snort. "How are you going to support yourself then? Sell yourself in the streets? Because you haven't a penny to your name and believe me, if you don't marry Sir Henry, it will come to that."

She could tell from his expression that he believed she still had no choice but to fall in with his plans. She didn't know what she could do—yet—but she'd think of something.

She rose from her chair. "I suggest instead of concerning yourself with my future, you give some thought to how you will support yourself. For the first time in your life."

He rose, and came toward her with an ugly look on his face. "You *will* marry Sir Henry Lester, if I have to drag you to the altar!"

"You wouldn't dare! And anyway, I would refuse! You cannot force me. Or trick me. I'm not a child any longer."

"You said that about marrying Hewitt, remember? And yet you did, despite your little brainstorm." He gave a nasty laugh. "So save your arguments, little sister—you'll marry whoever I tell you to."

Tessa stared at him, frustrated and angry. She did remember the arguments, and refusing to marry Lord Hewitt . . .

She'd never understood how it happened. She had no memory of the wedding—the loss was the result of a brainstorm, the doctor had told her. But she was irrevocably married—they even showed her the marriage certificate with her own signature—shaky but definitely hers—and she'd had no choice but to accept it.

Edgar sat there smirking.

"You are despicable! And I still refuse."

"How will you support yourself then?" Edgar sneered. "Become a courtesan? Sell your lush little body at Covent Garden?" She gasped, but he went on, his voice harsh, "Because that's all you're fit for. At least with marriage you'll have security."

"Oh yes, I can see that," she said sarcastically.

"That's why I've made two marriages and have not a penny to my name—and now even my own home is lost to me!" Furious, shaking with helpless rage, and feeling her eyes prickling with tears—which she refused to let him see—she swept out the door, brushing past Mrs Thracknell, who was loitering outside, doubtless waiting to report Tessa's unsanctioned absence to Edgar at the earliest opportunity.

Good luck with that, Tessa thought as she ran up the stairs to her bedchamber. No point shutting the stable door after the horse was out, and Tessa was well and truly out from under Edgar's thumb—mentally, at least. She had her own future to consider now.

She threw herself onto her bed, shaking. Any feeling of triumph at her rebellion had drained away after that last exchange. That comment about her brainstorm had rattled her. Edgar sounded so sure that a wedding to Sir Henry would happen, quite as if her strongest objections were irrelevant—even mildly amusing. It was more than unsettling.

She'd always known her brother didn't love her, but new depths to his callous ruthlessness had been revealed to her in the last few weeks.

She had to get away as soon as possible. But how? And to where?

It was all very well to tell Edgar to support himself for a change, but how was she to do the same? She had even less experience of the world and living at Ferndale was no longer an option.

She lay on her bed, staring sightlessly at a water stain on the ceiling, her mind racing.

His words came back to her, over and over. "*Sell your lush little body at Covent Garden?*"

Never! Though it hadn't been her choice, the brutal truth was that her body had effectively been sold in marriage—twice—and look where that had got her? She'd ended up worse off than when she'd been a child, running wild in Ferndale. She might have had ragged clothes back then, but at least she'd had freedom. And a home. And her body had been her own.

She'd never go home to Ferndale again. Tears welled up again. She scrubbed them away. She'd wept enough for what she'd lost. Weeping would get her nowhere now.

She thought again about Edgar's insistence that she must marry again. It stiffened her spine.

Never again would she let him—or any man—control her life.

She considered the options open to her. She would have to get a job. And somewhere to live that wasn't anywhere near her brother. She fetched a pen and paper and began a list.

<u>Jobs for females.</u>

— Governess

— Lady's Companion
— Nursemaid
— Saleswoman in a shop
— Maid
— ???

She considered the list. It wasn't very promising. Governess? She'd had minimal education. Nanny June had taught her to read and write and to do basic addition, multiplication and subtraction, and though she'd had the run of the library at Ferndale, that was the sum of her education.

Tessa had virtually none of the accomplishments that were required of young ladies today; she knew no foreign languages, had never learned embroidery or painted a watercolor or learned to play a musical instrument.

She crossed out 'Governess'.

Lady's companion? She could do that, she supposed, but she knew no old ladies to ask. She knew almost nobody in society. Mrs Thracknell? She'd been more of a prison wardress than a companion. Tessa would never do that to another woman. She didn't cross it out though.

Nursemaid? She loved children and thought she would enjoy caring for them. But again, she had no experience. And her experience of her first husband in particular had taught her that female servants, especially young, good-looking ones, were regarded as fair prey by gentlemen. And when she'd raised the question first with her father and later with Edgar, they'd both assured her that it meant nothing, that the servants expected it, even enjoyed it.

Tessa didn't believe them. She'd never enjoyed it herself, and she was sure it meant something to the servants concerned. And while it might not surprise them, she was certain they didn't enjoy it, otherwise why would there be such a high turnover of female staff in her husband's home?

Becoming a nursemaid would be risky, but she kept it on the list in case she had no other option.

Next on the list was saleswoman in a shop. Surely that was a job she could do.

The following morning, she put on her pelisse, hat and gloves and sallied out to Oxford Street and New Bond Street, where all the best shops were.

By noon, she felt utterly dejected. Her feet ached. She'd asked at every shop she could find, without success. She found a nearby park and sat down on a bench to eat some lunch.

Not that she felt like eating, but she'd made herself a cheese sandwich and filled a bottle with cold tea. There was the rest of the day to keep job-hunting; she needed to keep her energy up.

She took a bite, chewing slowly. A few people had

even been quite rude, thinking she couldn't possibly be serious. Most had taken one look at her and just shook their heads.

A movement at her feet drew her attention. A small, scruffy mongrel sat there, gazing up at her with a hopeful expression in his liquid brown eyes.

"Hungry, boy?" He was skinny and his coat was matted and crusted with dirt. "Of course you are. Here." She broke off a piece of her sandwich and held it out, careful in case he bit her in his eagerness to get the food.

The little dog sniffed it, then took it from her gently. Then with one gulp, it was gone. "More?" she asked.

His ragged little tail thumped on the ground, and she broke off another piece. Again, he took it from her gently, then gobbled it down.

"You're quite the little gentleman, aren't you?" she told him as she broke off another piece of sandwich. "I hope you're having a better day than I am."

She watched him eat. His coat was filthy, a ragged, indistinct grayish brown whose principal color was dirt. He was a street mutt, belonging to nobody, with no home and living off his wits. The sort of dog that nobody noticed, unless it was to kick it out of their way.

"You know, you've made me realize something," she told the dog. "I should have worn my plainest dress. All the girls working in the shops were dressed neatly but drably." The dog wagged its tail as if in agreement. "The trouble is, I don't have any drab dresses."

She gave the last piece of sandwich to the dog. "But it's not just that. Even the ones who took me seriously enough to ask a few questions, the minute they heard my accent they shook their heads And those that didn't, once they learned I had no experience, they just waved me away, too. One man even asked me to add up a string of numbers in my head—and I did, but it wasn't fast enough for him, so he sent me packing. It's most disheartening."

The little dog leaned forward and nudged her foot.

"Sorry little fellow, there's no more food. Off you go." She waved the little dog away, but he simply sat down again and eyed her expectantly.

"What's next, you want to know?" It was ridiculous having a serious conversation with a street dog, but it was oddly comforting.

"The next job on my list is maidservant." The little dog scratched behind his ear, then shook himself vigorously.

"You may be right. Maids live a hard life; up at all hours, at everyone's beck and call, doing all kinds of unpleasant jobs. I can do them of course—I can do anything I put my mind to—but it's not ideal." And hard work and long hours aside, there was the issue of being prey for the gentlemen of the house. The thought of that gave her the shivers.

The little dog gazed up at her, his head cocked curiously, all attention, even though there was no more food forthcoming. He was a fine little companion for a lonely lunch.

"Is that what you think I should do? Find a position as a companion? Find an elderly single woman or a widow, you think?"

The dog scratched behind his other ear and she chuckled. "I think you have fleas, my friend. But it's not your fault, I know. I'll need help in finding a suitable position, but the trouble is, I know almost nobody in London to ask. My first husband was quite sociable, but also very jealous of any attention I received, so when he did go out, he generally left me at home. Yes, not very nice, I agree."

She bent down and patted the little dog's head. "My second husband preferred to stay at home, day in day out, keeping me beside him, so I rarely went anywhere. And yes, it almost drove me mad. There's nothing worse than being shut in, day after day after day. You probably can't imagine it, having the freedom of the streets as you do." Not that scrabbling day-to-day, just to survive, was much to celebrate.

She looked down at the little scrap of canine refuse smiling up at her. Could dogs smile? This one could—it was something about his eyes. Liquid brown and bright with intelligence, they practically spoke.

"You didn't wait for someone to feed you, did you, fellow? Or try to snatch my sandwich, which a lesser dog would do. You *asked*, as plain as plain could be. And you're right—if I want to find a position as a companion, I'll need help. I must ask for an introduction."

The ragged little tail wagged. He was a living lesson, this small creature. No doubt he lived his life avoiding kicks and all kinds of abuse, scouring gutters for scraps, and yet despite it all, he retained a hopeful outlook. She bent down and patted him again. "Goodbye little fellow. Thank you for your company. And good luck."

She rose to her feet, feeling newly energetic. She'd try a few more shops. She wasn't about to give up after half a day, and from now on, she would refuse to allow any rejections to depress her spirits.

The next step—assuming she didn't get a job in a shop—was to find someone who might recommend her as a companion.

The only time she'd ever mixed in society was when Edgar or Papa was showing her off to some old man. And though on those few occasions she'd smiled at some of the ladies present, not one of them had smiled back. They despised her, she knew, for her marriages. She didn't blame them—she rather despised herself now for allowing herself to be used like that, young as she'd been—but it wasn't going to help her now.

She tried the next shop, a silk merchant and haberdashery. She loved fine fabrics and knew quite a bit about them. But though the manageress initially greeted her with fawning politeness, the minute she realized Tessa was not a customer, but a young woman seeking work, her expression changed. Looking down her nose at Tessa, she said, "We have no need of your sort in this establishment. I will thank you to leave."

What 'sort' she imagined Tessa to be was clear.

Tessa held her head high and walked out, fighting back tears. Why did other women always imagine the worst about her? And not just women. Even her own brother expected her to earn her living on her back.

Become a courtesan? Sell your lush little body at Covent Garden? Because that's all you're fit for.

As she exited the shop, the man on the door lifted an umbrella and growled, "Gedouttahere you little mongrel!" For a second Tessa thought he was talking to her, but when she turned indignantly, she saw who he was addressing in such a violent manner: the small scruffy dog sitting a short distance from the entrance.

"Don't touch that dog," she snapped. "He's with me."

The doorman gaped. "With you, miss?"

"Yes," she said haughtily. "With me."

She marched off down the street, the little dog trotting along beside her, and when they reached the corner, she burst out laughing. "Well, little fellow, that cheered me up no end. Horrid man. But you'd better go off now. I've got a few more places to try before I give up."

But she was given short shrift at the next five places as well—though none as rudely as at the silk merchant's. And each time she emerged from an unsuccessful interview, there was the little dog, waiting for her, his eyes bright, his ragged little tail wagging in welcome.

In the face of all her rejections, the scruffy little creature's welcome kept her spirits from plummeting. His was the friendliest face she'd seen in days. She looked down at him and made up her mind.

"You've adopted me, haven't you, little one?" she said. "Very well, Edgar will hit the roof when I arrive home with you—he hates dogs—but I need a friend. You're coming home with me."

As she walked, her feet aching with every step, she looked down at the little dog prancing happily along beside her. It was a rash decision, she knew. If she got a job as a companion or a nursemaid, she would never be allowed to keep a dog. But that was a problem for another day.

At the very least the little dog would get a few good feeds and a wash and brush. And if she did get a job, who knew, she might find someone who would take him for her.

CHAPTER FOUR

AVOIDING THE FRONT door, she entered the house by the steps down to the basement entering via the kitchen, and startling the maidservant, who said, "Oy, Miss Tessa, watch out! There's a nasty little mongrel follerin' you. G'wan, ya filthy little rat! " She went to shoo him out, but Tessa stopped her.

"He's not nasty at all, Lottie. He's mine."

The maid stared. "Yours, miss?"

"Yes. If there's any shepherd's pie left over from last night, please bring some of it. The dog is very hungry."

"Shepherd's pie? *For a dog?*"

"Or if there's none left, bring something else— bread and milk if there's nothing else. With an egg broken into it."

Muttering, the girl went off and returned in a few minutes with a bowl containing a mess of stale bread, milk and an egg. The little dog fell on it hungrily.

"Thank you," Tessa told the girl. "Now please set up a tin bath in the back yard, and I will want several large cans of warm water."

"Gunna drown 'im, miss?" The maid sniggered.

"Don't be silly. But as you observed, he's filthy and needs a bath." And there were fleas, but she wasn't going to stress that.

Lottie shrank back. "Don't look at me, I ain't paid to wash dirty mongrels—in fact, we all bin talking." She made an expansive gesture, as if to include the whole household. "None of us've bin paid in a good long while. It ain't right, miss, it ain't right."

"I know, and I'm very sorry about it," Tessa said, "but you'll have to take it up with my brother, I'm afraid. I can't help you. I don't have a penny to my name." She added in a coaxing voice, "But first, Lottie, could you please fetch me the bathtub and some warm water?"

Lottie sniffed. "I told you, I ain't washin' that thing. What if it bites me?"

"He won't," Tessa said. "I'll bathe him myself. Now fetch the tub, if you please."

Leaving the maid to carry out her tasks, and the dog licking the bowl clean, Tessa ran upstairs and fetched a cake of soap, a comb and then, as an afterthought, a pair of scissors. There was no way she'd be able to get a comb through that matted coat.

She set the little dog on a stool and began snipping off clumps of matted fur. He endured it, shivering, but made no move to escape. At first she just concentrated on the worst ones, but soon she realized the best thing, the easiest for her and the dog, would be to cut everything off. Which she did.

When he was shorn, she picked him up and placed him gently in the warm water. Shivering, he wriggled and struggled, and gave her piteous looks, but she stayed firm and, talking soothingly, lathered him from top to tail.

"The bucket please, Lottie." She rinsed him off and the water ran brown, so she had Lottie tip it down the drain and refill the tub, then lathered him up again.

The maid watched curiously. 'Cor, he's all skin and bones, i'nt he? Like a little skellington."

Still shivering, the little dog again made no move to escape, and this time when she rinsed off first the soap, then gave him a last rinse, the water ran clear.

Now he was clean, she could see his true color— no longer a dog that had looked like a colorless rag that had been dragged through a thousand gutters, he was now several shades of brown with a few touches of black, white feet, a white bib and a white-tipped tail.

"Quite a handsome little fellow, aren't you?" Tessa told him, as she toweled him dry.

Behind her Lottie snorted. "'Andsome?"

"And obviously intelligent," Tessa added. She put him down, and he shook himself mightily, even though he was almost dry, which made her laugh. While she and the maid tidied up, the dog explored the small back yard, found a suitable corner and relieved himself tidily.

"Good dog," Tessa said approvingly. "Now, if Lottie will fetch one of those meaty bones that cook saves for soup . . ."

Lottie shook her head. "Take one of Cook's precious soup bones? It's more'n me job's worth, miss."

"If Cook objects, you can tell her to take it up with me," Tessa told her. If Cook took it up with anyone—which was unlikely—it would be Edgar, and she'd get short shrift from him.

With the bone in one hand and the newly clean dog under her arm, Tessa had Lottie check for Edgar's whereabouts, and finding he'd gone out, hurried up the stairs to her bedchamber. There was just one small worn and shabby rug on her floor, so she gave the bone to the dog to chew on the wooden floor, figuring it would be easy enough to clean.

"What am I going to call you?" she mused as he gnawed happily. "Scrap? Patch?" He kept on chewing.

No, names like that were too close to dwelling on

his life as a street dog. He had a new life now. "What about Billy?" she said. The little dog looked up and wagged his tail.

"That settles it. Billy you are." Then she sighed. "I wish my own future was as easy to sort out." Today's unsuccessful quest for work had daunted her somewhat. She wouldn't give up, not after one day, but it obviously wasn't going to be easy. She needed to widen her search.

The idea of being a paid companion—even an unpaid one who would get meals and a roof over her head—was becoming more and more appealing. But she would need an introduction, at the very least. Old ladies would be unlikely to admit a complete stranger to their home without a recommendation, or at least an introduction.

But how, when she didn't know any old ladies? Or even any ladies at all? Both her husbands had kept her to themselves and she'd never had a chance to make any friends. Even as a widow, she'd never had any callers: Edgar didn't allow it. And the ladies of the *ton* who did know of her, scorned her as a heartless fortune hunter.

She thought again of Marcus. Lord Alverleigh.

'If there's ever anything I can do for you, let me know.'

She fetched the card he'd left, picked up the pen, and wrote a note asking him to call on her as soon as convenient.

She folded it, sealed it with a wax seal, wrote his address on it—thank goodness she'd kept his card—and rang a bell to summon a servant to get it delivered. She waited. And waited.

After his big meal, the little dog was snoozing contentedly so, carefully shutting him in her bedchamber, she stepped out and glanced around. The house was strangely silent. She frowned. They didn't have many servants, but even if some of them were taking a half-day off, there should still be someone left to keep the house running. She listened. The house was silent, not even the sound of a ticking clock.

She went downstairs and glanced into the drawing room. As expected there was no sign of Edgar. She went down to the kitchen area and was shocked to discover there was not a soul there. On one end of the big table was some partly made pastry, on the other, a small pile of half-peeled vegetables, the peels curling up and turning brown.

It was as if the servants had simply vanished while still in the middle of cooking. Even Hodges wasn't in his usual lair; the butler's pantry. There was no sign of Lottie either. Where was everyone?

She walked back upstairs and climbed the narrow stairway to the servants' quarters. They were bare of all possessions.

Everyone had left. She was alone in the house.

But why? Lottie had complained about their lack of wages, which was perfectly understandable, but she hadn't given any indication that she—and the rest of the servants—were leaving. Lottie must have known, but she hadn't said a word. Not even a hint.

It was very mysterious and unsettling. Edgar had clearly gone out, but he would return eventually, and she'd be alone and at his mercy. She shivered. All the more reason why she should send for Lord Alverleigh.

She added a few lines to the outside of her letter to him, then went out into the street and summoned a skinny little urchin she'd often seen hanging around the streets. Once she'd given him a currant bun and another time, an orange, and ever since he'd given her a gap-toothed smile on the few occasions she'd stepped outside the house.

"Will you take this letter to this house in Mayfair, please?" She read out the address, for of course the lad couldn't read.

He eyed her shrewdly. "Cost ya sixpence, lady."

Tessa didn't have sixpence. She said firmly. "I'll give you a penny now, and when you deliver it, the gentleman will pay you sixpence. See, I'm writing that here"—she added it to her note—"so the gentleman will know to pay you." She held up the penny, the only change she had been able to find. It had been in one of Edgar's coat pockets. She'd spent all her own money on the journey to Ferndale and back.

The boy hesitated, then held out his hand, saying, "Orright. Where did ya say to take it again?" She repeated the address—luckily it wasn't far— and he grabbed the penny and the letter and ran off. She hoped he would deliver it, but there was no guarantee.

She returned to the house and went to the front room to wait. It, too, looked strangely bare. Everything of value had been removed—the handsome ormolu clock that usually sat on the mantlepiece, the collection of silver framed miniatures that hung on the wall, and the small, expensive-looking knick-knacks that had been placed tastefully around the room to give the impression of prosperity in case there was ever a visitor. Everything was gone.

While she was out, perhaps even while she was bathing the dog, the servants had stripped the house of any small portable valuables and decamped.

She shuddered, imagining how Edgar would react. She prayed that he wouldn't return before Lord Alverleigh arrived.

Half an hour later the front doorbell jangled. She hadn't seen a carriage pull up, but since she was the only person left in the house, she supposed she should answer it.

She opened the door. "Lord Alverleigh," she exclaimed in relief. "Thank you for coming."

"Where is your butler?" he asked in a low voice as she hurriedly ushered him inside.

She shook her head, brushing the question aside. "It doesn't matter. Thank you for responding to my note."

"It's my pleasure. Now how can I help you? Is it money?"

She gave him an indignant look. "Of course not. I would never ask you for money." Then recalling the boy who delivered the letter, she flushed. "I can't repay the sixpence I owe you at the moment but—"

"Don't be ridiculous," he said. "You look worried. Now, what is it?"

Collecting the shreds of her composure she invited him to be seated, saying, "I'm afraid I can't offer you any refreshments at the moment but—"

"I didn't come here for refreshments." He waited for her to be seated on the settee, then chose an overstuffed armchair. "Now, tell me how I can help you." His voice resonated, deep and sure. It had a calming effect on her tense nerves.

She drew a couple of deep breaths. Where to start? It had seemed quite a straightforward request when she'd been looking at her list, but now, with this tall, handsome, assured gentleman watching her so steadily with those piercing gray eyes, it seemed suddenly like a dreadful cheek.

"You were right," she said abruptly. "About Ferndale, I mean. It was sold."

He nodded. "Your brother admitted it, did he?"

"I didn't ask him—I knew he would simply lie. No, I went there and saw for myself."

His brows snapped together. "You went to Ferndale? All that way? Alone?"

She nodded. "I could see at once that it was in other hands. It was all so tidy and prosperous looking, which it never had been before. Strangers live there now—the Sanderson family."

He frowned. "You spoke to them?"

"No, just the butler. I only stayed for a few minutes. I could see at once that new people were there and my old home was. . . was lost to me forever." Her voice choked a little on that last sentence.

He sat back. "What did Edgar say when you confronted him—I gather you did confront him."

"Oh yes, and he denied it and denied it—he must think I'm a complete fool. Though I suppose I am, given the way he has been deceiving me all along. But I stood firm and eventually he had to admit it. I don't believe he ever had any intention of getting a loan."

"It's not foolish to believe the word of your brother,

the head of your family. If anything, he is the fool for abusing his only sister's trust and alienating her."

"Perhaps." She swallowed and said, "He is still determined on my marrying Sir Henry Lester."

He sat up straight. "You're not, are you?"

"No, I've told him I won't do it. I made it very clear. However . . ." She bit her lip. She couldn't tell him how Edgar's smug confidence, and what had happened with her previous marriage frightened her. "I must find some way of supporting myself, a position of some sort. Which is why I'm asking for your help."

Marcus froze. For one appalled instant, he'd imagined she was talking about becoming a courtesan and for an even more shocking moment he'd almost considered it. She was very beautiful and would have no trouble finding a rich protector. At least she would be safe with him.

"What sort of help?" he said cautiously.

She clasped her hands over her heart. "I need to find some way to support myself."

"Yes of course. What were you thinking of?" He held his breath.

"I'm not sure. I made a list of possibilities, but I'm not qualified for positions such as a governess or even a dresser—I had dressers when I was married, and they were more skilled than I could ever be in the maintenance and repair of clothes. And I could never do hair as elegantly as they did."

Governess. Dresser. His breath escaped in a gust of relief. "I understand the difficulties, but why not marry? Not some ancient, but a much younger man, someone nearer your own age?" And then he found himself adding, "Myself, for instance."

He froze. Had he just proposed marriage? He had. Or close enough.

She shook her head. "No, thank you for the suggestion, but I don't ever intend to marry again."

He frowned. "What, never?" His brain was reeling. Any other woman would have snapped up that suggestion in a trice—and placed a betrothal announcement in the Morning Post at the earliest possible moment. But she'd barely seemed to notice.

"Yes, I find marriage doesn't suit me."

She would think that after two marriages to men old enough to be her grandfather. And he couldn't help persisting. "What about children? Don't you want children?" The way she'd cared about those wild animals when she was young, he was certain she'd make a wonderful mother.

She flushed and shook her head. "No, and please let us drop the subject. I won't marry again. I asked you here for quite a different reason."

"Of course," he said, feeling dazed. He'd virtually

proposed to her, and she'd acted as if he'd asked if she took sugar in her tea. And politely refused.

It was a lucky escape. Yes, it was. He had no plans to marry, so what on earth had prompted him to make such a foolish suggestion? He rallied his wits. "Then how can I help you?"

"Thank you. Do you know any lonely old ladies?"

He blinked. "Lonely old ladies?"

"Yes. They are on my list, you see."

"Your list?" He was all at sea.

"Yes, of jobs I could do. I don't have sufficient education to be a governess—well, you know how I was brought up. And though I couldn't be a dresser, I could be a maidservant, only I'd rather not if I could help it—not because of the hard work but because of the danger of um. . . predatory employers and older sons."

"Absolutely." The thought horrified him. She wouldn't last a week. "I see you've given it some thought."

"Yes. I thought I might be able to find work as a shop girl, but when I tried to find a position, nobody was interested."

Marcus was fascinated. "You tried, did you?"

"Oh yes, I visited every shop along Oxford Street, and any others I could find, asking about a job. I must have walked miles." She gave him a rueful smile. "Thank goodness I was wearing my most comfortable shoes."

His mind was spinning. She was serious. She'd rather slog around the streets looking for some dreary job than to marry again. Than to marry *him*.

Though maybe she hadn't realized that what he'd said was tantamount to an offer. What a relief.

It was relief he felt, he was sure.

"But I think I'd make quite a good companion for a lonely old lady," she continued. "Reading to her, fetching her shawls and slippers, keeping her entertained, making her life comfortable, that sort of thing. The trouble is, I hardly know anyone in society—or anywhere else for that matter—to recommend me. So, do you know any?"

"Old ladies? Yes, though off hand, I can't think of any who are in need of a companion." And he doubted any of them would want a beautiful, twice widowed young woman with an unsavory reputation—albeit an undeserved one.

Her face fell, and he hastened to add, "But of course I'll ask around. My Aunt Gosforth knows dozens of old ladies. She's bound to dig one up who will suit."

She clasped her hands together. "Oh, that would be wonderful." Then she sobered, adding in embarrassment, "Only it must be quick. Edgar insists that I marry Sir Henry Lester at once. He didn't say so, but I wouldn't be surprised if he was off at this very minute, arranging it."

Marcus frowned. "But you said you'd refused."

"Oh, I have, repeatedly. But Edgar doesn't care for that." She swallowed and added in a shamed voice, "I also refused to marry my second husband, but it made no difference."

Marcus stared at her, appalled.

"He forced you?"

She nodded. "I think so. It's all a bit vague. Anyway, Edgar is still insisting the marriage will go ahead. I will refuse of course, but it's rather unpleasant to be arguing all the time and he seems to think he can force me again. So you understand why I must make haste in finding a new position."

"Where is your brother now?"

She shook her head. "I don't know. He never tells me where he's going or when he'll return."

Marcus stood up. "Very well, I'll make the necessary arrangements. Will your brother be at home this evening?"

"Not after eight, he won't. He goes out every night, gambling, and is rarely home before dawn. But what arrangements do you mean?"

"Excellent. Pack your things. I'll come here at nine and collect you."

She raised her brows. "Collect me?"

"Yes, my Aunt Gosforth arrived in London this morning. You can stay with her until we sort out something more suitable. And in the meantime, you'll be out of Edgar's hands, and safe."

She hesitated. "It's very kind of you, but it's not necessary to discompose your aunt at the moment."

"She won't be discomposed." She would, of course, but he could deal with her.

"Thank you, but no. It will take several days at least for Edgar to arrange a wedding. Apparently Sir Henry is being difficult about the settlements, which I hope will give me time to arrange something, some kind of employment." She gave him an apologetic smile. "I prefer to be independent, you see."

"I see." She'd made up her mind, and he didn't blame her. Clearly the men she'd known in the past had all let her down, and in the worst way. And her father and brother had exploited her shamefully. Why should she trust him, simply because they'd been childhood friends?

"But it's very kind of you, and I am truly grateful.

He took her hands in his. "No need to thank me. We've been friends since we rescued that vixen, remember?"

She gave him a wobbly smile. "I'm not quite ready to chew off my paw yet, but if you could help me find a suitable position it'd be a huge relief."

He lifted one of her hands and kissed it. "Now, stop worrying. I'll speak to my aunt and see what we can come up with."

He closed the front door and started down the street, feeling strangely invigorated for a man who'd had his first and only marriage proposal rejected.

It was a salutary lesson in humility. Had he been looking for a wife—which he wasn't, of course—and thank goodness she'd refused him. What the devil had he been thinking? He'd imagined he only had to choose, and the job would be done.

How arrogant could a man get? She'd made it clear she'd prefer to scrub floors or sell shoes than marry him. She hadn't been tempted for a moment.

It wasn't exactly a cheering thought. He wasn't much of a ladies' man, not much of a conversationalist, could never produce a string of charming compliments and had no taking ways. And he preferred a quiet life in the country—none of which he understood would appeal to the eligible young ladies currently on the marriage mart. But he'd always believed his fortune and title would smooth the way.

Ironic to reflect that they'd made no difference at all to Tessa Blaxland, widely regarded to be a blatant fortune-hunter.

She clearly thought she could resist her brother's determination to marry her off again, but Marcus wasn't so sure. Her vagueness about the circumstances of her second wedding disturbed him.

How had her brother managed to force her when she'd been unwilling?

He didn't like the sound of that at all. Since first seeing Tessa at that ball, Marcus had given the question of Edgar Blaxland a lot of thought and now, after talking to Tessa again, he was feeling very uneasy about the whole situation.

His aunt might think him a countrified ignoramus, but though he might not have a lot of friends, Marcus did have excellent contacts, including one very useful fellow at the Horse Guards, Gil Radcliffe. He headed there now.

A short time after Lord Alverleigh had left, the front doorbell sounded loudly. Tessa was halfway down the stairs to answer it when it jangled again impatiently.

"What the devil are you answering the door for?" Edgar snapped, brushing past her. "Where the hell is Hodges?"

"I don't know."

He swung around. "What do you mean, you don't know? Didn't you ask one of the others, you ninny?"

"There are no others to ask," she said calmly. "All the servants have gone."

He glanced around as if the servants might be hiding somewhere. He scowled and swore. "That blasted Thracknell woman!"

Her chaperone? "I don't understand."

"I found her lurking outside the door when you and I were discussing your imminent marriage this morning. Listening in."

"There is no imminent marriage," Tessa said.

"There damn well is, but the stupid bitch must have believed your nonsense." He pulled off his coat and hat and tossed them at her, as if she had suddenly turned into a butler. "Hodge came to see me a short time later, asking for his wages—demanding them!—damn his eyes."

"We owe all the servants, don't we?"

He made a careless gesture. "A paltry few months, curse them. I told Hodge the dibs would be in tune again once you were married, but he obviously didn't believe me."

"Because I won't be married."

He turned on her savagely, his hand raised. "Contradict me one more time Theodosia, and I'll hit you!"

Tessa believed him. Edgar had a nasty temper, and he was clearly on the edge of losing it. She turned away to hang up his coat and hat and said in as calm a voice as she could manage, "Whatever the reason, it seems that all the servants have left. I even checked their sleeping quarters in the attic. They've taken all their belongings." She didn't tell him about the other items they'd absconded with. Edgar had a habit of taking out his temper on the nearest person.

He swore again and stormed off. Knowing he'd be soothing his temper, —but actually exacerbating it—with brandy, assuming he could find some, Tessa hurried to her room to keep herself and Billy out of his way. The little dog greeted her ecstatically. She ruffled his ears. It was so lovely to be greeted with such joy. But how would Lord Alverleigh or a prospective employer react to Billy?

She pushed the thought aside. She had enough to worry about at the moment.

First she needed to pack a bag, so she'd be ready the minute a position came up.

Or she had to flee.

She gave considerable thought to the kind of clothing she'd take with her. She'd learned her lesson when she'd been asking about jobs in shops—no fancy, fashionable clothing. An employer wouldn't wish to be sartorially outshone by a lowly hired companion.

The house was very still and silent as she sorted clothing into 'keep' and 'leave' piles. Edgar was no doubt drinking. Or he might have already gone out. Most days he slept through the daylight hours, the better to be fresh for his night-time gambling.

He only ever went out in the daylight when it was a matter of business, such as his current matter of business: arranging her marriage.

As the 'leave' pile grew higher, it occurred to her that she could probably sell these clothes. One of the maids she'd had in the past routinely sold the clothing Tessa cast off and gave her. It would be a handy source of cash.

But where did one go to sell second-hand clothing? She had no idea, and there was nobody to ask. Besides, time was running out: Edgar was determined to marry her off as soon as humanly possible, and from his complacency it seemed that he and Sir Henry might have come to an agreement.

Perhaps she should have accepted Lord Alverleigh's offer of shelter with his aunt. But no, she'd spent most of her adult life depending on a man—and look where it had gotten her. And he and his aunt were strangers, more or less.

She spent the next few hours unpicking lace and braid and any extra ornamentation from her dresses in order to look more like a companion. She couldn't do much about the rich fabric of some of them, but she could at least choose the drabbest colors and make them as plain as possible.

As well as removing braid and other ornamentation from her clothes, she made Billy a collar out of a piece of red velvet ribbon, and used another ribbon to fashion a leash so he'd look less like a stray.

She was glad she'd refused Lord Alverleigh's offer to stay with his aunt. She hadn't had much to do with society ladies—with women at all, come to think of it. There was only NannyJune when she was a child, and other than that the women she knew were either employed by her husbands as housekeepers—and they'd showed her token respect at best—or women like Mrs Thracknell, that her brother employed to watch over her like a prison warder.

She had little doubt that Lady Gosforth would be like the rest of them. Lord Alverleigh seemed fond of his aunt, but he was biased.

The thought of NannyJune reminded her: she needed to write to the old lady and tell her where she was going. She should have visited her when she was down at Ferndale, but she'd been so shocked and distressed at finding her home has been sold and that strangers were now living there, all other thoughts had been driven from her head.

Besides, it wouldn't be fair to land herself, penniless, on the old lady who would be just managing to survive on some sort of pension. She knew it wouldn't be much.

When she'd first been taken away from Ferndale she'd worried about NannyJune's and Phillips's welfare. Papa had been so dismissive of her arguments that he should make provision for their futures, after a lifetime of service to the family.

But a month after she'd left, she received a letter from NannyJune saying she and Phillips had found a cottage in the next village to live in, and now had pensions, sufficient to support them. Papa must have listened to her pleadings and relented after all. It had been a huge relief to Tessa to know that NannyJune and Phillips were safely housed and cared for.

She finished the letter, sealed it, and tucked it in her reticule to post when she could. Perhaps if she saw him Lord Alverleigh would consent to frank it for her. The mood Edgar was in, she wouldn't dare to ask him to do it: he'd probably rip it up and throw it in the fire.

At the Horse Guards, Marcus was swiftly shown to Gil Radcliffe's office. One of the perks of being an earl.

Radcliffe, who knew even more about the doings of practically everyone in London, knew all about Edgar Blaxland. "We keep an eye on people like him—member of the House of Lords, you know, government business," Radcliffe explained. "Edgar Blaxland is heavily in debt to some very unsavory fellows, namely the Greeling brothers, ruthless gangland moneylenders who don't take kindly to unpaid debts." He added grimly, "The Greeling brothers have their own extremely unsavory methods of enforcing payment. And their eyes seem to be everywhere."

"I see."

"If left to their own devices, the Greelings might deal with Blaxland in their own way, at the very least make an example of him as a warning to their other debtors. Break his legs, that sort of thing."

Marcus shook his head. "I'm not willing to risk that. Both her father and her brother viewed her as an asset to be used. The Greelings might well do the same."

Radcliffe nodded. "Quite possibly."

"I tried to get Lady Hewitt to leave her brother's house and stay with my aunt, but she won't do it. She seems to believe she can stand up to her brother, but I have my doubts." He told Radcliffe how vague she was about how her second marriage had come about.

"Sounds damnably fishy to me, too," Radcliffe agreed.

"I offered her shelter with my aunt, but she hardly knows me, and doesn't know my aunt at all, and she says she prefers to be independent." He made a frustrated gesture. "I can hardly drag her out of there by force."

"No, absolutely not." Radcliffe steepled his fingers and pondered the situation. "I'll give you Jackson and Sims—both very reliable—to keep an eye on her at the house. If anything changes, they'll notify you." He shrugged. "I know it's not much, but it's the best I can do. Of course, since it's not government business, you will be responsible for paying them."

Marcus thanked him, and a short time later he was briefing the men. He wanted a twenty-four-hour watch on the Blaxland house. He didn't trust Blaxland an inch, especially not with the Greelings after him.

Then, telling himself that he'd done what he could—and feeling nevertheless that it wasn't nearly enough— he went home.

Chapter Five

"A HOUSE GUEST? *A house guest?* Possibly coming to stay—*possibly?* And you don't know when, but it will be for an indefinite visit?" Marcus's aunt, Lady Gosforth, snorted. "What sort of house guest arrives with virtually no warning and at an indeterminate time and for an indeterminate period?" She raised her lorgnette and glared at him. "It is *not* convenient. You realize I've only just arrived in London."

"Yes, it was quite fortuitous," Marcus agreed.

"Well, I wasn't going to stay in the wilderness at Alverleigh when you so rudely abandoned me there."

"As I said, your arrival is fortuitous. I forgot to ask earlier—did you have a pleasant journey?"

She snorted. "Don't try that fiddle-faddle on me, boy—who is this *possible and indefinite* house guest?"

"A young lady."

Her eyes narrowed. "Do I know her?"

He strolled to the mantlepiece, picked up a small Tang horse and examined it. "I have no idea who you may or may not know, Aunt. Rather good, this horse, don't you agree? Marvelous workmanship."

"Marcus!"

He turned. "Yes, Aunt Maude?"

"What is the name of this possible house guest?"

"Lady Hewitt."

"Lady Hewitt? Lady Hewitt?" She pondered the name for a minute. "I don't know any Lady Hew— oh good God! You cannot mean the Ice Widow?"

"I believe that's what some people—in their ignorance—call her," Marcus said coldly.

"In their ignorance? *Ignorance!*" his aunt snapped. "You are the ignorant one! Don't you realize that, that"—she struggled a moment, searching for an acceptable word—"that *creature* has made a career out of entrapping foolish old men in marriage, men who, if my sources are correct, were wealthy at the time of the marriage but who died virtually penniless! I won't have her in my house! I won't, Marcus, and you can't make me."

"No, of course I won't," he said mildly. "Just let me know where you will be staying."

She stared at him, then said ominously, "What do you mean, 'where I will be staying'?"

He shrugged. "This is, after all, *my* house, and since

you refuse to share it with Lady Hewitt, I presume you will wish to find alternative accommodation."

She huffed and puffed. "*Alternative accommodation?* How dare you! I am your aunt!"

"Yes, Aunt Maude. And while I would be very grateful if you would reconsider, and agree to play hostess to Lady Hewitt, if you truly feel you cannot, I wouldn't dream of forcing you."

"No, you'll just push me into the gutter!" his aunt said bitterly.

Marcus hid a smile. His aunt had several excellent options, including an elegant house in Bath and a small but equally elegant London house in Mount Street, but after his father died, she'd let the house in Mount Street, preferring to stay, when visiting London, in Alverleigh House, his much grander and more convenient house in Grosvenor Square. And declared he needed a hostess. "Hardly the gutter, Aunt Maude. But it's your choice."

She hurrumphed and glared at him for a while. He rang for tea and waited for her to simmer down. She was short-tempered but her tempests never lasted long.

The butler brought tea, a plate of small, iced cakes and a variety of biscuits. After she'd drunk some tea and eaten several cakes, his aunt set her tea cup aside. "Explain to me why you wish me to play hostess to this notorious widow. How did you meet her?"

"I've known her since we were children. She grew up at Ferndale, the estate next to Alverleigh." He didn't want to reveal that as an adult, he'd met her on only three short occasions.

"So you don't know about her outrageous marital career."

"On the contrary. She told me herself about both her marriages."

His aunt snorted. "I'll wager she did. Poured some affecting tale into your receptive countrified ears, you foolish boy. And of course, you've always been a soft touch for a tragic tale. You realize, of course, that she's set her sights on marrying you."

Marcus shook his head. "She hasn't, as a matter of fact."

"Of course she has and—"

"I already asked her. She refused." And dealt his ego a severe blow at the same time.

His aunt's lorgnette dropped from her eye. "You *asked* her? To *marry* you? I thought you had no intention—" She broke off and said carefully, "You asked this woman to marry you?"

"Yes, and she refused."

She picked up her lorgnette. "What nonsense! There isn't a woman in London who'd refuse you."

"Apparently there is."

"What's her game?" She pursed her lips, eyeing him thoughtfully as she swung her lorgnette gently back and forth on its gold chain. "Are you sure you made your offer clear to her?"

He inclined his head. "Quite clear."

She sniffed. "She probably didn't hear you. You do mumble at times."

Marcus rolled his eyes. He hadn't mumbled since he was fourteen and one of his schoolmasters had drilled the habit out of him. "She heard me."

"And you're positive she refused?"

"She made it crystal clear." There was nothing ambiguous or hesitant about *I don't ever intend to marry again.*

His aunt shook her head. "I've no doubt it's some cunning ploy—all the better to lure you in, dear boy. Women like that run rings around men, no matter what their age."

"There was no need to lure me," he pointed out. "All she needed to do was to say yes. But she didn't. Quite the opposite, in fact. And then she added that she had no intention of marrying again."

His aunt gave a cynical snort. "Until she needs a new hat or another diamond necklace." She poured herself another cup of tea and ate a biscuit.

Marcus thought for a moment. He had to get his aunt to cooperate. She could be intensely difficult and was ruthless in cutting people she disapproved of, but once she approved of someone, she made a good and loyal friend, regardless of society's views.

She'd taken in his rejected brother and ill-gotten half-brother, after all, when their own father refused to acknowledge or support them. And raised them to manhood. And done her best to find them wives.

"Do you know how old she was when she married Lord Holgrave?" He bit into a biscuit and chewed.

"Her first husband? No. What does her age have to do with it? It's the gross difference in their ages that makes it so distasteful—and she did it *twice!*"

"So you would approve of wedding a child of fifteen to a man more than five times her age?"

His aunt frowned. "*Fifteen*? Are you sure?"

He nodded. "Only a few weeks before the wedding, she'd been running wild like a little gypsy in the forest at Blaxland, growing up with virtually no supervision except for her old nanny. But before she'd turned sixteen she was married."

"Good God!"

"The marriage—at least that's what she was told— was to save her father from creditors—violent ones. And it was her father and brother who then stripped Holgrave of his fortune."

She considered it a moment, then shrugged. "But she married a wealthy old man a second time, and she was no child then to be coerced into marriage. And old Hewitt went the same way as Holgrave— virtually penniless at the end, I heard."

"I know, but . . ." He hesitated. "This is pure

speculation on my part, so I must ask you to keep it confidential. If I'm right, I'm sure Lady Hewitt wouldn't want her very private business to be widely known."

His aunt made a cynical noise. "I'll wager she wouldn't," she muttered under her breath, then caught his eye. "Oh, go on then, I promise I won't tell a soul. What was her excuse this time?"

"She didn't make an excuse. But it's damnably vague. All she remembers is that she'd refused Hewitt a number of times, but somehow she ended up married anyway. I believe it was some sort of trickery by her brother."

"*Trickery?* What sort of trickery?"

"I'm not sure, and I don't wish to speculate further until I discover the truth." He vowed that Edgar would never be in a position to abuse her ever again. "I believe he's planning to force her to marry a third time—to another wealthy old man, but I'll be damned if I let him. I'm going to put a stop to Edgar Blaxland."

Aunt Maude sat up straight and stabbed her lorgnette in his direction. "You are *not* to call him out, Marcus. I forbid it!"

"Call him out? Don't be ridiculous, Aunt Maude. Dueling is illegal, and besides, I'm a magistrate." And he wouldn't sully a blade or even a bullet on a dishonorable swine like Blaxland.

She subsided slightly. "Then what do you plan to do?"

"I have some thoughts," Marcus admitted. "But though I offered—for her own safety—to bring her here this evening, she refused. She is determined to resist her brother's pressures. But I have my doubts of her ability to do so."

"I see." She poured more tea into her cup, took a sip, grimaced and set it aside. She looked at Marcus. "I can see that she's told you a very affecting tale and has awakened all your dratted protective instincts— you always were drawn to wounded creatures. I suppose she learned that about you when she was a child—no, don't interrupt me. Since you seem to have already become entangled in her toils, I'll accept this young woman as a house guest and judge her for myself. *I'm* not a gullible young man to be deceived by a pretty face and a sad story."

"Young? I'm one-and-thirty, remember?"

She snorted. "But an innocent in the ways of cunning and conniving females."

He rose, saying, "How could I be, when I've known you and Great-aunt Gert all my life?"

She snorted again, with laughter this time. "Get away with your nonsense—and show some respect for your elders."

Marcus bowed over her hand. "Always," he said softly. "Thank you, Aunt Maude. I'm sure it will be just a matter of time until I can prevail on Lady Hewitt to accept my invitation. You'll like her, I'm sure."

She sniffed. "We'll see about that."

The sun was low in the sky when Tessa heard Edgar leave the house, slamming the door behind him. Good. He wasn't staying for dinner. He rarely did, and in any case, he was very fussy about his food and with nobody to cook or serve it, he'd probably decided to dine with friends or at whatever gambling hell he was visiting tonight.

She hoped he'd remembered to take the front door key with him, for there would be nobody to answer the door for him, and she'd be asleep if he came home in the wee small hours, as was his habit.

Feeling hungry herself, she went downstairs to the kitchen. Not much had been left behind, but there were a few eggs and half a stale loaf of bread. And a couple of meaty bones, which would make Billy happy.

She was no cook, but she'd learned young to make herself a scratch meal, and the fire in the stove was not quite out. She fed it with wood chips until it was burning merrily, then she made herself a meal of toast and scrambled eggs.

In the pantry she found a small bowl of leftover

strawberry fool from the day before—her favorite—so she dug in a spoon. It tasted a bit peculiar—sharp—as if someone had mistakenly sprinkled some salt in it, so after a few mouthfuls, she set it aside.

Then she waited, until she realized she was waiting for Edgar to return, praying he wouldn't. Waiting to hear from Lord Alverleigh saying his aunt knew an old lady who needed a companion.

She hated waiting. And she hated feeling so helpless, depending on others, relying on their actions in order for her life to . . . what? Begin? What nonsense!

A huge yawn broke her train of thought. She was tired, sleepy and her thoughts were becoming muzzy. It would be easier to work out what to do once she'd had a good night's sleep. With another great yawn, she took herself to bed.

The downstairs bell jangled noisily. Marcus sat up in bed and eyed the clock on the mantel—not quite seven. Such an early caller at the front door could only be about one thing—Tessa!

He threw on a pair of breeches, grabbed a shirt and dragged it on as he hurried downstairs. There he found his butler arguing with one of Radcliffe's men.

"I tell you," his butler was insisting, "neither his lordship nor her ladyship accept callers at this hour. And if you're a tradesman you ought to go around to—"

"It's all right, Peverill," Marcus said. "What is it, Jackson?"

"Trouble afoot, your lordship. I come straight away."

Marcus turned to his butler. "Fetch my coat and boots—at once! And order the carriage! No time to waste!" Tucking his shirt in, he turned back to Jackson. "What happened?"

"An old gentleman arrived not fifteen minutes ago, all dressed up fancy and finicky like, as if for a special occasion, which is odd for this time of the mornin'. And then when I saw a parson getting out of a carriage—well, I knew what that meant. Trouble."

Marcus swore. Peverill arrived with his coat and boots. Marcus grabbed them and ran out the door. He looked for his carriage.

"I got us a hackney, m'lord," Jackson said and gestured to a shabby vehicle nearby.

"Excellent." Marcus turned to his butler, hovering anxiously in the doorway and called, "When the carriage arrives, send it to Cressy Lane. Number . . .?"

Jackson called out the number, and they both

jumped into the hackney, which sped off. Marcus pulled on his boots, shrugged into his coat and ran his fingers through his hair. He'd never gone out in such a state—he hadn't even shaved—but there was no time to lose.

"Sims is there, your lordship," Jackson told him. "He arrived for the changeover of the watch, so I come to tell you while he stays back and does what he can."

Marcus gritted his teeth. The men had done well, but dammit, it wasn't enough! What the hell was Blaxland playing at? A parson and an old man in formal dress? At this hour of the morning? It could only be one thing. A wedding.

The hackney turned into Cressy Lane. Marcus leapt out before it had stopped. He headed toward the front door, but Jackson grabbed his arm. "They won't answer the front door. But the kitchen entrance is down there." He pointed.

"Good man." The two men ran down the area steps and entered the kitchen, which was deserted. Upstairs they could hear voices raised—male voices. They followed the sound to the sitting room he'd visited earlier. Luckily the door was slightly ajar. They could hear everything.

"I'm not sure," a light, anxious-sounding voice was saying. "The lady seems to be indisposed. I cannot perform a marriage if she's—"

"Yes, she does seem to be unwell, Blaxland," a second voice said pettishly. The prospective groom, Marcus thought.

"She's not damned well ill," Edgar Blaxland snarled. "I tell you, she was nervous—all brides are, dammit—and she took a mild composer, that's all, and it went to her head. Women are like that, weak in the head. Now get on with it, man!"

Marcus edged the door open, and saw Tessa standing between her brother and the elderly gentleman, though standing was hardly the right word. She was sagging, swaying slightly, supported between them. Apart from the parson and the groom, there were two other men—Sims and a stranger.

Marcus burst into the room. "A mild composer?" For a moment, everyone froze. Tessa turned her head and mumbled something that might have been his name. Her eyes were slightly unfocused; the pupils shrunk to the size of a pin prick.

"You've drugged her, you swine," Marcus snarled.

The old gentleman gasped and released her arm. Tessa sagged against her brother.

Marcus took her arm, shoved Edgar away—hard—and passed the reeling Tessa to Jackson, saying, "Look after her."

"How dare you interfere with my business, you bast—" Edgar began. Marcus felled him with a furious punch. Edgar fell sprawling to the floor.

"Gentlemen, gentlemen," the parson began.

"Get out of here, vicar," Marcus snapped, "or you'll be charged with conducting a forced marriage."

"A forced marriage? You can't possibly think—oh good gracious me—I had no idea, I assure you. The lady's brother assured me—"

But Marcus had no time for him. Blaxland had scrambled to his feet and was trying to drag his sister away from Jackson. Marcus grabbed him by the collar, whirled him around and slammed another series of hard punches into him. Blaxland sagged, his eyes turning up, and collapsed in a heap.

Marcus turned to see who he needed to vanquish next. His blood was up and he was ready for anything. But the vicar, still bleating that he'd known nothing about any forced marriage, that he thought the girl had taken drink, that was all, was being hurried from the room by Sims.

The elderly gentleman, who was staring in dismay at the crumpled heap that was his erstwhile brother-in-law-to-be, saw Marcus prowling toward him and with a squeak of alarm ran out the door, calling "Petty, Petty!" which turned out to be not a commentary on the situation, but the name of the second stranger, who seemed to be in his employ.

In a few short minutes the room was empty, apart from Marcus, Blaxland, Radcliffe's two men and Tessa, sagging limply against Jackson, her eyes closed.

What the hell had the bastard given her?

Blaxland was breathing, but still unconscious, blood bubbling slowly from his nose, which was broken, Marcus hoped. He wanted to beat him to a pulp. He itched to give him a good kicking, but he'd been raised a gentleman, and kicking a man when he was well and truly down—well, there were times when a decent upbringing was a blasted nuisance.

In any case Tessa needed his attention.

The sound of wheels rattling on the cobbles outside drew his attention. "Your carriage is here, m'lord," Sims said, peering out the window.

"Good. You stay here with that swine." He jerked his chin at the inanimate heap that was Tessa's villainous brother. "Don't let him leave. Lock him in, if you must, but don't lose him. I haven't finished with Edgar Blaxland. But first I must tend to the lady."

Marcus lifted Tessa into his arms. As he did there was a flurry of barking, and something happening in the vicinity of his boots. "What the—" He looked down, with some difficulty as her skirts were in the way, and saw a small, scrawny mongrel attacking his boots. One of his boots, to be precise.

"Get off me, you." He tried to shake the creature off. Without success. Growling and snarling, the little dog continued to worry at Marcus's boot.

"Somebody get this blasted dog off me. Get rid of it."

Both Sims and Jackson tried to grab the little creature, but it wove and dodged and avoided them with ease. And returned to attacking Marcus's boot.

"Want me to shoot it, milord?" Jackson produced a small deadly-looking pistol from a pocket.

"No, just—" Marcus began.

"You can't shoot 'im! 'E belongs to the lady!" A small ragged boy appeared as if from nowhere, shouting at Marcus and dragging at Jackson's pistol arm.

Marcus hitched Tessa's insensible body higher against his chest and looked down at the child. It was the urchin who'd brought him the note from Tessa. What the devil was the child doing here inside her house—and in these circumstances?

"Her dog? Are you sure? It looks like a street dog."

"'Course I'm sure," the boy retorted. "I seen her walkin' him. An' look at that collar—does that look like a street dog's?"

Marcus had no idea what street dogs were wearing this season, but he didn't care about the dog. He had to get Tessa home and to immediate medical attention. The dog was back, dancing around him, barking and darting in to worry at his boots, which were undoubtedly ruined by now. "If you can catch the dog," he told the boy. "Bring it to my house. There's a tanner in it for you."

"Cost yer a bob," the child instantly responded.

Despite his worry for Tessa, Marcus couldn't help but be amused. "Very well, a shilling, now out of my way."

The child stepped in front of Marcus, grubby hands braced on his skinny hips. "Where are you takin' her?" he asked belligerently. "I look after over her, I do. She's a nice lady."

"I know. And I'm taking her to safety, to my home. You know where that is," Marcus said impatiently. He was touched by the child's concern, but enough was enough. "Now, dammit, let me pass."

Tightening his grip on Tessa, he strode from the house. She was barely conscious and, leaning her head against his shoulder, muttered something he couldn't make out. He levered her onto the carriage seat, holding her steady all the time and then climbed in after her and took her in his arms again. He didn't want to let her go.

"Home," he told the coachman in a clipped voice. Sims and Jackson stood at the door of the carriage. "I can't thank you enough," he told them. "Sims, you watch Blaxland. Jackson, be so good as to summon Doctor Price to attend me at my home as soon as possible. I will see to your payment after I have seen to the lady."

"Glad to help," Jackson said. "I'll call on you after the doctor has been, m'lord, if that would be convenient."

"It would," Marcus said as the coach moved off.

The physician arrived at Alverleigh House within the hour. With a maidservant sitting in, he examined Tessa carefully. She was by then completely comatose—but still breathing, thank goodness.

After twenty minutes, the doctor emerged from her bedchamber. Marcus, who had taken the time to shave and dress hastily, was pacing back and forth in the hall. "Well?" he said.

"The lady appears to have been drugged."

"I know that, but—"

"She is, in my opinion, in no immediate danger, my lord," he said soothingly. "Her vital signs are good, and she seems a healthy young woman. I believe she will sleep off the effects and wake with, I hope, no further repercussions."

In my opinion. I believe. I hope. Damned doctors, hedging their bets. But there was no point in arguing with the man. "How long will it take her to wake up?"

Dr. Price shook his head. "As I have no knowledge of the drug she took, or how much was ingested, I cannot say."

"But—"

"Leave a maidservant in the room with her. There is little anyone can do but it will assuage some of your anxieties. As well, when the lady awakens, she will be no doubt be confused and possibly anxious. A female face might help reassure her."

Marcus nodded brusquely and showed the doctor to the door. "Thank you, doctor. Send me your bill." As the doctor's carriage moved off, Marcus noticed Jackson waiting across the road. He beckoned him inside.

"Thanks again for alerting me to the situation, and for summoning the doctor. I don't imagine he liked being called out so early. The lady is sleeping off the effects of whatever filthy drug that swine gave her. You will be well rewarded, but first I have another task for you."

"At your service, m'lord."

"I'll be calling on Lord Blaxland shortly. I hope Sims has kept him securely confined. I have a job for him, as well. Your errand is a trip to the docks." He explained his plan to Jackson. The time he'd spent pacing outside Tessa's door had not been in vain.

As he showed Jackson out, his aunt made a stately descent down the stairs. "What is all the commotion, Marcus? People coming and going at such an uncivilized hour! And who was that man who just left? He looked like a positive ruffian."

He grinned. "Good morning, Aunt Maude. He probably is a ruffian, but a good one, I'm sure."

She snorted.

He continued. "As for the people coming and going, the guest I told you about has arrived and is sleeping in the best spare bedchamber, with a maid watching over her."

She raised her lorgnette and eyed him indignantly. "Your guest arrived at *this* ungodly time of the morning? And went *straight to bed*? Was she raised in a *barnyard* that she has so little understanding of basic good manners?"

"As you very well know, she was raised at Ferndale, the property next to Alverleigh, remember? I don't recall if there was a barnyard there, but if there was, I'm sure she would have played there as a child. Nash and I used to play in our barn, especially in wet weather."

She stamped her foot. "Do not try that fiddle-faddle on me, boy! I am not in the mood for it, especially at this time of day—I haven't yet broken my fast. You know perfectly well what I mean."

"Yes, Aunt Maude. Come into the breakfast parlor and while you drink your chocolate and eat your pastries, I'll explain."

After he'd breakfasted with his aunt and attempted to smooth her ruffled feathers—without conspicuous success, he had to admit—he headed out. It was not quite noon. "Still there?" he asked Sims when he arrived.

"Aye, m'lord. He came to and cleaned 'imself up a bit, then I put 'im upstairs in 'is bed. I reckon 'e'll be sound asleep by now. Or sozzled." He grinned. "'E weren't an 'appy chappy when I locked 'im in, I can tell you. The language 'e used! I din't know lords could swear like that. Right shocked, I was." Chuckling, he handed Marcus the key to the bedroom door.

"Good man." Marcus slipped him a sovereign. "I have more work yet for you and Jackson. I'll pay both of you when this affair is over."

He ran upstairs, found the only locked door and unlocked it. Then he knocked. And knocked again, more loudly. After a few moments Blaxland fumbled at the door, swearing angrily. It cracked open a sliver, and a bloodshot eye peered warily out, then it opened fully and Edgar Blaxland stood there, bruised, disheveled and fuming.

"Renfrew, you bastard! What the devil do you want?"

He was clad in a lurid dressing gown tossed carelessly over the crumpled clothes he'd worn at the failed wedding.

He stank of drink.

He wore a plaster crookedly stretched across his nose—Marcus hoped it betokened a broken nose—one of his eyes was swollen and was darkening nicely, and his face bore several cuts and luridly promising bruises.

He stood, glaring at Marcus then as Marcus moved forward, he scuttled back hurriedly saying, "You've got a damned nerve, calling here after what you did. Where's my blasted sister?"

"Safe." Marcus pushed past him and entered the house. "I want a word with you, Blaxland."

"Well, I don't want a word with you—unless it's to restore my sister to me."

"You'll wait in vain then."

"Dammit, she's my sister. You have no right to kidnap here, and so I'll tell the magistrate when I report you for it."

"Kidnapping is it? I thought it was more like a rescue. But go ahead, report me. I'm sure the authorities will be interested to hear how you were forcing your sister to get married by drugging her. And not for the first time," he added silkily.

"Drugging! what the devil do you mean by that?" Blaxland blustered. "No such thing. The silly chit took a composer, that's all."

"Both times? She told me she had no memory of her last wedding."

Blaxland's expression was shifty. "Lies, all lies. She, she drinks, and like all females she has a weak head, that's all."

"The doctor who examined her this morning was of the opinion she'd been given a dose of some drug. I'm sure he will be glad to confirm it to any court. In fact, I might report the incident myself."

Blaxland's face paled. "Dammit, you can't do that. I'm the head of her family. You have no right to—"

"To rescue her from an unwelcome marriage? As the head of her family, you are a disgrace. Now sit down, you fool—I'm not going to hit you again, much as I'd like to. I have a proposition for you."

Warily, Blaxland sat on the edge of the bed, clearly poised to leap from it if Marcus attacked. "What sort of proposition?"

"A monetary one."

His eyes narrowed. "Go on."

"I understand you are deep in debt."

He made a dismissive gesture. "Temporary shortage, nothing to be concerned about."

"Really? So you're not worried about the interest the Greeling brothers have taken in you?"

Blaxland stiffened. "The Greeling brothers? How the devil— What have you heard?" He glanced worriedly at the doorway, as if Marcus had brought the Greelings with him and they were lurking outside.

"I understand they are in pursuit of you—or rather, the rather large sum of money you owe them." He waited a moment, then added, "Of course, you could always explain about the temporary shortage, though they do have something of a reputation for impatience, I believe. But I'm sure if you explain, they'll understand."

Blaxland snorted. "They'll break both my legs first. And that'll just be the start."

"Tsk tsk, that sounds a trifle harsh," Marcus said pleasantly.

Blaxland glared at him. "What's it to you, Renfrew? And why the devil have you come back here? To taunt me?"

"No, to offer you a proposition."

Blaxland leaned forward. "Spit it out then."

"I will pay you five hundred pounds."

Blaxland's eyes narrowed. "In exchange for what? I've nothing to sell—" He broke off with a knowing smile. "Oh, I see. Sniffing around my sister, aren't you? Very well, you can have her, but I'll want more than a monkey. I owe more than five times that to the Greelings alone. A lot more."

Marcus frowned. "Are you offering to arrange a marriage between us?" he said silkily.

Blaxland said indifferently, "Marriage or not—it's up to you. She's used goods, no virgin after all."

Marcus clenched his fists—the man was despicable—but he managed to say in a cool voice, "So, you would sell me your sister for three thousand pounds?"

"Sir Henry would have paid more, but the bastard will be running shy after that wedding debacle—which is all your fault, I'll remind you." He added bitterly, "And as you pointed out, the Greelings are not known for their patience."

"No, I believe not. At any rate, I have no intention of buying your sister or any other woman—"

"Then what the devil are you playing at?"

"—and I certainly won't pay you three thousand pounds. The offer was for five hundred, but there are conditions."

"What conditions?"

"I will purchase you a one-way ticket to America, which will take you out of reach of the Greelings."

Blaxland thought for a moment, then his face took on a cunning expression. "I see, let the hue and cry die down. Very well, I'll accept your proposition. When can I have the money? I can arrange my own passage."

"I haven't finished yet," Marcus said coldly.

Blaxland gestured impatiently. "Get to the point then."

"I will purchase your passage to America and give five hundred pounds to the ship's captain, to keep safe during the voyage. He'll be instructed not to give you a penny until you've landed in Boston."

"Damn it all, I'm not a child—"

"No, you're a gambler, a liar and a cheat. And a total disgrace."

CHAPTER SIX

BLAXLAND FUMED SILENTLY for a few minutes, then he leaned forward. "What's to stop your precious captain from keeping the money? He could have me tossed overboard and keep it all himself. And for all I know there's no money at all. You might even pay to have me drowned at sea." He sat back, raking his fingers through his hair. "Why the devil should should I risk it?"

Marcus's voice was icy. "I hadn't considered those possibilities, it's true, but I don't actually care what happens to you. The captain could throw you overboard with my good wishes, but that's not our agreement. So, you have a choice: stay and face the Greelings or take the ship to America. Consider it a gamble. You like to gamble, don't you?"

There was a short silence, but Marcus knew the man would accept his offer. He had no choice. It was a better offer than he'd get anywhere else. It went against the grain to enrich Blaxland by as much as a farthing, but he could see no other way to permanently rid Tessa of her brother without harming him. And without involving her in some kind of public scandal, which it would, if the matter ever came to court. She'd suffered enough slander at the hands of her family.

"Of course, you would have to remain in America, or at least never come back to England."

Blaxland's jaw jutted aggressively. "Why the devil should I?"

"As I understand it, the Greelings charge quite high interest rates," Marcus pointed out. "The sum you owe them will be increasing daily, and they have long memories and vindictive habits, I'm told. Should you set foot in England again, they will be sure to find out." He gave a cold smile. "And then your life won't be worth living."

"They might not find out."

Marcus said gently, "Oh, but should you do anything so foolish, I will be at such pains to inform them."

"You swine!"

Marcus placed a slip of paper on the small bedside table. "This has all the details you need. Your ship sails tomorrow afternoon on the turning of the tide. My man Sims is downstairs and will escort you. If you leave within the hour, you should make it in time."

"Within the"—

"The captain already has your booking and your five hundred guineas, so if you fail to turn up, or arrive too late and the ship has sailed, the money and the opportunity will be lost to you." He smiled coldly. "In that event, the Greelings may have you with my good will."

Blaxland picked up the note and examined it, then shoved it in his pocket. "How do I know you've sent the money?"

Marcus shrugged. "You don't. You'll just have to gamble on whether or not I'm a man of my word. Goodbye Blaxland."

Blaxland swore long and horribly. Ignoring him, Marcus left. He gave a note and a small roll of notes to Sims who'd been waiting downstairs. "Stay with him. Make sure he gets on board this ship—I don't care if you have to deliver him in a sack, as long as you do it. Use whatever force is necessary, but I want him alive and on board that ship when it sails. Jackson will meet you there, and the captain will give you a receipt for Blaxland's arrival. The details are here, and the money for costs. I will pay you and Jackson the full amount I owe you when you bring me the receipt from the captain."

Sims pocketed the note and the money. "I'll make sure he's on it, guv'nor. Alive and kicking." He added with a grin, "Or not kicking an' tied up good and tight in a sack."

Marcus gave a brusque nod and strode away. He was wound tight with unexpressed rage. Blaxland had simply grabbed at the money and agreed to Marcus's conditions—albeit with bad grace. It shouldn't have surprised him—indeed, he'd expected his plan to work.

But after all that man had done to his sister, marrying her off again and again so he could bleed her elderly husbands dry—and now, not having any idea where she was or in what condition his filthy drug had left her, he would just walk off and leave her high and dry.

He'd just abandoned her without, apparently, a single thought. Saving himself and not giving a moment's consideration to any consequences his sister might face from his violent debtors.

Again, he wished he'd given the man a good kicking.

Marcus hoped the ship's captain was not the honorable man he'd thought him when he'd sent Jackson to make those arrangements. It never would have occurred to Marcus that he might toss Blaxland overboard and keep the money. But he supposed that being a dishonorable man himself, Blaxland would expect crooked dealing from others.

Marcus would never have made such a bargain if he hadn't found the captain to be a decent fellow.

Still, he wouldn't mind one way or the other if Blaxland were tossed overboard. As long as Tessa's brother was gone for good from her life, he didn't care what happened to him. From what Radcliffe had told him, those Greelings were ruthless, brutal men whose eyes were everywhere. The threat of their revenge would keep Blaxland from ever returning.

He walked home, breathing in the cold, crisp air. Getting rid of Blaxland had been easier than he'd expected. Now to wait for Tessa to recover from that drug. And then to get her to rethink her options.

He thought of the list she had spoken of. Even if she did find work as a maidservant or shop-girl, with her looks she would still be the target of unwanted attentions from unscrupulous employers. No, they weren't to be thought of.

He hoped Blaxland would be gone by the time she woke.

"Any news of Lady Hewitt?" Marcus asked his butler on returning home.

"I believe the lady is still asleep, m'lord. I have taken the liberty of assigning several of the maids to sit in rotation with her. They keep me informed."

"Good, good." He headed toward the stairs to check her for himself, when Peverill coughed, one of his Significant Coughs. Marcus turned back. "Yes?"

"Lady Gosforth asked me to inform you that she has gone out."

Marcus nodded indifferently. His aunt was always going out.

"In addition," Peverill added, "there is a Young Person, a *ragged* Young Person and an Animal he *claims* you asked him to bring."

Ah. The boy with the dog. "I did."

Peverill sniffed disapprovingly. "In that case you will find them awaiting you in the kitchen courtyard."

Marcus headed for the kitchen courtyard. There he found the urchin and his equally urchin-like dog. No, *her* urchin-like dog, the boy had told him. He paused in the kitchen doorway and eyed them thoughtfully.

They were playing, the boy tossing a stick, the dog fetching it. Neither of them had noticed him yet. It was doubtful which of them was the scrawniest. The boy was dressed in a hodge-podge of clothing—a shabby pair of too-short trousers that revealed a dirty pair of skinny white legs, a threadbare jacket that was too large for him, its sleeves rolled back several times, and worn over what appeared to be several knitted garments—all of them ragged and none particularly clean.

The dog at least looked relatively clean, but that was as far as it went. It was like no breed he'd ever seen; small, one ear up, one down, and so thin that every rib stood out. Its coat was brown but had been clipped so close it was almost shorn, except for the tail, at the end of which floated a scruffy clump of white, pretending to be a tassel. It wagged non-stop.

Marcus cleared his throat and the game instantly stopped. The boy snatched up the dog and with it under his arm, held out a grubby hand. "A bob, we said."

"We did." Marcus took out a shilling and flipped it toward the boy who snatched it deftly out of the air. He examined it carefully, then put the dog down. And waited.

Marcus raised a brow. "Is there something else?"

The boy's eyes darted toward the kitchen window where Cook had a tray of fresh-baked meat pies cooling. "I 'ad to give the dog 'alf a sausage to catch it," he said, as if in accusation.

"I see. And what happened to the other half?"

"Et it, din't I?"

"I see, so you are out of pocket by half a sausage."

"S'right."

"In that case," Marcus strolled to the window with the pies. "Take this as compensation." He lifted a pie, glanced at the boy's hungry expression and took two.

"She'll be mad," the child said. "She's a right scary one, she is. Nearly bit me head off when I was only trying to have a sniff. I hardly even touched it." He wiped his hands on his trousers. "Dunno what she'll do to you if she catches you pinching one pie, let alone two."

Marcus repressed a smile. "She won't mind." Cook ran a tight ship, but she'd always had time to feed a hungry boy. Well, a hungry Marcus.

The lad gave him a skeptical look, but took the pies, which vanished into the pockets of his coat. "Fanks, mister."

"What's your name?"

"What's it to you?"

Marcus picked up another pie. Neither the boy nor the dog took their eyes off it. "Your name?"

"Joey," he said sullenly.

"And where are your parents, Joey?"

There was a short silence. Marcus broke off some of the crust and dropped it for the dog, who gobbled it up in a trice. Marcus looked at the boy, who looked at the pie. "Your parents?"

Joey shrugged. "Ain't got none. Me dad ran off to sea when I was a nipper and never come back. And me mum died last winter."

"So who looks after you?" The child had to be seven, eight at the latest.

He straightened and looked Marcus in the eye. "I look after meself, I do, and nobody can say different." He reached for the pie in Marcus's hand.

Marcus raised it higher. "And where do you live?"

"Around." His tone was defiant, truculent.

Marcus nodded. The boy's bristles were well and truly up; he wasn't going to get much further. "Very well, if you come back tomorrow, I'll have some jobs for you to do. For money—and no I won't bargain with you. We'll see how well you work first. But it will be fair, and as well as pay, you'll get a good midday meal."

The boy glanced at the kitchen window. "From 'er what made them pies?"

"Yes, she's an excellent cook." He handed the boy the pie. He took a ravenous bite, glanced down at the dog, broke off another bit and gave it to him. Marcus was impressed.

"Orright then, I'll come, but if it's some trick. . ."

"It's an honest offer, partly in thanks for what you did for the lady this morning." Marcus would never forget the way this skinny urchin had stood up to him, trying to protect her.

The boy nodded, slipped out of the back gate and disappeared.

"That beggar-boy?" Peverill said in disbelief. "You're going to admit him to the house again, m'lord? And I'm to find him work to do?"

"That's it," Marcus agreed. Peverill had taken one appalled look at the dog tucked under Marcus's arm and had pointedly decided not to notice it.

"But he'll steal the silver."

"No he won't," Marcus said placidly, but with a firm undertone that his butler would recognize. "The only thing he's likely to steal is Cook's pies, and he's welcome to as many of those as he wants. That child is near starving."

"But he's dirty, really quite filthy. He, he *stinks*, m'lord."

"So would you if you'd been living on the street since last winter."

"My lord!" Peverill drew himself up in silent indignation at such a suggestion.

"But you make a good point. When he comes back, have him bathed before you set him to work. Oh, and get him some new clothes, not new— I suspect he'd hate wearing stiff new clothing—but clean and in good condition. As you say, he's dirty and ragged, and we can't have a child like that in the house, can we, Peverill?"

"No, m'lord," Peverill said miserably. "And The Animal? May I ask what is to be done with it?"

"It belongs to Lady Hewitt and will live here while she is with us, naturally."

Peverill sighed. "Naturally."

"You will take care of the dog while she's indisposed." Marcus handed him the dog.

The butler held the squirming dog gingerly and said weakly, "Perhaps one of the footmen . . .?"

Marcus hid a smile. He'd pushed his long-suffering butler far enough. "Naturally you will delegate the responsibilities as you see fit."

"Very good m'lord," Peverill said dryly.

Tessa woke slowly. Her head ached, her body felt heavy and lethargic, and her thoughts were . . . fuzzy. They made no sense to her. A series of images floated vaguely through her mind; a minister, Edgar, a . . . a fight? She must have been dreaming—at least she hoped that was it.

But these sensations . . . they felt unsettlingly familiar.

Her eyelids were heavy, sticky. She forced them open and found she was in a strange bed, in a strange room. The curtains were closed—blue velvet curtains. They didn't have any blue curtains, let alone velvet ones. She looked around the room. An elegant carved wardrobe, matching dressing table, a chair upholstered in blue velvet. Paintings she'd never seen. Not a single thing was familiar. Panic started to rise in her throat.

"M'lady?" a soft voice said.

Tessa turned. Behind her, on the other side of the bed stood a young maidservant. "Who are you?"

"I am Sutton, m'lady and I'm to be your maid."

Tessa stared at her dazedly. She had a maid? A ghastly thought knifed into her. "And who am I?" she said cautiously, dreading the answer.

The maid's brow crumpled in concern. "You're Lady Hewitt," she said gently. "Don't you remem—"

"Lady Hewitt? Still? Oh, thank God." Tessa fell back against the pillows. She wasn't Lady Lester. She hadn't married Sir Henry Lester.

Or had she? The anxiety seeped back in. Perhaps the maid didn't know her newest name. Perhaps she'd been told to lie to Tessa.

"How do you feel, m'lady? Would you like a glass of water?" The maid held out a glass.

"Where am I?" Tessa croaked, and accepted the glass from the maid. She drank thirstily and asked again where she was.

"At Alverleigh House, m'lady."

Tessa's brow wrinkled. Alverleigh House? For a few moments she couldn't think of where that was. It sounded familiar, but . . . She shook her head.

"Lord Alverleigh brought you here, m'lady. You were . . . ill."

"Ill?" Lord Alverleigh? It sounded familiar, but . . .

The girl nodded. "He brought the doctor to you. And you've slept now for nearly two days."

"*Two days?*" Tessa struggled to sit up. Her mind was full of dazed conjecture, terrible questions jostling in her fuzzy brain. Surely she hadn't had another brainstorm. Not again.

"There there, m'lady, just you rest a moment. I'll let Lord Alverleigh know you're awake. And, would you like me to order you some breakfast?"

"Breakfast?" Tessa repeated vaguely.

"Yes, you'll feel more the thing with some food inside you. How about a nice soft-boiled egg with some toast soldiers?" Sutton said coaxingly. "Or if you prefer, a cup of chocolate and some pastries. Lady Gosford always enjoys cook's pastries. Or maybe you just feel like a nice cup of tea."

Tessa shook her head. She felt quite nauseous; the last thing she felt like was food. She had an unpleasant acrid taste in her mouth. That strawberry fool last night that had tasted a bit funny. Had it been off? Did it make her sick? But she'd only had a couple of mouthfuls.

And if she could believe the maid, she'd been here two days, sleeping! Two days! So, the strawberry fool wasn't last night, but several nights ago.

What had happened? What was she doing in this strange house with a strange maid tending her and wanting her to eat? And why would this Lord Alverleigh bring her to his house and fetch a doctor to her? She was sure she'd heard the name before. Why couldn't she recall who he was? And why, oh why did nothing make sense?

The image of a minister in a long black cassock, a white surplice over it haunted her. Was it a memory or a nightmare?

Had there been another wedding? Was it too late?

No, the maid had called her Lady Hewitt, not Lady Lester. But maybe the maid didn't know . . .

The confusion, the blankness, the terrifying, unanswerable questions—it was all so dreadfully familiar. She clutched the sheets around her. She couldn't let herself panic, not now, not yet.

The maid slipped from the room, closing the door softly behind her. Immediately Tessa moved to get out of the bed. She had to get up, find out what was afoot, get out of this place.

But the minute she tried to stand, her legs quivered, then buckled beneath her. She would have ended up on the floor, but she managed to grab hold of the covers and haul herself back onto the bed.

Once she'd caught her breath, she tried to stand again, this time, holding on tight to a smooth carved wooden bedpost. Her legs wobbled, her head swam but she forced herself to keep standing while she breathed in deep, slow gulps of air. It helped to clear the dizziness somewhat, and her legs slowly gathered strength, but the questions whirling in her brain remained unanswered.

Realizing she was dressed in an unfamiliar nightgown, much too big for her, she looked around for her own clothes. A dressing gown hung from a hook behind the door. Lurching slightly as she walked, she reached the wardrobe and threw it open.

"What are you doing up?" A deep masculine voice came from the doorway.

She stepped back in fright and almost fell over—her dizziness hadn't yet passed. In two steps the man crossed the room, scooped her up and laid her gently on the bed. "You haven't yet recovered," he told her. The maid had followed him in, and he told her to help Tessa put on the dressing gown and get her properly into bed.

"Recovered from what?" she said accusingly, then faltered as she recognized him. "Oh. It's you." Even to her own ears her voice sounded thready, uncertain.

"Yes, you're safe, in my home," he told her. "Just rest and let yourself recover."

"Recover from what?"

"It seems your brother drugged you." He paused a moment, then added, "My physician confirmed it."

Edgar had *drugged* her? Tessa sank back against the

pillows and let the maid tuck her in. Her brain was whirling.

Drugged? And not for the first time, she realized slowly.

She should be more shocked, but in retrospect it made terrible sense. No wonder the sensations she'd felt on awakening—the taste in her mouth, the foggy brain, the lethargic limbs, the bewilderment—had felt so familiar. *Drugged.*

She drank another glass of water. It was very like when she'd woken to find herself married to Lord Hewitt, after she'd experienced what Edgar and her new husband had explained was an illness: she'd suffered 'a brainstorm' they told her.

That was why she'd been so confused and why she didn't recall her second wedding. She hadn't been ill at all; she'd been *drugged*. By Edgar.

Somehow, she wasn't as shocked as she ought to be.

It was as if, deep down, she'd known it was something like that, only she'd refused to face it. Edgar was, after all, her brother, her only living relative. He had his faults, to be sure, but . . .

And anyway, once they'd shown her the marriage certificate with her own wobbly signature . . . it had been too late.

She looked up at the tall man standing by her bed. She knew him, felt somehow safe with him, though she couldn't immediately think of his name. "So tell me, am I married or not?" she asked dully. No point in asking to whom—it would be Sir Henry, Edgar's latest choice. But if so, where was he? And why was she in Lord—she couldn't remember his title—in Marcus's house? Yes, that was his name—Marcus.

"No, we were in time."

She struggled to sit up. "I'm not married?"

"No. As I said, we stopped it in time." Seeing her confusion, he said firmly, "There was no wedding. It didn't happen. You are safe. And free."

There was a knock on the door. The maid opened it and another maid entered with a tray. "No, thank you." Tessa held up her hands to shoo it away. "Nothing to eat. I'm not hungry."

Marcus took the tray from the maid and laid it across Tessa's knees, saying. "The doctor who examined you advised me that once you woke, you ought to eat something light and nourishing. It will help you get your strength back. If you don't want this, I'll send for some soup."

She shook her head. She really wasn't hungry. In fact, thinking about what Edgar had done to her—twice—made her feel quite sick.

He ignored her. "The doctor also said food would help to clear the drug from your system. Now eat." He shook out a napkin, poured some tea from the pot, and added a little milk and a lump of sugar. Then he lifted a small, knitted cozy to reveal a boiled egg sitting in a little silver egg-cup, and a plate of toast soldiers.

She looked at it. The toast was still warm and smelled enticing.

He beheaded the egg. "Do you want me to feed you?" he said, reaching toward the toast.

She gave him a startled look. "No!" His rather hard gray eyes gleamed, and she realized he was teasing her. But in case he wasn't, she picked up a finger of toast, dipped it into the yolk and ate it. It was delicious.

And suddenly she realized she was hungry, after all. It had been years since she'd eaten an egg this way. It reminded her of cozy nursery suppers with NannyJune. And though she was hardly a child any more, she felt oddly pampered, cared for.

She was ridiculously aware of Marcus, now sitting on the end of her bed, watching her. No, it was Lord Alverleigh sitting there, and she had best remember that.

"Tell me what happened," she said while she ate.

His explanation was brief and crisp; he'd set men to watch the house, he'd been notified when the minister arrived, and when he arrived, he realized she'd been drugged.

Tessa frowned. She had no clear memory of any of it. Only hazy impressions.

"So I stopped the wedding and brought you here, and summoned the doctor," he finished.

Now there were even more questions clamoring in her head. Why had he set men to watch the house? How had he stopped the wedding? And what about Edgar? He'd be furious, she was sure, and she couldn't imagine him tamely allowing Marcus to stop the wedding, let alone removing her from the house.

"I don't understand—" she began, then broke off, as a memory floated to the surface of her mind. Edgar, calling her a fool, and forcing a small bottle of something nasty tasting down her throat as she struggled against him.

He hadn't been calling her a fool, she realized. It was because she hadn't eaten enough of the strawberry fool for the drug to work.

The realization sent the nausea swirling again. Her own brother . . .

She pushed the remnants of egg away.

"Finished? Good," Marcus said. He rose. "I'll leave you now. Any further questions can wait until after you've rested some more. The doctor was very firm that you should rest."

Tessa had no desire to rest, but a sudden thought occurred to her. "Where are my clothes?"

He gave her a blank look, then quirked an eyebrow at the maid.

"I have only the dress you were wearing when you arrived here, m'lady," Sutton said.

The dress Edgar had no doubt put her into for the wedding? Tessa had no memory of what she'd been wearing but whatever it was, she didn't want to wear it. "No, I don't want it. Throw it away. I don't even want to see it."

"But m'lady …"The girl looked at Lord Alverleigh.

"I'll have your belongings brought here," he said.

Tessa gave him a doubtful look. "I did pack a valise—I was intending to leave anyway—but I'm sure Edgar will refuse to give it to you. He must be very angry."

"Leave your brother to me. Drink your tea and rest. You will wish to be properly attired when you meet my aunt—perhaps this evening, if you're feeling well enough to come downstairs. In the meantime, let Sutton know if you need anything else." He strode from the room.

Marcus took two maids and a footman with him to Tessa's former home. He anticipated no difficulty in collecting her things—by now Edgar Blaxland would be well on his way to America—Jackson and Sims and a note from the ship's captain had confirmed it. It was too good for the swine, and

Marcus half wished he'd left him to the Greelings, or better still, instructed the captain to toss him overboard but Tessa, despite her hurt and anger, still had some loyalty for the man, and he doubted she'd ever truly forgive Marcus if he punished her brother as he truly deserved.

Arriving at Tessa's former home, he found the landlord, cursing his tenants' abrupt departure owing several months' rent.

"I know nothing of that," Marcus lied. "I am here to collect some personal belongings and to inquire as to whether any note or letter has been left behind?" Surely Blaxland would have left a note for his sister.

"No note, and not so much as a penny piece left behind, neither," the landlord said bitterly. "A few worthless bits and pieces, and a pile of female clothing—a young female at that!—and what am I supposed to do with them, I ask you? They won't fit my missus, and Lord save me if she finds me tryin' to sell 'em down Petticoat Lane. Nasty suspicious mind my missus has." He spat. "I ain't never going to rent to a toff again—saving your presence, your honor. They always expect endless credit, and I can't afford that."

"Not all aristocrats are without honor," Marcus told him coldly. "I will relieve you of the female clothing—and pay you handsomely." He sent the maids and footman inside with orders to take anything that they thought might belong to Lady Hewitt; clothes, books, knick knacks—anything.

He waited downstairs, listening to the landlord's complaints with a bored air. When his servants had finished packing up Tessa's things and packed them into his coach, he pressed a couple of gold sovereigns into the man's hand and left.

CHAPTER SEVEN

IT WAS LATE afternoon when Tessa woke again, much refreshed. Her mind was clearer and the headache had gone—though she still ached at how her brother had betrayed her. Again.

She lay there, brooding about how both her father and her brother had used her—repeatedly—and how in her ignorance and her pathetic, needy belief that they loved her and wanted the best for her, she'd allowed it. The realization simmered like acid in her belly.

Never again. It was time to take control of her life.

She rang for Sutton to order a bath, but when the maid came in she was not alone. A small nut-brown dog with a white flag of a tail bounced in ahead of her, and perceiving Tessa, gave a happy yap and a mighty leap and scrambled onto her bed.

"Billy!" she exclaimed delightedly, laughing as the little dog wriggled and capered in an ecstatic reunion.

"So, he really is your dog," Sutton commented, laughing at the little dog's antics. "We did wonder."

"Yes, but how did you know? And how did he come to be here?" She'd assumed he would have run off, back to his old life on the streets. Edgar wouldn't have tolerated a dog in the house.

"The boy brought him, on Lord Alverleigh's orders."

"What boy?"

Sutton shrugged. "Joey, his name is. A street boy, I think, but his lordship's taken him in for some reason. Oh, and his lordship said to tell you to keep the dog away from his aunt. She don't like dogs." She smiled. "Now, m'lady, what about that bath? You'll want to prepare for meeting Lady Gosforth. His lordship's had all your things brought here, so let me know what you'd like to wear. I'll just have the bath and hot water brought up."

Tessa cuddled her dog, so happy to see the little fellow again. Marcus had arranged it? And returned her belongings to her? How he had persuaded Edgar to let them go was a mystery, but she was grateful for it.

She slipped out of bed and looked into the wardrobe. Everything had been pressed and was tidily packed away: Sutton had been busy while she slept.

She recalled his comment as he left: *You will wish to be properly attired when you meet my aunt.* Something about the way he'd said it made her suspect his aunt might be somewhat of a high stickler. Most society ladies were, in her experience. Still, she wouldn't be staying long.

After a long hot bath, she felt a lot better—almost ready for anything. She considered which of her dresses to wear to meet the aunt—Marcus had brought everything, even her favorite books and some of the little knick-knacks she'd had in her bedroom. So thoughtful of him—she wasn't used to that.

Recalling that she was hoping for a recommendation from his aunt or one of her friends, she chose one of the dresses she'd altered to look plainer and more in keeping for a companion.

At half past six, with Billy left snoozing on a rug in her bedroom, Sutton conducted Tessa to a large, tastefully appointed sitting room. A fire blazed brightly. Marcus stood in front of it. Seeing him there, so solid and tall, caused a small ripple of relief to pass though her. She wasn't quite so alone.

An elderly lady rose to greet her—his aunt, Tessa assumed. Tall and thin—apart from a generous bosom—she was dressed in the first stare of fashion, not showy, but the kind of elegance that money alone couldn't buy. Her hair was silver and pulled back severely, highlighting both her elegant cheekbones and her proud Roman nose.

Marcus—she'd better start thinking of him as Lord Alverleigh: now that she'd recalled his title, it wouldn't do to address him familiarly, especially in front of this grim-looking aunt—introduced them.

She regarded Tessa through a lorgnette, her eyes gimlet hard, her demeanor stony.

He'd told her his aunt was a little intimidating. A *little* intimidating? More like Attila the Hen. She raised her chin and held the old woman's gaze.

Lady Gosforth scanned Tessa's outfit from top to bottom, and raised one elegantly plucked eyebrow in a disdainful, sardonic arch, as if to say, What is *that* you're wearing?

Tessa stiffened her spine. She would not be intimidated.

The old lady watched Tessa's curtsy with a critical eye and then bade them both to be seated. "Will you have tea or sherry?"

Spotting the small glass at Lady Gosforth's elbow, Tessa opted for sherry. She didn't much care for sherry but when in Rome...

Lady Gosforth glanced at the butler, who looked at Lord Alverleigh but before he could say anything she said. "My nephew does not require refreshments. He's leaving."

"Aunt Maude," he began in a warning voice.

"Marcus you know very well that while this . . . lady continues to sleep under this roof you must sleep elsewhere. For the sake of her . . . reputation," she added with a faintly malicious smile. It was clear to Tessa that those pauses were deliberate, to throw doubt on what followed. The old witch thought Tessa had no reputation to lose.

Lord Alverleigh leaned back in his chair, crossed one leg over the other and said, "I'll have a brandy, Peverill." He turned to Tessa. "Don't let my aunt alarm you, Lady Hewitt—I have already made arrangements to sleep at my club."

"I'm not alarmed in the slightest," Tessa said coolly. It wasn't quite true but she was determined not to let this steely old woman rattle her.

There was a short silence, broken only by the clinking of crystal as the butler filled glasses, and set a small dish of almond wafers at Tessa's elbow.

"That will do, Peverill," the old lady said when the butler had finished serving.

Once the butler had left, she turned to Tessa. "Tell me, Lady Hewitt, what is it you want of my nephew? You clearly have a plan."

"Aunt Maude—"

"Pish tush, let the gel speak for herself. Or are you worried about what she might reveal?"

"Not in the least."

Tessa set down her untouched glass. "What do I

want of your nephew? Introductions, that is all. It was his idea to bring me here, for which I'm very grateful, but—"

"Introductions? To whom? His friends? I'll tell you now, not one of them has a superior fortune."

Tessa glared at the old woman. "I want no introductions to his friends—or to any men. I have no wish to marry again, if that's what you're thinking. The introductions I sought were to elderly ladies like yourself—only perhaps to ones more open-minded."

Lord Alverleigh gave a muffled crack of laughter.

Lady Gosforth raised her lorgnette again. "Elderly ladies? Oh hush, Marcus. This is important. Why do you want to meet elderly ladies, gel?"

"Didn't your nephew explain? I am seeking a position as a lady's companion."

The old lady frowned. "A *lady's companion*. To what end?"

Tessa rolled her eyes. "Isn't it obvious? To earn a living, of course."

Lady Gosforth stared at her for a long moment, then said in an incredulous voice, "You would choose to become a lady's companion, to run endless errands and be at somebody's beck and call, in preference to marriage?"

Tessa sent an apologetic glance to Lord Alverleigh. "Yes."

"Why?"

Tessa lifted her chin. "That's my business."

Lady Gosforth considered that for a moment then shook her head. "If I'm to house you and introduce you to my friends, I'd say that it's my business too. I don't know you, after all, and what I do know of you is far from—"

Lord Alverleigh rose to his feet. "Aunt Maude, that's quite enough! I told Lady Hewitt that she would find safe haven here, not be obliged to endure impertinent questions."

His aunt bristled. "Impertinent?"

"Grossly."

Tessa also had had enough. She rose and walked to the door.

"Where do you think you're going, missy?" Lady Gosforth snapped.

Tessa turned to face her. "It's no concern of yours. I did not ask to come here, and I will not stay to sow discord between you and your nephew."

To her amazement, the old lady stared at her a moment then laughed. "*Sow discord*? What nonsense! There's no discord here, gel, just a . . . a robust family discussion. Nothing to get upset about. Now sit down."

Tessa didn't move. Her hand was still on the door handle.

The old woman stamped her foot. "Are you deaf, gel? I said, Sit. Down."

Tessa glanced at Lord Alverleigh. To her surprise, he looked amused. "That, Lady Hewitt, is what my brothers Gabe and Harry call the voice of General Gosforth. A great loss to Wellington it was, not admitting ladies to the army. But please, do sit down. I know it doesn't seem like the welcome I hoped you would have, but let us see where a civilized"— he gave his aunt a stern look—"discussion might lead."

Tessa hesitated. "I don't want charity." Ironic, because that's exactly what she was existing on at the moment.

"And you won't get it here," the old lady snapped.

Tessa glared back at her. Lord Alverleigh who had followed her to the door, cupped her elbow with his palm and said softly, "I never offered you charity and I'm not offering it now. But can't one old friend help another without being accused of charity?" She sighed, and let him lead her back to her seat. It was all quite confusing.

He turned to his aunt. "Now, Aunt Maude, behave yourself."

His aunt sniffed. "She's got a backbone, I'll say that for her. And too much pride for her own good."

Tessa stiffened. "Too much pride? How? I am looking for a position as a paid companion."

"Why a companion? Why not something else? No don't look at me like that, gel—I'm curious, that's all."

Tessa said wearily. "I have little education and few accomplishments, so I could never be a governess. And I was rejected by no fewer than forty-seven shop owners when I applied for a position as a shop girl."

The finely plucked eyebrows rose. "You applied to become a shop gel? At forty-seven shops?"

"Unsuccessfully. And it appears that you also consider me unsuitable as a lady's companion."

"Quite right. You do not have the temperament for it."

"With the right employer—"

"Pish tush! Enough of this nonsense." Lady Gosforth rose to her feet, leaning heavily on her cane. "It's late and I'm expected elsewhere for dinner. You can dine here alone—my nephew is leaving for his club, or I'll want to know the reason why—so you may eat yours on a tray in your room if you prefer. Anything else you require, ask Sutton or ring for Peverill."

Confused by the old lady's abrupt change in attitude, Tessa glanced at Lord Alverleigh. He winked.

"I told you," he murmured. "Intimidating on the outside, but underneath . . ."

"You mean it was a test?" she said in a low voice.

"Stop whispering!" The old lady held out an imperious hand to her nephew. "Take yourself off now, Marcus. You cannot stay to compromise the gel. I'll see you again in the morning."

Lord Alverleigh bowed over her hand then did the same to Tessa, saying, "Sleep well, Lady Hewitt. You're safe now."

His aunt snorted. "Of course she's safe. She's with me, isn't she?" And she prepared to go out for the evening.

To her surprise, despite the days she'd spent sleeping off the drug, Tessa slept like a log that night. No unpleasant dreams, no waking up in the night, startled out of sleep. It was the best sleep she'd had in ages.

The following morning Sutton woke her, bringing a cup of delicious hot chocolate and some sweet pastries and said, "One of the footmen took your dog downstairs to do his business, and Cook's feeding him now, m'lady. He's got a way with him, that dog. And Lady Gosforth would like to speak to you in the sitting room at ten o'clock."

Just before ten, Tessa went downstairs. She found Lady Gosforth dressed most elegantly in shades of olive green and pale gray. A flamboyant feathered hat sat beside her on the settee. She scanned Tessa's outfit with pursed lips.

"Good morning, Lady Hewitt, I hope you slept well." Tessa barely had time to respond, when the old lady swept on. "I have an appointment with my mantua maker this morning. Run upstairs and fetch your hat and pelisse. We're going shopping."

"Why?" Tessa said, surprised into bluntness.

"Isn't it obvious?" Lady Gosforth made a disparaging gesture with her lorgnette. "You can hardly go about society dressed like that."

"I don't intend to go about in society at all," Tessa told her, "and if you are suggesting I need new clothes, I neither want nor can afford them." The old lady opened her mouth as if to argue and Tessa added, "My clothes are suited to my future position, and I have all that I need."

"Pshaw! As a *companion*?" She said the word 'companion' in the way some people spoke of earwigs.

Tessa inclined her head.

"Pshaw! I told you yesterday you don't have the temperament for a companion."

"And I said that it would surely depend on the employer—except that you cut me off and didn't listen," Tessa said.

"How do you intend to find such an employer? Wander the streets asking strangers? Or were you planning to vulgarly register yourself at some employment agency?" the old lady said acidly.

"Oh, register at an employment agency, is that what one does?" Tessa said, relieved to know. "I shall do so immediately."

Lady Gosforth snorted and with a severe expression, trained the lorgnette on Tessa for a long few moments. Tessa sat, quite composed, and met her gaze, her chin held high. She would not be discomposed by a crabby old lady wielding a piece of glass.

Finally Lady Gosforth said, "That dress is horridly plain. Did you pick something off it?"

"Yes, some decorative piping." It had been quite a smart dress, light gray with an elegant piping design in scarlet and white. Now it was simply gray.

"Why? You've ruined it."

"I have learned that people expect a person in my position to dress plainly."

She snorted. "Plain? That dress is positively drab."

"The drabber the better. Most people prefer their subordinates to be almost invisible."

The old lady narrowed her eyes. "Stubborn, aren't you, gel?"

Tessa shrugged.

"Foolish gel, there's no earthly point in ruining your clothes. What are you going to do about that face of yours—wear a bag over your head?" And with that, Lady Gosforth picked up her hat and sailed out.

Shortly afterward, Tessa left Alverleigh House, clutching a list of employment agencies that she'd talked Peverill into giving her. He'd been quite uncomfortable about it, suggesting it was not the sort of thing a young lady like her should be doing. "I need to earn my living, Peverill. I have no choice," she told him.

"If you say so, Lady Hewitt," he said, his expression wooden. No doubt he knew her sordid little story—servants always knew everything. It was obvious he did not approve of her seeking employment—servants often had firm ideas of what was appropriate for the aristocracy—but he made a list for her in small, neat writing and she went off with it feeling almost triumphant.

She took Billy with her, on a lead made of a long ribbon. His presence and his bright eyes helped to keep her spirits up. Though it had to be said that he did not like being on a lead. He plonked his bottom on the ground and refused to move. It was rather like dragging loaf of bread for a walk. But with coaxing and encouragement he eventually got used to it.

At the first employment agency on the list, she

had to wait for almost an hour before a dauntingly formal matron consented to interview her. There were several others before her, waiting, looking nervous, or hopeful. One by one, they emerged from their interview looking excited or crushed. Her own nerves grew.

But she was clean, literate, polite and willing to work hard; surely there would be a position for her. Finally, it was her turn to be called.

A grim looking matron seated behind a desk gave her a long, searching glance, taking in, Tessa felt, every tiny detail. She made a few notes on a ledger in front of her. She did not invite Tessa to sit.

"You wish for a position as a lady's companion?" she said eventually.

"Yes, ma'am."

"You have a character?"

Tessa blinked. "A character, ma'am?"

"A character reference from a previous employer."

"No. I haven't been employed before. This will be my first position—I'm a widow—but I'm willing to work hard."

The woman sniffed and made another note. "We have nothing for you."

"Oh, but—"

"Did you not hear me, gel? We at the Howard Agency deal only with applicants of the highest standard. You do not meet those standards. Send in the next applicant."

When she left the building, she found Billy sitting beside the gas lamp she'd tied him to, untethered, the lead chewed quite through. "Oh Billy." She laughed and retied the ribbon again, much to the dog's disgust.

After that she had several more crushing interviews each by equally intimidating women who seemed to sum her up at a glance and decide she wouldn't suit. Some of them didn't even bother to interview her, just glanced at the form she had filled out and dismissed her, some politely, some brusquely, making it clear that she'd wasted their time.

It was quite confusing. When they did bother to ask her questions, they'd shaken their heads at her responses and cut her short. She'd been too honest, she decided in retrospect. She'd do better tomorrow.

She returned to Alverleigh House with dragging feet, Billy trotting ahead without a lead. He'd made his point.

Greeting Peverill with a bright smile, she went upstairs to her room and sat down to write herself a glowing 'character' from the widowed Lady Holgrave in her best copperplate handwriting.

She would not give up so easily.

"You're wanted downstairs, m'lady," Tessa's maid said.

"Thank you, Sutton but I don't really feel like afternoon tea," she responded. She was weary and dispirited and not in the mood to endure—or attempt to parry—the old lady's sniping.

"Lady Gosforth particularly requested your presence, m'lady."

"Very well. I suppose I'd better go then." Sutton tidied her hair and helped her into a fresh dress, and Tessa went downstairs.

"Well, miss, what did you get up to today?" Lady Gosforth greeted her. "Spent the day lolling on your bed, eating sweetmeats and reading some silly novel, I suppose."

"On the contrary, I visited a number of employment agencies."

"Did you now?" A finely plucked eyebrow rose, and the lorgnette was trained upon her. "And how did you fare?"

Tessa would die rather than tell this old woman how miserably she'd failed. "Quite well. I left my name with several very respectable agencies, and they will contact me when a suitable position arises."

"Indeed." It was a skeptical sort of 'indeed.

"Yes, it was most gratifying."

The old lady opened her mouth but before she could speak the drawing room door opened, and a footman carried in a tray bearing the tea things. And to Tessa's relief, Lord Alverleigh strolled in after him.

When the greetings were done, Lady Gosforth busied herself pouring tea. "Well, Marcus, what brings you here?" she asked handing him a cup of tea.

"Do I need a reason to visit my own house? And to enquire after my beloved aunt and my valued guest?"

His beloved aunt gave him a withering look. "I have been shopping and visiting friends. Your 'guest' has been out most of the day visiting *employment agencies*." Sounding as if Tessa had been visiting dens of iniquity.

For a moment she thought he'd frowned, but one blink and it was gone, and he was asking Tessa, "Did you have any luck?"

"They took my details but there are no suitable positions at the moment." It wasn't exactly a lie.

He put down his teacup. "I thought you might like to go out for some fresh air, but if you've been out most of the day attending interviews. . ."

She didn't hesitate. "No, thank you, I'd love it."

He rose. "Good, then we'll ride in Hyde Park. I'll be back here with the horses in an hour. It won't be the fashionable time, but there will still be enough light."

"Oh, but I can't," she said dismayed.

He turned back. "Why not? As I recall you used to be a keen equestrienne."

"Yes, but I don't have a riding habit."

He frowned. "Didn't the maids pack it? I told them to pack all your things."

"I don't own one."

His frown deepened. "You didn't ride as an adult?"

She shook her head. "Neither of my husbands approved of ladies riding." And oh, the arguments she'd had with them,—both of them—about that. All in vain. The first one kept her penniless and supervised all her clothing, so she couldn't purchase a habit, and since he didn't ride at all, there was not even a horse she could borrow. By the time the issue came up with Hewitt, her second husband, he'd been just as adamant, and she'd been more easily defeated.

Lord Alverleigh's lips compressed to a thin line. He turned to his aunt. "Aunt Maude, do you have a riding habit Lady Hewitt could borrow?"

"Yes of course, though it will be sadly out of fashion. And,"—she scanned Tessa through the lorgnette—"it will also be too long for her. She's shorter than I am."

"The length won't matter," Lord Alverleigh said, rising. "She'll be on horseback and ladies' habits drape low anyway."

"But it's dreadfully out of date," his aunt objected.

"It's been years since I've ridden. You don't want to look a dowdy, do you Lady Hewitt?"

"I don't care about fashion at all," Tessa assured her. "And I would be very grateful for the loan of a habit." The thought of riding again, after all these years, had her almost breathless with hope.

"That's decided, then. I'll see you in an hour," Lord Alverleigh said and strode from the room.

When Marcus arrived to collect Tessa, it occurred to him to wonder how the urchin, Joey, was getting on. "How is the boy working out?" he asked Peverill.

Peverill's normally impassive visage betrayed a faint grimace.

"Work-shy is he?"

"On the contrary, m'lord, the boy does his work well. He arrives promptly each morning and works hard until his various job are done."

Marcus frowned. "Then what's the problem?"

"It's not exactly a problem, m'lord. It's the clothing."

Marcus raised a brow. "Doesn't he like it?"

"I don't rightly know what he thinks of it. He arrives in his street rags, washes and changes into the clothes we—er, you— provided. Then he does his work—and he does it well, I admit—and when it's done, he collects his pay, eats the dinner Cook gives him—his appetite is prodigious. Then he changes back into his rags, only they are clean now, sir—Cook made it clear to him at the start that she would not feed a dirty boy—and he returns to his life on the streets."

Marcus frowned again. "Did you not make it clear that he can remain here?"

"I did, sir. I told him there was a room in the attic for his use, with a bed and blankets, and hooks to hang his clothing and so on. I even showed it to him, but it seems he wants none of it."

Marcus considered that. "Some wild creatures do not take readily to being tamed. Perhaps the boy would prefer to sleep in the stables."

"As to that, I could not say, m'lord, but I will offer him the choice." The butler hesitated, then added, "He's not a bad lad, m'lord. He's clever, respectful and diligent. I even gave him some silver to polish and not a single item went missing, not so much as a teaspoon. It's just his insistence on returning to the streets in his rags that's the problem."

"Ah well, give him time," Marcus said. "Now, be so good as to inform Lady Hewitt of my arrival—ah, no need. Here she comes now."

Tessa came skipping down the stairs, the long skirt of the riding habit hooked over one arm. Bragge,

Lady Gosforth's maid, had found the habit in a trunk in the attic, and with needle and thread had made a few hasty adjustments to make it fit. More or less. Tessa didn't care what she looked like, she was just so eager to go for a ride again. It had been years.

She resolved to take every opportunity to ride while she could. Once she was a companion, she doubted very much that anyone would allow her to ride, even if there were a horse available.

Lord Alverleigh waited out the front with a magnificent black gelding and a beautiful bay mare wearing a sidesaddle. A groom waited with a third horse: some kind of chaperon she assumed.

"Oh, she's beautiful," Tessa exclaimed. She fed the mare a piece of carrot filched from the kitchen and murmured endearments to her. "Thank you so much for this opportunity, Lord Alverleigh. I cannot tell you how much I have missed the freedom of riding."

He nodded. "It won't be like the freedom you used to have at Ferndale, I'm afraid. Mostly in London we just walk the horses and occasionally trot, but it will be better than nothing." He joined his hands and boosted her into the saddle. She arranged her skirts while he adjusted the straps.

Glancing down she saw his nose wrinkle. He took a few surreptitious sniffs. "Something wrong?" she asked.

"No, it's just . . ." He looked around as if for inspiration. "What is that smell?"

She knew at once what it was. "It's my new perfume," she said solemnly. "Do you like it?"

His expression as he searched for something polite to say, made her laugh aloud. "No, I'm teasing you. Your aunt's habit was stored in an oriental camphorwood chest, along with sachets of lavender, rosemary, mint and who knows what else—all to deter moths. Each scent is perfectly pleasant on its own, but the combination is admittedly peculiar. But I'm pleased to report we found no depredations by moths, so clearly it was effective."

His gray eyes glinted with appreciation. "Delighted to hear it." He mounted his horse and they rode off, the groom following.

When they reached the entrance to Hyde Park, she saw that despite the late hour there were still plenty of fashionably dressed people promenading. Men on horseback, too, as well as people in elegant vehicles of all kinds. Any one of them might know Edgar and tell him in whose company she'd been seen.

And then there would be trouble.

She reined in her horse.

"Something wrong?"

She hesitated. "I didn't expect to see so many people. Perhaps this wasn't a good idea after all." She scanned the clusters of people moving slowly along. No sign of Edgar, but who knew who else might see her?

Marcus must have noticed. "Don't like crowds? Then we'll avoid them." He turned his horse away from the crowd and led her down another path toward a much less populated area. As the green space opened up and the crowds fell behind them, Tessa should have felt more relaxed: instead, she was oddly restless.

Mostly we just walk the horses and occasionally trot, but it will be better than nothing.

But it was not better than nothing. It was infinitely worse. He didn't understand. It was like offering a starving person a dry rusk when there was a feast at hand.

There was nobody ahead, no pedestrians, nobody on horseback. Who knew when she would get the chance to ride again?

She glanced at Lord Alverleigh, and when his attention was elsewhere, she urged her mare into a canter. Hearing Lord Alverleigh's mount coming up behind her she glanced back, then urged her mare to a gallop. He increased his pace. He called out something, but she couldn't make out what. It didn't matter anyway. She just wanted to ride. And ride. And ride.

Oh, but it was glorious, the fresh air, the speed, the

scent of the grass, the damp earth, the warm horse. And most of all, the freedom just to ride. And ride.

Lord Alverleigh's horse was coming up behind her, but he said nothing, made no move to stop her. She pulled off her hat to feel the wind in her hair. For two pins she'd toss the hat away, but it was Lady Gosforth's so she couldn't. She pulled out her hairpins and shook her long hair free, laughing and she was almost fifteen again, carefree and happy.

Marcus stared at her off and galloping, a wild, untamed creature, her glorious hair streaming behind her as if she were riding the wind, like some equine goddess of old. Had he ever seen her like this, graceful and laughing, full of unfettered joy?

Not since she was a child.

But she was no child now; she was very much a woman. Lithe, lissome and . . . wholly, exuberantly, unselfconsciously sensual. Riding that horse as if she were part of it, reveling in the speed, the powerful animal beneath her, the fresh, moist air of the park.

He could barely breathe. He simply stared, stunned, unable to think. He followed her dumbly, unable to take his eyes off her, aware of the slow, dangerous coil of heat gathering in his body.

She was so beautiful like this, unselfconscious,

unconstrained, as if released from the burdens that had been weighing her down.

He swallowed, his mouth suddenly dry. *Beautiful?* He'd always known she was beautiful, but somehow, now, he *felt* it. Like a hard blow to his chest. And she wasn't just beautiful, but something much . . . more. He had no words, could not think, only watch, and wonder.

And want. Aching, insistently want.

CHAPTER EIGHT

EVENTUALLY TESSA'S MARE began to tire, and with it the reality of her situation closed in on her again. She slowed her mount and waited for Lord Alverleigh to join her.

No doubt she'd disgraced him with her unseemly behavior, but she didn't care. She'd had a few moments of glorious freedom and nobody could take that away from her. Whatever punishment he came up with, it would be worth it.

He drew up alongside her, and she braced herself. Would he be like Edgar and Lord Holgrave, who preferred to punish her in private? Keeping her waiting and wondering? Or would he be like Papa and Lord Hewitt who both tended to roar and react, not caring who witnessed it.

He glanced at her and gave her an odd look. "What is it?"

She scanned his face for any signs of anger, but could perceive none. "You didn't mind?"

"Mind what? Your galloping off like that? Of course not. It's not the done thing, but it's just what I wanted to do myself. Next time we'll go up to the Heath where you can gallop to your heart's content."

She wasn't sure she believed this matter-of-fact response. He might still wait and punish her in private. Recalling that her hair was flying free—wantonly, disgracefully loose and free—she replaced her hat and began to tuck her hair into it.

"Shame to cover it up," he said.

She blinked. "What?"

"Your hair. It's beautiful like that. Reminds me of when you were a little girl."

She ran a hand self-consciously over it. *Beautiful?* She'd always been told wearing her hair loose made her look like a hoydenish little gypsy. Or in Edgar's case, that she looked like a whore. She tucked the last few curls away.

They rode back in silence, Tessa wondering what Lord Alverleigh was going to say about her infraction. He seemed lost in thought, miles away. Not angry, but one could never tell with men.

She kept a wary eye out for Edgar or one of his cronies. Next time she went riding—if indeed she were given the chance—she would wear a veil.

When they reached his house, he leapt lightly down and held out a hand to help her dismount. She took it, still half-expecting him to rebuke her, but as she landed, her legs felt oddly wobbly. Staggering, she clutched onto him briefly and laughing, steadied herself. To her surprise, even briefly supported against his warm strong body, she felt a frisson of . . . what? Attraction? She wasn't sure; she'd never felt anything like it before.

Whatever it was, it felt . . . dangerous.

She stepped carefully away from him. "Sorry, it's been so long since I've ridden that my legs have gone a bit wobbly."

He seemed quite unaffected by the contact. "We'll have to take you riding more often, then, get you fit again. A hot bath will help. And I'll send around some liniment that will help, too. It smells a bit, but given your current 'perfume' I doubt you'll mind."

She gave him a cautious sidelong look. A joke? Was he not going to reprimand her at all, then? It seemed not, for he bowed, said he'd see her tomorrow, mounted his horse and rode off.

She mounted the steps slowly, feeling suddenly tired. As she entered the house, Peverill informed her that Lady Gosforth was dining out and would be attending the opera with friends, and if she liked, she could take her supper in her room. She accepted the offer gratefully. She had so much to think about.

The ride, much as she had enjoyed it, was not something she ought to expect in future. And that unexpected surge of . . . attraction? Whatever, it was disturbing.

She had stayed overlong at Lord Alverleigh's home, and she was sure his aunt must be getting impatient for her to go. She was clearly worried about Tessa's supposed designs on her nephew, even though Tessa had assured her repeatedly that she had no desire to marry again. And she hadn't changed her mind.

She didn't understand the old lady. One minute Tessa was sure the old woman despised her, and then next . . . It was almost as if Lady Gosforth sympathized with her. And why would she care whether Tessa was fashionably dressed or not? Surely she would prefer her unwanted guest to look like a quiz.

It was very confusing.

Never mind. She would try again for a post in the morning.

Deciding to walk back to his club, Marcus sent the horses to the stables with his groom. He'd enjoyed his ride more than he'd expected. She was easy company, riding along beside him in silence for the most part, a relaxed kind of silence, not awkward or uncomfortable. It suited him; he was not a natural conversationalist.

And then when she'd urged her mount into that most improper—though thoroughly enjoyable—

gallop, her face had been alight with pleasure. The sight of her delight had stolen his breath away.

Several times he'd heard her laugh. She'd shaken her long hair loose reminding him of when he'd known her as a child. That child had been full of life: warm, spontaneous and finding joy in the smallest things.

Perhaps that wellspring of joy hadn't been entirely driven out of her. A man could hope.

But then, when that exuberant, wild, gallop was over, she'd leaned forward, patted her mare's neck, and then straightened, turning to face him, the joy slowly drained from her face, leaving only that wary, somehow *braced* expression, that he hated.

What had drained the happiness from her? What did she think would happen? And when he'd stared at her, wondering what had caused that abrupt change in her demeanor, she'd hastily stuffed her hair, her glorious wild silver-gilt curls back under the ugly hat as if she were embarrassed or ashamed.

It disturbed him. What had her life been like? Not being allowed to ride, even though she loved it? And that disturbing change of expression at the end, almost like a child expecting punishment, not a grown woman entitled to enjoy herself in an activity she obviously loved.

He would make sure she had many more opportunities to ride.

Though what would happen if she found a job as a companion, or worse? He didn't like to think of that at all.

Tessa sat in front of the looking glass in her bedchamber, brushing her long hair. The action invariably sparked thoughts of Hewitt, her last husband. He loved brushing her hair—both her husbands had—but Hewitt's brushing was always a prelude to . . . unpleasantness.

Even though she knew he was long dead, she still found her body bracing itself for the moment when he would wind her hair around his hand and jerk her back. . . . She shivered and dropped the brush. How could she ever be free of the memories?

She sighed and tugged on the bell-pull to summon a maid to arrange her hair. It was too long and too unruly for her to arrange it in the smooth style that was required for a lady. As the bell faintly jangled downstairs she froze, then turned back to her reflection—and stared, as the realization dawned on her.

She didn't have to please anyone anymore: she could do whatever she liked with her hair. Whatever she liked.

She picked up her nail scissors and without further thought, hacked off a lock of the long, silver-blond hair. it floated to the floor, bright against the rich dark colors of the Turkey rug. That would do it. She snipped off another. It fell curling to the floor. Yes!

By the time the maid arrived, Tessa was concentrating so hard on cutting her hair that she didn't hear the girl come in. She did, however, hear her scream. "M'lady, m'lady, whatever are you doing?"

"What does it look like?" Wishing she had some bigger scissors, Tessa kept cutting.

"Oh, m'lady!" The maid started gathering up the fallen locks, then gazed at Tessa in dismay, her hands full of hair, for all the world as if she thought Tessa could put it back on her head.

Tessa laughed. "Take it away and burn it."

"Oh m'lady," the girl said dolefully, but she left the room, clutching handfuls of hair.

Tessa kept snipping until finally not a single long strand remained. She looked at her reflection and laughed. She looked like a scarecrow, her hair short, but all different lengths and sticking out in all directions. She ran her fingers through it and laughed again. Perfect! No man would want to marry her now.

A knock sounded on her door, and without waiting for her response the door opened, and Lady Gosforth stood there. She lifted her lorgnette. There was a long moment of absolute silence, then, "Good gad! What have you done to yourself, gel?"

Tessa stood slowly and shook her hair again. A few remnants of long blonde hair slithered from her shoulders to the floor. She faced the old lady defiantly. "I never liked it long."

"You look like a hedgehog!" the old lady said acidly.

"I like hedgehogs."

There was another long silence as the old lady glared at Tessa through her lorgnette and Tessa stared back. She would not be intimidated. Besides, what could anyone do? Her hair was gone. It was too late now.

Eventually Lady Gosforth turned and stalked away without another word.

A few minutes later, another knock on the door sounded. This time it was Bragge, Lady Gosforth's dresser. She gazed at Tessa, her hands clasped. "Oh, m'lady, your beautiful, beautiful hair."

"I wanted a change."

Bragge took a deep breath. "Yes, m'lady. Now, if you'd sit down here, I'll just neaten it a little."

Tessa thought of refusing, but then Bragge added in a low voice, "Her ladyship's instructions."

Knowing Bragge would get into trouble if she refused, Tessa sat. What did it matter if she were tidied up? She'd never have to brush her long hair again.

In one fell swoop—well, with lots of little snips—she'd banished the reminder of both her husbands handling it in that disturbing manner. She laughed again, thinking of it. She felt so much lighter and happier already.

"There you are, m'lady, that's better."

Tessa looked in the mirror and blinked. She didn't look like a scruffy hedgehog anymore; she looked like a . . . pixie? An elf? Tiny curls clustered around her head, framing her face in a way that was disconcertingly . . . pretty.

"Oh, Bragge, what have you done?" she whispered.

Bragge seemed pleased. "Luckily short hair is very much *à la mode*, m'lady. You look quite dashing."

"Dashing?" Tessa echoed dolefully.

"Yes, very. Lady Gosforth will be delighted."

Tessa sighed. "Thank you, Bragge."

The next morning Tessa went out job hunting again, a dowdy hat crammed over her head. She would never have cut her hair if she'd known it would make her look up-to-the-minute-fashionable. She'd intended to look plain and unassuming.

She left by the kitchen door, taking Billy with her. She didn't want to leave him alone all day, and he was used to the streets. Besides he was good company.

She was visiting the agencies lower down Peverill's

list, this time with higher hopes. But even though she now had a better story to tell, and a glowing reference from herself as Lady Holgrave to present, things went, if anything, even worse than the day before.

In the first interview, after waiting for forty minutes, the two women in charge took one look at her and dismissed her, saying, "We are an exclusive agency, Miss Blaxland,"—she'd decided to use her maiden name—"and our clientele is very select. You are not suited to our needs." They didn't even want to see her character reference. Even though it was from a baroness.

The final straw came when she'd stepped into the manager's office of second last agency on her list. She'd had to wait over an hour to be interviewed but when she was finally admitted to the interviewer's office she was made to wait again.

The well-dressed woman behind the big desk didn't even look up when Tessa entered. She wrote in a ledger, checked a file, took a sip of the tea at her elbow and grimaced, muttering, "Cold," before she even looked up to see Tessa standing there. Her eyes swept Tessa from head to foot. "Yes?" she said in an arctic voice.

Tessa explained that she was recently widowed and was looking for a position, perhaps as a companion or some such. She offered the woman her reference, but the woman ignored it. She looked Tessa up and down again, then gave a scornful snort. "Covent Garden fare, that's what you are, missy," she said, dropping her faux genteel accent. "Go on, get out of here. We're a respectable agency, we are, and we don't want nothing to do with the likes of you and your kind."

"Covent Garden fare?" she'd repeated. "I don't understand."

The woman explained in one pithy, brutal sentence, adding that with a face like hers it wouldn't be long before some rich gentleman would snap her up and she could then earn her living on her back. As she was no doubt used to.

Her cheeks burning, Tessa turned to walk from the room with as much dignity as she could manage. At the door she stopped, her temper rising.

Now she understood why so many agencies had stressed their respectability as they curtly dismissed her: they thought her some kind of courtesan. Or worse.

It was mortifying, not only for the undeserved slur on her character, but because Edgar had implied much the same fate awaited her if she refused to marry Sir Henry Lester. And she'd had enough of it!

She turned back and marched toward the desk. "As a lady I would not deign to acknowledge such a nasty, vulgar and unjustified slight, but then I'm not a lady, am I? According to you I'm *Covent Garden fare.* In which case—" She picked up the scummy cup of cold tea and threw it over the woman who let out squawks of indignation.

Feeling much better Tessa stalked from the room, but the minute she was back outside, even Billy's joyous welcome failed to cheer her up. A momentary rebellion, but a pointless result. She was still no closer to finding employment.

Disheartened, she trudged slowly back to Alverleigh House. As she entered the house again by the kitchen entrance, Peverill said, "Lady Gosforth asked to speak with you as soon as you came in, m'lady. She's in the small sitting room."

Tessa sighed and, deciding to get it over with, went straight to the small sitting room, leaving Billy to coax a treat out of Cook. There she found Lady Gosforth knitting some small, delicate white garment. The sight surprised her, but she wasn't going to ask.

The old lady looked up, set her knitting down and eyed Tessa through her lorgnette. "I see today's efforts have been as successful as yesterday's," she said sarcastically.

Tessa shrugged. "These things take time."

"I wouldn't know." She picked up her knitting and resumed it. "But it's clearly not as easy as you imagined. I suppose next you'll be advertising yourself in a newspaper."

"Oh. Good idea," Tessa said. "Thank you for the suggestion."

The finely plucked eyebrows flew up. The gnarled old fingers didn't stop knitting. "It was *not* a suggestion. Women of our class do *not* advertise themselves in newspapers."

"Perhaps they don't. But then, I'm no longer of your class, am I? I will soon be some kind of servant."

"Pshaw! Ridiculous. Blood is blood, and though your father and elder brother were a disgrace, their ancestry was distinguished and your mother was a lady from an excellent family."

"Nevertheless, needs must," Tessa said and left the room. She found Peverill and asked him for some recent newspapers.

"Newspapers, m'lady? For what purpose?"

"To read, of course." Tessa wasn't going to tell him her purpose. He was sure to disapprove as much as Lady Gosforth.

She took the newspapers up to her room and examined the advertisements, first to see if anyone was advertising a position that might suit her and, if there was nothing, to draft one advertising herself as a companion.

But to her delight, she found a notice requiring the services of 'a genteel female to act as a companion to an elderly lady.' It was in Yorkshire, which would be perfect. She knew nobody in Yorkshire and hoped nobody there would know of her background. She wrote a letter of application, describing herself as a widowed lady, sealed and addressed it.

Then sat staring at it. How to post it? It cost money to send letters, and she had not a bean to her name. In any case, she'd always had a husband or Edgar frank her letters to NannyJune. Dare she ask Lord Alverleigh to frank this for her?

The following morning at breakfast, Lady Gosforth almost made Tessa choke on her tea when, out of the blue, she said, "My nephew claims he proposed marriage to you."

"Yes, that's correct." Tessa hid a smile, recalling the fleeting look of shock in his eyes when he realized what he'd done.

The old lady raised her lorgnette. "He says you refused?"

"I did." She served herself a small portion of scrambled egg and added two spoons of grilled mushrooms. She liked mushrooms. She often used to collect them at Ferndale—she knew just which ones were good—and she and NannyJune would have them on toast for their supper.

"Hmm." After a moment's narrow-eyed contemplation, Lady Gosforth asked, "Why?"

"That's my business." Tessa took a mouthful of egg.

"A trifle reckless, wouldn't you say?"

"I don't think so."

The old lady pursed her lips at the implication. "So, you haven't had any second thoughts about refusing him?"

"Not one." It was true too, Tessa thought. He'd done quite enough for her. Even if she wanted to marry again—which she emphatically did not—marriage to her would ruin him.

"Most young woman would snap him up."

"These mushrooms are very good," Tessa said. Would the old lady never leave the subject alone? Did she believe Tessa was playing some convoluted game of hard-to-get? Nothing could be further from the truth.

There was a short pause, then the old lady said, "I know my nephew is cold and unapproachable—"

"Cold and unapproachable?" Tessa echoed. "Clearly you don't know him very well. I have always found him both kind and thoughtful." She returned to her breakfast.

Lady Gosforth raised her lorgnette again and stared at her through it for a long time. Tessa affected not to notice. Having finished her eggs and mushrooms, she spread marmalade on a piece of toast, then cut it into triangles. She would not let the old lady discompose her.

Eventually the lorgnette was lowered. "Be that as it may, prepare yourself for receiving morning calls this afternoon. Visitors will start arriving at about two."

"Morning calls?" Tessa looked up from her plate in surprise. "I won't be making morning calls."

"No of course not—you will be receiving them, with me."

"But I told you I had no intention of mixing in society."

Lady Gosforth eyed her down her long Roman nose. "You are a guest in this house, are you not?"

"Yes, but—"

"Then you will sit with me in my drawing room and meet my guests."

"But—"

The old lady raised her lorgnette. "You wish to become a lady's companion, do you not?"

"Yes, but—"

"Then you will need to meet ladies, and they will need to meet you. Which you will do here, under my eye. Bad enough that you vulgarly registered yourself at employment agencies," she said acidly. "We'll have no more of that nonsense!"

Peverill must have told her, Tessa thought. "I have applied for a position in Yorkshire. As a companion to an old lady." It wasn't quite true — she hadn't yet seen Lord Alverleigh to ask for a frank.

The old lady stamped her foot. "You will do no such thing! Who is this so-called old lady? A complete stranger? A person who advertises *in a newspaper*? Faugh! You know nothing about her— or him: it might not even *be* a lady. No, it's not to be thought of."

Tessa said nothing.

"You wish to be employed by the better class of lady, don't you?"

"I don't really care," Tessa said honestly. "It's not as if I have much choice, after all."

"Pshaw! Finish your breakfast and don't be ridiculous. A lady *always* has a choice. I will expect you downstairs at two." She turned a beady eye on Tessa and, with magnificent obliviousness, added, "And if you're not downstairs by two, I will have a footman carry you down—understand? And for goodness' sake wear something decent."

Tessa really didn't want to meet Lady Gosforth's visitors—she knew what they'd all think of her—but she also had no intention of being carried down by a footman, so just before two she went downstairs. But far from wearing something that Lady Gosforth would consider 'decent' she wore a very plain dress in dull charcoal gray.

When the old lady saw her, she sniffed and sent for a maid. "Run upstairs and fetch my pink shawl—the one with the embroidery," she told the girl.

The maid returned in a few minutes with a beautiful soft pink cashmere shawl, embroidered with a narrow black and silver design around the edge. At Lady Gosforth's direction, she then draped it around Tessa's shoulders. The old lady watched with a critical eye, then nodded. "There, that's better. Don't want people to think I've a crow for a guest, do I?"

Tessa didn't bother arguing—what was the point? Besides, the shawl was beautiful and warm, and the first callers were arriving. She could hear them in the hall. She tightened the shawl around her and braced herself.

It was a confusing afternoon.

Lady Gosforth made a point of introducing her to every caller as "My honored young guest, Lady Hewitt," which bewildered Tessa, as surely the point of making her attend was to let people know she was looking for a post as a companion.

The visitors' responses varied. Most were initially startled, and gave Tessa narrow looks, but good manners prevailed and they murmured a polite enough greeting. Several, however, pokered up indignantly, looking as though they would refuse to acknowledge her, but Lady Gosforth simply trained her lorgnette on them and waited until they condescended to greet Tessa, which they did with chilly hauteur. Not that she expected any kind of warmth, but Lady Gosforth's insistence on her guests' acceptance of Tessa confused her.

The old lady despised her, so what was she playing at?

There were several awkward moments. One was when Lady Gosforth, seeing her seated in a far corner made a point of calling her forward and instructing her to sit closer, pointing to a space between two ladies seated on the *chaise longue*. The ladies were not pleased and, as she reluctantly took the seat indicated, they made a point of twitching their skirts aside, as if they feared to be contaminated by her proximity.

One of them, a lady who had greeted her with ice dripping from every word, moved so far to the end of the chaise that the slightest nudge would have sent her sprawling to the floor. Tessa was tempted, but restrained herself. She was here to get a job.

Both ladies left soon afterward, cutting their visit ostentatiously short, and Tessa took the opportunity to move back to her previous seat.

Conversation soon became general—though Tessa had no doubt that she would be gossiped about later—and the serving of tea or sherry and dainty little cakes and biscuits helped relax the atmosphere. Each visit only lasted twenty minutes or so, and as some ladies left, others arrived. Few ladies addressed Tessa directly and when they did, Lady Gosforth answered for her.

In that respect it was almost like being married again.

They talked of people she didn't know, scandals she had no interest in, plays and operas she had no idea about—she'd never been to the theatre—and the weather. The weather changed so frequently in London it was always a safe subject of conversation.

Heartily bored, Tessa sipped her tea and nibbled on a biscuit and listened. If only she had something to do with her hands, but she had never learned embroidery or tatting or crochet or knitting, and wouldn't wish anyone to witness her beginner efforts.

But it was something of a relief not to have to make conversation herself. It wasn't a skill she'd ever developed. In both her marriages, visitors—male or female—had not been encouraged and she'd been required to stay at home most of the time. She'd been quite a chatterbox at first, but she'd soon learned that men preferred to do the talking. As her first husband told her a number of times, "I didn't marry you for your conversation, girl."

She'd never once had other ladies over for tea and cakes and chat, or had to exert herself to facilitate a conversation. It was quite a skill, she realized, one which, as a companion, she supposed she would have to develop.

And it was quite interesting considering which of the ladies she might like to become a companion to. None of them, she decided. While they were polite enough under Lady Gosforth's gimlet eye, she could tell that beneath the facade of good manners, most of them knew something of her history and despised her for it.

In any case, it didn't seem as though any of them needed a companion, for they mostly arrived in pairs. Only one of the ladies arrived with a companion in tow, a drab-looking female of about forty, and though she was greeted by everyone— some as an afterthought—she took a seat at the back of the room and spent the remainder of the visit in silence, ignored by all. And one lady sat with an older woman she addressed as 'cousin,' but the way the older woman addressed her was dismissive, verging on rude. Tessa decided that she was also a companion.

Now that she'd written that application to Yorkshire, she felt more hopeful. Lady Gosforth's strictures didn't bother her. She would be much more comfortable working with an employer who was not a member of the *ton*, someone who would know nothing of her marriages, and have no opinion about them.

To pass the time Tessa entertained herself by deciding which animal each lady looked most like.

Slowly the number of visitors dwindled, and Tessa was surprised to see one of the last to arrive was Lord Alverleigh. There had been very few male visitors up to then, and his arrival caused something of a stir among the ladies present. They sat straighter, were chattier and smilier and talked a great deal more. Fans fanned briskly, and young ladies blushed, though it wasn't at all hot in the room. And everyone tried to engage him in conversation. He responded politely but briefly, and made no attempt to encourage any of them.

He did however pay attention to Tessa, and asked her several questions, which were innocuous enough but the damage was done. The visiting ladies noted his attention to her, and Tessa could see they were drawing conclusions—erroneous ones. She wanted to explain that she had no interest in him, no interest in marrying every again. But of course she couldn't.

Finally the last visitor—except for Lord Alverleigh—left.

"Well, Marcus," Lady Gosforth said, "what do have to say for yourself, coming at this hour, when you know it is one of my 'at home' afternoons?"

"And are you not 'at home' to me?" He raised a sardonic eyebrow. "And here I was thinking I could come and go whenever I wish in my own home."

She snorted. "You know very well what I mean."

He turned to Tessa. "And how did you fare in the ordeal by hens—I mean ladies—that my aunt subjected you to?" His gray eyes gleamed.

Very aware that his aunt had stiffened at his words, Tessa said, "It was most interesting, and no ordeal at all. Everyone was very k—polite."

His eyebrow arched sardonically. Had he noted her switch from 'kind' to 'polite'?

"Of course they were polite," Lady Gosforth snapped. "My friends would not be otherwise."

"They would not dare," her nephew murmured.

"Marcus, before you go, I wish to speak to you—privately—in the small sitting room," the old lady said. She turned to Tessa. "I will dine at home this evening. You will join me."

She stumped away to the small sitting room, which was her favorite, leaving Tessa alone with Lord Alverleigh. She took advantage of the opportunity. "I have a letter to send, but I'm not sure how to send it. I've always had someone frank it for me."

"Yes, of course, give it to me." He barely glanced

at it before slipping her letter into his pocket. "Was that all? How did it go really, with my aunt's friends?"

She shrugged. "I didn't expect anything to come of it. Your aunt seems quite hostile to the idea of my seeking employment."

"You are still set on that?"

"Yes, of course. I must find some way to support myself, surely you can see that."

"Marcus!" Lady Gosforth called down the hallway. "I'm waiting."

"General Gosforth summons me," Lord Alverleigh murmured. "Would you be interested in a visit to Hampstead Heath tomorrow morning? It's quite a long ride, but I think you'd enjoy it. Weather permitting, of course."

Tessa smiled. "Thank you, that would be lovely." How could his aunt think this man was cold and unapproachable? Oh, during the morning visit he'd appeared cold and even a bit harsh—he almost never smiled, and she'd never heard him laugh—but if you discounted his severe mien and considered his actions, he was thoughtful and kind. And she liked the way he called his aunt General Gosforth, without in the least disrespecting her. It was clear to Tessa that he was, in fact, very fond of her.

Marcus had barely stepped into the small sitting room when his aunt snapped at him, "How long are you going to let that child exhaust herself applying for positions she's not remotely suited for?"

Marcus blinked. Tessa had apparently gone from being '*that creature*' to '*that child.*'

"It's what she wants, Aunt Maude."

"Pshaw! It's not what she wants, boy—it's all she thinks she can have."

"I know."

She stared at him. "You *know*? Then why the devil don't you do something about it?"

"I will. In my own good time" He had no intention of explaining his plans to his aunt. He'd only just made up his mind, and he needed to give Tessa time to get used to the idea. She'd had so few choices in her life, he wasn't going to join the line of men who'd ruled her.

Besides he wanted her to choose him freely, not be driven to it by poverty and desperation. Though he wasn't sure what he'd do if she did accept a post with one of his aunt's friends. Try to talk her out of it, he supposed.

"Well, time is running out."

"I know what I'm doing, Aunt Maude." Ignoring her derisive snort, he continued, "There is no need for you to worry. I have it all well in hand." He didn't, of course. It all depended on Tessa, and he understood her now much less than he had when he was a child. She had a past that had somehow . . . changed her. But he wasn't giving up on her.

CHAPTER NINE

AFTER A LONG hot bath, Tessa was feeling quite hopeful as she came downstairs for dinner. It would only be herself and Lady Gosforth, so she made no particular effort to dress up. Lady Gosforth would disparage whatever she wore so it made no difference.

"Well, gel? Any likely candidates?" the old lady asked her as a footman seated her at the table.

"Candidates? I'm not sure what you mean."

There was a short silence as the servants served the first course, a gently steaming creamy cauliflower soup. Lady Gosforth then waved them out, and she and Tessa were left alone.

Lady Gosforth picked up her soup spoon. "Several of my callers today are in need of companions, or will be shortly. Lady Portland brought her second cousin—the drab creature with no conversation— but the woman is shortly to be married to some elderly vicar or curate or some such. Though it has to be said, Lady Portland bullies her unmercifully." She sprinkled croutons into her soup with a lavish hand. "And I'm told Mrs. Bentink-Smythe's hired companion—she was the one who sat in the corner and didn't bleat a word—is shortly to remove to the country to help her sister-in-law with her children. Paid dogs-bodies both. Drink up, gel, your soup is getting cold."

"I will wait for a response to my application to the lady in Yorkshire."

Lady Gosforth snorted. "If you think my guests treat their companions poorly, cits will be even worse."

Tessa frowned. "Cits?"

"Mushrooms," the old lady said dismissively, and when Tessa still didn't understand, she continued, "People with wealth, but no background: the sort of people who would never be offered a voucher to Almacks."

Tessa had never been to Almacks so she couldn't comment. "I don't care if they're the sort you call cits or not." In fact, an obscure employer unknown to the *ton* and preferably in some small rural town would make her safer from her brother.

What was Edgar doing? Did he have people out searching for her? She hadn't heard a word, but he wouldn't give up so easily, she knew. Not because he cared about her, but because he still saw her as an asset.

Again, the old lady snorted. "That's because you don't have the least idea of what it would be like. There's a very good chance you could end up with someone like the creature who employed my nephew Harry's wife before she was married. The woman took enormous delight in loudly issuing orders, sending Nell running thither and yon, saying 'Lady Helen, pick up my gloves. Lady Helen, fetch my shawl—no not that one you stupid creature, the other one. Lady Helen, do this, do that'—all in the rudest, loudest, most scornful tone. The creature positively adored having an earl's daughter to boss and bully, especially in front of others." She eyed Tessa shrewdly. "Do you want that, gel, do you? Could you even stand it, you with your stubborn pride?"

"No, of course not. But I wouldn't use my title." And the sooner she rid herself of that the better. She wanted to take nothing of her husband—either of them—into her future. "I am using my maiden name."

"Yes, and Blaxland is such a common name," Lady Gosforth said sarcastically. "Besides, women like the one who employed Nell would ferret it out. That sort always do—and you're not exactly inconspicuous, you know."

"Then I would leave," Tessa said composedly. She'd been bossed and bullied enough as a wife. And a sister. She would not endure it again, no matter what.

"And find yourself looking for another position? Without a character reference? Because you wouldn't get one, and without a character, you'll never get another job."

Tessa shrugged. She could write her own character reference.

"And have you considered the danger of husbands and sons?" Lady Gosforth continued, pointing her spoon at Tessa. "There are plenty of nasty specimens who consider pretty young servants—especially pretty young companions—fair game for their vile, unwanted attentions."

Tessa lifted her head. "I have considered the possibility. Again, I would leave." She thought for a moment and said curiously, "Would you give me a character reference, Lady Gosforth?"

The old lady snorted. "Don't be ridiculous! Recommend you to someone as a hired companion? Preposterous!"

Tessa blinked, trying not to feel hurt by the open scorn in the old woman's voice. She was so difficult to understand. One minute she was displaying Tessa to her friends, and later asking Tessa if any of them appealed to her as an employer, the next minute she was heaping scorn on every suggestion Tessa made. And now she was refusing something that would actually help Tessa to be employed. Which would cost her nothing, just a sheet of paper and a few minutes of her time.

"But I have not a penny in the world so I must do something to support myself. You don't like any of my ideas, so what do you suggest I do?"

"Marry my nephew, of course! It's as obvious as the nose on my face!"

Tessa's mouth fell open. *Marry her nephew?* She couldn't believe it. Ever since she'd arrived, the old lady had been openly hostile toward her, and now she was offering her nephew up on a plate? The nephew she was clearly very fond of.

"Marry your nephew? You mean your nephew, the Earl of Alverleigh?"

"Well, you can't marry any of the others—they're married and I don't approve of bigamy," Lady Gosforth said acidly. "Of course I mean Marcus. What else do gels of our order do but marry? It's the way of the world."

"Well, the world is wrong!" Tessa declared. "Women should not be dependent on marriage and the good will of men. There must be other alternatives."

"Like scrubbing? Or reading dull treatises to bored old ladies in the wilds of Yorkshire?" She snorted. "You've married twice before, presumably for money and position, so why not do it a third time? My nephew is a good deal wealthier and a good fifty years younger than both your previous husbands."

Tessa shook her head. "I don't wish to marry again."

"Why not?"

Tessa met her gaze squarely. "My reasons are my own."

The old lady gave her a thoughtful look. "You are the stubbornest creature."

"Thank you," Tessa said calmly.

One finely plucked eyebrow rose. "It wasn't a compliment."

"I'm aware of that. But all my adult life, my wishes have been overlooked and ignored, and I refuse to allow it any longer."

"Is that so?"

Her skeptical tone flicked Tessa on the raw. "Yes, I won't be an obedient wife ever again. Besides, I'm not the kind of society wife your nephew needs. I have no interest in fashion, I don't wish to attend balls or host elegant little afternoon 'at homes' and entertain elegant ladies with tea and pretty cakes and petty gossip." She could tell from the old lady's expression that her shaft had hit home. She continued, "I had enough of doing what I was told when I was married and now, at last, I am standing up for myself. And I will *not* be bullied."

Lady Gosforth sniffed. "Then you won't last long as a hired companion." She spooned up her soup and pulled a face. She rang a bell and when the butler appeared, she said crossly, "This soup is cold, Peverill! Cold! Soup is meant to be served hot."

"I'm so sorry, m'lady," the butler murmured apologetically, removing her barely touched soup bowl. "I shall see to it immediately."

The following morning, when Marcus arrived to take Tessa for a ride on Hampstead Heath, he was about to mount the front steps, when as if from nowhere, the boy Joey, appeared and clutched his arm. "'E was there again yestdy," the boy said urgently.

"Who was?" Marcus said, calmly detaching the grubby fingers from his sleeve.

"The bloke—I dunno his name, but he's a bad 'un."

Marcus frowned. "How do you know?"

"I just know. I seem 'im 'anging around before, watchin' the 'ouse."

"Have you indeed? What does he look like, this fellow." Marcus wasn't sure he believed it. Was the lad being overly dramatic?

"Shifty-lookin', shorter 'n you, greasy dark hair, busted nose, wears a big overcoat."

"I see. Well, thank you for warning me, Joey." He produced a sixpence and flipped it to the boy, who snatched it deftly out of the air and secreted it invisibly somewhere in his ragged outfit. Marcus eyed him curiously. "Do you not like the clothes you were given?"

"No, they're grand. But I can't wear 'em on the street, can I? People would notice."

"Why would that be a problem?" Was the boy a pickpocket after all?

"It don't do to stand out on the streets."

"You're not thieving, are you?"

"Course not!" the boy said indignantly. "Me mum brung me up honest!"

"Good," Marcus said, then added, "You don't have to live in the streets, you know. You can sleep here if you wish. Peverill tells me you're a good worker, and Cook tells me you're a dab hand in the kitchen."

A grin split the boy's face. "I'd do anyfing for her cookin', even scrubbin' pots."

"I remember the feeling," said Marcus, who'd never scrubbed a pot in his life. "Well, keep an eye out for this shifty-looking fellow and if you see him doing anything suspicious let me or Peverill know."

"Letter for you, sir."

Barney Wimple glanced up. His landlady, having just delivered his breakfast, pulled a folded square of pale blue from her apron pocket and held it out.

Barney eyed it with deep suspicion and made no move to take it. People didn't send him letters—not people he wanted to hear from, at any rate. Bills, yes, unfortunately. Invitations, yes. *Billets-doux*, sadly not. But letters, infrequent though they were, invariably came from some relative—usually an aunt, of which he had dozens—castigating him for something some sticky-nosed busybody had reported, and demanding he reform his life and threatening dire consequences if he didn't.

Barney liked his life and had no intention of changing it.

He eyed the letter suspiciously. "What kind of letter is it?"

His landlady gave an exasperated huff. "I don't know, do I? I don't read other people's mail. Besides, it's sealed. It was hand delivered by some feller in fancy livery, and once I told him you was home— because he made a point of asking—he said there was no answer required. So here, take it. I got work to do." She placed the letter beside his plate and left.

Barney peered at it. It was a note, folded and sealed with an unfamiliar seal. Addressed to Barnaby Wimple Esq., which was quite auntly—none of his friends called him Barnaby, let alone esquire—but written in a hand he didn't recognize. Not an aunt then. Good. He looked at the fat sausages gleaming on his plate, the fried eggs and crispy bacon, the still steaming coffee and the toast that wasn't yet cold. No use letting a letter ruin a perfectly good breakfast. He'd read the wretched thing later.

Having demolished the excellent breakfast, he made his ablutions and settled back to allow his valet to shave him. His man lathered his jaw, and while he stropped the razor, Barney broke open the seal on the pale blue notepaper.

The razor had made its first smooth sweep when Barney gave a loud yelp.

"I'm so sorry sir, did I—" the valet began.

"No, no." Barney waved the valet away and scanned the note a second time. "Good God! What the devil?"

"Bad news, sir?" the valet enquired sympathetically.

"The worst!" Barney stared at the message again. It was from an aunt after all, but not one of his aunts, who mostly lived in decent obscurity in the country and could safely be ignored. It was worse, much worse.

Mr Wimple,

I would be obliged if you would call on me at your convenience on an urgent matter. I will expect you at ten of the clock this morning.

Maude, Lady Gosforth.

What the devil did Marcus's appalling aunt want with him? He'd been terrified of her since he'd first met her when he and Marcus were schoolboys. And she'd only grown more formidable with the years.

His first thought was to flee the city, but then recalled that her manservant had established that Barney was in residence. Damn and blast!.

"What time is it?" he asked the valet.

"Half past nine, sir."

Barney groaned. "Shave me then and be quick about it. And if you happen to slit my throat, I won't hold it against you."

At ten precisely, Barney presented himself on the doorstep of Alverleigh House. Before he could even enquire of the butler whether Marcus was at home—a fellow facing another fellow's aunt needed reinforcements after all—the butler informed him Lord Alverleigh had taken Lady Hewitt out riding, and before he could gather his wits, the butler had ushered him into the breakfast parlor. Lady Gosforth sat there like a spider in her web, drinking tea and nibbling on something that looked horribly like a rusk.

"Ah, Mr. Wimple, there you are," she said. "Have you broken your fast?"

"Broken?" he stammered, looking wildly around. "I only just arrived. I didn't break anything."

"Broken *your fast*," she repeated, and when he gave her a blank look, she sighed, and said in a voice geared towards the mentally deficient, "Have you eaten breakfast?"

"Oh," he said, hugely relieved. "Yes, yes, I have. Sausages and—"

"I did not enquire as to *what* you ate, only *whether* you had eaten," she said in a freezing voice.

"Ah, right. Breakfast, yes, had it already, thank you." He nodded, relieved that he wasn't going to be expected to chew on one of those rusk things.

"I have called you here to ask what you intend to do about the gossip."

"Gossip? What gossip?" he said cautiously.

"The gossip about my nephew, of course."

Barney thought hard. He hadn't heard any gossip about Marcus.

The old lady set down her cup with a snap. "Stop gaping at me like a gormless codfish, boy—the gossip about Marcus and Lady Hewitt."

Barney shook his head. "I haven't heard any gos—"

She made an impatient sound. "How on earth have you earned the reputation as a man who knows everything going on in the *ton*?"

"Oh, I say, have I?" he said, pleased.

She fixed her beady eyes on him and shriveled him through the lorgnette. "Clearly I was mistaken. If you've heard nothing about the rumors flying around about how my nephew kidnapped Lady Hewitt from the guardianship of her brother and installed her as his mistress—"

"Good lord, did he? Must say, it doesn't sound like M—"

"What my nephew may or may not have done with Lady Hewitt is beside the point!" she snapped. "You will quash these vile rumors, Barnaby. Quash them! Lady Hewitt is *my guest*—understand that? Mine!"

Barney nodded.

"You will make it your business to inform every one of your acquaintances that rumor has it wrong, that there was no kidnapping and that Lady Hewitt is my guest and not my nephew's mistress. Do. You. Understand?"

Barney swallowed. "But if I tell people that, it will only make it wor—" he began.

"Do. You. Understand?"

"Yes, Lady Gosforth," he mumbled, a thirteen year-old scrubby schoolboy again.

"Then go forth." She gestured magnificently. "Quash those dreadful rumors. Make sure *everyone* knows the correct version of events. Or I will want to know the reason why."

"Yes, Lady Gosforth." He scuttled out.

Several days later, Marcus's business was concluded earlier than expected so he thought he would invite Tessa for a ride in Hyde Park. His butler, Peverill, beckoned him inside. "Lady Gosforth wishes to speak to you—privately," he murmured. "In the small sitting room."

"It's an utter *disgrace!*" his aunt snapped as he entered the room.

He blinked. "Good afternoon, Aunt Maude. What's a disgrace?"

"I attended the rout at Lady Reynolds's last night."

Sir Allan and Lady Reynolds were excellent hosts. He couldn't imagine them producing a disgrace. He seated himself. "What happened?" he asked, resigned to a drawn-out revelation of whatever small thing had annoyed her. His aunt was addicted to drama, particularly if she was at the center of it.

"*Everyone* was talking about it. Asking me the

most *impertinent* questions." She snorted and drank a little tea.

"Questions?"

"Lady Hewitt is the one who will suffer, of course. Women are always blamed."

He stiffened. "Lady Hewitt?"

"It won't affect you, of course, not for long, at least. Not with your staid, not to say dull reputation. No, it's always the woman's fault. And it's not even true!"

"What isn't?"

"That you kidnapped her from her brother's protective guardianship—"

"What?" He could imagine how the tale might be twisted into a kidnapping, though how did it get out? Only a handful of people knew what happened.

"And installed her as your mistress!"

"What?"

"As I said, it's always the woman who suffers in this sort of situation. And with Lady Hewitt's unsavory reputation . . ."

"To hell with her reputation," he snapped. "What situation? There is no situation. Lady Hewitt has been living under your protection the entire time, and I've been staying at my club." He'd gone out of his way to ensure the proprieties were observed.

She shrugged. "I did deny it, of course, but . . ." She spread her hands in a gesture of helplessness.

He rose and began to pace around the room. After all the care he'd taken to protect Tessa. Blasted gossipmongers! He stopped pacing. He knew what needed to be done. He'd been planning it for a while. Giving her time to find her feet, explore her options, realize what needed to happen. This would just bring it forward.

"I suppose marriage would quash the scandal," he said in his best off-hand manner.

It was the perfect solution. He didn't want to make a love-match, didn't want to make himself vulnerable to desire, even though he was experiencing it, stronger than ever, each time he saw her. But as long as nobody else knew about it, he would be safe.

Tessa herself didn't need to know, he told himself. He'd been planning to offer her marriage as a low-key practical arrangement between friends, but now . . .

This blasted gossip problem could be a heaven-sent opportunity. *If* he could talk Tessa into it.

"*Marriage?*" his aunt declared. "*Good God, no!* I *know* how reluctant you've been to marry, dear boy. I wouldn't *for the world* see you saddled with an unsuitable gel, simply to stop a few tongues wagging." She snorted. "Besides, hasn't she told me a dozen times or more that *she* has no desire to marry again? Marriage, Marcus? No, no and no! You'll have to think of something else!"

Marcus stared at her and sat down, eying her cynically. What was going on? She'd been nagging him to marry for years.

His aunt added thoughtfully, "Actually, the best thing will be for the gel to take up that position up in Yorkshire. Once she's out of sight, the scandal will fade."

Marcus frowned. "What position in Yorkshire?"

She nodded to herself. "It's the perfect solution. I'll write her a glowing recommendation and she'll disappear from sight, never to be seen again."

Never to be seen again? Not if he could help it.

"Once she's gone, the gossip will fade in a sennight or two, take my word for it. Some other scandal will take its place in the *ton*'s imagination. It always does. Remember the fuss that was made over Lord and Lady Templeton last year? Such a to-do about noth—"

"*What* position in Yorkshire?" he repeated with grim patience. There were times when he itched to throttle his beloved aunt.

His aunt blinked at him and said vaguely, "Oh, she applied for a job with some complete stranger somewhere in the wilds of Yorkshire. Answering an advertisement *in a newspaper*, would you believe?" She snorted again. "It could be anyone, but gels these days . . ."

Marcus recalled the letter Tessa had given him

to frank, some address in Yorkshire. Dammit, why hadn't he thought to ask her about it?

Marcus rose. "I'll give the situation some thought. I must go now. Good day, Aunt."

"No need for any thought, dear boy," she said brightly. "Stashing the gel far away and out of sight in Yorkshire is the perfect solution. Let us just hope her new employer is someone respectable." Then she added, "Or at least someone safe."

The first thing Marcus needed to do was to check on this so-called rumor. He didn't trust his aunt at all. She had a tendency to exaggerate things, and unless it was indeed the scandal she'd claimed . . . Well, he would be as bad as her father and brother if he talked Tessa into a marriage based on a lie.

After checking the usual haunts, tracked his friend Barney to Tattersalls. Apparently there was an interesting auction coming up. Barney had a good eye for horseflesh.

Marcus had no interest in the auction; he wanted to pick Barney's brain, catch up on the latest gossip. His aunt claimed the damaging scandal about him and Tessa was everywhere. Naturally nobody would speak of it to Marcus's face, but Barney would know the truth.

As expected, he arrived just in time to see his

friend make a successful bid for a rather splendid-looking bay hunter. He made his way through the crowd.

"Did you see it?" Barney said when he clapped eyes on Marcus. "Such hocks, such a powerful, deep chest, and the temperament—"

Marcus cut off the enthusiastic horsey flow, which he knew could last for hours. "Congratulations, Barney. A fine looking beast."

"Yes, and—"

"A drink?"

Barney hesitated a moment then shook his head. "Sorry. No time, I'm afraid. There's another auction coming up soon that I don't want to miss. A beautiful little mare."

Marcus drew him to one side and said softly. "Heard any gossip lately?"

Barney jumped, and eyed Marcus warily. "Gossip?"

"About me and Lady Hewitt."

Barney's face crumpled with anxiety. "I tried to stop it, Marcus, I promise."

Marcus frowned. "Let me be clear: I'm talking about a scurrilous and nonsensical tale that I kidnapped Lady Hewitt, and made her my mistress."

Barney nodded miserably. "Yes, that's the one. Everybody is talking about it."

"Damn. My aunt was telling the truth. I wondered whether she'd made it up."

"I did try to stop—"

"Yes, yes, thank you." Marcus patted his friend on the shoulder in a distracted fashion and left. He knew now what he had to do.

In one sense it was a relief. The decision was out of his hands now.

He sent around a note inviting Tessa for a ride on the heath the following morning. She could have proper gallop, which would put her, he hoped, in a receptive mood.

He'd put the question to her then, where they'd be relaxed, there was no aunt to interfere and nobody to overhear.

For the first part of their ride there was very little opportunity for conversation, as they picked their way through traffic, pedestrians, beggars and dogs, and the noise of the streets, the rattle of carts and the sound of peddlers hawking their wares. But once they were out of the city, Marcus still couldn't think of how to phrase it.

It had been easier that time—it seemed so long ago—when it had just slipped out without his conscious volition. *Why not marry? Not some ancient, but a much younger man, someone nearer your own age? Myself, for instance.*

Now it seemed so much more difficult, regardless

of the fact that he now actively wanted to marry her. He swallowed, and edged his horse closer so they walking wide by side.

He cleared his throat. "Lady Hewitt," he began.

"Oh, please don't call me that, especially when we're alone. I'd much rather be Tessa to you."

"Very well, Tessa. I have been thinking . . ." Stupid way to begin, he decided. "The thing is. . ." She turned her head with a bright, encouraging expression, and all his words dried up. She was so beautiful.

"Watch out for that dog," he said feebly.

They avoided the dog, who ignored them, and continued on.

"You said you'd been thinking," she prompted him.

"Yes. Yes, I have," he agreed. And had no idea how to proceed. 'Will you marry me?' seemed so blunt, so bald, so unequivocal.

A small 'No' would kill it dead. And where would that leave him? He couldn't ask her again; that would be harassment.

She'd made it more than clear that she had no desire to marry again. Who was he to make her change her mind when she'd never had a choice in her life?

But society was cruel, and she'd be crucified by

the gossips, even worse than she had been in the past. And this time it was his fault.

They rode on, his thoughts in turmoil. How to explain, to persuade her to marry him, and not refer to the gossip?

And who was the fool who thought a proposal on horseback would be acceptable? It was probably disrespectful.

No, he would make her a formal offer when they returned to Alverleigh House. Or possibly in the morning. Yes, mornings were the correct time to make young ladies an offer.

He swallowed.

CHAPTER TEN

WHEN TESSA RETURNED from her ride, Lady Gosforth was out, visiting friends as usual. It was a relief, as she sometimes found the old lady's company exhausting. Her moods were so mercurial Tessa was never sure whether she was being attacked or complimented.

Her ride on the heath had been glorious. A sunny day with a breeze just crisp enough to be refreshing and not too crisp to be chilly. Most of the time Marcus had been quiet, apparently deep in thought, and she'd quite enjoyed knowing that he appreciated silence at times and that she needn't exert herself to make polite conversation. So she was free to let her own thoughts roam.

She still hadn't had an answer from the woman in Yorkshire, but she wasn't going to fret just yet. She'd continued scouring the newspapers for positions, and in the meantime was enjoying the treats of this new London life, chief among which was her almost daily rides.

She came down as usual for afternoon tea, and though everything had been laid out, there was no sign of Lady Gosforth.

"Milady said she might be late, but that you should start without her," Peverill told her.

So she did, but she'd only drunk half a cup of tea and eaten two dainty cucumber sandwiches and one of cook's wonderful wafer-thin almond biscuits, when Lady Gosforth entered the room like a tempest in full flow.

"Appalling!" she declared, ripping off her gloves and flinging them down on a chair. "Just appalling! Society is going to the dogs!" She took off her hat and sent it sailing across the room. "Peverill, brandy!"

"What is it, Lady Gosforth?" Tessa asked.

The old lady looked at her, pulled out her lorgnette and stared at Tessa for a long, unnerving moment. "My nephew didn't say anything of interest when you were out riding this morning?"

Tessa shook her head. "Nothing of any significance."

"Typical!" She sat down, seized the brandy and drained the glass. "Men are such asses! But he's always been ridiculously protective."

"I don't understand."

"Don't worry. He'll take all the blame for himself—he always did, even as a boy."

"The blame for what?"

"You don't know?"

Tessa shook her head.

Lady Gosforth explained about the gossip, and how everyone who mattered in London believed that Marcus had kidnapped Tessa and made her his mistress.

"But that's not true," Tessa exclaimed, horrified. "It's so unfair. Your nephew has been nothing but honorable!"

"I know that."

"Then how did such a rumor begin?"

"Who knows? Of course, my nephew knows all about it, but naturally he will pretend it never happened. It's the Renfrew Way. He goes about looking cold and formal and reserved, as if nothing could pierce that ego of his, but underneath he'll be mortified."

"Mortified?" Tessa frowned.

"Yes of course. As you say, he's always been the soul of honor. It would be different if he were a rake or a rascal, but that only makes it worse, don't you see?"

Tessa didn't respond. She was reeling from the knowledge that his gallant rescue of her from a third unwanted marriage had rebounded on him in such a dreadful way.

The old lady snorted. "Of course you don't. You've had no experience of men of honor, have you? But take it from me, my nephew's spotless reputation will make the gossips all the more gleeful and vindictive. 'How the mighty have fallen' kind of thing. Ill-disposed wastrels will positively delight in dragging his reputation through the gutter. But will he fight it? Never. His pride is too great."

She took a swig of the brandy Peverill had placed beside her, ate a slice of cake and eyed Tessa cynically. "I realize the gossip also concerns you, but since you hardly know anyone in society it will scarcely signify to you. Besides, you're going to Yorkshire."

"I don't have the job yet."

Lady Gosforth ignored that. "No, you'll be well out of it, far away in Yorkshire, leaving my nephew to face the music, the scandal, the shame alone."

"But—"

"Naturally I will support him, but the support of an aunt . . ." She shrugged. "Who would believe me?"

"But he *didn't* steal me from my brother—he *rescued* me! You *know* that. And he's been staying at his club the whole time."

"And taking you riding most mornings, where anyone could see the two of you together."

Tessa bit her lip. That his kindness should be so interpreted. "That's true, but he was just being kind. In any case, who would believe that *you* would allow any impropriety while you're living here?"

"Pfft! You would try to combat scurrilous gossip with *the truth*? How naive can you get? These people don't care about the truth. A nasty story, fabricated or not, is much more entertaining than the truth. Especially if it destroys the reputation of an honorable man."

Tessa sank back in her chair. This was dreadful. For Marcus's gallantry to be repaid in this dreadful way . . . It was unbearable. "Is there nothing I can do?"

The old lady sank back wearily. "No, no, my dear, you just run away, prepare for your new life in Yorkshire. Don't give us a thought."

"I won't go. Besides, I don't even have a reply to my letter yet."

Lady Gosforth waved that off. "*I* will stand by my nephew. Don't worry about us. You go and pack. My nephew and I will face down this atrocious scandal together. I just need a little rest first." She rose and tottered from the room.

Tessa watched her go, appalled at what she had learned No wonder Marcus had been so silent during their ride. She'd assumed it was some business or political matter that he'd been thinking about, but instead, it was a dreadful scandal she'd inadvertently dragged him into.

At eleven the following morning Marcus stood outside Alverleigh house. He was absurdly nervous. He was never nervous. He was carefully but informally dressed, in immaculate buckskins, a starched white shirt—no frills—and a gray waistcoat and navy coat. His boots gleamed with polish and he'd shaved twice.

Perhaps he shouldn't have sent that note to his aunt, asking her to be out when he called. He didn't want her sticking her nose in—which she would, of course. She couldn't help herself. But what if, forewarned of his intentions, Tessa had taken the opportunity to slip out to avoid him? He rang the doorbell.

"Is Lady Hewitt at home, Peverill?" he asked his butler.

Peverill stood back to let him enter. "She is, m'lord. If you will wait in the front drawing room, I will inform her of your arrival."

Tessa came downstairs a few minutes later, dressed in yet another plain dress, this one in dark blue, but it only served to highlight her natural beauty; her silken complexion, the silver-gilt color of her hair, which clustered in feathery curls around her face, the soft rose-pink mouth and those glorious violet-blue eyes.

After the usual greetings had been exchanged, he asked her the question that had been worrying him. "Has my aunt been treating you well?"

She hesitated and he tensed. Aunt Maude had a caustic tongue when she was displeased. Her family knew it often hid a kind heart, but Tessa wouldn't realize that.

"I can't work her out," Tessa said. "On the one hand she insists I meet her visitors, telling me I need to see if I could work for any of them as a hired companion—but then she introduces me as an honored guest."

"Which you are."

She dismissed that with a wave of her hand. "And yet in private, she heaps scorn on the idea of my finding a position as a companion, listing all kinds of reasons why I would not be at all suitable for that kind of employment."

"What does she suggest you should do, then?"

A blush colored her pale cheeks and she looked away. The silence stretched.

"Lady Hewitt?" he prompted.

She just shook her head again and looked away. "It's nothing."

He took a deep breath. "I gather she's told you about our little problem."

She looked up, frowning. "Problem?"

"The unfortunate gossip?"

She bit her lip.

"About you and me—all nonsense of course, but I'm afraid it's quite widespread."

She swallowed. "I'm sorry. I didn't mean to cause any trouble for you."

He made a dismissive gesture. "You didn't cause any trouble and, if anything ,it was my impetuous actions that caused the gossip. We both know the gossip is untrue, and quite ridiculous. But . . ."

"It affects your reputation."

He blinked. "What? Mine? No, not at all."

"But you're an earl, and a member of the House of Lords."

He shook his head. "Makes no difference. It's your reputation I'm concerned about."

"Mine? But I have no reputation—at least, not one that needs protecting. It's too late for me. You, on the other hand—"

"It's not too late at all, don't talk nonsense. Now, I have a solution, and while I don't think you'll like it, there is very little choice for either of us if we want to scotch the scandal."

"There's no need. I intend to take a position in Yorkshire."

"Won't make any difference. People—especially

women—write letters all the time. The gossip will follow you."

"But—"

"No, we need to marry." Curses. It came out blunt and bossy, not at all like the proposal he'd planned during the night and on the way here.

Startled, she looked up. "*Marry?* I couldn't. I've already told you—and your aunt, numerous times—I have no wish to marry again."

"I understand, but there is a scandal to be quashed, and if the choice is for you to look for employment in some menial position, with no security—I have to say, marriage will solve both problems."

"But I thought you didn't want to get married."

He shrugged. "Neither did you, but the situation has changed."

She frowned.

"At the risk of sounding like a conceited coxcomb—" he began.

"It's not that at all. You must know I am very grateful for all you've—"

"Gratitude makes a poor bedfellow," he said. *Bedfellow?* He swore silently at himself again. He was making a right mess of this, his first proper proposal.

She stared at him, as if a little shocked and he felt instantly remorseful, because of course he hadn't meant it literally. "But there, I won't press you. If you have taken me in dislike. . ."

"No, it's not that at all," she said quickly. Her blush rose again. "You have been everything that is kind. If I . . . if I had never married before, I would . . ." She broke off, shaking her head.

"Were your marriages so distasteful?" he asked gently.

She sighed. "Yes. . . no. It's not as if my husbands—either of them—were especially cruel or treated me harshly. It's just. . ."

Marcus waited. There were more kinds of cruelty than physical violence. Caging a wild little bird, for instance.

She stared at him a moment, then took a deep breath and said in a low voice, "I am not fit to be a wife. To anyone, let alone a man like you."

"A man like me? What's wrong with me?"

"Nothing," she said. "Nothing at all. I'm the one who's all wrong—me!"

Marcus waited. She was pale, and her fingers were knotted, her knuckles white with tension. The conversation was obviously distressing her. A gentleman would not press her further. A gentleman would accept her refusal and change the subject. But Marcus wasn't going to be a gentleman, not this time, when so much was at stake.

"In what way do you think you're 'all wrong'?" he asked gently.

She sighed again. "I was never a good wife.

Oh, I was obedient enough, and faithful and did everything that was required of me, though it was very hard for me at first. Well, you know how I was raised as a child. I was half wild and I had no idea how to be a wife. Holgrave, my first husband, had to work very hard to train me."

Train her? he thought savagely. Like a dog? She'd been fifteen, still a child. And her so-called 'wildness' had been charming.

"But even though I did what they told me, I—I was not happy being a wife, not with either husband." She met his gaze, sending him an anguished silent message. Was she talking about the marriage bed?

Looking down, pleating the fabric of her skirt in restless fingers, she said, "I could never be a good society wife—I hate all that. I don't like entertaining and, and people looking at me, and I know as an earl you would need to hold grand events and important dinners. But I dislike balls and parties, and I am hopeless at polite conversation, and I—"

He cut her off. "I feel the same. I dislike most society events and attend them only out of duty. I would never ask you to play the grand hostess. Having a few close friends around for dinner, yes, but not if you didn't like it."

She shook her head. "That's not all. You—you don't understand."

That was true. He waited.

She smoothed the crumpled fabric of her skirt and added in a low, desperate voice, "There is something broken inside me."

Broken? Her spirit, maybe—her family and those husbands had obviously knocked the confidence out of her, but Marcus was sure that deep inside her, beneath the careful, smoothly correct facade, some remnant of that wild, joyous little girl still existed. He'd glimpsed it on their rides.

"I don't believe it," he said gently.

She shook her head emphatically. "It's true." She rose and took a few agitated steps around the room, then turned and said in a burst, "I am barren, a barren wife twice over. And a man in your position needs children, needs an heir." Her eyes burned, her fists were clenched at her sides in white-knuckled knots.

Ah, so that was it. That explained her anguish, and her shame. As if the ability to bear children was her only value. He made a dismissive gesture. "I don't need to marry to get an heir. I have two brothers who are my heirs, both married and their wives are breeding."

Her forehead puckered. "Don't you want children?"

"Of course, children would be welcome, but if they don't come, I would accept it. I would never blame you." He paused to let that sink in, then added, "But how do you know you are barren?"

"Two husbands and I never quickened."

"Two husbands, both of whom were very old."

Again she shook her head in denial. "Hewitt had a friend who was only a year younger than him, and his young wife presented him with a healthy son. Hewitt was desperate to do the same and he tried and tried, but every month. . ." She swallowed. "I was a grave disappointment to him."

"Then he was a fool. Marry me and I'll give you a child—" He broke off. "I'm sorry, that was unforgivably arrogant of me. What I should have said is, marry me and we'll leave the question of children in the hands of God, where it belongs. I won't mind either way. I don't want a brood mare, I want a wife, a companion, a friend." And a lover he added silently to himself. He didn't want to alarm her. If she hadn't enjoyed the marriage bed. . .

She said heavily, "I fear I'll disappoint you there, too."

"We were friends as children, weren't we? And you enjoy my company when we go riding, don't you? It needn't be any more than that."

She sank down on the settee and eyed him solemnly. "Do you really mean that? Do you not want me in your bed?"

He considered that. "I do desire you, but I promise

I will never force you. I will respect your wishes." If celibacy was the price he had to pay to have her in his life, he would pay it.

But he hoped he wouldn't have to.

She was silent for a long time, thoughts and worries flickering across her face. Marcus waited. She rose again and made several more agitated circuits around the room, then stopped abruptly and faced him. "Do you truly mean it, Marcus, that my company would be enough for you? Just my company? You're not asking for any more?"

"I truly mean it. My word of honor on it." It was the first time she'd called him Marcus since she was a child. He took it as a hopeful sign.

Her eyes were troubled, and she said in lowered voice, "You're not hoping this will be a love match, are you? Because I can't promise that. I don't know if I can love anyone anymore."

"I've never wanted a love match." He saw the doubt in her eyes and said firmly, "It's true. Ask my aunt. She will confirm it. I haven't a romantic bone in my body. No, our marriage will be a practical solution for both of us: you will have a home and security for the rest of your life, and I will have a friend and a congenial companion for the rest of mine."

"And you'll marry me even knowing I've never quickened with child? And probably never will."

"Yes, it doesn't make the slightest difference to me."

She took a deep breath. Marcus held his breath and waited.

Tessa paced another few circuits of the room. What to tell him? Yea or nay? She really, really didn't want to get married again but equally, she couldn't bring herself to leave Marcus to face the scandal on his own. Lady Gosforth was right. He was a deeply honorable man, and he would loathe being spoken about in the kind of nasty, gleeful, faux-concerned, acid-saccharine manner she'd experienced herself in the past.

She was used to it: he wasn't. And he absolutely didn't deserve it. All he'd ever done was try to protect her.

Which was why he was offering marriage now— to protect her. But she knew how vicious gossip could get, and she just *couldn't* leave him to face that alone, not when he'd saved her from Edgar's dreadful plot.

Edgar—where was he, she wondered briefly. It was a relief not to have to deal with him. But it wasn't like him to simply let her go.

She pushed the thought aside. She had a decision to make. He was watching her calmly, his eyes steady.

Did she trust him? She did, unreservedly.

Did she love him? She'd been more than halfway in love with him as a child. And now . . . But he didn't want love, she reminded herself. Just companionship and friendship. A *practical* marriage.

He was kind, and he listened. And he hadn't tried to make her be someone she wasn't. He'd even said he wouldn't blame her for her barrenness. That was a relief. Hewitt had been furious with her, berating her every month, when it was clear that she hadn't conceived. As if she'd tried not to, when the truth was she'd yearned for a child. Ached for someone to love, who would love her in return. She'd been so desperately lonely in her marriages.

He'd promised he wouldn't force her to the marriage bed. She trusted his promises. She'd never enjoyed the marriage bed but . . . she would try. Men wanted it, she knew, and it would be unfair of her to accept so much from him without giving him anything in return.

She would have a home. Security. And a man who respected her. It was more than she'd ever had —or ever dreamed of.

She owed it to him for all he'd done for her.

She turned to face him. "Very well, I—" She broke off and moistened her lips, then said in a rush, "If you are of the same opinion in a week's time, I will marry you."

He frowned. "Why wait? If you have reservations, share them with me now."

She gave him an incredulous look. "My reservations? It's you I'm thinking of—your reservations."

"I have no reservations," he said firmly. "And I will not change my mind. And may I remind you that we need to quash those damaging rumors as soon as possible."

She bit her lip. "Oh. Yes." His reputation as an honorable man was at stake. How could it have slipped her mind? The turmoil of being asked to marry him, she supposed. And having to confess her infertility.

"Marriage is the very best solution for both of us," he said, his voice resolute. "In fact, it's the only solution. The gossip will only get worse. So what do you say?"

Tessa's throat was dry. Her palms were damp. She surreptitiously wiped them on her skirt, swallowed again, then cleared her throat and said in a voice that was slightly hoarse, "Then if you're sure, I will marry you whenever you want."

As soon as the words were out of her mouth, doubts assailed her. What had she done? She'd had no intention of marrying again, but now, with no home to go to, and no means of support—and with the other options open to her being so difficult and fraught with problems—*and* with that dreadful scandal, which he really didn't deserve—she'd given in and taken the easy way out.

Only now it didn't seem so easy.

It was 'a practical solution' she reminded herself. Necessary to stop the scandal from spreading. But it would mean everything for her, and what for him? Companionship? It was a very unequal bargain.

But it was what he said he wanted. So why was she shaking?

"Thank you." He rose to his feet.

Tessa stood and braced herself. What did he expect? Was he going to kiss her now? He stood before her—she was so glad he hadn't gone down on one knee, but had proposed in a cool, unemotional way—announced it, actually. *We need to marry.*

He held out his hands, and a little bemused, she placed her hands in his. Her hands were cold, his were big and warm.

He bent his head and kissed each hand lightly, first the left, then the right. She shivered at the touch.

Looking down at the dark head bent over her hands, she felt strangely moved, even a little bit tearful. As a gesture it seemed almost romantic, but then he released her hands and straightened, and his eyes were as gray and steady as ever.

She breathed again. He wasn't being romantic; it was just good manners. Theirs would be a *practical* marriage. He'd assured her he wasn't the slightest bit romantic. Friendship and companionship, that's what he wanted. She could give him that.

She would give him that with every fiber of her being.

Voices sounded in the hallway. Lady Gosforth had returned from her unusually early shopping expedition. The drawing room door opened and she stood there, casting a shrewd eye over them.

"Well?" she demanded as she entered the room, discarding shawl and hat and shopping as she went. The butler followed, picking them up as they fell. "Well?" she repeated, seating herself on the chaise. "Tea, Peverill, and some of those cat's tongue biscuits." She turned back to Tessa and her nephew. "And I say again, well? Cat got your tongue, Marcus?"

"Not at all, Aunt Maude," he said smoothly. "But 'well' is hardly a question. And good morning to you, too."

"Pshaw! Of course it's a question. You know perfectly well what I'm askin'."

Marcus inclined his head. "Lady Hewitt has agreed to marry me. You may wish us happy."

"Excellent!" The old lady stripped off her gloves, tossed them aside and turned to Tessa. "Thought for a while you didn't have the sense God gave a cat.

Now, off you go, Marcus. This gel and I have a grand wedding to plan."

"Oh, please, no." The words burst from Tessa. The thought of a big society wedding made her feel ill. Everyone—the women especially—would despise her. Bad enough that she'd twice married an old man for his money. But no young society lady dreamed of marrying an octogenarian, so although they might have despised her for it, their noses had not been put out of joint.

But virtually every match-making mama—and grandmother and aunt— had been angling to wed their darling to the handsome, wealthy and titled Earl of Alverleigh, one of the biggest prizes on the marriage mart.

They wouldn't just despise her; they would never forgive her.

"No?" Lady Gosforth echoed ominously. She fished out her lorgnette and trained it on Tessa. "Changed your mind already, gel?"

"No. I made a promise and will keep it, but I don't want a big society wedding."

"Of course you do," the old lady declared. "Marcus is an earl and earls, my dear, don't have shabby little hole-in-the-corner weddings."

Marcus cut in. "No, we have small, dignified, family ones."

His aunt gave him an incredulous look. "*Small?*"

"Small," he confirmed. Marcus glanced at Tessa, one eyebrow raised, and relieved, she nodded.

"No big wedding breakfast?" his aunt persisted.

"No."

She pouted. "What about a wedding ball?"

"No."

"Not even a small one?"

His lips twitched. "Not even a small one. In fact, if Lady Hewitt agrees, I shall obtain a special license, and we can be quietly married by the end of the week."

"That would suit me well," Tessa said.

"Nonsense!" his aunt snapped. "Marry hastily and everyone will assume the gel has trapped you into it. As if the scandal won't have everyone thinking it anyway. But Renfrews do not dance to the tune of gossip-mongers! You will have the banns called at St George's, Hanover Square, as is the correct procedure."

Marcus considered it a moment, glanced at Tessa, who nodded her agreement and said, "Very well, we'll have the banns called and marry at the end of the month. And now I'll take my leave and make the relevant arrangements."

"And what, pray, should we do in the meantime, since you're determined to deprive us of the pleasure of a wedding?" his aunt said acidly. "Am I never to arrange a proper wedding in this family? Harry and

Nell married in a rush, as did Gabriel and Callie—and she a princess! Even Nash and Maddy's wedding was in an obscure country church—though they did at least have a bishop present. *And* they allowed me to organize a ball, afterward. I thought I could at least count on you, Marcus, to have a wedding worthy of Alverleigh."

He smiled. "Sorry to disappoint you, Aunt Maude, but you know I've never liked a fuss, and I'm delighted that my bride agrees with me." Tessa glanced at him. Was that true, or was he simply saying it to support her?

His aunt snorted. "So, I'm to sit and twiddle my thumbs while the biggest catch on the marriage mart marries practically in secret."

"Hardly in secret. I shall be sending a notice immediately to the relevant newspapers, and the banns will also help spread the word. But if you're looking for something to do, you might take Tessa out and order her a couple of new riding habits. Oh, and you might drop a line to Harry and Nell to let them know. As the only relatives I have in England, it would be nice to have them present."

"Only relatives?" his aunt began indignantly. "You have dozens of cousins and—"

"I meant close relatives. I'd prefer only immediate family at my wedding." He turned to Tessa. "Is there anyone you'd like to invite?"

She thought of NannyJune and Phillips, but they were poor and elderly and it would be difficult for them to make the journey to London, so she shook her head. "No, I will simply write to the two most important people in my life. They will be happy to get my news." They would be, too. Neither of them had approved of her previous two weddings, but they would both know Lord Alverleigh, since he'd grown up on the next estate.

It occurred to her with a start, that she would be living at Alverleigh soon, and would be able to see NannyJune and Phillips whenever she wanted, and to make sure they were well cared for. She felt immensely cheered by the prospect.

"I hope you don't intend to invite that brother of yours," Lady Gosforth snapped. "I doubt he'll be at all pleased to hear about this."

"No, I don't want him at the wedding," Tessa said worriedly. Edgar would be bound to make trouble as soon as he heard.

"He won't be at the wedding, and he won't hear about it—if at all—until it's too late," Marcus said calmly. "Actually, I believe Edgar Blaxland is half-way to America by now."

"*America?*" Tessa gasped.

"Yes, an acquaintance of mine saw him board the ship and watched it sail."

"He left the country? Without a word to me?" Tessa couldn't believe it.

"Yes, I'm sorry."

"Oh, I don't mind," she said, her thoughts in turmoil. "In fact, I think I'm more relieved than anything. It's just so hard to believe."

"I assure you, it's true," Marcus said. "My source is quite reliable."

"But how could he afford a ticket? Though I suppose he might have won at the tables the other night. And why America? I would have thought Paris would be more his style."

"Whatever his reasons, it seems you'll have no need to worry about him turning up at the wedding like the skeleton at the feast!" Lady Gosford said briskly. "Not that there *will* be a feast!" she added with a baleful glance at her nephew. "So, in order to arrange the wedding of the Earl of Alverleigh I'm to supervise the ordering of a couple of riding habits and write a letter to Harry and Nell. Wonderful. I expect to be exhausted!"

CHAPTER ELEVEN

THE NEXT THREE weeks flew by for Tessa. Despite Tessa's reluctance, Lady Gosforth had dragged her off to order far more than a couple of riding habits.

"I don't need any new clothes," Tessa objected. She had no desire to play the beggar maid to Marcus's King Cophetua.

The old lady had snorted. "You don't want to disgrace my nephew, do you, by wearing those things?" she'd declared, gesturing distastefully at the clothes Tessa had deliberately chosen for their drabness.

Tessa bit her lip. She didn't really want to keep them, nor did she wish to keep the clothes that had been chosen for her by her husbands, but she also didn't want to feel like a charity case. Or a gold-digger.

"Pah, what nonsense!" Lady Gosforth declared when Tessa said as much. "You will go into this marriage with your head held high, my gel—or I'll want to know the reason why! My nephew is obscenely wealthy, and he wouldn't even notice the cost of a dozen trousseaux. However," she raised her lorgnette and eyed Tessa through it like an eagle eyeing a mouse, "he *will* notice if you dress like a servant! And even if he doesn't—and men can be ridiculously oblivious—the rest of society will! And you can take it from me, it will reflect badly on *him* if you dress out of the rag bag. Everybody will be talking about this wedding, and I intend to make sure that it is for the right reasons! Now, enough of your nonsense, the carriage will be here in half an hour and I'll take you to my own dressmaker."

"Um," Tessa hesitated.

The old lady's eyes narrowed. "Well, what is it, gel, spit it out."

"I would prefer to go to the House of Chance," Tessa said. The old lady was immaculately and stylishly dressed, but Tessa didn't want to go to her dressmaker: she was bound to take control, and Tessa had had enough of having others choose her clothing for her.

Both her husbands had had very clear notions of what they wished her to look like and had been present for every fitting. Tessa's opinions and tastes—when she ventured to express them—had been summarily dismissed.

And since Lady Gosforth was a woman of strong opinions, Tessa would sure it would be just the same. She didn't want to fall out with Marcus's aunt before the wedding, but this time she was going to stand up for herself.

"The House of Chance? Never heard of it."

"It's relatively new, but many of the, um, younger society ladies speak very highly of Miss Chance's designs," Tessa said. Society ladies might have ignored Tessa when she'd attended her few society events in the past, but that didn't mean Tessa had ignored them She'd passed the time by examining what the most fashionable ladies were wearing and picking up stray snatches of conversation. She'd overheard all kinds of gossip in passing, and had heard the House of Chance mentioned several times. By beautifully dressed young ladies.

Lady Gosforth snorted. "Mischance indeed! Younger ladies? You'd be better guided by an older and wiser head."

"Possibly. Nevertheless, if I must purchase a trousseau, I will get it from the House of Chance," she said firmly, hoping she wasn't making a dreadful mistake.

Lady Gosforth pursed her lips, then shrugged. "Be it on your own head then, but first we will go to the person who has been making my riding habits since

I was a young gel. Or do you have a preference for someone else?" she ended acidly.

"No."

But the carriage took them not to a ladies' dressmaker, as she'd expected, but to a gentlemen's tailor."

"Men make the best riding habits," Lady Gosforth stated. "I wouldn't dream of going anywhere else."

To Tessa's relief, the tailor had a young woman assistant who measured her up. Then she, Lady Gosforth, her dresser, Bragge, the tailor and Tessa chose the fabric and design. Tessa was looking through rolls of gray wool. Lady Gosforth sat tapping her fingers on her silver-headed stick.

Seeing Tessa's hesitation, Bragge pulled out a roll of fabric in a soft, dove gray-blue with lavender overtones. "This will bring out your eyes, I think, m'lady," she said quietly, and held it up against Tessa.

Looking at her reflection in the mirror, Tessa had to agree.

"Yes, yes, that would do very well," the tailor said, and pulled out a roll of darker purple velvet. We could use this for the collar, lapels and cuffs. What do you think, m'lady?" He looked at Lady Gosford.

Tessa followed his gaze. To her surprise, Lady Gosford simply waved the question aside. "Don't look at me, it's my niece who will be wearing it."

Tessa didn't know which surprised her more,

being given the final choice, or being called Lady Gosforth's niece.

Needing two habits, Tessa made her next choice bolder: claret colored wool, with silver facings and slightly military-looking ornamentation not unlike a hussar's uniform. This time, Lady Gosford gave her a thoughtful glance, then nodded briskly.

Then it was on to order riding boots. Tessa had been wearing Lady Gosforth's old ones, but they were too big, and the old lady insisted she needed new ones—again by the bootmaker who had supplied the Renfrew family for generations.

After the bootmaker's appointment they stopped for refreshments at Gunter's, a place Tessa had long wanted to visit but had never been given the chance. While Lady Gosforth and her dresser—Bragge sat outside: servants did not partake of tea with their employers—drank tea and nibbled on almond biscuits, Tessa ate her first ever ice—brown bread ice studded with brandied cherries. It was delicious.

Next was the dressmaker. Tessa braced herself. She'd always hated being fitted by dressmakers. With her husbands present and making all the decisions, she'd felt like a doll being dressed. She never wanted to feel that powerless again.

"Well, where is this mantua maker of yours?" Lady Gosforth asked her. "You'll need to tell the driver where to go."

Tessa blinked. She had no idea. She was just about to admit it when Bragge leaned forward and said, diffidently, "It's just off Piccadilly, m'lady. Shall I give the John Coachman the directions?"

Lady Gosforth directed her lorgnette at her dresser. "You know of this new dressmaker, Bragge?"

"I like to keep up with the developments in fashion," Bragge said demurely. "Miss Chance has an excellent reputation."

Tessa smiled gratefully at Bragge.

The old lady waved an indifferent hand. "Very well, Bragge, tell the driver where to go."

The House of Chance was a small, elegant-looking shop just off Piccadilly. The front window was quite bare, with a single long white satin glove draped elegantly over a stand, and green velvet behind. The window bore the name CHANCE in elegant gold lettering, and the stylized design of a daisy.

Inside, it was all green and cream, deep, soft carpet, velvet curtains, and several elegant, velvet-covered sofas and chairs. Very fashionable. Tessa heaved a surreptitious sigh of relief.

A young woman appeared from between the curtains at the back of the room. Bragge gave her Lady Gosforth's card, and she disappeared, saying, "Miss Chance will be with you shortly."

The woman who emerged was short, quietly but stylishly dressed and walked with a decided limp. And when she greeted them, her accent, much to everyone's surprise, was pure Cockney. She made no attempt at all to mimic a French accent, as had every dressmaker Tessa had ever visited.

Lady Gosforth stiffened. Tessa braced herself, hoping that the old lady would not say something to embarrass Miss Chance. She liked the little lady's friendliness and lack of pretension.

But though the old lady's disapproval was obvious, Miss Chance seemed not to notice. She questioned Tessa about what she wanted—Lady Gosforth sitting in a silent cloud of aristocratic disdain, and Bragge in nervous dread—and drew forth some bound booklets containing drawings of some of the dresses she'd made.

"I like these very much" Tessa told Miss Chance. They were simple, but beautifully stylish and there was something unusual about them. Tessa wasn't up on the latest fashion, but she could tell these were both up to the minute and at the same time, original.

"Right then, Lady Hewitt, let's get you measured up," the little lady said, and ushered her behind the curtain, where it was still clean and neat, but more workmanlike than luxurious. Sending an assistant out to offer Lady Gosforth sherry, champagne or tea, she had two more assistants taking Tessa's measurements.

"I'm sorry about my, um, friend's rudeness—" she began, but Miss Chance chuckled.

"Don't worry about it. They often start like that—a Cockney cripple?" she said in a horrified faux aristocratic accent. "But when they see me clothes, they soon come around. And if they don't"—she shrugged—"it don't bother me. I've got plenty of customers. Now, you mentioned a trousseau, so you're gettin' married?"

Tessa nodded.

"'Ave you thought about a wedding dress?"

"Not really. I thought I'd just wear one of my new dresses. I . . . I've been married before, you see. I'm a widow."

Miss Chance gave her a thoughtful look. "So, you don't want white then?"

"No. And there's not much time, either. The wedding is in three weeks' time."

"Right then, 'ow about a dress in a nice soft violet color. It'll match your eyes perfect. I've got a lovely length of silk here. A lace or gauze overdress'd soften the color even more, and you could use the dress—and the overdress—separately. I've got one here a bit similar in pink. Of course, yours won't be the same—all my designs are unique—but this'll give you the idea." She rummaged through a rack containing dresses hanging up and pulled out a pink dress with a lace overlay. It was very pretty, if a little fussier than Tessa liked.

"I'd keep yours simple with a gauze overdress instead of lace, with just a few touches of embroidery. For the wedding I'd make a small train, not so long that you'll need a string of bridesmaids to carry it, but it'll look elegant, and it can be removed later by your maid."

Tessa thought about it. It might be a small wedding, but though she'd prefer a simple dress, she knew Lady Gosforth was champing at the bit, fretting about what she was already calling a "hole in the corner" wedding. "I think the violet silk and the gauze would be perfect," she said. "My betrothed's aunt"—she nodded toward the waiting room and lowered her voice—"is very concerned that I look my best." Really, she was hoping Tessa wouldn't disgrace them all.

Miss Chance snorted. "Leave it to me, Lady Hewitt. You're gunna look like a princess—and it won't be too fussy, I promise. I can see you prefer a certain degree of simplicity."

Tessa just beamed at her, delighted to be so well understood.

A short time later, Bragge poked her head through the curtains and said, "Lady Gosforth has decided to go home."

"Oh, dear," Tessa exclaimed. They were nowhere near finished.

"It's all right," Bragge assured her. "I'm to go with her, then the carriage will bring me back and I'll stay with you until you're finished."

"Is she very cross with me?" Tessa ventured.

Bragge shook her head. "Bored, more like. Don't worry, she'll visit some of her cronies and they'll talk about the way the younger generation ignores older and wiser heads." She winked. "It's one of her favorite topics of conversation—her friends' too."

Tessa wasn't sure. It was one thing to assert her independence, and quite another to offend an old lady who'd taken her under her wing, quite against her own inclination. She would have gone out to the reception area, and spoken to Lady Gosforth herself, except that she was in her underclothes.

Bragge added softly, "If you ask me, m'lady, she's quite pleased by your show of spirit. Not that she'd ever admit it, but a little opposition refreshes her wonderfully."

Miss Chance chuckled. "I know a few old ladies like that. Me husband and I live with one."

Bragge smiled and withdrew, promising to return shortly, and Miss Chance briskly returned to the business of planning a trousseau fit for the bride of an earl.

As well as morning gowns, walking dresses, evening

gowns, traveling clothes, pelisses and spencers, there were underclothes, corsets specially designed to create the right flow of the dresses, nightgowns and more.

"I won't need half of these," Tessa protested.

Miss Chance just chuckled. "Most of these won't be ready in three weeks," she told Tessa. "But we'll do our best to get you gorgeous for your wedding and honeymoon, and then when you return, the rest will be ready for a final fitting."

Her honeymoon? Tessa hadn't given it a thought. She'd never had a proper honeymoon. After both her weddings, she'd been taken directly to her husbands' homes and there she'd remained for the duration of the marriage.

Would Marcus do the same? Take her directly to Alverleigh? She would have to discuss it with him. She had no objection to living at Alverleigh—though it would be very hard to look across to Ferndale and know that strangers lived there now—but she would like to see a little of the world first.

"You were right about the weather clearing up," Tessa commented.

Marcus nodded. It had been drizzling lightly when he'd called that morning to take her riding. He'd almost called it off, except that he was pretty sure the rain would stop before they were even out of the city. And so it had.

He'd taken her riding whenever he could, Hampstead Heath when he had no parliamentary or business engagements, and Hyde Park when he did.

Mornings suited them both, particularly since his aunt had returned to her old habit of rarely rising before noon. It gave them time alone, and he was pleased to see that the regular outings were having an effect on Tessa, relaxing her, and enabling easier conversation between them.

He no longer had to rack his brains for things to say—with Tessa it all seemed to come naturally. Even when there were periods of silence, they were not those uncomfortable silences he dreaded, and were usually broken by something inconsequential, like her pointing out a bird or a cheeky red squirrel.

He was comfortable with her, and she seemed the same with him. It boded well for their future

"I gather you've been doing quite a bit of shopping," he said.

She gave a guilty start. "Yes, I'm afraid it's going to be quite expensive. I haven't yet bought shoes or hats or shawls or... other things your aunt considers vital."

He shrugged. "Don't give it a thought. Buy whatever you like. I just hope Aunt Maude isn't bullying you." He sent her a sideways glance and was surprised to see a glimmer of a smile on her lips. "She isn't, is she?"

Tessa shook her head. "Not at all. But I'm afraid . . ."

"I'm afraid?" he prompted.

She took a deep breath. "She's finding me a bit of a handful."

"Is she indeed?" He tried not to smile.

"Yes. I refused to go to her own dressmaker."

"Understandable. You want something in a different style I suppose." He'd never shown much interest in feminine fashions, nor male ones either. His valet kept him sufficiently informed of what was appropriate for gentlemen.

She cocked her head and looked at him with a curious expression. "You don't mind?"

He laughed softly. "When you get to know my aunt better you will learn that a little opposition stimulates her. My brothers, especially Gabe and Harry make an art of it. She grumbles about it, but secretly it delights her. You'll see when you meet them."

She started and swiveled in the saddle. "They're coming, your brothers? But I thought Gabriel lived in Zindaria."

"He does, and he was very cross that he would miss my wedding. I'm the last single brother, you see. Head of the family." He grimaced. It couldn't be helped. There was simply not enough time for Gabe and Callie to make the trip in time for the wedding.

Marcus had worked hard at repairing the rifts in the family caused by his parents' quarrels—and by his own actions too, he had to admit. He was still deeply ashamed of the way he and Nash had treated Harry and Gabe when they were schoolboys.

"My other brother, Nash, won't be coming either. He and his wife and the children live in Russia, in St. Petersburg, and the journey would take weeks, if not months, depending on the weather, so they wouldn't make it in time. He's a diplomat." He glanced at her and added, "But if there is anyone you'd like to come to the wedding, make sure you tell Aunt Maude."

There was a short silence, then, "There's no-one," she said bleakly.

There was a short silence then Marcus said, "You don't mind that your brother won't be there?"

"No, of course not! It's a great relief to me that he hasn't shown any interest in me since I left his house. Of course, he wouldn't if he's gone to America." She glanced at him. "I know it sounds unnatural, a sister speaking so of her only brother—"

"Not unnatural at all. He treated you appallingly." Once again, Marcus wondered whether he should tell her about the role he had played in Edgar's removal from her life. He should, he knew, but though her brother had treated her badly and exploited her shamelessly, he wasn't sure how she'd react.

They rode on in silence until, Tessa silent and thoughtful. He wondered what she was thinking about. Life without Edgar?

As they approached the edge of the heath, she said, "I wish Louis, my other brother had lived. He died at Waterloo."

"I know. I'm sorry. I knew him—both your brothers—very slightly at school, and the general consensus was that Louis was a good fellow." And Edgar one of the worst.

She nodded, her lips compressed as if holding back emotion, but the minute they reached the heath proper, she said, "Race you to that old oak," and took off.

After a while, playing "catch me if you can" on horseback, their mounts were tiring, and they turned back, slowing to a walk.

"Thank you for sparing the time to take me riding," she said after a while. "I cannot tell you what it means to me. And I know how busy you must be."

"Not at all," Marcus assured her. For the first time in his life, he'd delegated much of his business—and even some parliamentary matters, when that was possible—to his very efficient secretary, who was delighted to be given more responsibility. Marcus didn't even feel guilty about it. After all, he was getting married in a few weeks, and he'd be off on his honeymoon after that. Which reminded him. "By the way, have you thought about where you'd like to go on our honeymoon?" he asked her.

She blinked and looked at him in surprise. "Honeymoon? You're asking *me*?"

"Yes. Anywhere you'd particularly like to go?"

She gave him a long look then nodded. "Belgium." It burst out of her.

"Belgium?" he repeated, bemused. "Do you mean France? Paris?" People had been flocking to Paris since Napoleon's final defeat.

"No, Belgium. Waterloo, in fact. I would like to visit Waterloo."

"You mean the site of the battle?" It was a strange choice for a honeymoon.

She nodded. "I would like to visit my brother's grave. Louis's grave. But I suppose it's not possible."

"I see." Marcus nodded, keeping his doubts to himself. Most of the Waterloo graves were unmarked and likely to be invisible by now. Some wealthy English families had had their sons' bodies shipped home, to be buried in the family graveyard or crypt, but clearly Edgar hadn't bothered with the expense. If he had, she would surely know. Louis Blaxland had likely been buried along with the thousands of undistinguished dead. Should he tell her that now or wait? Wait, he decided.

"Very well, if that's what you want, we will go to Belgium and visit the battle ground."

Her face lit up and she reached across and touched his arm. "Thank you, Marcus. I cannot tell you how happy that makes me." Her smile stole his breath and caused his mouth to dry. He swallowed.

Her delight seemed a disproportionate reaction, and made him curious as to where her other honeymoons had been. But before he could ask, she added, "I've never been anywhere, you see, not out of England. Not even to other parts of England."

He frowned, but she continued, "Both my husbands took me directly to their homes after the ceremony, and there I remained."

"You've never been to the beach? Not to Brighton or Worthing or Scarborough?" he said incredulously, naming some of the more fashionable seaside resorts. "Or to other fashionable places, like Bath or the Lake District?"

"No. I've never even seen the sea. My second husband often visited Bath to take the waters, and he always brought several bottles of the water back and made me drink them." She pulled a face. "It's nasty stuff, but he said it would help with my infertility."

"He didn't take you with him?"

"No, never. I never went anywhere. So, you can imagine how happy it makes me that we will travel to Belgium," she said brightly. "I will get to see the sea *and* visit a foreign country."

Marcus held onto his temper. She'd been virtually imprisoned by both of those husbands of hers, like a wild bird in a cage. And her blasted brother had connived to do it again. "If there is anywhere you'd like to visit—anywhere in the world," he said grimly, "just say so and we will go."

She gave him a surprised look. "Thank you." She glanced at the sun. "I suppose we'd better be getting back. Lady Gosforth will be stirring soon, and I'm sure you have more important matters to attend to."

"None more important than you," Marcus murmured as she trotted ahead.

"Drat! Harry and Nell won't be coming," Lady Gosforth announced at breakfast. She was perusing a letter that had just arrived.

"Why not?" Marcus asked. He'd made a habit of joining them for breakfast since the betrothal had been announced in the papers. "There's plenty of time. The wedding's not for another week."

She shrugged. "Harry's gone to Zindaria with Mr Delaney, to help him bring his latest crop of yearlings back. And one of Nell's precious mares is due to foal any day and she can't leave it. It's always horses with those two!" She dropped the letter and scrabbled through the rest of the correspondence that Peverill had brought in.

Marcus explained to Tessa, "Delaney is Harry and Nell's partner— they breed horses—and each year Delaney is entitled to take his pick of the yearlings from the Royal Zindarian Stables."

Tessa nodded, not very much more enlightened. She knew that Zindaria was the small European principality where Marcus's brother Gabe was Acting Regent for his wife's son, little Prince Nicky, who was heir to the throne. But she knew nothing about horses and why Mr Delaney would get the pick of their stables.

"I'll explain later," Marcus murmured, as with a cry of triumph, his aunt pulled an elegant-looking letter with gold edging from the pile, ripped it open and scanned the contents.

"Blast and botheration! Gabriel isn't coming to the wedding either—though it doesn't surprise me." She glared at Marcus. "And that's what you get for having a hole-in-the-corner wedding with not enough time for people to plan! Nobody, not one relative, will be there to see the Earl of Alverleigh marry!"

"Why? Are you not coming, Aunt Maude?" Marcus asked with an innocent expression. His eyes glinted in amusement. Since their betrothal had been announced, Marcus seemed so much more lighthearted. It was, Tessa hoped, a good omen.

His aunt gave him a baleful look and said in an austere voice, "Don't be ridiculous, Marcus. Though it would serve you right if I didn't go. I will attend, of course, to ensure it's done properly!"

Marcus gave his aunt a lazy smile. "I did say we wanted a small wedding, after all. This sounds perfect."

His aunt gave him a long, irritated look, then snorted and returned to her correspondence.

"There y'are, m'lady. You're gunna look gorgeous." Miss Chance stepped back to let Tessa view her reflection in the large mirror that took up half the wall of the back room at Miss Chance's.

It was Tessa's final fitting. The wedding was only a few days away. Her nerves weren't getting any better, but she was determined: she would be a good wife to Marcus. He was nothing like her previous husbands. Or her father or brother.

He listened to her. And she cared for him. She was determined to make him happy. She turned to look at her reflection.

"Ohhh." The dress was lovely. And it was nothing like she'd worn for her previous two weddings where she'd looked—and felt—like a stiff little doll. Here, she looked like . . . herself. The soft violet fabric of the dress shimmered beneath the fine, floating gauze overlay, which was embroidered here and there with tiny violets.

"We made you this, too. D'ya like it?" Miss Chance reached up and popped a little circlet of silk violets over Tessa's short curls.

"It's perfect," Tessa told Miss Chance. She adjusted the circlet and swished the dress back and forth. "It's all just perfect."

"Oh, m'lady, you do look beautiful," murmured Bragge, behind her. Bragge had attended all Tessa's fittings with her—part chaperone, part advisor. "Congratulations, Miss Chance, the dress looks even lovelier than I'd imagined."

The little woman grinned. "Told ya it would be. Now, let's get it all off, and we'll make those last few adjustments. I'll send it round to Alverleigh House tomorrow."

Tessa dressed in her usual drab street clothes, feeling a little like Cinderella after the ball. Once she was married, she wouldn't ever wear these clothes again. Lady Gosforth said she intended to burn them, but Tessa was giving them to Sutton to sell.

All her new dresses were lovely. Miss Chance had somehow divined the exact styles that suited Tessa, without making her feel uncomfortable or as if she were playing a part.

She felt, for the first time in her adult life, like herself.

Dressed again in her street clothes, she put on her hat and gloves and said, "Ready, Bragge?" The carriage had been sent for. Thanking Miss Chance and her assistants again, Tessa and Bragge stepped out onto the pavement to enjoy the fresh spring breeze while they waited for the carriage to arrive.

Wheels rattled over cobbles, and without warning two men jumped out of a shabby carriage. One of them knocked Bragge into the gutter while the other shoved a bag over Tessa's head. She screamed and struggled, but the sound was muffled, and before she knew it, she was picked up and flung into the vehicle. It moved off with a jerk.

She struggled, and received a blow to the head that left her dizzy. A rough voice said, "Shut your mouf if you value your life." Rough hands tied her wrists together.

The bag smelled musty and dusty and she wanted to sneeze. She could hardly breathe. They'd twisted something around her neck to keep the bag fastened tight.

Who were these men? What did they want?

The vehicle rattled along at a fast pace, swerving and bumping. Tessa rolled back and forth, struggling in vain to keep herself stable, until a pair of boots landed on her stomach, keeping her relatively still. Though less comfortable.

"What do you want?" she said through the bag.

"Shaddup." He kicked her.

"Where are you taking me?"

"I said, shaddup!" He kicked her again, harder this time. It really hurt. She subsided, her head and now her ribs aching, dizzy. She was dizzy but her brain was whirling with questions. What on earth was going on? She was being kidnapped, but for what reason? Ransom? And by whom?

There was only one answer: Edgar

Marcus thought he was half-way to America, but he must be mistaken. It seemed Edgar had decided to return and try one more time to marry her off. Ooohh, it was just like him, she decided, her fear turning to fury.

Her ribs ached from those kicks. Yes, he was angry with her for escaping him and causing him so much trouble.

It felt so much like something Edgar would do. When they got to wherever the kidnappers were taking her, they would probably be met by a minister and Sir Henry Lester. Or some other rich, ancient groom.

Of course it was Edgar. Who else would want to kidnap her?

Chapter Twelve

MARCUS WAS ABOUT to enter the front door of Alverleigh House when his carriage pulled up, the door flew open, and before the groom had time to let down the steps, Bragge, his aunt's dresser, jumped unsteadily out and staggered toward him. She looked dusty, disheveled and very distressed.

"Bragge?" Marcus exclaimed. "Whatever has happened?"

"M'lady," she gasped. "Kidnapped."

"*Kidnapped?*"

She nodded. "Taken off in a carriage."

"Who was it? Could you describe them?"

She shook her head. "I'm sorry, m'lord. It happened so fast I didn't see their faces. I couldn't stop them. They knocked me to the ground and—"

"Never mind that. It wasn't your fault. Where did this happen?"

"Outside the House of Chance. Lady Hewitt was getting her final fitt—"

Cutting her off, Marcus turned to the butler who'd been hovering and uttering small distressed sounds. "Peverill, take Miss Bragge inside and see to her needs. And send your two strongest footmen to come with me. Oh, and inform my aunt as to what has happened."

In minutes he was inside his coach, returning to the scene of the crime, with a groom riding on the back and two footmen inside. And with two loaded dueling pistols in the capacious pockets of his coat.

His brain was racing. His stomach knotted in fear. Who would kidnap Tessa? If Edgar had remained in England he would be the obvious choice, but he was gone.

Or was he? Had he escaped from the ship? Returned to England?

He scribbled a note, then handed it to one of the footmen. Take this to Mr Gil Radcliffe at the Horse Guards. Hand it to him and only him—don't allow anyone to fob you off. Tell them it's urgent. A matter of life and death!" A cold sliver of ice ran down his spine as he said it. Pray he was wrong about that.

Pray Radcliffe could help. He might know something. Radcliffe was uncanny like that.

The carriage slowed. The footman jumped down

and ran off, the note clutched in his hand, and they continued on to the House of Chance.

Standing outside was a small, elegantly dressed woman clutching the arm of a burly-looking fellow in a luridly colored waistcoat. She was clearly distressed.

"That's the dressmaker," the remaining footman said. "I dunno who the big bloke is."

Marcus jumped down and the little woman rushed up. "Oh, Lord Alverleigh, I'm that sorry about—"

He brushed her apologies aside. "What happened?"

She shook her head. "I didn't see it. The first I knew was when I heard a scream, and by the time I came outside, there was a carriage driving away and poor Miss Bragge in the gutter, struggling to get up."

"Which direction did the carriage go in?"

She pointed. "But then it turned the corner and I couldn't see it no—anymore."

The burly man said, "I've questioned a few people who saw what happened. There were two men and a driver. The carriage was old and shabby, but the horses pulling it were good." He was Irish by his accent.

Marcus frowned. Who the devil was this fellow? Was he part of this?

The Irishman seemed to read his doubts. "Me

name's Flynn. This is me wife's shop. She's mighty upset about such a thing happening to one of her clients—we both are. And she's especially fond of Lady Hewitt. So, I'm here to help." He proffered his hand and as Marcus shook it, Flynn added, "I'm accounted a fair hand in a fight."

Marcus could believe it. The man looked fit and brawny, and despite the obvious expense of his clothing, and the colorful silk waistcoat, his hands were big and bore scars from a hard life.

And he was obviously a quick thinker, having questioned any onlookers. Marcus glanced around hoping for inspiration. "Nobody saw anything?"

Flynn grimaced. "Nothing useful. It was over so quickly, all most people knew was a scream and a poor lady fallen into the gutter—never mind a kidnapped one. I did get one description: Two men in plain coats, both with hats pulled low and one with a scarf around his mouth." He grimaced again. "Could be anyone."

At that point a hackney cab pulled up, and Marcus's footman jumped down accompanied by Radcliffe's men, Sims and Jackson. The footman handed Marcus a note. It was from Radcliffe.

My men are 100% reliable. If they said they'd put Blaxland on a ship to America, they did it. I'm sending them to help in the search. In the meantime I'll do my best to dig out any useful information. If I find anything, I'll let you know.

Best of luck, Radcliffe.

Marcus nodded at the men. It was all very well having help, but where the hell had they taken her? He had no idea where to look. There was no point just randomly rushing off and searching. This was London, the largest city in the world, with a thousand hidden alleyways down which criminals could dive, and dozens of rookeries that were home to the poor, the desperate and the criminal.

Doubtless the rational thing to do would be to go home and wait for the ransom—surely there would be a ransom demand. But he wasn't feeling rational: he was beside himself with worry. He couldn't possibly go home and wait tamely for a ransom note. In any case his aunt was there to receive any demand.

If one came.

He prayed one would. He'd pay anything to get Tessa back, safe and sound. Oh lord, what if they hurt her? Or worse? He couldn't bear it.

He needed her to be safe, to be with him. But what could he do? Where had they taken her?

He paced back and forth in front of the elegant little shop, trying to work out what to do, fruitlessly scanning his surrounds for any hint of where they'd gone, the questions eating at him. Who would kidnap her? Some unknown enemy? He couldn't think of any. What were they doing to her? Was she terrified? Of course she was. Any woman would be.

He paced, trying to think of what to do, flooded with anxiety and fuming at his own impotence.

Just then a grubby, ragged urchin came running up, gasping for breath. It was Joey, the boy he'd been trying to tempt off the streets. He grabbed Marcus's sleeve. His mouth opened and closed like a fish as he gasped to catch his breath. "Me lady," he finally wheezed.

"What of her?" Marcus said, suddenly intent.

Joey continued his fight to catch his breath, his narrow chest heaving with exertion. A few precious moments later he rasped huskily, "I saw 'em take her."

"What?"

A few more gasping breaths and the boy said, "An' I know where she is."

Marcus grabbed him by the shoulders. "How? Where?"

In between gasps, the boy said, "I been watching 'im—that bad'un I told you about. He's bin follerin' her around, so I bin follerin him. 'E's the one what took her. I saw 'im do it."

Marcus clamped down on his impatience. After a few more deep, ragged breaths Joey continued.

"I saw 'im grab 'er, so I nipped across the road and jumped on the back of 'is carriage an' hung on like blue blazes—it din't 'alf go fast."

He stopped to gulp in another few deep breaths. "An' when it stopped and they took me lady out— she's got a dirty great bag over 'er head and she couldn't walk—they 'ad her feet tied—but I fink she's all right. She wasn't crying or nuffin'. So I hid and watched, and when they took 'er inside, I legged it." On a final great gasp, he finished, "An' then I come back here coz I figgered you'd be here. Plus, it was closer than your place."

"Good lad. Can you show us where they went?"

The boy nodded. "Course."

Marcus sent one of the footmen back to tell his aunt what was going on. Radcliffe's men, the brawniest footman and Flynn piled into the carriage—the extra pairs of fists would be useful. He and Joey sat up top with the coachman and groom, so that Joey could direct them.

They wove in and out of the traffic, down ever smaller, narrower and more noisome lanes and alleys, young Joey telling the coachman where to go.

Marcus was beside himself. The questions pounded through his brain, the same questions over and over. Was she all right? Had they hurt her? Who'd kidnapped her? And why?

If they'd hurt her, or worse. . . His chest seized. He couldn't bear it. Couldn't bear to live without her. She *was* his life.

Finally, the streets became so narrow they had to get down and go by foot. "Not far now," Joey said.

Marcus prayed he was right. So much was riding on this small scruffy boy's sense of direction. His whole happiness in fact.

"She's in there," Joey whispered, pointing at a narrow, ramshackle building, seemingly unoccupied, with roughly boarded-over windows. "You can see in through that crack."

Marcus was so tense he could hardly breathe. He peered through the crack in the boarded-up window. His breath came back in a rush. There she was, tied to a chair by the look of it. As the boy had said, a bag had been tied over her head, but it was Tessa, he knew. She sat up straight, seeming quite calm—or maybe it was because she was tied up so tight and couldn't move.

Relief rippled through him. *She was alive.* Suddenly he was calm—furious but calm. He knew exactly what to do.

Through the crack he examined as much of the

room as he could. Only two men with Tessa. But there could be more, out of his vision range.

"Good lad," he told Joey again. "You wait behind when we go in."

"Oh but—"the boy began.

Marcus said firmly, "On no account are you to enter. There will be a fight, and I don't want you there when that happens." The boy had done enough. He didn't want him to get hurt. Or in the way. "Do you understand?"

The boy gave him a rebellious look.

"I need you to keep watch," Marcus told him, "And if anything goes wrong, you must take the news to my aunt. It's a very important job." But nothing would go wrong, he vowed silently. His blood was ice in his veins.

The boy hesitated, then reluctantly nodded and secreted himself in a nearby alcove.

Marcus glanced at his men. "Ready? On the count of three."

They burst in the door—there were three men. The odds and the element of surprise were in their favor. There were a few scuffles, and several punches were thrown, but Marcus had no intention of letting the fight run its course, not when Tessa was sitting tied to a chair in the middle of the room, in the path of the violence and unable to see or move.

"Stop!" He pulled out his pistols and fired one.

The fighting stopped for an instant. Then one of the men made for the door, and Marcus fired the other pistol, wounding him in the leg and sending him sprawling.

His men moved to restrain the remaining kidnappers.

Flynn produced a small, wicked-looking knife from somewhere and handed it to Marcus, saying. "Cut the ropes."

Marcus took it, first drawing the bag carefully over her head, murmuring, "Don't worry, it's me, Marcus."

Incredibly, she laughed. "I knew as soon as you spoke. I knew you'd come for me."

Her trust in him humbled him. He'd had no idea what to do. If it hadn't been for young Joey's heroism . . .

"Can you stand?" She tried and wobbled and fell back. "My legs are numb," she said rubbing them. "The ropes were so tight, I lost all feeling in them. And now it's all pins and needles."

"Ow, ow, that hurts!" a voice wailed. The two uninjured men were now trussed like fowls, and Flynn was standing over them wielding an even more wicked looking knife. "Now talk," he growled. "Who's behind this?"

Both men, clearly too frightened to talk, just shook their heads. But their eyes wandered to the wounded man who was moaning and wailing. The meaning was clear. He was the ringleader.

Flynn strode over and bent to examine the wound. "Barely even a scratch," he said in disgust. "Big fuss about nothing. You're lucky 'is lordship missed killin' you."

"I didn't aim to kill," Marcus said coldly. He was an excellent shot and though he could happily have slaughtered the lot of them, he had no intention of having his wedding tied up because of legal nonsense. If Tessa had been hurt—or worse—it would have been a different matter.

"Take them all to Radcliffe. He'll know what to do with them." Sims and Jackson pulled the two bound the men to their feet. Flynn dragged their leader to his feet and dumped him on a chair.

A sharp whistle spilt the air and an instant later the door burst open and five men rushed in. Two of them were pointing pistols.

Marcus cursed. He'd discharged both his pistols.

One of the men was very elegantly dressed—in other circumstances Marcus would have called him a dandy. Of middle height he was dressed in the first stare of fashion, his thinning hair brushed à la Brutus and lavishly pomaded.

"Freeze," he announced almost languidly and of course, Marcus and his men had to obey. They were outnumbered and outgunned. Again, Marcus cursed himself for not getting them all out of there sooner.

"Dear me, what a to-do," the languid man murmured in a faint Cockney accent.

He strolled into the room, raised a quizzing glass and surveyed them dispassionately. "Oliver Greeling at your service," he said to Marcus and bowed mockingly. Despite the thin veneer of gentility, he had the coldest eyes Marcus had ever seen.

One of the notorious Greelings. Marcus's heart sank. This was a case of thieves—or kidnappers—falling out.

Marcus pushed Tessa onto the chair and stepped in front of her, putting himself between her and the Greeling brothers.

Greeling eyed Marcus with a cynical expression, but his real attention was on the kidnappers, one in particular; the wounded one who Flynn had dumped on a chair. "And this sorry specimen is my little brother Albert."

Now that Marcus looked, he could see a distinct resemblance.

Sliding his pistol in his pocket the elder Greeling sauntered over, bent over the wounded man and examined his wound through his quizzing glass.

Albert Greeling sat up eagerly. "Ollie, I'm glad you came. We can get the money out of—ow!"

Oliver Greeling gave his little brother a backhander, hard across the face.

Marcus blinked. He and Flynn exchanged glances. What was going on?

"That's from Muvver," Greeling the elder said calmly. "And this is from me." He punched him hard in the face. Blood trickled from Albert's nose.

Through Albert's sniffles he managed to say, "But Ollie, din't you see the notice in the papers? We can't find Blaxland, but 'is sister's marryin' a rich lord. That's him over there." He jerked his head toward Marcus. "He can pay—Ow!" Another hard slap.

Edgar Blaxland's debts, Marcus thought. Of course. It all made sense now.

The older Greeling continued, "And that's just for starters. You know why Muvver is angry with you, don't you?"

The man nodded and mumbled something incoherent, sounding whiny and aggrieved. Marcus realized Albert was quite young, perhaps twenty or twenty-one.

"Speak up!"

"I know," the young man said sulkily. "But—Ow!"

"No buts."

Marcus watched with a sense of disbelief. This was bizarre. He glanced at Flynn to see if he was following. Flynn gave an infinitesimal nod and indicated one of the men holding a gun. He would tackle that one, while Marcus took down the leader. And Jackson and Sims would do their bit.

"*Greelings don't hurt ladies*, isn't that what Muvver has told us, over and over all our lives?"

"Yeah, I know, but—Ow!" Albert whined as his brother slapped him again.

"No. Buts. An' despite that rule—which you've known all your life—you harmed this poor lady." He gestured at Tessa, waited a moment, gave his brother another hard backhander and said, "Din't you?"

"Yes," the young man mumbled. "But not very mu—ow!"

"Worse," his brother continued. "You kidnapped her without the family's permission—not from me, not from Muvver—taking it upon yourself to decide what to do about Blaxland's debts."

"Well, how else can we—?" He was stopped with another slap.

The elegant Greeling brother turned to face Tessa and Marcus. Marcus braced himself for action.

Greeling bowed gracefully. "Please accept our apologies, Lady Hewitt, Lord Alverleigh. My little brother overstepped his authority."

All at sea now, Marcus waited.

"We Greelings don't make war on ladies." He turned back to his brother and snarled, "Lady Hewitt was Blaxland's victim too! Idiot!"

He turned back to Tessa. "Lady Hewitt, my mother was most distressed to hear you had been kidnapped by her youngest son. I hope he wasn't too rough. Please accept our most sincere apologies. You may leave."

Marcus blinked. Tessa gave him a doubtful look, put a hand on his arm, then rose and looked at Greeling. "What are you going to do about my brother's debts to you? Forgive them?"

Marcus gave her a sidelong look. "Don't argue, just go," he murmured and tried to usher her out.

She refused to move.

Oliver Greeling snorted. "We Greelings never forgive a debt," he said smoothly. "As I understand it, your fiancé here had your brother smuggled out of the country. America, was it not m'lord? Boston?" he said to Marcus. Beside him, he heard Tessa gasp.

Greeling added, "Or should I ask these two fellows who loaded him, trussed like a chicken, onto the ship?" He indicated Jackson and Sims.

Marcus inclined his head slightly. Radcliffe hadn't been exaggerating when he'd said the Greelings' eyes were everywhere.

"Then how do you intend to get the money?" Tessa persisted.

"That's my little brother's responsibility now."

"What?" Albert, who had busied himself wiping blood off his face, looked up at his brother. "How am I supposed to get it from Blaxland, or even make a lesson of him when he's in America? Breaking his legs is only good for frightening others, and nobody will even know about it if he's on the other side of the world."

"That's your problem, little brother. You're sailing for Boston on tomorrow's tide."

"What? No, I'm not! All the way to America? I won't go! Does Muvver know about this? Because—"

"Muvver made the arrangements," his older brother said silkily. Albert paled and reeled back in shock. His brother continued, "You wished to act independently of the family? Here's your chance. Once you have recovered the debt, you may return to England. But not before. Take him out, boys."

Two of Greeling's henchmen grabbed the protesting young man and dragged him out, struggling and yelling and pleading with his brother. One of them glanced at the older Greeling, who nodded. A swift thump to the head and the yells and struggles stopped abruptly. They carried his insensible body out.

"Please don't be distressed, my lady," Greeling said smoothly. "He will recover when he's aboard the ship. Again, my mother sends her apologies for your distress and inconvenience. We Greelings do not harm ladies, and you are not responsible for your brother's debts. You and your husband-to-be will not be bothered by us again. My felicitations on your upcoming marriage." With another elegant bow, he and his entourage left.

There was a short, shocked silence in the room.

"Well! That's a rum do if ever I saw one." Flynn said eventually. "I was gettin' ready for another fight." He cracked his knuckles.

Marcus nodded. "A smooth and slippery rogue, and a totally unexpected outcome."

"Do you think he meant it?" Tessa asked. "That he won't bother us again?"

"Bizarrely, I think he does," Marcus said.

"And if he doesn't," Flynn said with a grin, "'Muvver' will give him what for!"

Marcus slipped his arm around Tessa's waist. "Are you all right to walk?"

She nodded. "The pins and needles have quite gone."

"Then let's go home," he said, tightening his embrace. She was safe. It was all that mattered.

"Can I come out now?" a little voice said. From a dingy corner of the room a small figure stepped out from behind a pile of broken furniture.

"I told you to stay outside," Marcus growled.

"I did whistle, but they was too quick for me. And anyway, I wanted to watch. I can't learn nuffin' if I don't watch, can I? Besides, I needed to see if me lady was all right. You are, ain't ya miss—I mean me lady?" He fixed her with an anxious gaze.

"Yes, thank you, Joey dear, I'm perfectly all right," she assured him.

"It was really Joey who saved you." Marcus said, and explained the lad's role in leading them to her.

Tessa smiled down at the boy. "So, you were my guardian angel, Joey?" She bent and kissed him on the forehead. Blushing, the boy swelled with pride. Marcus tried not to feel jealous of a small scruffy boy. Tessa glanced up at him, squeezed his arm and added softly, "My other guardian angel."

They returned to the waiting carriage, where the coachman was brandishing his whip, holding off potential thieves. Marcus helped Tessa in. Jackson and Simms decided to ride on the roof and Joey eagerly joined them. Flynn would have too, but Marcus stopped him, saying, "No, please ride inside with Lady Hewitt and me. The least I can do is return you to your wife, who will be waiting anxiously." Besides, in the short time he'd known the Irishman, he'd come to like him.

The carriage set off, and the inside passengers leaned back in relief. It was over. Tessa was safe. Marcus, knowing she wouldn't want a fuss, kept a subtle eye on her. She must be badly shaken, but had too much pride to display her distress in front of others. Not that he'd mind if she did need comforting. He would be a whole lot happier if she was in his arms right now.

He could have lost her.

He'd never been so frightened in his life.

And it could have ended a great deal worse if it wasn't for the intervention of the older Greeling brother. What a bizarre turn of events.

A small, muffled sound beside him made him turn to her. Her face was hidden, and her shoulders were shaking. She was weeping. The realization pierced him to the heart. He reached to draw her into his arms.

She looked up, and to his amazement it wasn't tears he saw in her eyes; it was laughter.

"Their mother!" she said between giggles. "You should have seen your face when the slapping started." She turned to Flynn. "And yours, sir—I'm sorry, I didn't catch your name."

"Flynn," he said. "Daisy Chance is my wife."

"Oh, dear Daisy," she said. "I hope we didn't worry her too much."

Flynn didn't answer. He just shook his head and glanced at Marcus.

Tessa laughed again. "Such tough and ruthless men—and they *were* terribly ruthless, I could tell—but both in so much awe of their mother."

Flynn shrugged. "A pretty ruthless mother, I would have said."

"I think you will find that the correct term is Muvver," Marcus said carefully, and they all laughed.

"What I would give to meet her," Tessa said.

"Shall we invite her to our wedding?" Marcus suggested dryly, which sent her laughing again.

They fell silent again, but after a moment, Tessa turned to Marcus. "What are we going to do about Joey?"

"What do you mean?"

"We can't let him continue spending so much time on the streets. He's bound to get into trouble. When I think of him clinging to my kidnapper's carriage . . ." She shuddered.

Marcus nodded. "I know. I'll give it some thought."

They reached the House of Chance and found Daisy pacing up and down in front of her shop. The carriage had barely stopped when Flynn leapt down. The worry wiped from her face, she raced to him and he immediately scooped her up. Marcus wished he'd done the same with Tessa, but years of having gentlemanly behavior drummed into him had prevented him. Besides he wasn't sure that after all she'd been through she would appreciate being manhandled. Not by him, at any rate.

Peering over Flynn's shoulder as he carried her into the shop, Daisy Chance called out, "Glad to see you're all right, Lady Hewitt." And Tessa waved back, smiling.

"A fond couple," she said, and Marcus glanced at her. Was that wistfulness he heard in her voice. Should he scoop her up and carry her inside when they reached Alverleigh House?

But no, he was too stiff and proper for such a thing. He knew it, and he cursed his rigid upbringing, but she would probably be embarrassed by such a departure from his usual demeanor. No, he couldn't be other than he was.

She seemed remarkably calm after her ordeal— even making jokes and laughing. Marcus was stunned by how calm she seemed. Most women would fall apart after such an experience. "Weren't you terrified?" he asked her. He certainly had been, terrified on her behalf. Even now, after it was all over, he wanted to sweep her into his arms and hold her tight. But she sat in the coach, looking out quite calmly at the passing scene, not shaking or shivering and with no sign of tears at all.

She shook her head. "No, I was angry, more than anything, especially when one of them kicked me."

"He *kicked* you?" Rage swamped Marcus. How dare that swine kick her! He wished now that he'd given him a greater hiding than he had.

"Yes, but I thought he was Edgar. Or one of his men."

"You thought he was *Edgar*?" he echoed.

She shrugged. "Edgar could be violent when he was angry. And he'd been severely thwarted, you know, by your rescuing me from that wedding and spiriting me away so he couldn't find me. I knew he'd be furious."

Marcus wished he'd beaten Edgar to a pulp as well.

"So, because I thought the kidnappers were Edgar's men, I was more angry than frightened. I knew he wouldn't hurt me, not really. I knew he would have needed me for some plot or other."

"I see." It helped to know she hadn't been truly frightened, but that *not really* still angered him.

"So, was Oliver Greeling correct?" she asked after a moment. "That you were the one who sent Edgar to America?"

He'd hoped she'd missed that, but it was time to admit the truth. "Yes, I got rid of him. I thought it was best."

"I kept wondering why he hadn't come after me. It was very unlike Edgar, so I thought something drastic must have happened. You didn't kill him, did you?" There was a faint note of doubt in her voice.

"Of course not," he said, shocked that she might think it of him, even for a minute. "I merely got him out of your hair."

"How?"

"I bribed him, gave him a ticket to America and a small sum of money to start him off."

"And of course he took it."

He nodded. She didn't need to know how eager her brother was to take the money and abandon her. "The fact that the Greelings were searching for him was an added inducement."

"So you sent him away. *Trussed like a fowl,* the elder Greeling said.*"

Marcus shrugged. "Apparently he resisted."

She laughed. "Oh, how I wish I'd seen that. And you're sure he won't be back?"

He shook his head. "Even if young Albert doesn't find him, the Greelings will be waiting for Edgar if he ever returns to England. He's a fool if he does."

There was a short silence, broken only by the sound of the wheels rattling over cobbles and the noise of street hawkers calling their wares. "Why didn't you tell me what you'd done?" she asked.

"I thought it would upset you, knowing I was responsible. He is, after all, your brother and only living relative." And she was a very loyal person.

"Blood isn't everything," she said tightly. "Edgar lost the right to my love and loyalty a long time ago. He showed none to me. Quite the contrary." She slipped a small cold hand into his and added, "And I'm not at all upset. In fact, it's a relief to know he's so far away. For a long time I expected him to pounce on me any minute. Every time we went out riding or walking in the park. So when I was kidnapped, I naturally assumed it was Edgar."

He squeezed her hand. It was small and soft. "I'm sorry. I should have told you."

"Yes, you should have. I'm very grateful to you for it, but I've had quite enough of secrets. I would prefer it if there were none between us in future." She looked up at him. "Agreed?"

"Agreed," he said. Again, he wished he could just pull her into his arms and hold her, but somehow, while she sat beside him, so quiet and composed, he just couldn't. He was the Earl of Alverleigh, and rectitude was his middle name. Dammit.

When they reached his house, he politely helped her down from the carriage and escorted her inside—no carrying her off romantically like Flynn had of his wife.

So very proper and dull of him, he thought in disgust as his aunt surged forward and embraced Tessa warmly, exclaiming over her horrid adventure and demanding to know all the details. Talking non-stop, she led Tessa into the sitting room, leaving it to Marcus to arrange tea, refreshments and brandy. He also ordered a bath for Tessa to be ready as soon as his aunt had finished interrogating her. He knew she'd want one.

Chapter Thirteen

"I HAVE A JOB for you, young Joey," Marcus said the following day. He'd tracked the boy down to the kitchen, where he was energetically scrubbing carrots.

"Orright. But I gotta clean these carrots fer Cook first," the boy said importantly.

Marcus hid a smile. It was clear that he ranked rather lower in the lad's estimation than his cook. He glanced at her and winked.

"Yes, of course, you must always do what Cook asks of you."

"I know," he said darkly. "She won't feed me, else."

Marcus nodded. "Indeed. I doubt you'll find this job onerous."

The boy frowned. "What's onerous?"

"Difficult. Your task is to look after her ladyship's dog while she's away. We are traveling and cannot take him with us. So, you must walk him every day, clean up after him, brush him, and feed him. Cook will give you his food—"

"And mine?" Joey said anxiously.

"Yes, as long as you do what she tells you."

Joey nodded. "Course." He added in a confiding whisper, "She's a good 'un is Cook."

Marcus smiled at Cook. "I know. As well, I want you to do whatever Peverill tells you to do."

Joey grimaced. "Aw right," he said reluctantly.

"And Peverill will pay you each week."

At that, Joey brightened. "'Ow much?"

"That will depend on how well you do your work."

"Oh." Joey subsided.

"As well," Marcus continued, amused by the boy's transparency, "from now on you will wear the clothes that were purchased for you at all times—not your street clothes."

"Oh but—"

"Her ladyship is worried about you roaming the streets, so that will have to stop," Marcus said firmly."

The boy opened his mouth to argue.

Marcus said, "You don't want to worry her, do you?"

"No," Joey muttered.

"Good. And every night you will sleep in the house. An attic room has been prepared for you."

Joey heaved a sigh. "'S gunna be hard."

"I know, but only at first. And by the time her ladyship and I return from our honeymoon, she will be very proud of the new improved Joey, I am sure. So, do you agree?"

There was a long pause, then Joey said, "I s'pose so. Orright then."

To Marcus's surprise the boy straightened, spat in his hand and offered it. The street version of a gentleman's agreement, he perceived, if rather . . . slimy. Ignoring his cook's horrified expression, Marcus gravely shook Joey's hand. "We are agreed then."

Tessa's sleep was restless, and she woke just as the faint gray light of dawn slipped through the gaps in the curtains.

Her wedding day.

Third time lucky? Oh, but she hoped so. She lay thinking. Worrying, really, even though she told herself that there was no point in worrying. The die was cast. She'd said yes, the date was set, the banns called, her bride clothes had been delivered the day before and there was no changing her mind.

Not that she wanted to change her mind. But she still had doubts about Marcus. He wanted a *practical* marriage, he'd said. Companionship. A friend.

She could do that.

Her barrenness wasn't an issue, he'd assured her.

So . . . why was she worrying?

In a few hours she'd be promising to love, honor and obey. Honor and obey she could do, but love? He wasn't looking for love, he'd said so. *'I've never wanted a love match.'*

But today she was going to promise to love him—before God and the congregation.

She hadn't loved her previous two husbands, and yet she'd made those same vows. So what was the difference?

Marcus was the difference.

Had she met him again when she was eighteen—without any marriage to spoil things—she would have happily, joyfully married him. She'd been more than half-way in love with him then, even as a young girl.

Now, as a widow with no illusions left, she was more in love with him than ever. How could she not love him? He was irresistible, not only because he was so kind and thoughtful and respectful of her feelings and opinions, and that subtle, wry, dry sense of humor, the dancing light that warmed his gray eyes, eyes that were often so grim looking. But not for her, never for her.

She turned over in bed and hunched into the bedclothes. It wasn't just a list of qualities that made her love him. You might like a man for his qualities, but love? Love just happened.

Love for the whole man, qualities and quirks, faults and all.

Not to mention those times when his mere presence made her shiver with what she suspected was desire.

Only how could she burden him with her feelings, when he'd made it clear—more than clear—that he didn't want love from her?

But love came in many forms, she reminded herself. Perhaps, as long as she didn't speak her love aloud to Lord *I-haven't-a-romantic-bone-in-my-body*, she could love him quietly—'reverently and discreetly' as the wedding service said. Without embarrassing or burdening him with her unrequited, unwanted love.

Footsteps sounded outside in the corridor. The servants were up and about. Soon one of the maids would bring Tessa a cup of hot chocolate and ask her when she would want her bath.

Time to put fruitless worries away. She had a wedding to get on with.

The previous day Daisy Chance had sent around the finished wedding dress and a number of others to wear on her honeymoon. They were, Tessa decided, the nicest clothes she had ever had in her life. Every single clothing decision had been hers—taking into consideration Miss Chance's advice, of course, and

Bragge's gentle suggestions. But the final decision in every case had been hers. For the first time in her life. It was an amazing feeling.

Unlike her previous husbands, Marcus had not offered a single suggestion.

After rejecting any breakfast—she couldn't eat a thing—Tessa bathed and washed her hair. How much easier it was to wash and dry short hair. She slipped into her underclothes—all new. She was taking nothing from her old life into this new one.

A short time later Bragge arrived to help her dress. She lifted the soft violet silk dress over Tessa's head, and then the gauze overdress embroidered with tiny knots of violets.

It looked lovely, Tessa decided, examining her reflection in the long mirror in her room. A little bit bridal, without looking virginal. She was achingly aware of the shadow of those two previous weddings.

Bragge put the final touches to her hair—not that there was much to arrange, but the tiny wreath of silk violets was perfect.

"His lordship sent this," Bragge added, and handed her a flat velvet-covered case.

Tessa bit her lip as she took the case. A wedding gift. Should she have given him something? She wasn't sure. It had never come up before.

She opened the case and gasped. A beautiful delicate pearl and amethyst necklace lay inside, along with a dainty bracelet and a matching pair of earrings.

"Oh, how pretty," Bragge commented, looking over Tessa's shoulder. "He must have known the color of your dress. Here, let me help you with the fastenings."

And then it was time to go downstairs. She found Lady Gosforth waiting for her, looking magnificent in a gold and purple dress, with a large gold and purple turban on her head.

She eyed Tessa critically through the lorgnette, and sniffed. "You'll do. We're both a little overdressed for a *quiet* wedding that *nobody* will come to," she said with ill-disguised disgust. "But we don't need to lower our standards. At least it's in St. Georges, Hanover Square, and not in some nasty little hole-in-the-corner church in some obscure out-of-the-way place. Now come along, the carriage is here."

Tessa knew why the old lady was in such a grumpy mood: apart from being denied a grand wedding fuss, suitable to an earl, she was even more put out that she wasn't even an official member of the wedding party.

Knowing that Tessa had no female friends or relations, she'd offered to be Tessa's matron-of-honor, but Marcus had said a firm no to that. And then Lady Gosforth had announced that in that case, she would give the bride away, Tessa having nobody to perform that office either. But again, Marcus had said no, that he'd arranged something else. And refused to explain.

At the entrance of the church, Tessa hesitated.

"Nerves?" Lady Gosforth said. "Should have thought you'd be used to this by now." She stomped into the church.

Marcus waited by the altar. He hated waiting. He itched to pace back and forth, but one didn't pace in church, not with the vicar standing by and the pews slowly filling before him. His hand drifted up to loosen his neckcloth, but he forced himself to stop. One didn't greet one's bride with a disarranged neckcloth either.

Where was she?

Beside him his best man, Barney Wimple was wittering on about something, his voice low and confiding. Marcus wasn't listening. Barney was a good fellow, but he often wittered on about things Marcus had no interest in.

He pulled out his watch and looked at it for the umpteenth time. She wasn't late. But where was she?

"So, I'm sorry about it, Marcus."

Marcus half-turned. "Sorry about what?"

"Those rumors."

Marcus shook his head. "Not your fault." He went back to staring at the church door, willing Tessa to appear. And not pacing.

"I've always found her terrifying. You know that."

"Mmm." Marcus was listening with half an ear. Less. "Why is that, d'you think?"

"Dash it all, Marcus, you *know* your aunt is a, a *gorgon*."

Marcus blinked. "My aunt? What has she to do with anything?" He glanced at her, sitting upright in her pew, wearing a massive gold and purple turban, glaring at him through her lorgnette. Still crabby at not being included in the wedding party, no doubt.

"She *made* me do it. I tried to tell her it would only make things worse. But she stares at a fellow through that glass thingummy and it turns a fellow to stone, I swear it. She's a gorgon!"

"What things? What are you talking about? When did you talk to my aunt?" As far as he knew Barney avoided his aunt like the plague.

"Last month, when she summoned me. Yes, summoned, that's the word. Sent a footman around to my lodgings. Before breakfast! Dashed if I know how she discovered my direction. Might have to move. Though my landlady does make an exceptionally good breakfast."

"Hang your landlady and her breakfasts. What did Aunt Maude want?"

Barney rolled his eyes. "I already told you. I knew you weren't listening."

"Hang it all, Barney, I'm waiting for my bride to arrive. Of course I wasn't listening. So what did she want?"

"For me to scotch the rumors about you and Lady Hewitt."

"*What?*"

"I told her I hadn't heard any rumors, but she insisted. Tried to tell her, too, that denying them would only stir things up, but would she listen?" He snorted.

Marcus's fingers clenched into fists. So that was it. The cunning old witch. He'd thought there was something off about those rumors. And there was definitely something fishy about his aunt's supposed opposition to his marriage. He'd walked right into her trap. Galloped, more like.

But he wasn't the one who'd been trapped.

It was Tessa.

He'd *wanted* to marry her even before the rumors. But she hadn't wanted to marry *anyone*. His aunt had convinced her she had to, in order to protect his good name. His honor.

"Damn you, Barney, why didn't you tell me sooner?"

His friend shrugged. "Never had the opportunity.

Why? Does it matter? It all worked out in the end, didn't it?"

Does it matter? His fists tightened. He thrust them into his pockets and turned away.

He would have to tell her. Now. Today. Before the ceremony began. Tell her the truth. Let her make her own decision—free and clear of his aunt's blasted trap—without any nonsense about rumors or scandal or honor hanging over her.

A chance to choose to marry or not. For the first time in her life.

The organ played a chord. He whirled and there she was, standing hesitantly in the doorway of the church, a vision of loveliness. She looked down the aisle at him, and gave him a small, shy smile.

He found himself smiling back and her whole face brightened.

Her attendants came forward, fussing around her and in that split second he made up his mind. He wasn't going to tell her. Not now. Not until they were married.

It was dishonorable of him, but he was going to do it regardless.

Tessa took a deep breath end stepped inside. It took a moment for her eyes to adjust to the relative gloom inside the church. As expected, there was a scattering of people already inside, most of whom were unknown to her. Her gaze was drawn to the sight of Marcus, standing at the altar, waiting for her. He looked tall and stern and magnificent and grim in formal black and white with a silver and gray embroidered waistcoat that she knew would match his eyes.

She blinked, seeing that beside him stood his friend Mr. Wimple. He had a best man? And yet he had refused to allow his aunt be Tessa's matron of honor, or give her away? Oh well, what did it matter?

She took another breath, ready to march down the aisle alone, when a low cough and a movement on her left attracted her attention. She turned, and gasped.

"NannyJune?" Tessa's eyes blurred as, beaming, her beloved old nanny came forward and embraced her. And behind her stood . . .

"Phillips? Is it really you?"

Grinning, the dear man who'd taught her to ride stepped forward and awkwardly patted her on the shoulder. "There there, lass, don't take on." It was so very like him that it only sent more tears running down her cheeks.

Phillips drew a crisp white handkerchief from his pocket, shook it out and handed it to NannyJune, who blotted Tessa's cheeks, saying, "Now come along, child, his lordship is waiting."

Tessa glanced at Marcus, waiting by the altar. His posture was as stiff as ever, but he seemed to be smiling too. "How did you know? How did you get here?" she asked the two dearest people from her childhood. They'd been more like parents than her real parents.

"His lordship arranged it all." Phillips said. "Arranged everything, even sent his own carriage to bring us up to London."

"And ordered us new clothes," NannyJune added proudly. And now that Tessa could see again, she saw that they were both dressed in smart new clothes. NannyJune was wearing a new, smart version of her favorite old hat with the faded pink silk roses.

"Now come along, lass," Phillips said. "Let's get you married." He presented his arm, and when Tessa looked at him in surprise, he added, "It's all arranged. I'm givin' the bride away, and June here is your matron of honor."

"Bridesmaid," NannyJune corrected him. "I never did marry, you know." She adjusted the fall of the Tessa's gauze overdress.

Somewhere an organ began to play and, half-blinded again by tears, Tessa was led by her old groom and nanny down the aisle towards the dear,

dear man who'd given her such a gift to make this quiet little wedding so special for her.

Phillips handed her over to Marcus, Nanny June fussed a little, arranging her dress, and then stepped back. The minister began. "Dearly beloved, we are gathered here . . ."

Tessa barely heard the service, her heart was so full, but she managed to make her responses in the correct manner. When it came to the part about 'let any man speak' she felt him tense, but nobody spoke. And when Marcus slipped the ring on her finger, she felt no despair, as she had in her previous weddings, only a sense of relief. And when they were declared man and wife, more tears threatened, but were overwhelmed by a surfeit of happiness.

On the way out, she saw that the church was not quite as empty of people she knew as she'd thought. Flynn and Miss Chance were sitting at the front, in a pew opposite Lady Gosforth, claiming the bride's side.

And a number of the servants from Alverleigh House had sneaked into the back pews and sat there beaming at her: Bragge, Peverill, Cook and others. Even young Joey was there, scrubbed to within an inch of his life, dressed in his new clothes and with Billy half hidden in his jacket. He waved the little dog's paw to her.

She and Marcus stopped to talk briefly to Flynn and Daisy—Marcus invited them back to Alverleigh House for a small, informal wedding breakfast—and the next time she looked, all the servants, and Joey and her dog had vanished.

The wedding breakfast was amazing. Cook had outdone herself. There was a large raised game pie, several cold roast chickens, a platter of crab patties, two dressed lobsters, a ham shaved to wafer thin slices, several salads, a basket of warm bread rolls, fresh from the oven, two large jellies decorated with whipped cream, an enormous trifle, dishes of strawberries and other fruits and a large elaborately decorated wedding cake. Champagne fizzed gently in tall, fragile glasses.

And this was what Cook deemed necessary for a small informal wedding breakfast for a handful of people. Tessa wanted to laugh. Cook obviously was in the Lady Gosforth camp when it came to celebrating an earl's wedding.

She sat with Phillips and NannyJune, who were a little intimidated by being in such a grand house with such grand company. Marcus sat opposite, tending to his guests, as was proper—Flynn and Daisy on one side and his best man, Mr Wimple, on the other—but glancing at her from time to time with a slightly worried look on his face. She smiled to reassure him. Everything was perfect.

"But how did Lord Alverleigh know where to find you?" Tessa asked Philips and NannyJune.

They looked at her in surprise. "Didn't you know? He's the one that gave us the cottage to live in," NannyJune told her.

"And the pensions," Phillips added. "Generous they are, too."

"Otherwise we'd a'been done for," NannyJune said darkly. "On the parish, in the workhouse. Your pa left us nothing." Phillips nodded.

"I'm so sorry." Shame flooded Tessa, and not for the first time. She'd assumed her father had had second thoughts and done the right thing by these two loyal old family retainers. Who meant more to her than family.

NannyJune patted her hand. "Not your fault, lovie. Your pa didn't do right by anyone, from what I heard—and you most of all. Marrying you off the way he did when you were still just a child—and to such an old man! Shocking it was."

"But all behind you now," Phillips said firmly. "You've got a good man there, a good husband. He'll take good care of you."

"I know," Tessa said, looking across the table at the man who seemed so cold and remote to people who didn't know him, but was capable of such quiet generosity and kindness. She frowned slightly. He was having some low -voiced conversation with Mr

Wimple, and looking quite grim about it. Whatever was that about?

"But why didn't you just refuse?" Marcus said in an undervoice. He was keeping his voice low so as not to disturb the other guests.

"Do you even know your aunt?" Barney said indignantly. "I told you before, she's a gorgon—turns a fellow to stone with that dratted glass of hers. Makes you completely helpless. She's as terrifying now as she was when we were at school." He chewed thoughtfully on a chicken leg, then added, "More, actually. She insisted I deny to everyone that you had kidnapped Lady Hewitt from her brother's house and made her your mistress."

"But I *didn't* kidnap her and she's *not* and never has been my mistress," Marcus said through gritted teeth.

"I know you didn't," Barney assured him. "Don't know the gel—dashed pretty though—but have known you forever. Soul of discretion. Honorable to the back teeth. You'd never do anything so blasted sordid. Or vulgar. Or illegal." He added a mound of ham to his plate. "I say, this breakfast is dashed good. Compliments to your cook. Weddings always give me an appetite. Other people's that is."

"So if you knew I didn't kidnap Lady Hewitt

and she wasn't my mistress, why the hell did you go around denying it to all and sundry?" Marcus demanded. "Because if anything was guaranteed to give credence to such a nonsensical rumor it would be energetic denials!"

"Well I know that," Barney said indignantly. "And I tried to explain it to Lady Gosforth. But the old b—er, lady insisted. And don't tell me I should have resisted—you know what she's like! Apart from turning fellows to stone, she's a dashed what-d'you-call-it, that Indian thing?"

"What Indian thing?" Marcus said, bewildered. He glanced at his aunt, holding court on the other side of the table. She might not be too keen on Cockney dressmakers who couldn't even be bothered to feign a French accent, but she had no objection to being charmed by a handsome Irishman. "You mean her turban?"

"No, of course I don't mean her turban," Barney said irritably. "What on earth would that mean— 'she's like a turban'? Make sense man. A turban is not the least bit alarming. Though depends who's wearing it. No, I mean the other Indian thing. The one that your aunt is like."

Marcus couldn't think of any Indian thing that his aunt resembled. Her nose was admittedly large, but it was Roman rather than Indian. "This conversation is getting out of hand. Forget the blasted Indian thing.

Why didn't you tell her that denying the rumor would only make any gossip worse?"

"As I said, I did try, but listening ain't her strong suit," Barney said, and took another long draft of champagne. "Oh I say, look at that! What a splendid cake. And that trifle looks delicious. Very fond of trifle, I am. Did I say, my compliments to your cook?"

Marcus gave up. Despite Barney's confusing explanation, one thing was clear to him: his wretched aunt was behind the rumors that had made it necessary for him and Tessa to marry. And she'd bullied Barney, poor sap, into spreading them.

For himself, he didn't mind being tricked, though he loathed being the subject of gossip, especially false gossip. Marrying Tessa was exactly what he wanted. But she'd been forced into marriage twice before, and now it had happened again—or if not exactly forced, she'd married him on a false premise. And he hated that this time it was his fault. Or at least his aunt's.

He dreaded having to tell her.

Barney tugged his sleeve. "Juggernaut!" he declared triumphantly.

Marcus stared at him. "*What?*"

"Your aunt, the Indian thing—she's like a Hindoo juggernaut! M'uncle told me about it once. Saw it in India. Terrifying thing. Unstoppable force. Crushes everything before it. Your aunt does that. Pass me that bowl of trifle, will you?"

The wedding breakfast was drawing to a close and Marcus gave Tessa a nod to indicate it was nearly time to leave. She went upstairs and changed into more suitable attire—a traveling dress in sage green with a collar and cuffs in dark purple, a pelisse in a darker green, and darling green hat with a jaunty little purple feather.

Their carriage departed with everyone spilling out into the street, waving and wishing them well, but once they were on the road south, they fell silent. Tessa was happy just gazing out of the window, watching the passing scenery, and when she glanced at Marcus, he seemed to be dozing.

Her husband. She took a few moments to gaze at him; she'd never really been able to do so before, not closely, because whenever she looked at him, he always seemed to be looking at her.

She was married. To one of the handsomest men in the *ton*. And the kindest.

They were to spend the wedding night in one of Marcus's friend's country house just outside Folkestone.

"Why Folkestone?" she'd asked when he told her

his plans. "Isn't Dover the usual place to depart for the Continent?"

"Yes, Dover would make the trip shorter, but my yacht is currently moored at Folkestone, so we'll cross the English Channel from there." He'd given her a searching look. "I don't suppose you know whether you get seasick or not? No, of course not, since you've never even seen the sea."

"Why would that matter?"

"It will make a difference to our destination," he explained. "If you're seasick, we'll take the shortest route to the continent—to Calais—to cut your suffering shorter. Otherwise, we'll make for Ostend."

"Ostend?" She'd never heard of it.

"It's the most direct route to the site of the Battle of Waterloo. I thought you'd want to go there first. And after that, I thought we'd head for Paris, if you wish."

Tessa was delighted with his thoughtfulness. He'd taken her wish to see where Louis had died seriously. And Paris was 'if she wished.' And he was concerned that she be as comfortable as possible on the sea journey. She hoped she wouldn't get seasick.

For a time, the journey passed in silence. Tessa didn't mind. She was enjoying the scenery. But she knew Marcus was tense; she could feel it. He fidgeted, and crossed and recrossed his long legs, as if uncomfortable.

After a while he said in a heavy voice, "Tessa, I have something to confess to you."

"Yes?" She gave him an enquiring look.

"We were married—*you* were married—on a false premise."

She frowned. "False premise?"

He nodded. "I didn't discover it until it was too late to call things off."

She stiffened. "You wanted to call things off?"

"No, I didn't. But you probably would have."

"Why would you think that?"

"Because those rumors about you being my mistress and so on. They were false."

"I know."

"Yes, but what you don't know is that the rumors were started by my aunt."

Her jaw dropped. "By Lady Gosforth?"

He nodded. "And spread—under her orders—by my cloth-headed idiot friend Barney Wimple. Which he spread by energetically explaining to everyone that the rumors were false."

"Which they were."

"Yes, but denying them increased people's interest and made them all the more certain the rumors must be true."

"Oh, I see."

"It was all a plot to ensure you married me. My aunt has long been determined to get me married."

Tessa thought about that. "But you were taken in by those rumors, too. And if you hadn't been, you would never have married me."

"Not at all!" he said firmly. "I wanted to marry you almost from the beginning. The rumor nonsense was, I gather, to make *you* agree to marry *me*. To protect my reputation." The carriage wheels jolted and rattled along a rough patch of road. Tessa thought about what he'd told her.

After a time, Marcus added, "I'm sorry. I only learned of it the morning of our wedding. In the church."

So that was why he'd looked so grim before the wedding. And what he'd been talking to Mr Wimple about at the wedding breakfast—the serious discussion. Not because he didn't want to marry her, but because he thought his aunt had tricked them both.

Which she had, finely.

Tessa recalled how distressed she'd been, thinking how Marcus would suffer from the slur to his reputation. How the old lady had urged her to run off to Yorkshire and abandon Marcus to face the scandal alone. Knowing that Tessa didn't have it in her to abandon anyone. Oh, the old lady was cunning indeed. Outrageous—worse!

And both she and Marcus had taken the bait which, now she looked at it in hindsight, wasn't even terribly subtle. She ought to be angry. Furious. She hated being manipulated. But actually, looking back at what happened . . . She snorted.

Marcus blinked and looked at her.

Another snort escaped her and then it became a chuckle. Then another.

"Are you *laughing*?" Marcus demanded incredulously.

Now helpless with laughter, she nodded, gasping out between chuckles, "She is wicked, I agree, but oh, we're a fine pair of fish, aren't we?"

"Fish?" Marcus frowned.

Tessa kept laughing. "We positively leapt onto her hook, hardly needed any bait at all."

His lips twitched. "We did. You don't regret our marriage then?"

"No." She took his hand and squeezed it. "Not one little bit."

The expression on his face stopped her laughter cold. He leaned toward her. She waited, breathless. Was he going to kiss her? Oh, she wanted him to, had wanted it for such a long time.

But after a moment he sat back against the seat and said only, "I'm glad."

But he didn't let go of her hand.

Chapter Fourteen

THEY ARRIVED AT his friend's house in the late afternoon. It was quite a grand house, but not intimidatingly so, she thought. Built of warm brick, it was originally Jacobean, Marcus explained, with additions made by various generations over the years. The family had owned it for hundreds of years, and it was only one of their properties. His friend was a keen yachtsman and only visited when he wanted to go sailing, which was less frequently since his marriage. His wife disliked the sea. A bad sailor—which Tessa gathered was not about any lack of sailing skill, but a tendency to seasickness.

Tessa noted a subtle unvoiced hope that she wasn't going to be a bad sailor, but it wasn't something you could choose to be. They would both find out tomorrow.

There was a wedding night to get through first.

"I think you'll enjoy the gardens," Marcus said as they drove up the drive. "It has a yew hedge—

like the one at Alverleigh, only it's not a maze, it just encloses part of the garden. But there's a wild garden as well, which I'm sure you'll like. Not as wild as your wood at Ferndale, though."

She bit her lip and tried not to think of Ferndale, knowing how her wild and lovely wood would by now be cleared and neat and bereft of all her precious wildlife. Where would they go? She couldn't bear to think about it.

The front door opened just as their carriage pulled up: clearly they were expected. An elderly butler directed two footmen to bring in their luggage and a groom took the carriage and horses around the back to be stabled. The family must be quite well off, keeping so many servants for a house not often used, she thought.

The butler was obviously proud of the house—he'd worked there all his life, he explained, pointing out various features to be admired; the medieval hall, the various family portraits, the beautiful carving on the staircase, and so on. Tessa barely took it in. She was tired—she'd slept badly the night before—and was starting to get nervous about the night to come.

Which was ridiculous, she told herself. After two husbands, she was hardly a virgin. She knew what was involved.

"Everything is prepared, m'lord," the butler told Marcus. "Tea and refreshments are available immediately if you wish, and dinner a little later if you prefer. We keep country hours here."

Marcus looked at Tessa. "I'd love a cup of tea," she said. She was hungry, too; she hadn't eaten much at the wedding breakfast.

"Very well then, "Marcus said. "Fifteen minutes in—?"

"In the drawing room," the butler said. "I'll send a maid up to tend to m'lady."

Tessa had a bedroom to herself, she noted: Marcus's room adjoined it, with a door connecting them. She tried not to think about the night to come. Her wedding night.

They were on the second floor. She peered eagerly out of her window, hoping she'd be able to see the sea from the house, but there was just a line of trees.

The 'maid' turned out to be a woman of at least sixty years, but she was a comfortable soul and Tessa felt instantly at ease, as the woman bustled about, bringing hot water for a wash and freshen up.

Tea was a pot of strong tea, warm coconut biscuits straight from the oven, crisp gingernuts, and a moist, delicious fruitcake topped with almonds. Tessa ate two slices.

Afterward she and Marcus went for a walk. They explored the "wild" garden, but though it was pretty, it wasn't the sort of wildness that Tessa loved and still missed. They reached a rise at the edge of the property, but though she could see miles of rolling pastureland Tessa still couldn't see the sea. Twilight was falling, a clear lilac sky that darkened above them minute by minute.

Dinner was plain country food, simple, but well-cooked and very tasty; a hearty vegetable soup, roast beef, chicken pie, and plum tart with lashings of thick cream.

Afterwards they played billiards. Tessa had never played before but found it fun. Being a beginner, she was not very good, and her game wasn't helped when Marcus kept bending over her, his strong hands positioning her hands on the cue as he showed her how to line up a shot. With his hands covering hers and his big body warm behind her, she found it impossible to concentrate.

He'd recently shaved—they'd both changed for dinner—and he smelled delicious, some sort of cologne water, sandalwood, with a hint of citrus and some spice that she didn't recognize.

She had also washed and changed before dinner, but hadn't had any perfume, so had to content herself with the soap provided, which was pleasant enough, faintly vanilla-ish and soapy, but not very glamorous.

After several games, in which Tessa managed to pot several balls, much to her delight, Marcus put the cues back in the rack, saying, "I think that's enough for this evening. It's late. Shall we retire for the night?"

Tessa swallowed. "Yes, of course." It came out sounding a little scratchy.

He said gently, "We don't need to consummate the wedding tonight. You must be tired. If you would prefer it, I'm happy to wait."

She shook her head. "No, I made vows today before God and I will honor them. I am and always have been a dutiful wife." One part of her was nervous, but another part of her wasn't. Though she'd never enjoyed being bedded, she knew what to expect and was determined to do her duty by him. And putting off the moment would only make the anticipation worse.

There was a short silence, then his eyes darkened. "I don't want a dutiful wife."

"*What?*" She stared at him in shock, trying to work out what he meant. Did he mean he wanted her to be undutiful? No, no husband would want that, she was sure. So was it some strange game he was playing? Getting her to defy him and then . . . what? Some kind of punishment? She shivered.

"I want you to do what *you* want," he said. "Not be bound by what you imagine I want. If I propose something that you don't wish to do, tell me, and we will work something out, a compromise perhaps."

She frowned. Was he still talking about the marriage bed? He must know that women didn't enjoy being bedded: everyone said so.

He took her hand. "Don't look so anxious," he said gently. "I only meant that if you don't wish to consummate the marriage tonight, I will respect that."

She shook her head. "No, I'd rather get it—" She broke off. "I'd rather we consummate it tonight. We need to make the marriage legal."

He lifted her hand and kissed it lightly. "Very well then. I'll join you in half an hour."

Marcus turned away, not wanting her to see his expression. He heard the click of the door as it shut behind her and released the breath he hadn't realized he'd been holding.

He poured himself a brandy. So . . . He was under no illusion; she wasn't looking forward to it at all. What had she said? '*I'd rather get it—*'

Over with, he supplied.

Most brides would be at least a little nervous on their wedding night, he supposed. No matter how experienced. He was guessing she'd found little pleasure in the marriage bed.

He drained his glass, picked up a cue and shot a few balls around the table. He'd hoped billiards might relax her, but it hadn't. He'd felt the tension in her body every time he showed her how to hold the cue.

He sank another few balls. So she didn't expect to enjoy their wedding night. It was up to him to change that.

He hoped he was up to the job.

He'd had several mistresses in the past—opera dancers and actresses for the most part—but mistresses had a tendency to flatter and praise, whether he deserved it or not. It was no doubt a condition of the position.

One mistress had been downright obsequious. She hadn't lasted long. He couldn't stand toadeaters.

And he sure as hell didn't want that in a wife.

It was what he'd meant when he told Tessa he didn't want a dutiful wife. He'd explained it badly, he saw, when the color had leached from her cheeks. All he meant was that he wanted honesty between them, that's all.

God knew what she'd imagined he meant.

He glanced at the clock on the mantel. Another ten minutes. He loosened his neck-cloth.

His first night as a married man. He'd better not mess it up.

Someone had lit a fire, and her bedchamber was lovely and warm. Tessa opened her portmanteau, looking for her nightgown and wrapper. As they were only staying for one night, the maid had not unpacked for her. She preferred that. Bragge and one of the maids had packed her luggage for her.

She blinked. Sitting on top of everything else was a soft, tissue-wrapped parcel, with a small card saying, "With my very best wishes, Daisy Chance."

Curious, she unwrapped it and found two garments, the like of which she'd never seen. She lifted one out. Could this possibly be a nightgown? In shades of cream, palest pink to a dark crimson, it was made of finest, sheerest silk, so soft and—she held it up to the firelight—practically transparent. And bringing to mind the seven veils of Salome.

The second garment was some kind of wrapper in the same shades, but just as fine and soft and translucent.

Both garments were quite improper. Why on earth would Miss Chance send her such scandalous garments? Was this what sophisticated ladies of the *ton* wore to bed?

She thrust them back in the portmanteau, stuffing them under the rest of her clothing and searched for her own nightgown: she was no Salome.

Her own nightgown was long and white and warm, with a dainty line of lace at the neck and cuffs. Spreading it out on the bed, she looked at it and pursed her lips.

It was a perfectly ordinary white flannel nightgown but now, having seen Daisy Chance's gift, it looked to her eyes rather . . . virginal.

And that reminded her of her previous husbands, who preferred her to look and play the innocent little girl at all times.

She shuddered. Never again. She was a grown woman.

She folded her long white nightgown, put it away and took out the Salome one.

Marcus undressed in his bedchamber and slipped a dressing gown over his nakedness. He knocked softly on Tessa's door and, after a moment, entered. The room was dim. Apart from the fire burning in the grate, only two candles were alight.

She was shy. She was sitting up in bed with the bedclothes pulled up to her chin. She looked nervous and her eyes were huge.

He bent and stoked the fire with more wood, then turned to face her. "I didn't explain myself well earlier. About . . . expectations. And your being dutiful." The heat from the fire warmed him.

"Yes?" It came out like a squeak. Nervous as well as shy, he thought.

"I've never been good at expressing myself." He cleared his throat. "I was thinking about how we were as children. Back then, you said and did whatever you wanted, without worrying about what I might think. And sometimes I was a little bit shocked—well, we were brought up differently. But knowing I didn't always approve never stopped you. Do you remember?"

"Yes." She nodded but looked a little wary.

"That's how I want you to be."

Even in the dim light he could see her face fall.

"You want me to act like a little girl?"

"No! Of course not!" he said, horrified. "You're not that little girl anymore—neither of us is a child now. No, I want you to be like yourself! However that is. Saying and doing whatever you—we—want. And if the other is unhappy about something, they should speak up and we will sort it out. Together."

There was a short silence, broken only by the crackling of the fire. Her expression was still faintly troubled.

He groped for the words to explain. "I know you vowed to obey me, Tessa, but you don't have to—that's what I meant by not wanting a dutiful wife. When we were children we were friends, equals, and that's how I want it to be now, as adults and as husband and wife."

"You mean we really should be honest with each other? Totally frank?"

"Exactly."

"And if I should say that I didn't want to lie with you tonight? Or any night?"

His heart sank. "As I said, I would respect that."

She looked thoughtful. "And if I said I wanted to slip out at night and explore the woods?"

"You could. Though I would probably ask to come with you. But it would be your choice."

There was another long silence as she thought it over. "So you're really saying I'm free to do whatever I want?"

He devoutly hoped he was doing the right thing. '*Whatever I want*' was risky. But he had to get her to trust him. And he needed to trust her in return. "Within reason, yes. And if I'm unhappy about something—or you are—we would talk things over and hopefully reach a compromise." He took a deep breath. "When you were a child, you were full of exuberance and, and life. Somewhere along the way you've lost that, but I would be very happy if it returned. Though not as a little girl and not if you feigned it to please me."

"I see," she said slowly after another thoughtful silence. "Then in that case . . .

He held his breath.

She slipped out of bed and came to him. "In that case, dear Marcus, I agree. And I would be happy to consummate this marriage tonight." She reached up on tiptoe to kiss him on the cheek, but he turned his head and captured her mouth instead. Briefly. Just a taste. Because she was trembling.

His own hands were also shaking slightly. He drew her closer and cupped her face gently. Her skin was like warm silk. He slipped his fingers into her cool, soft curls, and tipped her chin up with his other hand. Despite her apparent willingness, she was tense, strung tight. A pulse fluttered just below her jawline.

He took a deep breath and eased back slightly, and that was when he noticed what she was wearing. Or barely wearing. Silhouetted against the firelight, every slender curve showed. The nightgown was practically transparent, a froth of silky shadows tantalizing in what they almost but not quite concealed. Her nipples peaked, and the shadowed triangle at the base of her stomach enticed.

His eyes devoured her and he rubbed the silky stuff between his fingers. "What is this?"

"A gift from Daisy Chance."

"Remind me to thank her," he murmured and bent to kiss her again.

Her eyes, reflecting sparks from the firelight,

darkened. A man could drown in those eyes. He stroked his thumb lightly, lingeringly over her lower lip, warm and full and satin-soft.

Her breath hitched. She moistened her mouth with her tongue and waited, gazing up at him expectantly, her lips slightly parted. How could a twice-married woman look so deliciously, deceptively innocent?

He bent and brushed his mouth over hers, lightly, barely touching, and he felt her sigh and soften against him, just a little. He was desperate to take her now, make her his, but he knew he had to take things slowly, to make it good for her.

He was, after all, a civilized man.

Coals settled in the grate. Outside the wind stirred the leaves in the trees. Her eyes fluttered.

Forcing himself to resist the enticement of her mouth he pressed kisses along her jawline, feathered them over her eyelids; slow, light, tender kisses, skin barely brushing against skin.

He breathed her in, the fragrance of her skin, of her hair. A hint of vanilla, soap and nothing else except scent of woman scent of Tessa. Intoxicating.

Again, he brushed his mouth over hers, teasing, tasting, nibbling gently until, with a soft little sound her lips quivered, then parted. And oh Lord, the taste of her. Sweet, luscious, honey-dark. Addictive.

Slowly, leisurely he explored her mouth, her soft, gloriously responsive mouth. He wasn't used to leashing his desire like this, but the tension it created in him was delicious.

And her response was everything he could dream of.

He felt her knees give and her body soften against him, and he moved them to the bed. "We won't need this delightful bit of nonsense." He drew the nightgown up over her head and tossed it aside. Before she could react, he lifted her onto the bed. He swiftly dropped his dressing gown to the floor, joined her in the bed and continued kissing her.

She returned his kisses eagerly, pulling him against her, and pressing her lovely body against him. He fought against the ravening desire it released in him. Not yet, not yet. There was an inexperience to her movements that surprised him, but he didn't want to think about her past. Not now, not yet.

He explored her slender body with his mouth, his hands, brushing against her aroused nipples, and worshipping her breasts. She moved against him, responding to each touch with small incoherent murmurs. Of pleasure, he hoped.

He slipped a hand between her thighs, and she opened to him, moist and warm and ready.

"Now?" she gasped, and he agreed.

She reached for him, touched him, gasped—and pulled back in shock.

"What is it?" he asked her. "What's the matter?"

She didn't respond. She was staring at him, at his nakedness—his manhood—with wide eyes. "You don't . . ." Her eyes, wide and confused, met his. "You don't need me to . . . to . . ." With her hand she indicated what she had expected to do.

And he realized what the problem was. She'd been married to two very old men, men who needed help from their very young wife to raise their member to action.

"And you're very . . . big," she added doubtfully.

He tried not to smile. "No, I don't need any help to er, perform," he said gently. "I'm a young man. All I need is you, here in my bed with me."

"Oh." She continued to stare at his erect, his very erect member.

"Shall we continue?"

She jumped. "Oh, yes. Sorry."

He leaned over her, his arms braced on either side of her. "You don't need to be sorry," he murmured. He gazed down on her in a possessive hungry manner that half thrilled, half alarmed her. "It will be all right, you know."

Tessa managed to nod. She hoped it would be all right—no, she knew it would. She trusted him. Nevertheless, she was still shaking. She told herself to stop it, but she couldn't help it. She knew what would happen next, at least she thought she knew. This wedding night had been unlike any other night in her life.

It was all very well for him to say she should do what she wanted, but how did she know what she wanted? Everything so far had been a surprise, not least the sight—and feel—of his hard, erect member. Without any effort on her part.

She wanted to touch him there again, but she wasn't sure if it would be all right.

He kissed her again, slow and lingering and she felt it shimmer right through her, right to her bones. She ran her palms over his face, enjoying the faint prickle of dark bristles under his skin. He smelled clean and warm and his cologne was light, spicy, enticingly masculine, his kisses laced with a beguiling hint of tooth powder and brandy.

His mouth and hands—oh, the sensation of those large warm, firm-skinned masculine hands moving against her skin, teasing, tantalizing, arousing. Wanting more, she rubbed herself against him like a cat, running her hands over him, enjoying the feel of the hard, young, muscular male body. So hard. So deliciously hard.

With every kiss, the taste of him flowed into her, potent, dark. The heat of a man. Desire as she'd never known it. His mouth and hands sought, caressed, aroused, demanding a response she hadn't expected, hadn't known was in her.

Wherever he touched her, ripples of sensation followed, shivering through her like ripples on a lake. His mouth ravished her, nibbling, licking, finding places on her body that she had no idea were so sensitive. It was like nothing she'd ever known. Almost as if she were being . . . cherished.

She melted, clutching mindlessly onto him, feeling as though she were falling, but knowing she lay pressed beneath his hard heated body. Deliciously pressed. The warmth of his body soaked into her.

She heard soft little sounds, and realized they came from her. Did he dislike them? She didn't care; she couldn't help it.

All awareness blurred as he lavished her with kisses and caresses, soothing the yearning ache of loneliness that had been part of her for so long.

His mouth lavished attention on her breasts, while he caressed her in the dark, moist place between her thighs. His cunning fingers drove her mindless, teasing, soothing, drawing ripples, waves, shudders from her body and she cried out and writhed in response as bolts of pleasure-pain-heat speared through her, the sensations building, pushing her to. . . where?

Her knees fell apart and he moved over her, his

thighs pushing hers wider as he rubbed and rocked against her in a rhythm that her body tried to match.

"All right?" he murmured, but she had no words to answer.

"Mmm." She writhed restlessly against him, pulling him closer, not knowing what she craved, except *more, more, more.*

She felt him, hot and heavy and blunt at her entrance, and her body clenched with longing. She must have made a sound for she felt him hesitate. Without thought, without hesitation she pushed herself against him and with a groan, and one long smooth movement he was inside her.

He drew back, as if to leave her so she tightened her legs around him, pulling him closer, taking him deeper.

And then he was moving inside her, slow at first, then faster, plunging . . . thrusting . . .

Lost to everything, she shuddered and thrashed around him as the pressure built and built. He gave a final, deep husky groan, and she felt a gush of warmth deep within her. For a long moment she trembled on the pinnacle of . . . something . . . and then he stroked her—there—again and she . . . shattered.

The room was almost dark when Tessa finally opened her eyes again. The candles had guttered. The fire had burned down to ashy, barely alive coals.

He slipped out of bed, naked, and built up the fire again. Sparks danced up the chimney. His strong, beautiful body was limned in firelight. She watched him coaxing the fire back to light, feeding the flames.

He'd done that to her, too. Set her body alight in a way that had never happened to her before. A way she'd no idea was even possible.

She stretched. How much time had passed? She had no idea, but even now she felt the echo of small tremors deep inside her. Her whole body hummed with . . . satisfaction? Delight?

The fire crackling merrily, he turned and saw her watching him.

"How are y—I mean are you—?"

She smiled and stretched again. "I feel wonderful."

"Oh good. I was worried that—I lost control at the end. I'm sorry."

"There is nothing to be sorry for. It was . . . amazing. I'd never. . . .um." And it was her turn to break awkwardly off. She had no idea how to explain.

But he was smiling now. "I'm glad. It will get better."

"Better?" she repeated incredulously.

"As we learn more about each other."

It was hard to believe. She would have to take his word for it. A yawn surprised her.

"It's been a long day. You're tired. Would you like me to leave you now?" he asked.

Both her previous husband had left her bed immediately after intercourse—or what passed for it with them—was over. And she'd been glad to have her bed to herself.

But tonight she didn't want Marcus to leave. She was tired, that was true, but she didn't want the night to end yet. "I don't mind—" she began, then stopped herself. He'd told her to do or say whatever she wanted. Well, this is what she wanted. "I would like you to stay," she told him. And then added, "But only if you want to, that is."

He gave her a slow smile. "Oh, I want to, believe me." He slipped back into bed with her and pulled the bedclothes up. "Good night, Lady Alverleigh," he murmured and kissed her, a sweet and simple kiss, tender and quiet. It was a sharing of feeling, an act of communion. . . and it stole Tessa's heart right out of her body.

He wrapped his arm around her and pulled her close, spooning his big warm body around her. "Mmm, I love the scent of you," he murmured. "It's addictive."

"But I'm not wearing any perfume."

She felt the smile in his voice. "I'm not talking about perfume. It's the scent of *you*," he said with a slight emphasis on the last word. "Intoxicating."

She felt herself blushing.

He pulled her closer, and together, they drifted off to sleep.

Chapter Fifteen

Tessa woke to slivers of light coming through a gap in the curtains. It took her a few moments to realize it—she felt so warm and relaxed and sleepy—but Marcus was still in her bed. Neither of her husbands had ever stayed with her after marital congress. But he'd slept with her the whole night through.

She lay curled up against him. He was still asleep, wrapped around her, her back against his chest, one heavy arm over her. It gave her a glorious feeling of warmth. And safety. And . . . rightness.

That wasn't the only difference. Something nudged her in the small of her back. Was that what she thought it was?

She felt cautiously behind her, and felt his member, hard, warm and erect. He was ready again? Already? She was used to once a fortnight, if that. But after the amazing experience of last night, she would be happy for more frequent congress.

She could still hardly believe the difference.

She stroked him experimentally and he stirred and gathered her to him.

"Good morning, Lady Alverleigh," he murmured. "How are you feeling?"

"Wonderful."

"Then would you mind?" He caressed her breast. "A little morning delight?"

Blushing, she smiled. "Yes please."

He kissed her deeply and proceeded to make love to her again.

By the time she woke again, the sun was well and truly up. She never slept in so late. It felt deliciously indulgent.

Marcus, too was awake. He kissed her and said, "Do you want me to get breakfast sent up?"

She sat up. "No. I'd rather get up. It looks like a lovely d—" She broke off. He was staring at her, and she realized she'd let the sheet drop. She wasn't even wearing Daisy's nightgown, she was naked. Totally naked. Blushing, she pulled the sheet up.

He laughed softly. "I've made you self-conscious, but there's no need." He kissed her again. "You're beautiful, and I'm a very, very lucky man." He slipped out of bed, and naked, walked to the door to his bedchamber.

Speaking of beautiful. . . Tessa had never imagined a man could be beautiful, but his strong, lean-but-muscular body was breathtaking. She'd explored that powerful body last night. And he'd explored hers. She shivered deliciously in remembrance.

The maid knocked at the door, opened it a sliver and said, "Will you want a bath now, m'lady?"

"Yes please," Tessa said, and the door opened fully. The maid entered carrying an enamel bathtub and several more maids carried in buckets of steaming water.

Afterward, feeling fresh and clean and eager to face the day, she hurried downstairs and found Marcus waiting for her in the breakfast room. He rose and kissed her hand. "My lady."

She felt like a queen as he seated her.

An oak sideboard was laden with a range of covered silver dishes. She could smell toast and coffee and a variety of other delicious smells, and suddenly she was ravenous.

She ate a hearty breakfast, starting with hot chocolate and porridge. She hadn't eaten porridge since NannyJune had made it for her when she was young. According to her husbands, porridge was peasant food. But she liked it.

Next she filled a plate with eggs, ham and a small serving of kippers.

"Perhaps you shouldn't eat all that," Marcus suggested, looking at her plate.

"Why not? I'm hungry.

"We don't know yet if you'll be seasick."

She gave him a mischievous grin. "All the more reason to eat it now. Whether I lose it later over the side of your boat—

"Yacht."

"—will make no difference to my enjoyment of it now. And anyway, whose fault is it that I've worked up an appetite this morning?"

His complexion darkened and he looked a little embarrassed.

"'Morning delight' is the loveliest way to greet the morning," she said softly. She buttered some toast, topped it with plum jam, and poured herself another cup of hot chocolate.

After breakfast they set out for Folkestone where Marcus's boat was moored. Tessa smelled the sea before she actually saw it, fresh, a little salty and something else, distinctive and unfamiliar.

"Seaweed, probably," Marcus said when she wondered aloud.

A few minutes later she gained her first sight of the sea, at first just a sliver of glittering blue on the horizon. "Oh, oh" she exclaimed. "Is that the sea?"

"Not quite. Just the English Channel."

"It's so big," she marveled as they came closer. "You can't even see to the other side."

"The sea, the real ocean, is many times larger. We can cross the Channel in half a day if the wind is right, but it can take many days and months to cross an ocean."

It was hard to fathom.

The wind was brisk, each wave topped with white caps. Tessa gazed at it, mesmerized, as their carriage made its way into Folkestone and down to the docks. The sea changed color all the time, just like the sky; one moment gray and dark, the next brilliant blue in the sunshine. And the waves, steady and never-ending, but each one different. She doubted she could ever find the sea boring.

She eyed the smaller boats that were dancing on the waves and hoped they wouldn't be traveling in one of those.

"Which boat is yours?" she asked looking at the forest of masts.

"Yacht. That one. The Aurora." He pointed to a sleek white boat, with several masts. She didn't know anything about boats, but this one looked elegant, as well as being large enough to cope with waves. She hoped.

A couple of sailors appeared and collected their luggage. A man who she presumed was the captain waited by the gangway and a young woman stood behind him. Marcus introduced her to Captain Saunders, and then said, "And this is Betsy Madden, who will act as your maid while we're aboard."

The girl smiled, bobbed a curtsy and said, "This way to your cabin, m'lady." She led Tessa to a set of stairs—rather steep; she was glad of the railing—and they went below.

The cabin was small, with a wide bed built into the side of the wall, and a rail along the open side. "That's to stop you fallin' out of the bunk if we get rough weather," Betsy said matter-of-factly. She demonstrated how it could be raised or lowered.

Tessa hoped it wouldn't get rough enough for that!

There was also a little round window, a porthole, which was fastened shut at the moment, to stop the spray getting in.

"I hope it won't be too rough," Tessa said, peering out of the porthole. "I've never been on the sea before."

Betsy smiled. "Don't you worry none, m'lady. This is a grand yacht, and Captain Saunders knows what he's doin'. I've sailed on the Aurora many a time and we've never had a problem."

"Do you work here all the time?"

The girl laughed. "Lord love ye, m'lady, no. Only when 'is lordship has lady passengers. Me dad and brothers are all fishermen, so I knows me way around boats. And I'm glad of the extra pay—I'm savin' up to get married."

"Does his lordship often have lady passengers?"

The girl shook her head. "Nah. Only when his brother comes over from Zindaria and brings his wife and the boys—she's a princess, you know. And a couple of times Mr Delaney 'as brought 'is wife, only it's always one-way with him. He won't bring 'is precious 'orses onto a yacht like this." Seeing Tessa's confusion she added, "Every year 'e brings seven young 'orses over from Zindaria."

Tessa, recalling that Marcus's half-brother, Harry Morant and his partner Ethan Delaney bred horses, nodded.

Betsy showed her where various things were stowed and, with a certain degree of pride, showed her something she called the head, which was a small closet in which she could relieve herself. Apparently fishing boats had nothing so civilized. There was also a little alcove with a wash basin built in, so it couldn't slip in rough weather. It drained away all by itself, Betsy told her. "Just pull this little plug, miss."

Everything was so neat and cleverly designed. Tessa found it fascinating.

"We're about to cast off, m'lady," Betsy said, "so if you want to watch, you'd better go up."

Tessa hurried back up on deck and joined Marcus by the rail. "This is exciting," she told him.

He smiled down at her and circled his arm around her waist. They watched as the sails were hoisted up and bellowed out as they caught the wind. And in no time at all the land was growing farther and father away as The Aurora skimmed over the waves.

Entranced, Tessa watched it all—the busy sailors, the fast-disappearing shoreline, the seabirds that circled, shrieking. The wind was brisk, and the boat bounced a little as it breached each wave.

"Feel all right?" Marcus asked her. "Not feeling queasy or anything?"

"Not at all." She actually did feel a little peculiar, but she didn't want to miss a moment.

"The fresh air will help," he said. "You won't be able to see the White Cliffs from here, but if it's clear enough, we might be able to see to France."

"The White Cliffs?"

"Yes, of Dover. The cliffs are chalky which makes them so pale."

"Oh."

"Never mind, we'll see them when we return. It's a sight that causes a lot of people to feel emotional—especially people who've been away from England a good long time. The White Cliffs of Dover is the first sight of 'home' to them."

Tessa nodded vaguely. She'd only ever seen them

mentioned in books, so she didn't miss seeing them. She squinted in the direction they were heading, but she couldn't see France either. But she was enjoying herself immensely, watching the prow of the boat breach wave after wave, sending spray up, and at the other end, watching the trail where the boat had been.

After a while she got cold—the wind was very brisk and seemed colder out on the water than it had on the shore. Marcus noticed her shivering and scrutinized her face. "Are you sure you don't feel sick? You're a little pale. We can easily change course and head for Calais if you prefer. It's a much faster journey."

"No, I'm fine. I'm enjoying this," she assured him. She didn't really feel sick—just a little peculiar with the movement of the boat on the waves.

"Then why don't you go to your cabin and take a nap? It will take us the rest of the day, at least, to get to Ostend. I'll come down and join you later."

She nodded and made her way unsteadily to her cabin.

Betsy met her there. "Feeling a mite queasy, m'lady?"

Tessa was about to deny it—she was determined not to be a bad sailor—but Betsy said, "Don't worry m'lady, I got just the thing for you." She produced a flask and poured out a cupful. "Cold tea with ginger and a few 'erbs me mam swears by—just the thing to settle your stomach. Now, drink it all down."

Tessa wasn't sure about that, but she drank it obediently. The ginger taste was quite strong.

"Now, just you lie down and try to get some sleep, and when you wake up, you'll be fresh as a daisy. And if you do need to be sick, use this." She pointed to a small bucket on a little hook beside the bed, then helped Tessa to remove some of her clothes and tucked her into the bunk.

Tessa woke to a sense of warmth and well-being. Marcus lay in the bunk with her, sound asleep, his arm circling her, holding her against him. Water lapped gently against the side of the yacht, but otherwise there was very little movement. Had they arrived?

She carefully disengaged herself from Marcus's embrace, sat up and looked out of the little porthole. It was fairly dark, but she couldn't tell if it was night or very early morning. Through faint drifts of mist she could see several lights glimmering ashore and there were several other boats floating gently at anchor on the harbor. They'd arrived, but where, she wondered — Ostend or Calais?

She lay down again, snuggled up to Marcus who murmured something unintelligible, tightened his arm around her but otherwise didn't stir. She closed her eyes again and, rocked by the rhythmic gentle rocking of the boat, drifted back to sleep.

She woke some time later. Marcus had gone and it was much lighter outside. She stretched, sat up and looked out of the porthole. The mist was gone and the harbor was dotted with boats of every size. The water was blue and gleaming and the sky was clear and very blue, with just a few fluffy little clouds.

"You slept well, I think." Marcus said from the doorway, startling her. He was fully dressed and even shaved. He bent and kissed her, and she could taste his tooth powder. "I'll leave you to make your ablutions. There is a jug of hot water there," he said, indicating it. "We'll disembark as soon as you're ready and break our fast ashore."

Tessa washed hurriedly but thoroughly, and was dressing just as Betsy arrived to assist her with the last few buttons and her hair. "Don't worry about your things, miss. I'll pack 'em up and the men will bring 'em later. The master is anxious to get ashore." She winked. "Lookin' for his breakfast, I reckon."

Tessa made her way upstairs and found Marcus waiting at the rail. "Do you think you can climb down?" he said.

She looked down and saw a small rowboat bobbing gently at the bottom of a narrow ladder. Two men waited in it.

"I can get you lowered if you prefer," he added.

"No, I, I'm sure I can manage," she said, sounding more confident that she felt.

"I'll go first then." He disappeared over the side and stood in the small boat, legs braced and arms up, ready to receive her. She took a deep breath, did her best to wrap her skirts around her and climbed over the rail.

"I did it!" she exclaimed as she landed, and then grabbed onto Marcus as the little boat bobbed and wobbled. He laughed, sat her down and gave the order to move off. She gazed around her, enjoying the sights and sounds of the harbor, men calling out in accents she didn't recognize, sea birds screeching and shrilling raucously as they dived for fish and fought over scraps. And the smell, not just salty and seaweedy, but . . . ew. She wrinkled her nose.

In no time at all she was being handed ashore. She stood there, shaking out her skirts and looking around her. "Breakfast first," Marcus said, "And then we'll see about transport. Are you in a hurry to get to Waterloo or would you prefer to spend a day or so exploring the town?"

"Look around the town, please," she said, pleased that again he had consulted her wishes first before making a decision. "I've never been outside England, remember?"

"Very well. There is an inn—quite respectable I'm

told—and I wrote ahead to bespeak a suite there in case you preferred to stay a while. I also plan to hire a local fellow to organize our arrangements. We'll take breakfast and then explore the town."

"Have you been here before?"

"No, I never did the Grand Tour when I was of an age to do it, as Europe was too unsettled to be regarded as safe for foreign travelers. If I had, I probably would have gone straight to Paris first and skipped Belgium completely. However, the question never arose, as my father was failing and I could not leave. Now, shall we?"

She took his arm and they walked into the town.

Breakfast was delicious, with fresh, warm, crusty rolls and butter with ham or soft white cheese, or plum or cherry jam and boiled eggs. Marcus ate several rolls with ham and cheese, while Tessa spread her rolls with delicious cherry jam, washed down with hot creamy chocolate. Marcus drank coffee.

Tessa was intrigued to see that, though Marcus spoke to the innkeeper and servants in French, the servants conversed with each other in a language that sounded quite different. Not that she understood any of it: she'd never been taught French or any other language.

"Many people here speak Flemish in preference to French," he explained. "Flemish is related to Dutch,

I believe." In a lowered voice he added wryly, "And whether they're Flemish or French, few of them love the English."

Then they explored the town.

The following day they set off, heading eventually for Brussels and then Waterloo. Marcus had hired a local man, Tomas, to arrange things, and, since a light drizzle was forming, they set off in a hired carriage.

"We could also hire horses if you wished to ride," Marcus said. "I can't. promise you a side-saddle, though, as choices in such small towns will be limited."

Tessa laughed. "I often used to ride astride as a girl, though Phillips used to scold me for it. And I would love to ride"—she glanced outside—"when the weather improves."

The journey passed quickly with so much to see, villages of pristine white cottages with bright red roofs, little fields like patchwork, acres of what looked like cabbages and potatoes, apple and pear orchards and lush green fields with beautiful black and white cows grazing.

The weather cleared up in the afternoon, and when they came to a small clear river, Tessa said, "What about a picnic lunch here?" She was enjoying traveling and looking out at the passing scenery, but the carriage did jolt and bounce along the road and her bones could use a break.

Marcus shrugged. "Why not? We're in no hurry, after all, and we should enjoy the good weather while we can."

So they picnicked beside the river on bread, cheese and sausage, washed down with a local wine. Afterwards Tessa paddled in the shallows. How long since she had been able to do this? Not since she was a child, at Ferndale. It gave her an idea. With a mischievous glance at Marcus, she pulled off her loose traveling gown, waded in and plunged in dressed only in her chemise.

"What the—" Marcus began, and then, when she laughed up at him, and sent a splash in his direction, he stripped down to his drawers and dived in after her.

Laughing and splashing they frolicked like children.

Afterward, seated on the bank, she watched him dry his chest, and let out a big sigh of contentment. "I'm so glad I married you."

He gave her a sharp glance. "Because?"

She spread her arms out wide. "All this."

He frowned, not clear on what she meant.

She lay back on the grass—indifferent to possible stains—and stretched out, still in her damp chemise.

"The water was chilly, but so fresh and glorious. Thank you."

Marcus said nothing. She was unlike any woman he'd ever known. He hadn't given her anything, but she acted as though an impromptu swim in a river was a precious gift.

Her hair clustered around her face, forming tiny curls as it dried in the sun. The damp fabric of her chemise clung to her every curve. He could see the dark circles of her nipples, still hard from the cold water, the shadowed vee at the base of her stomach, but she didn't seem the slightest bit self-conscious.

He sat down beside her on the grass.

She gave another contented sigh and added, "I haven't been swimming since I was a girl, at Ferndale. I didn't realize how much I'd missed it." She stretched, and added with a smile of dazzling sweetness. "I didn't really know what people did on a honeymoon, but I can see now why they enjoy them."

"Swimming isn't the only reason," Marcus murmured and bent over her. She laughed softly and pulled his head down.

They made love in the open air, on his spread-out coat. Marcus had never done anything so frivolous or improper in his life.

He didn't regret a moment of it.

Though he was very glad their driver and guide were back with the carriage beside the road.

They spent a night in Ghent, and then on to Brussels. After a couple of days exploring the beautiful old city, where Tessa came away with several lengths of the exquisite, hand-made lace for which the city was famous, they made plans to go to Waterloo the following day.

"It's about ten miles," Marcus said. "The weather is looking to be fine, so I thought we could ride there, send the carriage on with Tomas, and meet up with him at the next stop after Waterloo. What do you think?"

"Ride there, on horseback?" Tessa exclaimed. "That would be delightful. So much better than being cooped up in a stuffy carriage."

Marcus smiled. She was very easy to please. "Then I will hire some horses."

The following morning after breakfast, a groom arrived at their inn leading two rather fine horses. To Tessa's surprise, one, a dainty-looking gray, part-Arab mare, wore a side-saddle.

Marcus shrugged. "As soon as they heard one of the riders would be a lady, the stables insisted on this. They seemed rather proud to have it. I hope you don't mind. I know you wanted to ride astride, but the mare is trained for sidesaddle."

She laughed. "I don't mind. I'm just happy to be out in the open air and riding. And she looks very sweet." She offered her mare a sugar lump on her palm and the mare lipped it delicately. "Beautiful manners too," Tessa added.

Their belongings loaded into the carriage, Tomas headed off with it, and Marcus tossed Tessa up into her sidesaddle.

Once out of the city, they enjoyed a refreshing fast gallop, but after that they took things fairly slowly, enjoying the scenery—at least that's what Tessa seemed to be doing, stopping every so-often to admire this little cottage or that orchard, though he could see nothing remarkable about them at all. She took delight in all kinds of small things.

She was putting off the moment they arrived at the battlefield, Marcus decided. He didn't blame her. It was bound to stir up memories of her brother, Louis. Still, it was what she'd wanted.

They slowed their horses as they entered the village of Plancenoit, and as they passed the church he noticed the cemetery wall was pocked with holes. Musket balls, Marcus decided, hoping Tessa hadn't realized it.

"There was fighting here, wasn't there?" she said.

"Yes." They rode on in somber silence. In Brussels

he had acquired a pamphlet that had been prepared for English tourists wishing to visit the site of the great battle, and was able to direct her attention to some of the sights.

Marcus led them straight through the village of Waterloo without stopping, Tessa glanced at him with a puzzled expression. "I thought this was where the battle was."

"No, Waterloo was the village where Wellington wrote his final report from, and that's how the battle got its name, but the actual fighting was further along."

As they passed close to the village of Braine-l'Alleud, Marcus pointed to the church of Saint-Étienne. "See that church? They used that as a field hospital to treat the wounded."

She nodded, but said nothing. He glanced at her. Her eyes had sheened with unshed tears.

Next was the building that had become the hospital at Mont-Saint-Jean.

When he pointed it out, she gave him a troubled look. "I don't even know whether Louis was wounded or killed outright. Only that he went to war and never came home."

Marcus frowned. "You never received a letter?" Her brother was an officer after all. Surely someone would have sent an official notification.

She shook her head. "Edgar might have, but if

he did, he never told me. It's one of the reasons I wanted to come here. The only thing I know for certain is that Louis was at the battle of Waterloo. And never came home."

Marcus clenched his teeth and hoped the captain of the ship had decided to throw Blaxland overboard after all.

Finally, the main part of the former battlefield lay before them, a wide sward of gently rolling green grass, dotted with little white daisies and tiny wildflowers. Marcus gave a quiet sigh of relief. Nothing here too obviously distressing.

He pointed to a large elm tree. "I think that tree might have been where Wellington's command post was."

"Do you mind if we walk for a bit?" Tessa asked, and without waiting for his response, she slipped off her mount, looped the long skirt of her riding habit over her arm and began to walk slowly across the field, scanning the ground before her, as if looking for something.

Wildflowers perhaps? Or maybe just grieving for her brother.

He left her to it, not wanting to break in on her reverie and private grief.

He strolled on, leading the horses, deep into the pamphlet guide. Names of places he had only heard of, or read in English newspapers had now become unsettlingly real to him. Hougoumont, La Haie Sainte, Plancenoit, La Belle Alliance, Papelotte, the Chemin d'Ohain, the ridge on the Mont-Saint-Jean. Just names to him before; now they carried a weight of emotion, and not just for Tessa's sake.

He'd avidly followed the various reports of the battle at the time, consumed with anxiety for his brother, Gabriel, and his friends, and to some extent, his half-brother Harry from whom he was estranged.

He hadn't realized how much detail he'd absorbed.

It was hard to imagine this peaceful green scene churned up with blood and mud and the horrific sounds of battle, and men and horses screaming and the constant shattering sound of gun and cannon fire. His own brothers had fought here.

Not that they'd ever spoken of it.

It seemed to him that most soldiers—men who had known war—real war—rarely talked about what they had seen and done. Not to him, anyway.

Raised voices caused him to look up and turning, he saw Tessa had been surrounded by a small group of men and boys he had seen earlier, loitering in the distance. They clustered around her, jabbering at her in a mix of French, Flemish and broken English.

She flinched from their importunities, and Marcus hurried to intervene.

"Get them away," Tessa pleaded. "It's hideous.

They are selling people's *bones*! That's some poor boy's fingerbone!"

"*Souvenirs, madam, monsieur,*" the men insisted, holding out their 'wares'— a jumble of white bones, teeth, pieces of shrapnel, musket balls, and bits of lead, brass, bronze and rusted iron. He saw several brass buttons with the Imperial eagle grasping scattered thunderbolts, presumably from a French uniform and pieces of fabric bearing British regimental insignia. It was a grotesque collection.

Cursing himself for not paying closer attention, Marcus chased them off with a mixture of French and English and some threatening gestures.

"Are you all right?" he asked her, pulling her close. She was shaking.

"Y, yes. I'm all right," she stammered, leaning into him "I just didn't expect it, that's all."

After a few moments she recovered and they walked on a little, their horses trailing behind them, cropping occasionally at the grass. "Why would they imagine I'd want to buy such gruesome things?" She shuddered.

"People do, I'm afraid," he said gently. "It's nasty, I know, but I suppose it's one way to make a living."

She shuddered again. "That could have been L–L–Louis's finger bone." And tears spilled from her eyes. "S–s–sorry," she began, trying to scrub the tears away, but he just drew her into his arms and held her. "It's all right," he murmured. "Let it out."

His soft words released a torrent of tears. He held her for a long time, until the raw sobs slowed and juddery breaths took their place. Eventually she stepped away. "I'm sorry," she began again.

"Don't be. I think you needed it." He handed her a handkerchief. She took it, wiping her eyes and staring at him as if bemused. After a few minutes, calmer but still a little shaky, she tucked her arm in his and resumed her slow examination of the ground.

"Those horrid men are still hovering, aren't they?" she said.

Marcus glanced back and nodded. "To be fair, the way you've been examining the ground, they probably think you're looking for some kind of souvenir."

She looked up at him in dismay. "But I'm not! Of course I'm not!"

"What were you looking for then? Wildflowers?"

"No, somewhere to plant these." She pulled a small bag from the pocket she'd had made in her riding habit and tipped the contents onto her palm.

Marcus frowned. "Acorns? And. . . bulbs?"

She nodded. "English acorns and bluebells. I was looking for a good place to plant them. Somewhere where they won't be dug up by farmers—or horrid scavengers." She continued scanning their surroundings, and explained, "When he was a boy, Louis loved to climb into the biggest of the oak trees at Ferndale. He'd sit there for hours, just thinking and dreaming and listening to the birds chattering. And he used to pick a big bunch of bluebells every spring and give them to my mother."

She paused and glanced up at Marcus. "That was before I was born, of course. NannyJune told me about it. Mama loved bluebells too. So I want Louis to have a little piece of England, here in this foreign field where he died."

"I see. It's a nice idea." He glanced around. "What about over there, where there seems to be a natural border between fields? Less likely to be ploughed."

Yes." She headed over there, then glanced back at the souvenir sellers, who were watching her avidly. "I suppose they'll imagine I've found some horrid souvenir. I don't want these dug up." She thought for a minute. "Pretend I am relieving myself, will you? They won't want to dig *that* up."

Her back to the observers, she squatted down, spreading her skirts carefully, and Marcus, quietly amused by her practicality, drew the horses closer and tried to look as if he was protecting his lady's modesty.

She drew out a small trowel, dug a hole in the ground and placed an acorn in it, then covered it over. Then she made a small ditch and surrounded the acorn with half a dozen bluebell bulbs. She filled in the holes and stood, pressing down the dirt. "We brought water, didn't we?" she asked.

Marcus pulled a flask of water from his saddle bag and handed it over.

"Now, move out of the way," she said. "I want them to see this." She proceeded to wash her hands, being careful to ensure the water fell on the disturbed earth, giving the acorns and bulbs a start in life.

She dried her hands and as she handed the bottle back, gave him a mischievous smile. "They won't want to disturb that now."

Twice more she found a place to plant an acorn and some bluebells.

The men were still watching. "They'll be suspicious now," Marcus commented.

"No, they'll think I have a weak English bladder."

He laughed and she slipped her arm through his, smiling up at him. "Thank you for this. You don't know how much it means to me. I've never had a grave to leave flowers on—Edgar wouldn't even organize a proper funeral service for him—so planting a tree or two and some bluebells in his memory has been immensely comforting."

Not to mention the outpouring of grief that had briefly overwhelmed her. He bent, cupped her chin and kissed her. "I'm glad. Now, have you finished here?"

She nodded. "Yes, I've done what I came for." She glanced across to where the men with the gruesome 'souvenirs' had approached several other visitors. "I don't want to spend another minute in this unhappy place."

"Very well." He tossed her into her sidesaddle, mounted his horse and side by side they headed south.

CHAPTER SIXTEEN

THEY LET THEIR horses amble along for a while. They were in no hurry. There was plenty of time to get to the town where Tomas and their carriage would be meeting them.

Tessa was lost in a reverie, but she seemed lighter, somehow, as if visiting the scene of the battle and planting her acorns and bluebells had lifted some weight off her shoulders.

"I'm sorry for crying all over you," she said after a while. "But thank you for letting me. For some reason it has made me feel better—that and planting the acorns and bluebells. I didn't really ever get to mourn Louis. I was married by then, and . . . well,"— she grimaced—"I wasn't allowed. It wasn't appropriate."

He gave her a sharp glance. "Not appropriate? To mourn your own brother."

Looking straight ahead, she said in a peevish

tone, "Must you do that, woman? The noise is bad enough, but tears make you look hellish ugly, demmit! I didn't marry you to look ugly." It was clearly a quote.

One of her damned husbands, he thought grimly. He didn't even try to work out which. He despised them both.

"So I stopped. Bottled it up." She glanced at him. "But all that's in the past. With you, it's different." She was silent a moment then added, "I feel . . . seen."

"Seen? What do you mean?"

"Oh, just that both my husbands liked my looks, but not who I was. They preferred me to be like. . . like a doll. No opinions, no thoughts except ones related to them. And when they went out it was as if they had placed me on a shelf, to only be useful or even active unless they were present."

"Their loss," was all Marcus said, but underneath he was boiling at the thought that the lively and spirited little girl he'd once known had been treated like a doll.

"But today, when I was weeping for Louis and all those other poor boys and men killed in the battle, you didn't seem to mind how it made me look. You just held me and let me cry as long as I wanted to."

"Well of course I did." She didn't need to know how helpless it made him feel, not to be able to do anything except hold her as she wept. And give her a handkerchief.

"It was exactly what I needed. You didn't reproach me or even hurry me." She gave a little laugh and wiped away another couple of tears. "Sorry to be so melancholy. It's all water under the bridge now."

They rode on, rounded the curve of a small hill and saw below them a village. Barely deserving of the name, it was just a few scattered houses down a narrow dusty lane, off the road on which they were traveling. The village looked deserted, but the road looked cool and shady, lined with trees, and they could see the glint of water from a small stream.

"Oh look, a stream," she said. "Could we go down there? Water the horses?"

"Of course."

"Race you," Tessa said and urged her horse forward.

Marcus let her lead at first, but he soon caught up. As he passed her, he heard her laugh, and his heart swelled. She really was feeling better after visiting the battlefield. As if a weight had been lifted.

By the time they were approaching the village, he was ahead by several lengths. A slight curve of the road into the village, and there was movement ahead. A toddler emerged from a tangle of weeds and stopped, right in the center of the narrow road.

Tessa saw the child at the same time as Marcus. She

screamed a warning, but he was moving too quickly and was unable to stop in time. In desperation he urged his mount to leap over the little creature—who seemed frozen. To his relief the horse jumped. Wrenching his horse to a halt, he flung himself out of the saddle and raced back to check on the child, praying that it was unhurt.

Tessa, who had stopped in time, was crouched beside a ragged little toddler. Who made no sound.

"Is he all right?" he gasped. "I didn't hit him, did I?" He could see no blood but that didn't mean anything. "I tried not to hit him, but he just burst from the undergrowth, right in my horse's path."

"*She* seems to be unhurt," Tessa said.

"She?"

"She's a little girl."

The child turned her head and looked up at Marcus. She still hadn't made a sound. She was trembling a little but not crying. He crouched down beside her. "Are you all right?" he asked gently in French.

She just looked up at him curiously. Maybe she was in shock. Maybe she didn't know French, and only spoke Flemish or whatever dialect they spoke in this place. He looked around, and still the place seemed deserted.

He tried again, but again she said nothing.

"Do you think she's in shock?" Marcus said.

"I don't know. She doesn't seem very upset, poor little mite." She gently stroked the child's dirty face. "Are you, *p'tite*?"

As if to prove Tessa's words, the child held up the ragged bunch of wildflowers clutched in her grubby fist and offered them to Tessa with a small hesitant smile.

"*Merci, p'tite,*" Tessa said in halting French. "*Les fleurs sont très jolies.*"

The little girl's smile widened.

"Thank God," Marcus muttered to himself. She understood. And was all right.

He breathed out several slow deep breaths. He could have killed her, but she was all right.

But who did she belong to? He looked around again. The village was barely worth the name, just a straggle of run-down houses and what looked like a blacksmith's forge, also looking the worse for wear.

They'd probably had several armies run over them.

But smoke came from one of the chimneys and a dog was tied up outside the smith's premises. So where were the people? The child's mother?

They'd made something of a dramatic entrance; the thunder of hooves alone should have been noticed, let alone Tessa's desperate scream, but nobody had come to investigate.

"She's terribly neglected, Marcus," Tessa

murmured. He looked. The little girl was skinny and dressed—if you could call it dressed—in a few filthy and inadequate rags; barefoot, bare-legged and bare-bottomed. Her hair was a dusty indeterminate color, matted and with dead leaves and clumps of various unknown substances caught in it.

She looked from him to Tessa and back again, with wide, bright blue eyes shining from the dirty face.

She didn't seem distressed at all, but still hadn't spoken. Why? She was very small. Did children of that age even speak? When did children learn to speak? He had no idea.

As if she'd heard his unspoken question, the little girl touched the ragged flowers that Tessa held and said, "*Fleurs.*"

He gave another sigh of relief.

"Is she hurt?" a voice said behind them. It was a woman of about his own age. Her face thin and careworn, she was clad in a faded blue, threadbare dress.

"Are you the mother?" Marcus asked.

She shook her head. "The mother died weeks ago, God rest her soul." She crossed herself.

"Then who is responsible for the child?"

The woman hesitated, then pointed to the smithy. "It should be him, but. . ." She pulled a face and shrugged. "I would have taken her in, but I have my own brood to feed." She gestured behind her. A gaggle of small faces peered from the door of one of the cottages.

As he watched, a boy of about ten or eleven detached himself from the group and caught the reins of their horses, who were lazily cropping grass. In silent gestures, he asked whether he could take the horses to the stream.

"My son," the woman said. "He is a good boy."

Marcus nodded his assent and the boy led the horses toward the stream. Marcus returned his attention to the child. She was barely more than a baby. How could anyone let her get into a state like this? And wander about unsupervised.

The woman followed his gaze and added with dignity, "I am a widow, m'sieur. My husband died fighting for the Emperor. I help this little one when I can, but when my own children are going hungry. . ." She gave another fatalistic shrug.

Marcus nodded. "I'll speak to the smithy," he told Tessa. Will you be all right here?"

"Of course."

The smithy was dusty and unlike the one in his home village, it was untidy and looked neglected, with tools dropped where they fell. There was no sign of life. He called out, but nobody answered. Yet the forge was still warm and he could see faintly glowing coals inside.

He called again, and heard a grunt inside. He followed it through a door and found a man of fifty or more, disheveled, unshaven and dirty, sitting on a chair. On the table beside him was a board with cheese, half a loaf, a bowl of olives and a tumbler of wine.

The man gave him a hostile look and swilled a mouthful of wine around his mouth before swallowing. He made no attempt to get up. He merely eyed Marcus with a baleful expression.

"You are the smith?" Marcus said, hoping the man spoke French.

The man lifted his shoulder slightly, which Marcus took to be assent.

"I understand you are responsible for that little girl outside."

The man spat. "Not my blood, not my responsibility." His accent was thick, but understandable. A native Flemish speaker, no doubt.

Marcus held his temper. "Then whose is she?"

The smith shrugged, as if to say, 'who cares?'

"The woman outside said she was yours," Marcus persisted.

The smith gave him a long look, drained his glass and said, "My son, he go off to fight for l'Emperor"—he spat again, seeming not to care that it was his own floor, albeit filthy. "He bring back a woman—a wife, or so he say. A foreigner. From Avignon." He snorted.

"Then l'Emperor returns and the fighting starts again." He gestured in the rough direction of Waterloo. He shrugged. "My son never come home. "His woman go looking for him, but instead she come back with a wounded man. An English aristo!" He spat perilously close to Marcus's boot. "An officer." He spat again.

"And so?" Marcus prompted grimly

"She look after him. He get better. He go back to Angleterre." He spat again. Much more and he could mop his floor with it, Marcus thought.

"Two weeks later she tell me she have a bellyful." He pointed outside. "With that."

"Then the child is your respons—" Marcus began.

"Not my blood, not my problem!" the man snarled again.

"She's filthy and neglected and starving to death."

The smith gave him an insolent look. "Is in the good lord's hands." His tone was mocking. "When the priest come he can take the brat, give her to the sisters to raise. In the meantime. . ." He gave an evil smile. "She sleep with the dog."

Marcus's fists were tight knots of rage, but he wasn't going to let this sorry excuse for a man to provoke him. "Very well then," he snapped and strode out the door.

Tessa was holding the child on her hip. She had twisted the ragged bunch of flowers into a little tiara and placed it on the matted curls.

"M'sieur, he claims he will give the child to the next priest that visits, to be raised by the sisters," the shabby woman told him in a low voice. "But there has been no priest here for over a year and the Abbey at Nivelles was destroyed during the revolution, more than twenty years ago. Who knows what happened to the sisters?"

He nodded, pressed an unobtrusive handful of coins into her hand, and signaled the boy to bring the horses.

She looked at the coins in her hands and gasped. "Gold Louis? Mais m'sieur. . ." she began.

"You did what you could," he said brusquely. "Look after your children."

She pocketed the money, her eyes filled with tears. "Bless you, m'sieur, God bless you."

He turned to Tessa. "We're leaving," he said curtly.

Tessa gaped at him. "But what about this little one?"

He held out his arms. "Give her to me."

Her eyes riddled with doubt, she handed the child over. "But—"

"Mount up," he said. The boy held her horse still so she could mount, and Marcus flipped him a coin. The lad caught it, glanced at it and grinned. "Merci m'sieur."

Tessa gave Marcus an unhappy look but, seeming to realize his temper was on a knife-edge, obeyed. With one hand he boosted her into the sidesaddle, the little girl clasped against his body with the other. "Now take the child." He held her up and Tessa settled her onto her lap.

"Eh, what you doing, Englishman?" There was a spate of swearing from the door of the smithy. Marcus ignored it.

The smith staggered out toward them. "You can't take that child."

"Not your blood, not your problem," Marcus said in an icy voice.

The smith spluttered for a minute, then a cunning expression spread over his face. "You can have her for ten gold Louis."

Marcus ignored him.

"Five then," the man shouted.

Marcus inclined his head to the woman. "Get yourself and your children to safety, madame. Ride on, Tessa." He swung up onto his own horse and they rode out of the village together, the little girl clasped, wide-eyed but otherwise unperturbed, in Tessa's arms.

"Filthy thieving Anglais!" the smith shouted after them.

As they reached a bend in the road, Marcus glanced back and was glad to see the woman and her children had vanished into their cottage. The smith stood swaying in the middle of the road, shaking his fist and roaring with frustration.

They ambled along at a steady walk. Any faster and little girl's head would have jiggled on her skinny little neck. Besides, they weren't in a hurry. She seemed quite content to be sitting on Tessa's lap, gazing all around her with bright-eyed interest and occasionally glancing up at Tessa as if in reassurance. After a little while the child relaxed and wriggled back to lean into Tessa's arms as if perfectly content to be there.

And oh, the feeling of holding the small, warm body in her arms. Tessa had never held a small child before, had never had the chance, and the feeling was indescribable. The trust, the acceptance. The surge of protectiveness she felt.

After so many years failing to conceive, she'd thought she'd learned to accept her barrenness, but now all the yearning for a child of her own returned.

From time to time, she felt Marcus's gaze upon

her. "All right?" he asked, one time when she'd noticed him watching her.

"Perfect," she said. "I think she's enjoying herself." It was remarkable how quickly the child had adapted to being on horseback, how quickly she'd accepted being held by Tessa.

Marcus reached into his saddlebag and drew out a wrapped parcel. "Leftover bread and cheese," he said. "A bit stale, but she won't mind that." He passed a slice of bread and a piece of cheese to Tessa who gave it to the little girl.

She sniffed each cautiously, then fell to chewing with a blissful expression. Marcus waited until she'd finished, then passed Tessa a water flask. "She'll be thirsty too."

She drank the water thirstily. "Is there any more food?" Tessa asked. "I think she's still hungry."

"A bit, but who knows when she last ate. She'll be sick if she eats too much too fast. It had better be small meals and often until she becomes used to not feeling hungry."

They rode on. The further they got from the village, the more Tessa began to worry. What would become of this little scrap? It was all very well to have rescued her from the dreadful situation they'd found her in, but what now? She held the child close as they moved along. A convent with nuns?

If there were any convents and nuns left after the revolution.

An hour or two out of the village, a brisk breeze sprang up. The little girl snuggled closer to Tessa. Goosebumps formed on her skinny little arms and legs. "Marcus," Tessa said, "she's getting cold."

Marcus glanced across at her. The little one was shivering. Those rags were totally inadequate. And Tessa's fashionable riding habit was designed to closely fit her slenderness. His coat was not so tight. "Pass her over." He unbuttoned his coat, moved his horse closer and held out his arms.

The child stared at him in faint suspicion and clung to Tessa. "It's all right," Tessa said softly. "Go to Marcus."

But of course the child spoke no English.

"Come here little one," he said in French, hoping she could understand. If her mother was from Avignon, she might have spoken French rather than Flemish to the little girl. "I'll keep you warm."

With some reluctance the child allowed Tessa to unclench her fingers and pass her over to Marcus. He tucked her into his coat, and did up several buttons, supporting her on his arm.

"See?" He told her. "Like a nest. Warmer."

The big eyes gazed back at him. Her little body was stiff and tense at first, but after a while she slowly relaxed against him. He felt small, cold fingers wriggling between the fastenings of his shirt and then her palm pressed against his skin. She gave a big sigh and relaxed more fully against him. Trusting him to keep her safe.

He swallowed a lump in his throat and silently vowed that he would. Poor little scrap.

They continued steadily on their way. From time to time. he peered inside his coat to check how she was traveling. Each time those bright eyes blinked back at him, like a little bird, but an hour later he saw she'd nodded off, her small body warm and relaxed against him.

"She's asleep," he said quietly.

"Oh, good," Tessa said.

They rode on in silence, Marcus deep in thought.

After a while, Tessa said, "What are we going to do with her, Marcus? Do you plan to give her to the nuns—assuming we can find some."

He glanced at her. "Hmm? I was just wondering, what did Louis look like?"

She blinked at the abrupt change of subject. "A lot like Edgar, only with kinder eyes."

"So, blond with blue eyes?"

"Yes. But why—"

"And he was an officer, wasn't he?"

"Yes, a lieutenant. But what does that have to do with anything?"

He paused for a minute, then said, "What would you like to do with the child?"

"Keep her," she said immediately. No hesitation, and said with a faint air of defiance.

"Good," he said mildly. "Because that's what I was thinking, too. Raise her as our own."

"You did?" She stared at him. "Keep her? Really? That's wonderful. But, but you're an earl."

His mouth twitched. "I know."

"I mean, yours is an ancient, well respected family. With blue blood."

He smiled. "Everyone's blood is red, Tessa—prince or peasant."

"Well, I know that, but if we arrive back in England with a child of this age, people will talk."

"Let them. People will talk anyway, no matter what the provocation. We'll let it be thought that she's Louis's child, your niece. Orphaned. But we'll raise her as our daughter."

"Really? You would do that? As our daughter?" Her voice was husky. He glanced at her. Her eyes shimmered with unshed tears.

They rode on a little. "If you'd already planned to keep her, why did you ask me what I wanted to do? What if I'd said no? Some women would be offended at the suggestion they take in a dirty little foreign urchin to raise."

He shot her an amused look. "Those women

didn't spend their childhood watching over fox kitts and otter pups and badgers."

"Yes, but what would you have done if I had refused to take her in?"

Again he lifted a shoulder. "Place her with a kind childless couple on one of my estates, I suppose. But we won't, will we, Blossom?" he added, glancing into his coat. "We're keeping you."

As he spoke, she woke, stretched, and began to wriggle. "Pipi, pipi!" she said urgently.

Her second word, and he had no idea what she meant.

She continued to struggle, pushing at his coat as if trying to get out.

"Pipi?" he repeated to Tessa with a bemused look.

"Does she want to relieve herself?" she suggested.

"Oh. Right. Come on, Blossom, let's pop you down." Keeping her firmly in his embrace, Marcus swung down from his horse and set her on the side of the road. She took two steps into the grass, then squatted down and relieved herself.

"What a good girl," Tessa said in a warmly congratulatory tone.

Marcus glanced at her, bemused. "Why? It's a natural process."

Tessa grinned. "Yes, but she could have done it all over you. She's very young, after all."

"Oh." Marcus blinked. "Yes, right, good girl, Blossom. *Very* good girl."

The child, having finished, jiggled her bottom, then held up her arms to be picked up. Gingerly, Marcus lifted her and passed her to Tessa who, laughing, took the child from him.

He mounted, Tessa passed her back, and Marcus settled her again in his coat, shutting his mind to any potential dampness. It could have been much worse, he told himself.

"At least we know she can speak—that's two words now," he remarked as they set off again.

Twilight was falling and they were still a good distance from Genappe where they'd arranged to meet Tomas and their carriage. "Let's see if we can find an auberge or an inn in the next village—somewhere to spend the night," Marcus said. "This little one is tired, and I think you are too. And I don't want to travel in the dark—after years of war, poverty will be rife here, and we don't want to become a target for desperate people."

Tessa nodded wearily. She was indeed tired. It had been a very emotional day; first visiting the site of the battle where her brother had died, then encountering the ghoulish souvenir sellers, and then letting go the grief she'd bottled up for so long. And finally, the drama of finding the neglected little girl. As well, it had been a long time since she had spent almost an entire day in the saddle. Her back ached and her spine wanted to droop.

Luckily at the next village, they found a small inn, shabby but clean looking. The outside area had been swept clean and there were pots of bright geraniums on either side of the door.

"Wait here. I'll enquire within," Marcus said and dismounted, the child still snuggled under his coat.

He came back a few minutes later with a motherly-looking woman and a young boy of around ten or eleven, who swiftly moved to the horses' heads. Tessa dismounted in a weary slide, and the woman, clucking sympathetically, hurried to usher her inside and up the stairs to a small but clean bedchamber—just a large bed, a small table, a wooden settle and a row of pegs behind the door on which to hang clothes.

Marcus gave the landlady a string of orders in French, and when she'd hurried away, he explained, "I asked her for a bath, hot water, and food, including bread and some milk. Is there anything else we'll need?"

She shook her head. "I don't know. I've never had much to do with babies. I suppose we'll learn as we go along."

In a short time a sturdy young girl of about sixteen

arrived with a tin bath in one hand and a large can of hot water in the other. She dumped them in front of the fireplace, swiftly bent to light the fire, which had already been set, and hurried away, explaining she'd bring more water and soap for madame shortly, and that Tante Jeanne would bring food up soon. And that her name was Clothilde.

Marcus still had the child bundled in his coat. The bulge had been given a few odd glances, but nobody had asked.

Once the extra hot water and soap had arrived, and Clothilde had left, Marcus unwrapped the little girl. "Is that water hot enough?" he asked Tessa.

"It's not terribly hot, but I think that's a good thing for babies," she said, swishing the soap around to make some suds.

"Let's get her in, then."

It took a few minutes to strip the noisome rags from her, almost glued on to her skinny little body. Some they had to dampen to loosen. She was so thin her ribs stuck out.

"Poor little plucked chicken," Marcus muttered.

He gently slipped the little girl into the bath, and she reacted with initial anxiety and then, after a minute, with cautious pleasure, dipping her fingers into the warm water and trying to catch the soap suds. Tessa soaped the little body thoroughly and the dirt came off in streams.

Her hair, though was another matter—matted with knots and leaves and God-only-knew-what caught in it. After unsuccessfully trying to ease some of the tangles out—much to the displeasure of the little girl who wriggled and resisted—Tessa sat back on her heels and shook her head. "I don't know how we're going to clean her hair."

"Just cut it all off," Marcus said. He produced a knife and began to slice off clumps of hair, not an easy matter, as the child wriggled and squirmed.

Tessa tried to distract her by playing "pat-a-cake" which only bewildered the child, and then 'splash' to which she caught on quickly. Soon Tessa, laughing, was damp from head to foot with dirty water.

"I'll need a bath too after this,"

In the meantime, clump by clump, strand by strand, Marcus carefully cut the matted hair from the little girl, tossing each bit in the fire as he went. It hissed and then as it dried, shriveled and burned. The room filled with the smell of burning hair, but soon it was done.

Tessa stood her up in the bath and Marcus carefully rinsed the child using the last can of water.

"She really does look like a plucked chicken, but at least now she's a clean one," Tessa commented, as she lifted the child out and wrapped her in a drying cloth.

"That hair," Marcus said thoughtfully, "is going to be very blonde when it dries—as blonde as yours."

Tessa gave an absent nod. What did it matter what color her hair was? She was going to be their daughter. A daughter! For years she'd prayed for a child, and now, she had one, a child who needed her, needed them desperately. Needed love and care and a home. And a family.

Just what Tessa needed too.

And oh, she had so much love to give. She gave her a gentle hug, kissed her, carried her to the hard little bench and settled her into her lap. The little girl gazed up at her, bemused.

"That's better isn't it, Blossom?" Marcus said, gently running his fingers through the ragged remains of her hair.

"Is that what you want to call her," Tessa asked. "Blossom?"

He shook his head. "I hadn't actually thought of it as a name, but we do need to call her something other than 'the child.' The blacksmith never told me her name. Or her mother's. You don't like Blossom as a name?"

"Not really. It's all right as a term of endearment, but as a proper name, people will think it's odd," she added, jiggling the little girl on her knee. "And having been christened Theodosia I know what it's like to have a peculiar name. Why Blossom?"

He shrugged. "I hadn't really thought about it. Possibly because she was clutching some flowers when we first saw her."

"Then how about Flora?" she suggested.

"Flora, Flora," he repeated. "Yes, I like it. It suits her, doesn't it Flora?" he added to the little girl. She smiled up at him. "And see, she likes it, too."

Tessa laughed. "She has no idea what you said."

"But she likes it anyway," he said firmly.

A knock at the door signaled the arrival of two boys, who lugged out the bath and dirty water, followed a few minutes later by the landlady. She was carrying a tray filled with two bowls of delicious-smelling stew. "*Lapin*" she explained.

"Rabbit," Marcus translated. As well, there was half a loaf of bread, some cheese, half a bottle of wine and a cup of milk.

Noticing the child, she beamed, threw up her hands, and turned to Marcus with a flow of French. He responded, and they had quite an exchange. Not for the first time, Tessa wished she understood French. Finally, the landlady gave a brisk nod, Marcus handed her some money, and she hurried away.

"She's going to bring us some food suitable for a baby," he said, "and she's sending Clothilde to fetch clothes for Bl—for Flora. I told her our baggage was lost, and though you and I can manage until we get to Genappe, we need things for the baby."

"Oh, that was clever," she said. "I hope Clothilde knows what she will need."

He snorted. "She can't know less than we do, at any rate. Now, eat your food while it's hot." He dipped a crust of bread in his stew, blew on it, then gave it to Flora to gnaw on while they ate.

A few minutes later the landlady returned with a soft-boiled egg for Flora. Without asking, she took the baby from Tessa, and sat down to feed her, clucking and making soft motherly sounds.

Flora ate greedily, much to the woman's delight. She kept up a stream of conversation, which Marcus tried to follow and respond to, in between mouthfuls.

CHAPTER SEVENTEEN

ONCE THEIR LANDLADY had collected their dishes and left, they sat in the quiet, the only sound the muted crackling of the fire and the wind in the trees outside. It was beautifully peaceful, Tessa thought. Flora, clean and well fed, was snuggled sleepily on her lap. Her precious new daughter. Tessa could hardly believe it.

Marcus was sipping wine and staring into the flames, seemingly deep in thought.

Tessa broke the silence. "How are we going to explain Flora when we go back to England?" The question had been nagging at her ever since they'd decided to keep her. It was one thing for Marcus just to announce it, but he was an earl and used to everyone obeying him without question.

But arriving with a toddler out of the blue would be bound to cause gossip and speculation. She didn't care about her own reputation—that was lost long ago—and Flora was too young to care. But when it came time for her to marry, things would not be so easy. *Ton* families were very particular about who they admitted into their ranks, whose blood they allowed to mingle with theirs.

Of course, all that was a long way off, but still, it needed to be considered.

"I've been pondering that very question." Marcus set his glass of wine aside. "That blacksmith said this little one's father was an aristo, an officer—an *English* officer."

"Yes. What are you getting at?"

"Louis was an English aristo and an officer. And this wee one has the same coloring at Louis."

"Yes. but . . . You can't possibly be imagining that Louis was her father? He died at Waterloo, long before this little girl was conceived."

He nodded. "I know that. But how many others do?"

She frowned. "Marcus, what are you suggesting?"

"What if your brother didn't die at Waterloo, but crawled off somewhere, wounded with a head injury. He was taken in by a Frenchwoman who cared for him until he was back to health, but unable to recall his name or anything else. In gratitude, he married her, and they had a child."

"It's a fairy tale. Who would possibly believe it? And then what? We found her by accident?"

"No, we sought out the child. Louis died after

she was conceived—perhaps a piece of shrapnel migrated to his heart or brain or something. It does that sometimes, I'm told. But it doesn't matter what he died of—we'll keep it vague. It would be speculation on our part anyway."

Tessa nodded. She could see how that might be plausible. "It's not too far from what we know about how Flora."

He continued, "Just before Louis died, he got his memory back and wrote to you, to let you know he was alive. But he died before he could send it. His widow forwarded it with the news of his death scrawled on the outside, but it was addressed to Edgar, who never told you."

"Anyone who knew Edgar would easily believe that," she agreed. "But after he left for America, we found the letter."

"Exactly. So you received the letter—you hardly know anyone in society so nobody can say you didn't—which is why we decided to visit Waterloo on our honeymoon, not only to visit the battlefield where your brother was so gravely wounded, but to enquire after his widow."

She nodded slowly. "That would work."

"Only when we went looking for Louis's widow it was to discover that she had recently died, and little Flora was an orphan. Naturally we would take in your niece."

She thought about it for a minute or two. "It sounds all right, but will we need to explain that to everyone? I'm not very good at lying. I go bright red whenever I try."

He gave a slight smile. "We won't have to explain it at all. I will share a few salient snippets of the story with people like my aunt, and my friend Barney, both of whom are inveterate gossips. They will do the rest, all unwitting. Soon there will be a dozen different versions circulating in the *ton*, and we will not deign to even discuss it. All you would ever need to say—and only if someone were ill-mannered to ask intrusive questions—is '*We are raising Flora as our daughter.*' Do you think you could do that?"

She nodded eagerly. "I could. That would be perfect."

"It will help matters that Flora also has blue eyes and blonde hair, like you."

Tessa blinked. She hadn't thought of that. "Oh, that's why you were talking about her hair. Yes, and her eyes are very blue, like Louis'." She thought for a minute. "Could we call her Flora *Louise*, after my brother?"

"An excellent suggestion." He picked up his wine and drained the glass. "A good thing he wasn't the brother called Edgar—Flora Edgarina or Edgarella would be quite a mouthful."

She laughed. It was all happening, she thought.

Becoming real. It was a good story—close enough to the truth for it not to feel much like a lie. And Flora would have a home with people who loved and would care for her.

And Tessa would have what she'd always wanted: a child to love. A family. And a home, even if it wasn't Ferndale.

A knock on the door signaled the arrival of Clothilde with an armful of small clothes in a large willow basket behind her. "Nothing new, I'm afraid m'sieur," she explained to Marcus. "The basket is for the little one to sleep in. I hope that is all right."

When Marcus translated, Tessa hesitated. Clothilde, seeing her doubt, added hastily, "Everything is very clean, I promise you, madame. And nobody will be deprived—in fact they were grateful for the money."

"But won't they need these for their own children? Tessa asked.

Clothilde dumped the basket with the pile of clothing onto the bed, and shook her head. "Non, madame. There will be no babies born in this village now, not until the children grow up." She added softly, with a matter-of-fact gesture, "No husbands or unmarried young men left in this village, madame. Only boys and old men. The war, you understand."

Tessa bit her lip.

Clothilde placed the basket on the bed. "Choose whatever you want, madame. The women need the money."

Tessa handed Flora to Marcus and came to examine them. Most of the tiny garments were mended and some were patched, but every one of them was clean and sweet smelling, of lavender, or soap and sunshine, and washed so often the fabric was downy soft.

She imagined each mother sorting through the small garments, deciding which ones she could spare, and realizing perhaps that the next time they would be needed it would be for a grandchild. And they needed the money now.

She picked one of the little garments up. It looked like a christening gown, beautifully embroidered, white on white. There were no patches, no trace of any mending. The fabric was fine, and though soft, it felt. . . new?

She turned to Clothilde, a question in her eyes.

The girl dropped her gaze and said quietly, "Never used, madame. Her baby died."

Tessa needed no translation to understand that. She felt her eyes fill, and, blinking, turned quickly away. "If you're sure the women want to sell these?" Clothilde nodded. "Then we'll take them all."

The girl beamed at her. "Merci, madame. It will make a big difference to their lives. The living must be fed and clothed, after all. Now, shall we put the little miss in this one?" She selected a tiny nightdress and passed it to Tessa.

With some difficulty, Tessa managed to get Flora into it. Clearly, she preferred being naked, and wrapped in just a towel, riding high in Marcus's arms.

Next Clothilde passed Tessa a large square of well-washed flannel. Bemused, Tessa accepted it. What was it for?

The girl, recognizing her uncertainty, said, "For the little one. For bed. So she doesn't wet it."

"Oh, a napkin. Yes." Wondering how to fasten the thing, Tessa tried to tuck it under the little girl on her lap. Flora resisted, kicking the cloth away.

"You permit, madame?" Clothilde said, trying to hide a smile.

"Yes please." Tessa handed the child over.

Clothilde laid the cloth on the bed, placed Flora on it, briskly flipped the nightdress up and began to fasten the napkin around her nether quarters. Flora resisted mightily, arching her back, squirming and thrashing her little legs, doing her best to avoid being imprisoned by the evil cloth. "Non!" she said. "Non!"

"Her third word," Marcus commented, amused. He leaned over Clothilde, caught the baby's eye and said firmly. "Oui!"

"Non!"

"Oui!"

"Non!" Flora glared up at him.

Marcus scowled down at her. "Oui!"

She scowled back at him. "Non!"

Tessa, seeing the two almost identical expressions on man and baby, began to laugh. The sound distracted Flora, who paused in her struggles as she glanced across at Tessa. In a flash, Clothilde had the cloth wrapped around her bottom and between her legs and knotted it firmly.

The little girl tried to unfasten it, but Clothilde knew her business. She stood back, smiling. Flora scowled.

"You're a stubborn little creature, aren't you?" Marcus told the little girl. He scooped her up into the air. "You're going to be the devil of a lot of trouble when you're older, aren't you?"

Tessa laughed.

Flora stared down at him, frowning and puzzled, her little legs dangling. He tossed her up in the air and caught her. Her eyes widened, then a peal of baby laughter came from her. "Encore!" she demanded. "Encore!"

"And thus she adds a fourth word to her vocabulary," Marcus commented, and tossed and caught the little girl again.

Tessa laughed again. It was a delightful surprise

seeing Marcus so at ease with the little one. She'd half expected him to be awkward, but she was obviously the inexperienced one.

"You have nieces or nephews, don't you?" she said.

"Yes. Both." He tossed Flora up one more time, and set her down beside Tessa, saying, "That's enough, young lady. Much more and you'll throw up that nice egg you had for your dinner."

Flora frowned, clearly wanting to understand the words, though she snuggled against Tessa contentedly enough. Clearly she'd forgotten about the hated napkin.

"Madame?" Clothilde hovered. "Would you like me to put the little one to bed?"

When Marcus explained, Tessa shook her head. "No thank you, Clothilde. I'd prefer to do that myself." Her first night with her new daughter. She was going to savor every moment.

"Merci, Clothilde," Marcus said in clear dismissal.

Clothilde turned toward the door, hesitated, and turned back, twisting her hands in her apron. She opened her mouth as if to say something, then closed it, half turned away, then, with a determined expression, turned back to face them.

Tessa nudged Marcus.

"Is there something else?" he asked the girl.

She swallowed. "Monsieur, you said you had lost

all the baby's clothes. Did you lose her nursemaid as well?"

He glanced at Tessa, made a quick translation, then said to the maid, "Why do you ask?"

"Because if you did lose her, then . . . what about me?"

"You mean hire you as our nursemaid?"

She nodded eagerly. "I would work hard for you and madame, m'sieur. And as you saw, I am good with little ones."

"What about your aunt? What would she say to such an arrangement?"

"Tante Jeanne is not really my aunt. She was my mother's friend and after Maman died, she took me in. Papa and both my brothers had perished in the wars and I was young and alone." Marcus hesitated and she added eagerly, "Tante Jeanne will probably be glad of one less mouth to feed. We don't get many guests here. It is hard to make a living, and she has other children to help her—her own children."

Marcus explained it to Tessa, who had been listening, frustrated at not understanding. "Does she realize we will be living in England?" Tessa said in a low voice.

Marcus turned to the girl. "We're going back to England. What would you do then?"

"Go with you, of course."

His brows rose. "Even though your country has been at war with England for years?"

She snorted. "War does not belong to women, m'sieur. Men make war. Women are left to pick up the pieces, care for the children and try to go on." She added with a mischievous look. "I might even marry an Englishman one day. Enemy or not, under their uniforms men are all the same."

Marcus explained to Tessa, who hid a smile. They would need a nursemaid to help with Flora, and this girl had already proved herself capable and willing. And had initiative. Besides, Tessa liked her.

"You don't speak English," Marcus said. "How will you manage?"

Clothilde shrugged. "I learn fast." She twisted her apron into a tight coil and eyed them anxiously. "So m'sieur, madame, will you give me a chance?"

Tessa might not speak the language, but she understood the question. She nodded, smiling. "Yes, of course. *Oui,* Clothilde."

"As long as your aunt agrees," Marcus added.

"Oh, she will, I know," the girl answered excitedly. "Merci, madame, m'sieur. Merci." She bobbed a hasty curtsy and almost skipped out.

Breakfast next morning was porridge all round, thick and hearty, with creamy milk. But first Flora needed to be introduced to a chamber pot. Tessa sat her on it. Flora tried to get off it.

"Non," Tessa said firmly and put her back, holding her gently with a firm hand. The little girl looked confused.

"Pipi." Tessa said. "Pipi."

After a moment a small trickle of liquid was heard.

"Good girl," Tessa told her warmly. "Very good girl." And from the expression on Flora's face, she was starting to understand what that meant.

But when Clothilde then washed her bottom and went to tie a fresh napkin on her, it was a different matter. "Non!" she said indignantly.

"Oui," Tessa and Marcus and Clothilde all said at once, and with a mutinous expression the little girl reluctantly allowed the hateful thing to be fastened on her.

"Good girl," Tessa said warmly. The child then turned to Marcus.

"Yes, good girl," he said and she looked reluctantly satisfied.

They left for Genappe after breakfast. He should have made arrangements to meet Tomas and the carriage back in Brussels, Marcus thought, but at the time he thought they would be making their way to Paris.

But now, with the child, Paris might not be convenient. Ah well, he would see what Tessa thought once they were in Genappe.

Once Tessa was mounted, he handed Flora up to her, but as soon as he was in the saddle, she held her little arms out to him in a clear demand to ride with him. She was warmly clothed now, so there was no reason for her to want to ride with him, other than she wanted to.

He tried not to feel pleased.

The landlady's oldest son, Léon, the boy who'd cared for their horses the previous night, had borrowed a mule from one of the neighbors, and he and Clothilde, along with her small bundle of belongings were to ride it. Léon would bring the mule back. It was not very far to Genappe.

The little cavalcade set off, Tante Jeanne with tears and hugs and many words of advice to Clothilde and her son, while her other children and several neighbors waved them off.

They ambled along the quiet country road.

Now warmly clothed and no longer traveling in his coat, Marcus's little passenger sat up brightly watching everything they passed. From time to time she would point at something, and Marcus would nod gravely and make some kind of comment.

Tessa was enjoying his interaction with the little mite, one-sided conversation though it was. After a short time he started teaching her English. "That's a tree. Yes, so is that one. And more than one tree is trees—trees. Can you say trees?"

But though she seemed to understand, she never repeated the word.

His deep voice continued, "Mind now, you are not to go climbing trees like a little hoyden, do you understand? Though if you are anything like your mama you will. And knowing her, she will probably join you. She was a terror for climbing trees when she was a little girl."

Tears welled up in Tessa's eyes. *Your mama.* He really did mean it when he'd told her all that time ago that he didn't care about an heir, that his brothers were already his heirs. Her barrenness didn't seem to bother him at all.

After a while he produced an apple from his pocket and proceeded to cut slices for the little girl to eat. When all that was left was the core, he was ready to feed it to Tessa's horse, when Flora said "Non!" and grabbed it from him. She ate it, seeds and all, until only the stem was left. She inspected it gravely, decided she had no use for it and gave it to him.

"Thank you," he said in all seriousness. She frowned up at him in puzzlement. "Good girl," he said, nodding, and her brow cleared.

On the way, they passed the stark stone skeleton

of a ruined abbey. "Is that the abbey the landlady mentioned? The one the smith said he would take Flora to?

"No," Marcus said. "We passed the turnoff to Nivelles a while back. This is .." With some difficulty he pulled his pamphlet from a pocket and consulted it. "According to this, that one is—or was—the *Abbaye de Villers.* I suppose it was destroyed in the revolution as well."

They rode on in a somber frame of mind. The destruction of war and revolution was all around them.

The accommodation Tomas had found for them in Genappe was clean and comfortable and, after a good meal, they'd all settled in for an early night. Clothilde and little Flora were housed together in a separate small room, as was Tomas, who was sharing with young Léon.

It was the first time Tessa had been entirely alone with Marcus since Brussels, and he had wasted no time taking her to bed and making love with her. It was blissful.

"Are you sure you don't want to go to Paris?" Marcus asked Tessa some time later. "The Army of Occupation left France several years ago, but it's perfectly safe. I'm told the French are relieved to have the war behind them and are anxious to rebuild their country."

She stretched luxuriantly and ran her hand down his chest. It was still hard for her to believe that the activity she had endured in her previous marriages had such potential for . . . bliss. She could never get enough of the feeling of his skin against hers. "I don't really care about Paris, but of course, if you want to go there—"

"I don't." He smoothed her hair back and kissed her. "I just wanted to check with you. Women are usually keen to shop in Paris."

She laughed. "I'm happy to do any shopping I need in London, thank you. You forget, for most of my life, I've never been allowed to go shopping at all."

Looking back, it was almost as if her previous two marriages were just one long, unpleasant dream. For all her initial reluctance to accept Marcus's proposal, and despite his very lukewarm declaration when he made it—*we need to marry. . . I haven't a romantic bone in my body . . . I've never wanted a love match . . . Our marriage will be a practical solution*—this marriage was turning out wonderfully well.

He wasn't the cold, repressed, proud man so many people thought him. Underneath that reserved, hard-to-read exterior he was kind, and thoughtful, and he had a wonderfully dry sense of humor.

And she didn't just feel listened to, she felt *seen*. Respected, as if she were an equal partner in their marriage.

And when they made love, she felt . . . cherished.

The following morning, Marcus made the arrangements to begin the journey back to England. First he had to hire a carriage and driver.

"But we already have Tomas and a carriage," Tessa said when he told her.

"I've decided to send Tomas and the carriage back with young Léon," he said brusquely, and before she could ask why, he added in a gruff voice, "Léon is only ten. I won't send a child of his age on the journey back to his village—not alone, for all that he considers himself the man of the family. He and the mule would be targets for any passing villains. Tomas will look after them."

Tessa simply nodded, understanding. Of course Marcus would feel it his responsibility to see Léon safely returned to his mother. He was always protective of children—witness the way he'd looked after young Joey back in London, and Flora, currently playing at her feet.

He would make a wonderful father. She felt completely safe with him too—not that he treated her like a child. She smiled to herself, thinking of the way they had made love the previous night, and again this morning. Very much not like a child.

Deliciously not like a child.

"We will make for the coast—to Calais I think, depending on the roads," he continued. "I'll send a note with Tomas to have my yacht sent there. He'll no doubt make better time than we will—we're not in a hurry, are we?"

"Not at all," she agreed. "And I think it will be easier, traveling with Flora, if we're not cooped up in a carriage all day. Besides, the countryside is so pretty." And having had so little opportunity in her life to travel anywhere, she was enjoying every minute of it—apart from the endless jolting of the carriage. It took her a little time every morning to get used to the swaying and bouncing. Another reason to travel in short stages.

He gave a brisk nod. "Very well then. We'll take our time, and do a bit of exploring along the way."

They made a slow, leisurely trip to Calais, stopping whenever they felt like it, to view the sights, or to have a picnic, or simply to stretch their legs in a pretty area. And of course for 'pipi' because, napkin or not, Flora insisted on stopping to relieve herself and became almost frantic trying to get the napkin off. They decided in the end to use a napkin only at night.

The little girl took to carriage riding as easily as she'd taken to being on a horse, gazing out of the window at the scenery passing by. She'd also taken to Clothilde, though only as a secondary choice, her preference being to be with Marcus or Tessa, preferably both.

"She's a bright, happy little soul, isn't she?" Marcus commented as, sitting on Tessa's knee, she pointed out some sheep in a nearby paddock. "Remarkable that the neglect she was suffering when we found her doesn't seem to have made a permanent impression."

"Only at night," Tessa said. The child became quite clingy at night and seemed anxious not to be left alone. Tessa usually lulled her to sleep, cuddled on her lap, and then Marcus would carry her to bed, accompanied by Clothilde.

"She'll soon learn that we're not going to abandon her," Marcus said.

"Do you think it's true, what that man said, about her sleeping with the dog?"

He shrugged. "No way to know. But it's all in the past now. At least she's talking more. Even some words in English." He looked at her. "No regrets?"

"Never," she assured him, her arms wrapped around the little girl. "You?"

"None."

"I wonder what your aunt will say when she sees her."

Marcus gave a half-smile. "We'll just have to wait and see."

"She won't be nasty about it, will she? I would hate Flora to be upset." It was a worry. Lady Gosforth was a terrible snob. Tessa hated to imagine what she would think of her nephew—the head of his family—arriving home from his honeymoon with a strange child.

Her *niece*, Tessa reminded herself. They must never reveal how they'd actually found her. An illegitimate, half-English foundling—in the home of an earl? Unthinkable!

No, she was the legitimate daughter of Tessa's late brother, Louis.

Tessa smoothed Flora's hair. In Genappe she had tidied Flora's haircut with her nail scissors and she looked quite sweet. And she was clean now, and not so scrawny as she had been.

She was a bright, pretty little girl, with big blue eyes and pale blonde hair that would curl when it grew. And when she smiled—which happened more frequently every day—it lit up her little face. How could anyone be nasty to her? And if Lady Gosforth dared. . . Well, Tessa would show her!

"There they are, the white cliffs of Dover." Marcus stood at the rail of his yacht, Flora held firmly against his chest, the other arm around Tessa. The voyage had, thankfully, been quite swift, but to Tessa's dismay, the sea had been rough and she had been miserably ill, only recovering slightly in the last hour when Marcus brought her on deck. The fresh air helped but she was still unsteady on her feet.

"They're more gray than white, aren't they?" She leaned against him, still feeling a trifle queasy.

"It depends on the light. In some lights they can be positively dazzling, but when it's overcast, as it is today, they're less so. But for most Englishmen it's their first sight of home, and a very welcome one."

They disembarked, made a very swift pass through Customs—the benefit of being married to an earl— and found Marcus's carriage waiting for them. Soon they'd be in London.

Tessa wasn't sure whether she was excited or not. It all depended on how Lady Gosforth treated Flora.

CHAPTER EIGHTEEN

IT WAS LATE when their carriage turned into Grosvenor Square and pulled up outside Marcus's house. To their surprise the house was still bright with light. "My aunt is still awake. Maybe she has guests," Marcus observed.

A groom hurried to let down the steps and Marcus alighted first then helped Tessa down. She took a deep breath, then turned and said to Clothilde, who was staring open-mouthed at the grand house. "Pass Flora to me, please, Clothilde."

Begin as you mean to go on.

With Flora in her arms and Marcus by her side, she began to climb the steps. The door opened before they reached it and Peverill, Marcus's butler, came to meet them. "Welcome home, m'lord. We weren't expecting you home so soon. I hope you'll forgive—"

"Marcus? Is that you?" Lady Gosforth appeared in the entry hall. "What on earth are you doing home so early? We didn't expect you for at least another month. What happened?"

"Change of plans. Good evening, Aunt Maude."

She presented her cheek for him to kiss, glanced past him and saw Tessa with Flora in her arms. And froze.

After a moment she produced her lorgnette and raked Tessa and the child up and down with it. "And who is this?"

"My wife, Tessa," Marcus said mildly. "Surely you haven't forgotten her."

"I meant the child, as you very well know," his aunt snapped.

Tessa lifted her chin and met the old lady's stare boldly. "This is my niece, Flora." Her tone dared Lady Gosforth to make something of it.

Lady Gosforth stared at Flora. Flora stared back.

Lady Gosforth wrinkled her nose. Flora wrinkled hers, though it was just a button and no match for the old lady's proud Roman nose.

"Your niece, you say?"

"Yes. My late brother Louis's orphaned daughter."

The old lady sniffed. "Then why is she dressed in rags?"

"They're not rags," Tessa said defensively. "Patched, yes, and mended, but—"

"*Rags!* Peverill!" Without taking her eye, horribly

magnified by the lorgnette, off the little girl, Lady Gosforth addressed the butler who was supervising the luggage being brought inside. "Have the basket in my dressing room brought down here at once—the big one, with the lid."

As the butler hurried upstairs Billy, Tessa's little dog appeared on the landing of the stairs. With wuffs of joy he bounded down and began to gambol around Tessa's feet. Her arms full of little girl she tried to pat him, but at the sight of him, Flora almost launched herself out of Tessa's arms, reaching for the dog.

Feeling sure Billy wouldn't harm her—and clearly the little girl was not the least bit frightened of the dog, Tessa set her onto the floor. It was an instant love-fest—dog and child acted as if they'd been best pals all their lives. Flora laughing and speaking unintelligible baby talk to the dog, and Billy wuffling and snuffling and wriggling with delight, licking any bits of her he could get to.

A short time later Peverill arrived carrying a large wicker basket.

"Ah, Peverill, the very thing. Put it on the table in the morning room." To Tessa she said, "Bring that child into the morning room. Never mind the dog, he can come too."

Tessa blinked. Lady Gosforth despised dogs. She glanced at Marcus, who shrugged and gestured her to go ahead, so she picked up Flora and followed the old lady into the morning room. Billy trotted after them.

Lady Gosforth undid the fastening of the basket and flipped it open.

Tessa gasped. It was full of the most exquisite little knitted, sewn and embroidered baby clothes. Lady Gosforth, muttering to herself, sorted through them quickly saying, "How old did you say the child was?"

"W-we're not exactly sure," she began. "Her mother died before—"

"Never mind, hold her up." She measured a beautiful, embroidered smock up against Flora. "Yes, that will fit. Here—" She pulled fistfuls of baby and toddler clothes from the basket, dumping them on the table. "She's smaller than Torie, and about the same size as I expect Jane will be, only I haven't seen Jane yet, so I can't be sure. But at least she won't be dressed in rags—will you?—what did you say her name was? Flossie?" She pulled a face at Flora, who promptly pulled one back.

The old lady chuckled. "She's going to be a handful, mark my words. Now, take that child up to the nursery and get rid of those dreadful rags! Peverill, send a maid to take these things up—oh, you have one, I see," she added, noticing Clothilde loitering in the doorway. "Here, you, gel, take these."

Understanding the gesture and tone, if not the words, Clothilde gathered up the small pile of garments and followed Tessa, who was a little dazed by Lady Gosforth's unexpected reaction, from the room.

Marcus wasn't surprised. His aunt, unhappily childless her whole life, hid, under her brusque manner, a fondness for children that few people knew about. He remembered her doing much the same when his half-brother Harry had arrived with his wife's daughter, little Torie, dressed in nothing but a pillow slip.

With a critical expression, Lady Gosforth watched them go. "That maid will have to be outfitted properly too. Can't have the child's nursemaid looking so shabby."

Marcus was seated in the morning room with his aunt. He had just finished explaining how they had discovered Flora.

"She eyed him cynically. "So that's what you're claiming, is it? That the child is Tessa's niece. Her late brother's child? His *legitimate* child?"

Marcus said mildly, "Yes, though we intend to raise her as our daughter."

The old lady gave a scornful snort and arched one finely plucked eyebrow. "You expect me to swallow such a farrago of nonsense?"

Damn her sharp, suspicious mind. He was on

shaky ground here, but he had no intention of failing at the first fence. He raised his own, much thicker brow and said stiffly, "You doubt—?"

"*A farrago of nonsense?*" Tessa sailed into the room. "I expect you are an expert on that, given the farrago of nonsense *you* spread about Marcus and me before our marriage." She folded her arms and faced Lady Gosforth, a militant light in her eyes.

The old lady shrugged. "I have no idea what—"

Tessa cut her off with a sharp gesture. "Piffle! You know exactly what I'm talking about, so don't try to deny it. We know all about it, don't we Marcus?"

Marcus, deciding Tessa was well able to handle his aunt by herself, merely nodded in agreement.

The old lady pouted. "Well, what of it? It worked, didn't it? You two would never have married otherwise, hiver-havering around as you were. You needed a nudge. And look at the two of you now, smelling of April and May!"

"You have no idea what we might or might not have done. Yes, we are happy now," Tessa admitted, "but you weren't to know that." She glared at the old lady.

The old lady glared back.

There was a short, tense silence.

After a minute, Tessa gave a meaningful glance at Marcus, slipped her arm through his and said,

"We *were* planning to ask you to become Flora's godmother, but if you refuse to acknowledge her. . ."

The old lady's brows snapped together. She sat up. "*Godmother?* You want *me* to be that child's godmother?"

Marcus pressed his lips together to hide a smile. They hadn't discussed it, but it was a master stroke. It was a sore point with his aunt that none of her nephews had invited her to be godmother to any of their children.

"We *did*," Tessa told her. "But since you're claiming our miraculous discovery of Flora is *a farrago of nonsense. . .*"

Wearing his best serious expression Marcus nodded wisely.

His aunt made a dismissive gesture. "Oh pish tush, how you do take one up, gel. It's an extraordinary tale, I admit, but as we all know, truth can be stranger than fiction." She glanced at Tessa's adamant expression and added, "And miracles do happen, after all." She turned to Marcus. "Besides, who am I to doubt the word of the head of the family? So, yes, I would be delighted to sponsor the child."

Tessa glanced at Marcus, then eyed the old lady thoughtfully. "I'm not so sure anymore. If we thought you might cast aspersions on the story of how we found Flora . . ."

Again Marcus nodded solemnly. He was enjoying this hugely. It wasn't often anyone got the better of his aunt.

"Cast aspersions? I? What nonsense!" the old lady said indignantly. "I've never cast an aspersion in my life!"

Marcus choked, and tried to turn it into a cough.

"Because we would be *very* unhappy if unpleasant rumors were to spread," Tessa continued. "Would you undertake to ensure that didn't happen, Lady Gosforth?" Her expression hardened and she added in the sweetest voice, "Because we *know* how skilled you are at handling gossip and rumors. Aren't you?"

Lady Gosforth gave her a haughty stare. "No shadow of doubt will fall on my goddaughter, I assure you."

"Nobody would dare," Marcus murmured.

His aunt shot him a basilisk look. "As long as you don't continue to dress her in rags!"

Tessa smiled. "Of course we won't, not with those beautiful clothes you've given her. So thank you, we'd be delighted for you to become our daughter's godmother, Aunt Maude. Now, I must go and see how she's settling in. You can make the arrangements with Marcus." She hurried out.

There was a short silence after she left. Then Aunt Maude said, "I'm surprised the child hasn't been christened before this."

"We're not sure she hasn't been, but from what we saw there was a distinct lack of priests in the area."

Lady Gosford turned an appalled lorgnette on him. "*Priests*? That child is *Catholic?*"

He shrugged. "We assume her mother was—she was born in a Catholic country, after all. Though religion was frowned upon by the revolution."

The old lady snorted. "What nonsense! We'll have her decently christened in the family chapel at Alverleigh, like the rest of the Renfrew family, with a proper Anglican vicar presiding!"

"Strictly speaking Flora is a Blaxland," Marcus said mildly.

Lady Gosforth turned her lorgnette on him. "We'll hear no more of that! She will be christened as a Renfrew in the family chapel at Alverleigh!" She frowned momentarily. "Or would it be better done in St George's, Hanover Square?" She shook her head. "No, we don't want curious busybodies wondering why she wasn't christened before now. It must be the family chapel at Alverleigh, where Renfrews are always christened."

"Very well, Aunt Maude," he murmured, well pleased with the outcome. Little Flora would now have her own personal champion in his aunt. "Now, if you don't mind, I'll see how everything is going upstairs."

She inclined her head graciously. "You are excused. Tea will be served in half an hour. Don't be late."

Marcus had just put his foot on the first step when there was a discreet-but significant cough behind him. He was well acquainted with the sound. "Yes, Peverill, what is it?"

His butler glided forward. "It's about the boy, m'lord. Young Joey."

"Has he been behaving himself?" Marcus asked, expecting to hear that he hadn't. Not surprising, expecting a boy raised on the streets to adapt easily to a gentleman's house.

"Very much so," Peverill assured him. "In fact . . ."

"In fact?" Marcus prompted him.

"He's spirited, I'll grant you and sometimes mischievous as boys are . . ."

"But?"

"But he's also very intelligent, m'lord. Unusually so."

"Indeed?"

"Yes, m'lord. It took him barely a week to learn his alphabet and start deciphering words. And as for arithmetic—he took to that like a duck to water. You should see how quickly he can add up a column of numbers. In his head!"

"Really?"

"I was wondering . . ." The butler hesitated.

"Go on."

"What are your intentions for the lad, m'lord? Only I doubt he has the makings of a footman, or indeed anyone in service. He . . . he's a good boy, but not really . . . a respecter of rules if you take my meaning. He's what you might call an independent thinker."

That didn't surprise Marcus. Joey had bent and broken rules from the beginning of their acquaintance. What did surprise him was Peverill taking such an interest in him. He'd taken the boy on with the utmost reluctance. His current enthusiasm for the boy's abilities was unexpected, but Marcus had known Peverill for many years and had great respect for his insight.

"What do you think I should do with him then?"

"It's not for me to say, m'lord"— Peverill took a deep breath—"but if the lad were my grandson, I would . . . I'd send him to school." He swallowed.

Marcus considered the suggestion then nodded. "Very well, we'll take him down to Alverleigh with us when we return, and he can attend the village school. Life in the country will give him a chance to catch up on his education and explore his options,. If he proves to have the potential you see in him, we'll send him to a good school. Train him up to some profession. What do you think?"

Peverill's normally impassive face broke into a smile. "Thank you m'lord. That's very generous of you. I assure you, the boy won't disappoint you. He'll be as good as gold, I promise you."

Marcus laughed. "Let's hope he's not a complete angel. It's good for a boy to get up to mischief now and then, and mischief in the country is not nearly so grim as it can be in the city." Joey had recognized the danger to Tessa long before anyone else. He himself had discounted the boy's warning, thinking it was just an imaginative boy's tale. But if it hadn't been for Joey . . . He shook his head to clear his mind of the dreadful thought.

The boy deserved every chance Marcus could give him.

He turned to mount the stairs, then paused. "The dog, Peverill. My aunt has always been utterly antipathetic to dogs, and yet I noticed earlier. . ."

His butler allowed a faint smile to appear. "The animal has winning ways, and appears to have charmed her, m'lord. Any night that m'lady has no visitors and no plans to go out, she sits knitting or sewing in her sitting room, the little dog at her feet. She even talks to him—I gather he's good company. She also ordered a basket made for the little fellow to sleep in *and* sewed a cushion to line it herself."

Marcus raised his brows. "So, miracles do happen?"

Peverill permitted himself another small smile. "Indeed, my lord."

The christening of Flora Louise Blaxland Renfrew was to be in six weeks. Marcus had written to his brothers to invite them, but their replies indicated they were unlikely to make it. Even if were able to get leave, it was too far for Nash to travel from St. Petersburg in the time given. Gabriel was busy with events in Zindaria, of which he was the Regent. And Harry said he would try to come, but it depended— as it always did with him and Nell—on the horses.

Not that Marcus and Tessa minded. Marcus understood the demands on his brothers' lives, and Tessa was uncertain of how Marcus's family would respond to her. All of them descending on her at once was an alarming prospect, so she was happy to have it delayed

Though now she had both Marcus's and Lady Gosforth's support, things would be easier.

Lady Gosforth, giving up the notion of a family gathering at the christening, had decided that an Easter ball at Alverleigh would suffice, and had already begun negotiations with her nephews for their attendance. She wasn't worried about the *ton* attending. "Where I lead the *ton* will follow" she declared, and nobody dared argue.

After a few days in London, mainly to purchase supplies for Flora and Clothilde, and for Tessa to have final fittings for the clothes Miss Chance had made for her, they traveled down to Alverleigh. Marcus, in particular, was eager to get there—he'd been a long time away from his estate and knew there would be work to catch up on.

Tessa was happy to be leaving London. She was still uncomfortable with the way people stared and whispered about her, as she knew they would once they learned of her marriage to Marcus.

Before they left on their honeymoon, he'd send a notice to the newspapers announcing their marriage, but it wasn't 'old news' yet, and the gossips were still busy. And once people realized they'd come back with a toddler in tow, well, the tongues would wag even more, and she'd rather not be there to witness it.

Nevertheless, she had mixed feelings about going to Alverleigh, mainly because she would be only a stone's throw from her beloved Ferndale, and wasn't sure she could bear it.

They arrived in rain, gray, dreary drizzle. As their carriage turned in between the impressive high stone pillars that supported the gates to Alverleigh, Tessa swallowed.

The gently curving drive lined with ancient oaks straightened bringing the carriage to a perfect view of the house. She'd never seen it from this angle, never actually ventured onto Alverleigh property when she was a child, and the drive approaching it had been designed to impress visitors.

Even through the drizzle, the house was impressive. It was huge, several stories high with wings spreading out each side from a central tower-like structure. Tessa received an impression of many windows gleaming in the rain, numerous turrets and chimneys. She swallowed. Marcus was explaining some of the history of the house, but his words became a background blur and she didn't take much in.

She would be mistress of this enormous house. She'd never been the mistress of anything. In her previous marriages she was merely 'the wife'—her husbands made all the decisions and the staff more or less operated without her. How many servants were employed here?

She was very thankful that Peverill and Cook were in the second carriage behind them. And that Lady Gosforth had engagements to attend and would come much later, so she wouldn't be here to watch Tessa trying to learn the ropes. Peverill and Cook would help her adjust, she was sure.

The next morning dawned clear and sunny and, when Tessa threw open the windows of her bedchamber, the air was fragrant with the scents of damp earth, damp leaves, and the last flowers of autumn. It cheered her. It smelled like home.

Marcus had already told her he would be having a very busy day, catching up with his estate agent and dealing with tenants and various local matters. "You familiarize yourself with the household and staff," he told her over breakfast. "I'll see you at dinner."

As she'd hoped, Peverill introduced her to the main staff. And as she'd feared, there were too many servants for her to learn all their names at once, though she vowed to herself she would. But she was treated from the first with deference and respect— and welcome—as the mistress, which was a relief, if also a little unnerving.

Alverleigh was her home now, she kept reminding herself. Yes, it was a magnificent house, quite intimidatingly so, but she would get used to it. Eventually. Even the gardens were spectacular, the neatest she'd ever seen, with an army of gardeners to keep them spick and span.

But more important than too-big houses and too-neat gardens and too-many-servants, she had a husband and a child to love.

She played with Flora whenever she could. The little girl seemed quite happy with her new home, the nursery with all its toys—old as they were—and she delighted in the garden, where she and Billy played.

The staff all seemed to delight in the little girl too, which was a huge relief. "It's been too long since there were children at Alverleigh," was something she heard a number of times, from Mrs. Allen, the housekeeper, down to the lowliest maidservant. "Such a happy little soul. And look at the smile on her—lovely it is."

For Flora was smiling and talking more and more, seeming not just unfazed by all the new places and new people, but delighting in all the attention.

Even the gardeners welcomed the child—despite her and Billy once relieving themselves on the lawn, much to her embarrassment. But the gardeners just laughed.

Her first day as mistress of Alverleigh was a busy and challenging one, and when the long day came to an end and she and Marcus sat down to dinner Tessa was exhausted. She wanted an early night to bed, preferably with her husband.

But Marcus had other ideas. "Let's go for a walk," he said to her after dinner. "I need to stretch my legs after all the sitting I've been doing. And it's a lovely evening."

It was a lovely evening, she had to admit. The sky was slowly fading to a soft lilac, the air was warm with a light, fragrant breeze and she could think of no excuse to refuse. Flora had been put to bed in the beautiful nursery, with Clothilde sleeping in the adjoining room.

It was just that Tessa didn't want to see Ferndale and what had become of it.

Which was cowardly.

And foolish as well. Most people would be glad to see the restoration of a fine old estate that for years had been neglected, overgrown and falling to ruins. She fetched a shawl, and arm in arm they stepped out into the balmy night.

"Let's go this way," Marcus suggested and began to lead her in the direction she least wanted to go—toward Ferndale.

"What about over here?" she suggested. "I haven't explored the maze yet. It looks most enticing."

"We can do that another day. It's better in full daylight." Marcus led her firmly onward.

Tessa swallowed. Change was inevitable in life, she told herself. She needed to face the changes at Ferndale, accept that her old home was no more, that there would be no fox cubs to visit, no otters frolicking in the pool, no badgers to watch by moonlight. They belonged to her childhood, and her childhood was well and truly gone.

He was heading straight for the forest. She bit her lip. She needed more time to prepare for this.

She could have told him, insisted they go the other way—he would listen, she knew. He always did.

But she said nothing. She could not look, however, and kept her eyes on the ground in front of her, trusting in Marcus to keep her on the path.

She knew when they entered the forest: she could smell it all around her, that fragrant melange of damp earth and fallen leaves and a million green scents. So dear and familiar.

Marcus said nothing, just led her on and on, while Tessa kept her eyes on the ground and silently berated herself for her cowardice.

He stopped and she stumbled to a halt. "Look," he said softly.

She took a deep breath and raised her gaze. And gasped. The forest—her beloved forest—was unchanged. Well, of course it wasn't, but it hadn't been cleared and chopped and pruned neatly back into unrecognizability. It was still the forest she'd grown up in and loved—with ferns and tangled undergrowth—and teeming with life.

Bewildered, unable to talk for the emotions flooding her, she turned to Marcus. "What? But I thought . . ."

He wrapped his arm around her waist. "I should have told you this before, but I was a coward. When your brother sold Ferndale, I bought it."

"You?" She stared. "*You* bought it?"

He nodded. "I was the one who had the orchards brought back to productivity, and the gardens weeded and restocked, and the house repaired and refurbished."

"But this . . ." She gestured all around them.

"I gave orders for minimal interference here. I knew you loved it wild and untamed." His gaze flickered, and he turned her around. "Look."

And across the lawn they'd come from ran a fox, a fox who limped slightly.

Tessa gasped. "Is that—it can't be —it's Russett! But how has she survived all this time?"

"It's not Russett," Marcus said gently. "Foxes don't live that long."

Tessa nodded. "Of course. I forgot that. My Russett would have died years ago. But there are still foxes living here?"

"More than ever. When I came into my inheritance, I banned hunting on all my estates. And traps are forbidden, so I don't know how that one hurt her leg." He smiled ruefully. "It's not a popular move, especially from those who raise chickens, but I remind them that foxes are God's creatures too and they have to eat." He shrugged. "It doesn't impress anyone, but still. . ."

Tessa watched, her heart full as not-Russett disappeared into the underbrush. Marcus continued,

"And badgers still live in that sett, and otters still frolic in the pool. Your forest creatures are all safe."

She turned in his arms, her eyes full of tears and embraced him. "Oh, Marcus, I don't know how to thank you. I do love you so much!"

He stiffened, and she realized what she'd said. She hadn't planned to say it—it had just burst from her full and overflowing heart. She bit her lip. "I'm sorry, Marcus," she said. "I didn't mean to say it."

There was a short silence. Neither of them moved. His eyes bored into her. Finally he said in a curious voice, "You didn't mean it?"

"No, of course I meant it. I just planned never to tell you, to burden you with my . . my feelings."

"Burden me?" he repeated in that same curious voice.

She nodded. "You made it clear when you proposed that you didn't want a love match. I should have told you back then that I thought I was falling in love with you, that I've been half in love with you since I was a little girl. But I didn't." She hung her head.

There was another long silence, broken only by the breeze fluttering the leaves, the far of cry of an owl, and the distant bark of a fox.

"You love me," he repeated, as if checking his ears hadn't deceived him.

She nodded. "I'm sorry."

He took a deep breath. "I've been in love with you almost from the start." He paused, looking down at her, gripping her shoulders in a light firm hold. "I was so sure you didn't want to marry, that I made you think a practical marriage was all I wanted." He swallowed. "But we don't have a practical marriage, do we?"

Her heart to full to speak, she just shook her head.

His arms tightened around her. "At the time, I thought that's what I wanted, too. But I was in love with you long before I realized it. I'm not very familiar with love, you see, so I didn't recognize it at first." His ice-gray eyes burned as he said in his deep voice, "But I love you, Tessa, darling, so very, very much."

"And I love you, too, so very, very much," she responded. And then they were kissing, and for a long time there was no more talking, only the giving and receiving of love.

Later they walked to the otter pond, and saw two otters playing and diving. It was getting dark, and the clouds were coming back, so by mutual consent , arm in arm, they walked slowly back to the house. "I first realized I felt more for you than I knew that time you were kidnapped. I was beside myself, fearing you'd be harmed—or worse. And I could do nothing—nothing!—to help you. The thought of going the rest of my life without you in it—" His voice broke and he kissed her again, hard, his kiss showing her what he couldn't find the words for.

"And then," he said as they resumed strolling, "on our honeymoon everything just kept getting better and better."

"It was the same for me," she said. "I was bursting to tell you what was in my heart—oh, so many times—but having married you under false pretenses I couldn't burden you with my unwanted feelings."

"False pretenses?" he laughed. "What a pair we are. But it's not a burden—far from it. I'm a changed man from the one you married, all cold and repressed and buttoned-up. In fact, I'll show you! I was longing to do this after you'd been kidnapped, but I couldn't bring myself to do it." And without warning he swept her up into his arms and carried her, laughing and exclaiming that she was too heavy—to which he merely snorted. He carried her up the front steps of Alverleigh, where he paused. "Could you ring the doorbell please? I don't want to put you down."

She pulled the bell pull and Peverill opened the door. "My lord," he began, with a perturbed expression.

"Just carrying my bride over the threshold, Peverill. Nothing to be concerned about," Marcus said airily and, with his precious burden, headed toward the stairs.

"Very good m'lord," the butler said and beaming,

he began to clap. Within minutes another half dozen servants appeared and seeing what was happening, joined in the applause. A shrill wolf-whistle showed that young Joey had joined them. Attempting to maintain his habitual dignity, Marcus continued carrying his laughing bride up the stairs, kicked open their bedchamber door and deposited her, with a sigh of relief, on the bed.

"And now, my darling Lady Alverleigh. . ."

She opened her arms to him. "Yes, now please, Marcus darling."

EPILOGUE

AS SHE DID most days, Tessa was walking in the forest with her daughter, observing the small seasonal changes and delighting in the creatures of the forest.

"I like it here, Mama," Flora said confidingly. "I like it best when it's just you and me, but it's nice when Papa's here, too. And Joey."

Tessa smiled. "I like it here too, sweetheart. It's a very special place for me. And you know where Papa and Joey are, but they'll be home later today."

Having taken an interest in young Joey, and then adopting Flora, it had occurred to Marcus that there were too many unwanted and uncared-for children in the world. So he'd talked it over with Tessa, and they'd decided to establish a number of small homes for orphans—not big impersonal institutions, but smaller ones, with no more than six or so children, and a motherly woman and a good man to take care of them. More like a family than an orphanage. And today he was establishing the third one, and had taken Joey with him. Tessa was so proud of them both.

"You know I lived here when I was your age," she told Flora.

"In the forest?"

"No, in the house beyond the forest, the one that the Sandersons rent." Flora sometimes played with the Sanderson children. "But I spent a lot of time here in the forest, watching the animals and just playing. Papa used to come here too, when he was a boy. That's how we first met."

Flora nodded, satisfied. "And you and Papa saved the vixen." She liked hearing the story about how they met, and often had Tessa or Marcus retell it. Flora also spent a lot of time playing unsupervised in the forest, as Tessa had, but she was invariably accompanied by Joey. With no prompting from anyone the boy had appointed himself Flora's guardian.

Billy, who spent most of his days with Flora and Joey, usually remained safely at home on these excursions, dealing with a meaty bone under Cook's supervision. Billy was inclined to chase forest creatures.

"Ferndale will be yours one day," Tessa told Flora. "The forest and the house and the orchards and everything. Papa and I have set up a trust for you."

Flora looked up at her with a faint frown. "Will I have to live there?"

Tessa hugged her. Flora was still a little insecure. "No, of course not, darling. Not ever, if you don't want to. But when you turn twenty-five, it will belong to you and only you. So you'll always have your very own home that nobody can ever take away from you."

Flora thought that over, then nodded. "That's good. And Joey too?"

"Joey will have a home of his own, too. Papa will arrange it." Joey had worked hard and was proving more than capable and Marcus was very proud of him. They both were.

Flora pursed her lips. "Joey's going away to school next year, but I won't have to leave, will I?"

"No, you'll have years and years with Papa and me first, and you'll only leave if you want to." It was three years since they'd found her, and she was growing up fast—too fast, Tessa sometimes thought. But she was a joy to them both.

"There's our vixen again," Flora whispered and pointed. Tessa smiled at the possessive note in her daughter's voice.

They watched for a minute, as the vixen sniffed around, exploring.

"She's getting fat," Flora observed.

"Not fat," Tessa corrected her. "She's going to have kitts—babies—soon."

Flora turned and patted her mother's stomach. "Like you, Mama. Fat with a baby."

Tessa nodded and said tremulously, "Yes, darling, like me."

It was her own personal miracle. After years of thinking she was barren, she had hardly even noticed when her courses had stopped—they'd always been erratic. But six months ago Lady Gosforth had noticed her putting on weight and asked her bluntly when her last courses had occurred. And Tessa, thinking back, had realized.

Still unable to believe it, she'd had herself checked by the local doctor, as well as the village midwife, who had brought hundreds of babies into the world. They both confirmed it. And now, in a few weeks, she was to have her very own baby.

The unexpected possibility of an heir for Alverleigh had delighted Marcus, but Aunt Gosforth was utterly over the moon, and acted as if she were wholly responsible. And after years of believing herself barren, Tessa was simply thankful.

She placed a palm on her belly, feeling the baby moving inside her. Alive and healthy. It was an incredible feeling.

"Can you make it a girl?" Flora said. "Aunt Maude says it will be a nair for Alverleigh." She wrinkled her nose. "But we don't need a nair, do we, Mama? I want a girl, a baby sister."

"A baby boy would be nice too," Tessa told her daughter. "We don't get to choose."

"I suppose not," Flora admitted grudgingly. "But a girl would be *much* better, Mama."

Tessa laughed. "The baby will be whoever God sends us, and we'll love them whether they are a boy or a girl."

Flora nodded. "Yes. But especially if it's a girl."

The sound of rustling bushes and footsteps caused Tessa to turn. "It's Papa and Joey," Flora exclaimed and ran towards them.

Marcus caught the little girl as she hurled herself bodily into his arms. Laughing, he swung her around in a circle, making her shriek with delight.

Tessa watched with a lump in her throat. This man, this quiet, contained, austere, outwardly stern man was so full of love. He was a born father. Both Flora and Joey adored him.

And so did she. More than she would ever have dreamed was possible.

He put Flora down, and she grabbed Joey by the hand and the two children rushed off saying something about the otter pool. Marcus turned to Tessa with a smile. "How is it that when Flora is by herself, she makes not a sound running through the forest—just like you, when you were a child—

but when she's with Joey, they sound like a pair of excited little elephants?"

She laughed. "I know. I doubt they'll see any otters today."

"In that case, we'd better make the most of our temporary solitude." He gathered her in his arms, his gray eyes gleaming. "Have I told you lately how much I love you, Lady Alverleigh?"

"You have. And I love you, my darling Marcus, so very, very much."

THANK YOU FOR reading *A Bride for Marcus*. I hope you enjoyed it. Reviews help other readers find my books, so I would really appreciate it if you could leave reviews and/or ratings, whether positive or not, and if you like them, to recommend my books to your friends.

© Anne Gracie 2026

ACKNOWLEDGEMENTS

Heartfelt thanks to Carol Marinelli, Mary Jo Putney, Patricia Rice, Alison Reynolds, Julia Byrne and Kelly Hunter for advice, feedback and encouragement, and to all the other Word Wenches for general encouragement and support. (www. wordwenches.com)

Thanks also to my writing friends, Carol, Kelly, Barb, and Rosie for keeping me going when the going got tough!

And though I might be repeating myself, thank you once again to every reader who wrote to me asking for Marcus's story. I wouldn't have written it if not for those wonderful encouraging letters.

A FEW HISTORICAL NOTES

Salome: I have taken some liberties with using the name Salome in relation to Tessa's scanty night dress. Salome was not explicity named in the Bible. (The name comes from the Jewish historian Josephus.) She dances for Herod and, prompted by her mother, demands the head of John the Baptist on a platter.

The name "Dance of the Seven Veils" was chiefly popularized in modern culture with the 1894 English translation of Oscar Wilde's 1893 French play Salome, in the stage direction «Salome dances the dance of the seven veils».

But though it is something of an anachronism for Tessa's time, I decided modern readers would understand the reference and implications, so I hope you forgive me.

"That Indian thing" — In the 19th century a common spelling of Hindu was Hindoo, which is what I've used.

1827. "About the year 1790, no fewer than twenty-eight Hindoos were crushed to death.. under the wheels of Juggernaut."

J. Poynder in *Asiatic Journal & Monthly Register*

Juggernaut — The word originally came from Europeans describing a Hindu procession. "*A title of Kṛishṇa, the eighth avatar of Vishṇu; spec., the effigy of this deity at Pūrī in Odisha where an enormous 'car' was dragged through the streets, and fanatical devotees threw themselves under its wheels and were crushed.* (The first European account of the Juggernaut festival, and its attendant immolations, is that by Friar Odoric, *c*1321." From the Oxford English Dictionary.)

These days, of course the word is used more generally to describe an unstoppable force that crushes all in its path. Or certain aunts …

Souvenir-selling at the site of the battle of Waterloo.

This really happened.

"Souvenir-selling at the site of the Battle of Waterloo began almost immediately after the conflict in 1815, turning the blood-soaked landscape into one of the earliest and most intense sites of "dark tourism". Locals quickly pivoted to an economy based on supplying British tourists and relic-hunters with items taken from the battlefield, a trade that soon included mass-produced, counterfeit, and even macabre items. You can read more here: *https:// daily.jstor.org/souvenir-hunting-on-the-battlefield-of-waterloo/*

#2 His Captive Lady
ISBN-13: 9780425223246
Also available in Audio

Romantic Times Top Pick! 4 1/2 stars & K.I.S.S. (Knight in Shining Silver) Award to my hero, Harry

"There was an enchanting ring to this tale that just had me totally addicted to the charming tale of love and romance. A page turner that will move you on a emotional level. A Delightful tale that will warm you heart and leave you aching to read more from this author!!

(https://addictedtoromance.org/book-review-his-captive-lady/)

Universal link to the e-book: books2read.com/u/3yzv2L

#3 To Catch a Bride
ISBN-13: 9780425230220
Also available in Audio

"Threaded with charm and humor, this action-rich, emotionally compelling story is the third in Gracie's popular "Devil Riders" series. Though it stands on its own, it is sure to entice readers to read the others." — Library Journal (USA) Best Books of 2009 - ARRA (Australian Romance Readers Association) Finalist

Universal link to the e-book: books2read.com/u/4NXQ5W

#4 The Accidental Wedding
ISBN-13: 9780425233825
Also available in Audio
A DIK-Desert Isle Keeper-AllAbout Romance

"Gracie takes conventions of the romance novel that have been done to death—amnesia, injured hero, heroine who does too much—and turns them into a story that is fresh and new and interesting. That takes talent. And this, plus two charming main characters, a suspenseful subplot, and some delightful love scenes, makes for a near-perfect read."

Universal link to the e-book: books2read.com/u/mKyxP5

#5 Bride By Mistake
ISBN: 9780425245798
Also available in Audio
RITA Finalist 2012 (Historical) Romance Writers of America

"Bride by Mistake, a marriage of convenience story, is my favourite Anne Gracie romance to date. The romance between Luke and Isabella, two individuals each determined to have their way, is impetuous and heartbreaking, joyous and sad. It is a story of adventure, fun, family and the peeling back of wounding secrets but most of all, of the healing power of trust and love. A lovely take on the story of the ugly duckling, and a beautiful read that will warm your heart." (Lolly Russell)

Universal link to the e-book: books2read.com/u/me7B8V

WHERE TO BUY:

Anne Gracie's books can also be ordered through any bookshop by using the ISBN — the number attached to each individual book.

About Anne Gracie

ANNE GRACIE SPENT her childhood and youth on the move, thanks to her father's job which took them around the world. The roving life taught her that humor and love are universal languages and that favorite books can take you home, wherever you are.

Anne started her first novel while backpacking solo around the world, writing by hand in notebooks. Published by Harlequin, and Berkley (PenguinRandomHouse, USA) her regency-era romances are national bestsellers in the USA, have won many awards, been translated into more than eighteen languages and include Japanese manga editions (which she thinks is very cool). Anne has now embarked on a new adventure—self publishing—and hopes readers will support her.

A lifelong advocate of universal literacy, Anne also writes books for adults just learning to read.

When not writing, Anne frivols on FaceBook, cooks, gardens and flings balls for her rescue dog, a black kelpie-cross called Milly.

You can visit Anne on *www.annegracie.com,* where

you can sign up for her monthly newsletter and/or her weekly personal blog. She loves to get emails from readers.

www.ingramcontent.com/pod-product-compliance
Lightning Source LLC
Chambersburg PA
CBHW021219060726
47590CB00005B/1560